ECHOES OF APOLLO

G.A. THOMPSON

Echoes of Apollo
Copyright © 2015 by George A Thompson
First Print Edition: March 2015

ISBN 13: 978-0-9961223-6-8
ISBN 10: 0996122362

Cover and Formatting: Streetlight Graphics

This is a work of fiction. Names, characters, places, and incidents either are the product of the author's imagination or are used fictitiously, and any resemblance to locales, events, business establishments, or actual persons—living or dead—is entirely coincidental.

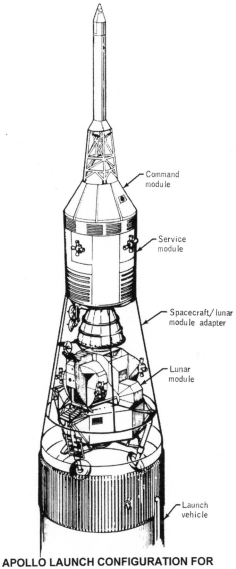

Command module

Service module

Spacecraft/lunar module adapter

Lunar module

Launch vehicle

**APOLLO LAUNCH CONFIGURATION FOR
LUNAR LANDING MISSION**

DEDICATION

For the moonwalkers,
and the generation who sent them.

PROLOGUE

CIA Headquarters
Langley, VA

STEPHEN AUSTIN STARED AT A bank of six widescreen plasma monitors. The impressive array was one of the CIA's most sophisticated portals for data collection and information fusion. Data streamed in from a wide variety of platforms: spy satellites of the National Reconnaissance Office, powerful military space-based tracking radars, and communications and data relay stations on the ground, in the air, and high above in the dark reaches of "milspace." This was of little comfort to Austin though, as his situational awareness beyond Earth orbit was extremely limited. And in the vicinity of the lunar surface, the senior intelligence officer was virtually blind. He would instead have to depend on tiny, elusive threads of data from the satellites and moon-based sensors of other nations—at least those nations not openly hostile to the American way of life.

The CIA's mission analysis center had been a hive of activity during China's manned Shenzhou spacecraft launches, but was operated today by a relatively small crew. Austin watched anxiously as the data trickled in, creating a sketchy mosaic of China's first attempt to land an unmanned sample return vehicle on the lunar surface. His head cocked to the side as he stared at the screen. It just didn't add up. The global scientific community was only slightly interested in the mission since they'd had moon rocks to study for decades. The US military was relieved to see such effort and expense directed toward a mission that diverted assets from more secretive—and potentially dangerous—offensive counter-space projects. And most CIA analysts agreed, such missions would merely allow China to acquire a base of experience using the same incremental approach that NASA had used during its early space program, experience that could be used by Chinese *taikonauts* during a manned lunar landing attempt sometime in the next decade.

This was certainly not a threat to US national security.

Austin scratched his head. *Then why attempt this baby step on the far side of the moon?* As hard as he tried he couldn't seem to make sense of the unfolding events. Even though the Chinese appeared to have a leg up on the Apollo program by having a radio relay platform in lunar orbit, the China National Space Administration, the CNSA, had reported weeks earlier that the Chang'e 4 communications satellite had been lost to solar orbit following a miscalculated engine burn. Now they would have to attempt to land the sophisticated Chang'e 5 on the far side of the moon with only limited assistance from ground controllers.

"We have loss of primary radar return," Mark Gregor, the mission controller, announced as he typed away on his keyboard. He input several key pieces of data from the ghostly-faint radar returns into a program he had written himself. The change in velocity, or delta-v, between the start of the engine burn and loss of radar return would give him a good estimate of the Chang'e 5's planned landing site. But the Chinese spacecraft was now in the shadow of the

8

moon, and even the marginal signals Gregor had to work with were suddenly occulted by the moon's rocky surface.

Austin felt like a blind man. And it was this feeling that had led him to submit a special request for data to the Japan Aerospace Exploration Agency. If he had to be blind, he would rather not be deaf too.

Austin tapped Gregor on the shoulder. "Mark, bring up the seismic feed from JAXA." Austin's forehead wrinkled as he considered the odds. The coarse seismographic sensors, originally designed to detect and catalogue major meteor impacts on the moon, might be capable of identifying a disastrous event like the crash of a lunar lander. They might even be able to detect a hard landing, one that would render a delicate spacecraft useless. But Austin was doubtful that they could accurately detect a successful soft landing by the Chang'e 5.

Xi'an Satellite Monitor and Control Center (XSCC)
Shaanxi Province, China

"Chang'e 4 is now established in the L2 halo orbit." The man who made the report sat behind a placard that identified him as the Satellite Communications Officer. "Stand by for COS in three, two, one...change of signal."

Computer displays throughout the room blanked momentarily and then flickered back to life as the Chang'e 5's telemetry stream—now successfully rerouted through the reportedly "lost" Chang'e 4—was reacquired from behind the moon. Each man checked the data he was responsible for, ready to report any changes to the landing coordinator. Absence of communication would indicate no degrade in telemetry or systems status for all controllers except two.

"Propulsion...go," shouted one Chinese controller.

"Guidance is go," his colleague echoed.

"Stand by. Six minutes to touchdown," the landing coordinator announced.

The Chang'e 5 hurtled in silence toward the desolate cratered landscape. Computers on board the spacecraft throttled the main engine and adjusted the flight path of the unmanned vehicle with small vernier thrusters, even as engineers back on Earth monitored its progress. Tension in the crowded control room mounted with each passing second. Among the nervous members was China's first official *taikonaut*. Colonel Li Yang released his grip on the attitude controller and reached up to wipe the sweat from his forehead.

Yang sat inside an unusual array of six pentagon-shaped video screens that surrounded him like the panels of a soccer ball. Encased in the awkward cockpit simulation, he streaked along through virtual space as though he were *inside* the spacecraft on an intercept course with the long forsaken face of the moon. The Chinese lander would fly under automatic guidance to a minimum-error-of-probability point in space where a landing attempt could be made. Once inside this "basket," Yang would take over and fly the craft manually to a safe landing. Using cameras mounted around the vehicle's exterior, he would see the lunar landscape exactly as if he were inside the spacecraft— with one significant difference. The roundtrip transit time for the video signal would take three precious seconds. He would have to anticipate the correction required nearly two seconds from now, apply it, and then wait to see if the reaction was appropriate.

"Two minutes to touchdown. All systems are still go," the landing coordinator reported. "Release the decoy."

Yang's virtual world shook as the small explosive

10

device rocketed clear of the spacecraft and dove toward the center of the giant crater. Yang secretly hoped that the seismic signature of the impact would be enough to disguise the lander's true location. But that would only happen if he could successfully do what had never been done before.

Yang wiped his face again.

"Approaching the basket. Stand by for manual control."

CIA Headquarters

The countdown display ticked down through one minute. Austin dragged a clammy hand through his thinning brown hair. Each second seemed like hours. His mind raced. He still couldn't figure out why the Chinese were pushing so hard for a soil sample mission. He could only hope for a clear signal, positive proof of the outcome that was less than a minute away. If the mission failed, he could quit worrying about the ulterior motives of the Chinese Communist Party. If the mission succeeded, he knew that every detail released by the CCP would be suspect. His thoughts wandered to the plaque that hung on the wall in his office, a gift from an old Chinese acquaintance. Carved in the beautiful hardwood were the ancient words of Sun Tzu:

> *All warfare is based on deception. Hence, when able to attack, we must seem unable; when using our forces, we must seem inactive; when we are near, we must make the enemy believe we are far away; when far away, we must make him think we are near. Hold out baits to entice the enemy. Feign disorder and crush him.*

Austin and Gregor stared intently at the data

11

coming in from the JAXA lunar seismographs. Three cylinders rotated slowly on the screen. On each one a computer-generated stylus traced a smooth, straight line across the virtual paper.

"Thirty seconds," Gregor said, as if Austin were unaware.

One stylus suddenly spiked, followed quickly by the remaining two. Three jagged peaks appeared on the simulated seismographic display and quickly ratcheted back down toward the noise level represented by the straight lines. Austin blinked and looked at the clock again. *Twenty-eight seconds to go.* But that was only an estimate, he reasoned.

"Looks like a definite kill, sir. A soft landing would have peaked way down here," Gregor said, pointing to the screen. "For the estimated mass, I'd guess an impact of several hundred feet per second." He clicked on a separate window and looked at a different display. This one was a spherical graphic of the lunar far side topography. A segmented line arced toward the landing point calculated by the young operator's program. A small red dot appeared and marked the actual impact point, well beyond where the segmented arc intersected the lunar surface. "My guess is that they lost thrust right about here," he said, pointing to the trajectory prediction. "Gravity took over from there, accelerating it to an impact at this point."

Hands on his hips, Austin arched his back until it popped several times. He ran the scenario through his mind one last time. Chang'e 4, a Chinese lunar communications satellite, lost to a lonely solar orbit. Chang'e 5, the country's first lunar sample return vehicle, destroyed in a spectacular crash on the far side of the moon. *Just bad luck...or too much coincidence?*

When the countdown clock scrolled through zero, Austin slapped Gregor on the back. "Nice work, Mark," he said, and then pointed to the JAXA feed. "Make sure we save a copy of that for reference, though. I've got a request for data in at NASA. If they can reactivate the cameras on the Lunar Reconnaissance Orbiter, I'd really like to get some imagery of the crash site for analysis." Austin then pivoted away from the console and strode for the door.

"Thanks, sir. I will." Gregor smiled proudly. His first mission with the Agency was a categorical success. It was his program that had tracked the Chinese mission, and his program that had recorded its failure. He checked the clock one last time. It was counting up through three minutes. He had waited long enough. Gregor began securing the computer systems one by one. The final monitor displayed the lunar seismographic feed. But as he reached down for the power button, Gregor failed to notice the three small seismic echoes made by the Chang'e 5—and recorded by the styluses—just seconds before the monitor went dark.

CHAPTER 1

Launch Complex 39
Kennedy Space Center, FL

OV-104, KNOWN TO THE PUBLIC as Shuttle *Atlantis*, sat poised for liftoff on the northernmost launch pad in the swampy environs of Merritt Island, Florida. The display had been a familiar one to residents of the space coast for three decades, but today was a spectacle almost beyond belief. Following many months of preparation devoted to turning the crown jewel of America's space program into a museum piece, an unthinkable order arrived on the desk of the NASA administrator: *Atlantis* was to be returned to flight status—in a hurry. For the Department of Defense, the urgency was a package that could only be carried into orbit in the shuttle's cargo bay. For NASA, the rationale was much simpler: every day that the retired orbiter was grounded made it that much harder to reactivate.

That *Atlantis* had been restored to an operational vehicle so quickly was nothing short of a miracle of logistics and technology. Thousands of components had to be located, inspected, tested, and either refurbished or replaced. No one had the time to stop and consider whether it had been a fortuitous organizational decision, or just dumb luck, that had made the mission possible at all; the improvised and risky mission would have been dead on arrival had the external tank not been ordered as a spare nearly two years before the shuttles were retired. Luckily, the remainder of the critical pacing items—the launch pad itself, the orbiter's main engines, and the powerful solid rocket boosters—had all been slated for use in NASA's next generation rocket system, the SLS. While the Space Launch System was still just a "paper" rocket, the components critical to its ultimate design were very real and therefore still available for retrofit back to the *Atlantis*. Still, hardware was only half of the problem.

Thousands of key personnel had been laid off or reassigned when the shuttle fleet was retired. The untimely lack of expertise at the agency forced NASA to turn to the one aerospace contractor that seemed to be overflowing with ex-rocket scientists. The Shuttle Services division of Freer Industries had in recent years become an impressive repository of shuttle talent and had performed heroic efforts to resuscitate a program that, according to its namesake CEO, had been "prematurely taken off of congressional life support and left for dead." Still, the margin of safety was perilously thin, and would almost certainly test the NASA axiom coined long ago by Apollo 13's flight director, Gene Kranz: "Failure is not an option."

But while initial planning and preparation for the mission had been kept under tight security, the sudden burst of activity at the space center could no longer be hidden from the public. And once the shuttle stack began inching its way out of the vehicle assembly building for the long crawl to Pad 39B, months of obfuscation by various government agencies evaporated in an instant. The result was hundreds of miles of clogged Interstate and thousands of overbooked hotel rooms. Those who flocked to the once-vibrant spaceport felt as if they had suddenly been given a rare opportunity to relive history. Millions more around the world would be watching via television and the Internet, but the fever pitch surrounding the launch site was dutifully ignored by the four men who had climbed atop the massive stack and strapped themselves to the tip of the spear.

High above the crowded beaches and packed bars surrounding Kennedy Space Center, *Atlantis's* crew had spent the last three hours on their backs running through countless checklists. Jack Harden, the mission commander, wiggled his toes again, hoping to regain some feeling in his lower extremities. Behind the glass faceplate, he drew in a deep breath and tried to shrug it off. Numbness in his legs and feet was just one of the many occupational hazards that he had grown accustomed to over the years, but there seemed to be more to it than that today. Harden had already reached the pinnacle of an astronaut's career. He had already flown three shuttle missions, commanding the last one himself. At NASA there were no higher mountains to climb. The timing of his decision to retire along with the shuttles seemed perfectly natural. The idea was wholly supported by everyone who knew him—anticipation greatest perhaps from the one person he had hoped to please most with the announcement—his wife. Yet here he was once again, lying on his back and wondering why he had said yes to such an inherently dangerous mission.

The silence on the comm link was finally broken. "*Atlantis*, this is Launch Control. Good luck and Godspeed. You are go for launch. Resume the countdown at T minus nine minutes."

"Okay, this is it, boys. Time to buckle up," the mission pilot said on the shuttle's intercom loop. Lying in the seat to Harden's right, astronaut Russ

Batema tugged on the straps of his restraint harness and gazed past the external tank vent arm into the clear blue Florida sky.

"Yep, I suppose it is," Harden said as he reached up to the rows of switches overhead and pressed a large button. "Control, *Atlantis*. The event timer is running."

"You're not having second thoughts, are you, boss?" voiced Pat Dennis on the intercom. Seated on the aft flight deck, Pat Dennis and Mark Bernegger were the two Air Force mission specialists assigned to assemble and deploy the latest in national defense assets, the hub of a satellite system that would finally give the US Air Force a capability it had sought for decades.

Harden glanced over his right shoulder and smiled. "No. But in case you missed that part of the brief, this would be a good time to put your game faces on. I don't think you'll be having dinner with the missus tonight." Harden didn't mind the good-natured ribbing, but his tone had nothing to do with a lack of confidence. In fact, he had come out on top of one of the most competitive professions in the world, where every assignment was a hard-won battle to outperform the competition. It should have been flattering when he was told that he was the best man for the job. But as he replayed the events of the past year in his mind, the decision to forgo his retirement suddenly seemed bittersweet. "I'll just be happy once this thing is safely on orbit."

"I have to remind you that this *thing* you keep referring to is the most important weapons system ever fielded by the US Air Force, *Commander* Harden," Dennis fired away at the only Navy member of the crew. "I know you don't like hearing this, boss, but the aircraft carrier is about to become a dinosaur of
18

twentieth century warfare. Once HALO is operational, those tubs you used to fly off of will all be dry-docked."

"Keep dreaming, my friend," Harden shot back. "And don't forget that this spacecraft we're about to launch in was once considered obsolete too. So you'd better watch what you say about dinosaurs, lest one rear up and bite you in the ass." Harden was only half kidding about that, but he didn't need to remind everyone what they already knew. Everyone at NASA considered the HALO mission, with an orbit and inclination even higher and steeper than the final Hubble repair mission, to be its most dangerous. And it was Harden's flawless command of that mission, STS-125, that made him the administrator's first choice. Still, had *Atlantis's* reprise been just another scientific mission like Hubble's, saying no wouldn't have been so hard. It wasn't until Harden was finally convinced of the importance of the military satellite buried twenty feet below in the cargo bay, that he finally gave in.

The satellite in *Atlantis's* cargo bay was actually just one element of the expansive High Altitude Launch Operations constellation. Many smaller satellites would eventually follow the enormous HALO control node into orbit on various, unmanned rockets. But the critical piece of Cold War technology secured inside *Atlantis* had been conceived in an era when everything was designed to launch in the shuttle—an era when it was naively assumed that American astronauts would always be available to conduct spacewalks to deploy such complex satellites.

"T minus six minutes. *Atlantis*, Control, you are cleared for APU start."

"*Atlantis*, roger," Batema said as he recalled the tired old joke about shuttle pilots. Right-seaters, he was told, had only three tasks during any given mission. The first, before launch, was to start the auxiliary power units, the APUs. The final task, just before touchdown, was to lower the landing gear handle. But it was the remaining task that had been deemed the most important by nearly every mission commander. For the remainder of the mission, his sole job was to "make the commander look good." Batema smiled as he completed the first task flawlessly.

Harden could sense the junior pilot's excitement. Shining through the thin glass bubble, Batema's perpetually optimistic toothy grin highlighted a feeling of confidence that was only possible on an astronaut's first spaceflight. Harden shifted again in his seat. He had no doubts about Batema's ability. He was fully qualified to fly the mission—but so was Jeff Burns. Yet his old squadron mate had spent the last week as far from the action at the Cape as an astronaut could possibly get as Burns fulfilled his NASA responsibilities at an obscure air base in southern France.

"T minus four minutes."

Atlantis once again stirred to life. Her wing elevons, body flap, and massive rudder cycled methodically through a preprogrammed test pattern as hydraulic fluid circulated throughout the spacecraft. The spasmodic motion jerked Harden out of his untimely reflection and forced him to pay particular attention to the short but crucial test. The aircraft-like flight controls may have been useless in space, but they were nothing short of critical during the atmospheric portion of the shuttle's precarious glide back to Earth. And if they failed during reentry, there would be no hope for a fix.

"T minus three minutes. Hydraulic checks complete."

Beneath the majestic spacecraft, the tripod of

space shuttle main engines, the SSMEs, danced swiftly through another important test of the shuttle's flight worthiness. If the main engines failed to swivel properly at liftoff, it would be impossible for the unwieldy stack to maneuver clear of the encroaching umbilical tower during launch.

"*Atlantis*, Control, main engine gimbal checks complete."

Batema's heart rate nearly doubled as the external tank vent arm finally retracted and severed *Atlantis's* last visible tether to the fixed service structure.

"T minus one minute."

It was all business now on the flight deck of *Atlantis*. The nervous banter that had helped Harden and his crew pass away the anxious moments of the past three hours suddenly gave way to the somber realization that their fates may well be decided by the rapidly approaching eight minute chasm in time.

Enormous valves swung open at the base of the launch platform. Water from a nearby storage tank rushed in to flood the thousand-foot-long flame trench, the resulting deluge ready to absorb the intense acoustical energy generated by nearly seven million pounds of thrust.

"T minus ten seconds."

"Five, four...we have main engine start."

The shuttle's main engines roared to life in rapid succession. Blue shock cones pounded the earth. *Atlantis* strained against her mechanical restraints.

"Two, one..."

High up in the cockpit, Harden's eyes were glued to the main instrument panel. When the pressure in each main engine climbed above 90 percent, all three engine status lights awoke with a reassuring green glow. He swallowed deeply as the interlock that lit

21

the solid rocket boosters was ultimately satisfied; and any reservations Harden may have had about the impending mission ended with a bang as the restraining bolts finally blew—and *Atlantis* exploded away from the launch pad.

CHAPTER 2

Air Base 125
Istres, France

JEFF BURNS STOLE A QUICK glance at the Omega Speedmaster strapped loosely to his left wrist. The Learjet he was piloting had been locked in a boring racetrack pattern above southern France for nearly two hours. It was the least glamorous astronaut duty he could possibly imagine, but mission rules were quite specific. The Transoceanic Abort Landing Communicator, or TALCOM, was a designated NASA astronaut who, along with ground personnel, was assigned to a base somewhere in Western Europe and certified the shuttle's emergency landing site as "safe for launch."

Burns had successfully completed the airborne checkout of the airfield's navigation aids and had long since run out of things to talk about with his copilot. The boredom left him with too much time to think about his unpalatable situation. When the shuttle program finally came to an end, Burns had all but given up hope of ever making it into space. He had been next in the rotation when the nation's manned space program slipped into chaos. He was reminded daily of the unpleasant prospects. But when rumors surfaced that the Department of Defense had a one-off payload in the pipeline, he decided it might be worth the wait.

For months the ad-hoc mission had been camouflaged as an unmanned test flight deemed necessary for the development of the shuttle's successor, the SLS—but Burns knew better. And when NASA finally acknowledged that a minimal "security" crew would accompany *Atlantis* to orbit, his dream seemed to be within reach once again. He wasn't at all surprised when they brought in his old friend to command the top-secret mission, but he was devastated when NASA managers announced the remaining crew members. Burns was one of only two shuttle pilots who hadn't flown a mission, and he was senior to Russ Batema. The decision made no sense.

His first instinct was to retire. Quit. Part of him still wished he had. Instead, he was won over by his friend's predictably grounded advice. "Wait until the mission is over," Harden had said, "and make the decision on *your* terms—not theirs."

Deep down, Burns knew that was why Harden had made it and he hadn't. Throughout his entire career, the world had been changing around him, and he failed to notice. Or perhaps he had chosen to ignore it. Either way, Burns had made it as far as he could on skill alone; his approach to problem solving was no longer part of the recipe for success in a system that had a book thick enough to conceivably cover all contingencies. It was a system that had served Harden well. Burns struggled with it at first, but in the end he decided that it was possible to respect Harden—and resent him—both at the same time.

Burns shook off the distraction as the final seconds ticked down. He closed his eyes and imagined himself inside *Atlantis*, behind the controls of the only spacecraft in history that launched vertically, but could be piloted from the vacuum of space to a winged landing—still the ultimate feat in aviation.

"Liftoff! We have liftoff of shuttle *Atlantis*...an unexpected rebirth...her final flight...and a new end to the STS era."

Shuttle Atlantis

Atlantis rose from the water's edge on a ragged stream of liquid-yellow flame that grew in length as the shuttle rolled eastward and slowly tilted away from the vertical. On the flight deck, the launch had been an assault on Batema's senses. But as the shuttle rolled to its heads-down attitude for the climb to orbit, the pilot was slowly recovering from the onslaught and beginning to enjoy the ride. After making a quick scan of *Atlantis's* flight instruments, he glanced down to the small mirror he had strapped to the right knee of his pressure suit and drank in the memory of a lifetime. There, at the edge of the azure blue Atlantic, a pristine white ribbon of sand sparkled with waves of cheering spectators as the scattered cloud deck fell away quickly beneath them.

"Control, we are at max-*q*," Harden radioed.

"Roger, *Atlantis*, you are go at throttle up."

Harden held his breath as the engine pressure gauges rolled back up toward 104 percent. He fought the urge to fixate on the solid rocket boosters—a distraction that had haunted every shuttle crew since the *Challenger*—and instead forced himself to scan the multiple instruments that together would paint a picture of the overall health of the ship in his command. He wasn't sure exactly when the ABORT panel caught his attention, but he suddenly found himself staring directly at the cryptic Range Safety ARM light. For a brief second he was confused. *Holy shit!* It didn't matter *why* the light was on—it only mattered that it was *on!*

As Batema's hand shot up to point out the undeniable fact, Harden made the call. "Houston, we've got a problem."

White Flight Control Room
Johnson Space Center, TX

Flight Controller William Paxton quickly surveyed the reactions of his controllers around the room. He was met by a sea of confused faces. He looked back to his capsule communicator, CAPCOM Joe Fosse, and shrugged.

"We copy, *Atlantis*. Say again your problem," Fosse said coolly.

"Houston, we have a range safety light. Not sure how long it's been on, but our trajectory looks good from up here. What's the story, Joe?" Harden's radio transmission echoed through the room like words spoken into an empty tin drum.

"We're getting range control on the phone right now, *Atlantis*. We'll get to the bottom of this. We currently see no conditions that would require action from the range safety officer. Your trajectory is right down the middle. All systems are still go. Might just be a bad light." Fosse knew his last statement was bordering on unprofessional, but until they found a better answer, he decided on the optimistic tack. The alternative was too painful to think about. It was the range safety officer's unenviable responsibility to destroy the shuttle's solid rocket boosters and external tank—and by default the orbiter vehicle and its crew—if any part of the system strayed out of the prescribed corridor or threatened the public in any way. One tenuous radio link was all that separated residents of the space coast from a runaway launch vehicle with the explosive equivalent of a small atomic bomb.

26

Paxton already had the direct feed to range control pressed hard against his ear. Every word was pivotal, and even the smallest detail could affect his course of action. He nodded to each of the terse statements that Major Archer delivered with machinelike efficiency. He concurred with the range safety officer. The current situation was adequately covered by mission rules.

"Okay, Arch," Paxton said calmly. "I agree. First send a SAFE command, and let's see if we can't get that light to go out. We'll decide what to do next if it comes to that."

Shuttle Atlantis

The ride had smoothed out considerably after *Atlantis* punched through the region of maximum dynamic pressure, max-*q*. But that went unnoticed by Harden and his crew, who were sitting on top of an armed bomb with no way to know if—or when—it was going to explode. As the shuttle roared toward staging and booster separation, Harden noted the mission clock. *Approaching two minutes.* Every muscle in his body tightened. And with the weight of nearly three-g's of acceleration on his chest, he suddenly found himself fighting for every breath.

Inside the bulky helmet, Harden winced as he watched the P_c readings on the solid rockets drop below 50 percent. "Houston, we have SRB burnout." But when the explosive bolts on the massive boosters finally fired, the flash outside his window was enough to convince Harden that he had just made his final transmission. Surging from an unfettered flood of adrenaline, his heart raced near the limits of human endurance.

"Houston, we have SRB SEP," Batema reported.

"*Atlantis*, we confirm booster separation," CAPCOM

replied with relief. "Two minutes to negative return. What's the status on your ARM light, Jack?"

Harden struggled to keep his voice calm, his words crisp. "Houston, the light flickered off just before staging. What's the word down there? Is this an equipment fault, or did someone arm the flight termination system?"

"Jack, we just got off the phone with range control. They definitely *did not* activate the FTS circuitry. Your cockpit light was the only indication. They did send a SAFE command though, and it sounds like it worked."

"I don't like the sound of that, Houston. If there's a mechanical short in the system, then it's possible for this thing to cook off on its own."

"We'll have to get back to you on that, *Atlantis*," Fosse said flatly. He didn't have the answers he needed, and he was done speculating.

White Flight Control Room

The flight control console had suddenly become a beehive of activity. The Mission Management Team, a group of NASA executives who made decisions in situations that mission rules did not cover, normally occupied the viewing booth high above the rear of the control room. But when the first hint of trouble permeated the thick glass skybox, the managers quickly congregated next to one of NASA's busiest employees, the sweaty man currently occupying the flight control console.

Paxton cradled the phone and turned to address the group. "Gentlemen, that was Major Archer at range control. He believes that someone *outside* of the 45th Space Wing may have armed the flight termination system. If he's right, then they could conceivably detonate the external tank and destroy the vehicle."

"That's not possible, Bill," the shuttle program manager interrupted. "The FTS uses coded plugs installed on the orbiter that are crypto-keyed prior to launch, and—"

Paxton waved a hand. He didn't have time to let the man finish. "I know you know how the system works. So do I. But Major Archer thinks it's a possibility and will be scanning for foreign signals. If he detects any signal close to our frequency, it's the last thing I want to do, but I'm going to call for a return-to-launch-site abort."

"Bill, you can't just—"

"That's not going to help!" General Patrowski shouted. "For an RTLS abort, you still need to burn the main engines. It'll take several minutes to reverse their flight path and burn off enough fuel to jettison the external tank. And if the ET is detonated while it's still attached to the orbiter, it's sayonara, *Atlantis*. If we're going to burn those engines, let's at least shoot for an ATO and get this damned package to orbit."

The general's argument about the abort-to-orbit made sense, but he lost all credibility in Paxton's mind when he let slip his real motivation—to get his precious military satellite into orbit. "Yes, General, but they won't have to burn the engines as long, and every second might count if someone out there has compromised our codes."

The shuttle communications loop opened up again, and Harden's strained voice filled the room with more bad news. "Houston, the ARM light is back on. We show sixty seconds to negative return, and we still have a thirty-second gap to transoceanic abort. What's the word on this thing cooking off? Are we press to orbit?"

Paxton was picking up the phone to range control as CAPCOM looked to him for an answer. Paxton raised his hand, putting the man off until he had more

29

information. Fosse keyed the mike and stalled, "Uh, Jack, we're looking into that right now, and we copy your last on the abort gap." But the stoic CAPCOM suddenly felt his gut tighten as he heard Paxton scream into the phone.

"Jam the fucking signal!" Paxton slammed the handset against the cradle, his voice loud enough to be heard by controllers down in the Trench even though he wasn't on headset. He then turned to the growing crowd of NASA managers and summarized the conversation. "Range control is jamming the frequency, but we have no way of knowing where they're transmitting from or if they can send the FIRE command before MECO, Main Engine Cutoff. If they have the right codes and a strong enough transmitter... *shit!"* Paxton ran his sweaty palm over the stubble of his fresh crew cut. "We have no choice but to execute an RTLS abort. Or else we'll be dredging up pieces of *Atlantis* across a thousand miles of open ocean."

"Now wait a minute, Bill," one NASA manager objected.

"We don't have a minute!" Paxton shot back. "Look, I'm sorry, gentlemen. This decision is time critical. I'm making the call to abort and bring *Atlantis* back to Kennedy." But as Paxton turned toward his CAPCOM, he felt like a quarterback who had just watched the play clock expire before he could take the snap.

Fosse keyed the mike and reported, "*Atlantis*, we show you at negative return."

"Bill, we might as well have them abort to orbit now," General Patrowski bargained. "This thing will be over in less than five minutes."

"They can still do a manual shutdown and ditch the shuttle," Paxton said as he turned his back on the general.

"You can't do that, Bill!" the NASA mission manager shouted.

Paxton abruptly squared off with the noisy man in the pressed blue suit. "If we want the crew back alive, I see that as our best option, *sir*."

Shuttle Atlantis

400,000 feet over the Atlantic

Harden knew the rest of his crew heard the same thing he had on the CAPCOM's open mike. He also knew their odds were diminishing rapidly. If someone had the code to arm the flight termination system, then it was just a matter of time before they would detonate the huge orange bomb that *Atlantis* was strapped to.

"We've got to find a way to cut power to the FTS," Harden finally said.

"There are two main batteries in the external tank," Batema thought out loud.

"Yeah, but are they tied in directly? Or is there a breaker or relay that we have access to?"

"Wait. That's it! There's an ET power panel in the aft cabin. There might be a circuit breaker in there for the FTS."

Atlantis was still accelerating toward space with more than three times the force of gravity. Harden knew that climbing into the aft cabin would be like hiking down a steep canyon with a three-hundred-pound back pack. He thought quickly. "Mark, Pat, do either of you know the panel he's talking about?"

The two mission specialists shook their heads.

Harden knew he didn't have a choice. "Russ, we don't have much time. Unstrap and see if you can cut the power to those batteries."

Batema was already releasing his restraints.

Outside the spacecraft, deep blue had given way to

the blackness of space. Somewhere in the darkness, a coded electrical signal quietly slipped through *Atlantis's* defenses and triggered the explosive detonation cord embedded in the thin skin of her external tank. The massive fuel tank peeled open at the seams, instantly spewing its deadly contents into the vacuum of space. The volatile liquids expanded violently in all directions, mixing into a lethal brew of fuel and oxidizer that quickly engulfed the doomed orbiter. Ignited by flames from the main engines, the noxious cloud exploded in a white-hot fireball. And in an instant, the majesty was over.

CHAPTER 3

Shuttle Atlantis
350,000 feet over the Atlantic

THE POWERFUL CONCUSSION WREAKED HAVOC on the *Atlantis*. Harden and his two mission specialists convulsed violently in their seats, limbs flailing uncontrollably. But at least they were still strapped in. On the aft flight deck, Russ Batema was not as fortunate.

Batema's helmet smashed against the aft cabin ceiling, shattering his faceplate and transmitting the deadly forces directly to his spinal column. Three cervical vertebrae were irreparably crushed before the pilot lost consciousness and was thrown clear.

When *Atlantis's* fuel pumps ran dry, thrust from the powerful main engines vanished in an instant. The three seated astronauts slammed forward in their straps against the rapid deceleration. Batema shot into the forward cabin, barely clearing Bernegger's head before slamming into the forward cabin window. With a velocity now equal to his surroundings, Batema floated weightlessly above the empty pilot seat.

The vicious onslaught ended just as quickly as it began.

Harden's world was suddenly moving in slow motion. *Atlantis* was stranded on a ballistic trajectory that would not reach orbit but reenter the atmosphere and plunge to a fiery destruction. The violent thrashing had stopped, but the cockpit was swollen with a cacophony of bells and warning horns. As Harden recovered from the physical shock, he began silencing the alarms. He had no idea how bad things were or whether he could land the crippled spaceship, but before he could take stock of their situation he had to be able to think, and he couldn't think until he muted the incessant wails of the ailing *Atlantis*.

"Jesus!" Harden screamed into his helmet when he noticed Batema hovering next to him in midair.

"Russ, Russ, can you hear me?" Harden grabbed a fistful of Batema's pressure suit and pulled the floating figure toward him. He was horrified by the sight. A crimson mixture bubbled from the crack in Batema's faceplate. Looking deeper into the smashed helmet, he saw frothy red blood spilling from a gash above the pilot's left eye. Two inconceivable problems were immediately apparent. His pilot was seriously injured—and there was a leak in the cabin.

Make that three serious problems!

"Get him strapped in," Harden ordered as he stared in horror at the ADI. The Attitude Director Indicator, a half-grey, half-black sphere used to display spacecraft attitude relative to the earth below, was tumbling wildly. *Shit, this only happens in the simulator.* But when Harden looked through the forward window, his worst fears were confirmed. A sudden wave of nausea crashed over him. Deep concentration and sheer will were the only things holding back the vomit. The view through the orbiter's window spun rapidly—black space...blue marble...black space...blue marble. The earth's curvature was pronounced, and it rotated around in a dizzying circle as the orbiter pitched dangerously end-over-end. The only reason they were still alive was because *Atlantis* was high above the dense atmosphere—and the destructive forces of parasitic drag. But that wouldn't last for long.

"*Atlantis*, Houston. Over."

The frantic voice finally penetrated Harden's consciousness. "Houston, there's been an explosion," he panted. "The main engines are out. I think the ET is destroyed. We have uncommanded rates in all axes, and my pilot is seriously injured. Stand by."

Harden was busy activating the shuttle's reaction control system, the RCS, when Houston finally responded. "Roger, *Atlantis*. It's good to hear your voice. We've lost all telemetry. We're completely in the dark down here." The CAPCOM paused momentarily before adding, "We're calling for a contingency abort."

"Roger," Harden said, quick to dismiss the absurdity of the request. His immediate fears were centered on the alligator closest to his canoe, not the one he would have to wrestle twenty minutes from now.

Atlantis was confused. Still in auto-flight mode, but without the thrust vector control of the main engines, she didn't know how to steer and continued to tumble wildly out of control. Harden instinctively reached forward and punched the CSS pushbutton. His training told him that the control stick steering mode was his only hope to correct *Atlantis's* dangerous tumble. He gripped the joystick controller with his right hand and took a deep, cleansing breath. He worked on the smallest of the rates first, twisting the rotational controller gently to the left. Thrusters buried in *Atlantis's* nose, aided by those in the orbital maneuvering system, or OMS, pods on the aft end of the orbiter, worked in concert to counter the unwanted yawing motion. The effect was slow, yet positive. But Harden knew he had to hurry. If he didn't stop the dangerous tumble before *Atlantis* reached 250,000

35

feet, the shuttle would disintegrate in the rapidly thickening atmosphere.

Bernegger and Dennis had just finished strapping Batema into his seat when the injured pilot regained consciousness. Batema struggled to remember where he was. Then he felt the pain, and the hopelessness of the situation came flooding back. "Where are we?" he moaned.

"Three hundred and forty thousand feet—and falling," Harden said, smiling for the first time since the Range Safety ARM light illuminated. He still didn't know the extent of his pilot's injuries, but he knew that if he could keep him conscious until they got on the ground, Batema might have a fighting chance. *On the ground? Shit!*

"Russ, give me altitude readouts every ten thousand feet, and get set up for manual ET SEP," Harden ordered as he watched the yaw rate indicator on the ADI slowly center up.

"Coming up on...three hundred...and twenty thousand feet," Batema slurred, staring deep into his altimeter.

The crippled ship was slowly responding to Harden's inputs. The ADI now displayed a purely end-over-end looping tumble. But even as their chances of survival appeared to increase, so did the pressure to perform. Beads of sweat swelled on Harden's forehead. He reached for his face with the back of his gloved hand, but the pressure suit and its aquarium-like helmet denied him the simple relief. Instead, he was forced to blink away the sting as he fought to ignore yet another of his profession's occupational hazards.

Atlantis may have won many battles against gravity in the past, but she was about to lose the war. Harden knew the shuttle couldn't withstand the heat—or stress—that the dense atmosphere would soon inflict on his ballistic cocoon. He had to finish reorienting the spacecraft with its thermal tiles facing forward, and he had to do it fast.

"Three hundred thousand." The distortion in Batema's voice intensified as the g-force increased and transferred the weight of his bobbing head to his fractured spinal column.

"Almost there." Harden was finally able to arrest the dangerous pitch rate and gently relaxed the hand controller to the neutral detent. *Atlantis* was still heads down, but nose above the horizon. "Russ, go ahead and punch off whatever is left of the ET, and then I'll roll us back upright for reentry." Harden could only hope that there was no damage to the thermal protection system, or the umbilical doors that would seal the holes in *Atlantis's* belly when the remnants of the giant fuel tank finally detached.

"Roger." Batema reached for the button, but the mounting pressure in his neck suddenly exploded into a torrent of pain. Batema screamed inside his helmet, then lowered his hand as he began to sink back into unconsciousness.

Harden grimaced as he watched Batema recoil. He then leaned over, lifted the plastic cover, and punched the ET SEP button.

"I think he's out again, sir," said Bernegger.

"Shit. Mark, give me a status report."

"Altitude two-niner-zero. Both fuel cells are okay. One APU is out; the other two are running. Do you want me to try to start number two?"

"No. We don't have enough time. Just make sure those umbilical doors are secured. I'm going to roll us upright."

The wounded *Atlantis* plunged deeper into the hostile atmosphere. Harden had finally managed to roll the spacecraft upright and orient the thermal tiles for reentry. His crew had been spared a fiery demise, but they were far from out of the woods. He still had to maneuver the weakened shuttle through a series of trajectory-shaping S-turns using the backup flight control system. Then, if they were still alive at sixty thousand feet, he would have to fight yet another alligator and do what he still couldn't believe Houston had ordered. He had to *ditch* the shuttle.

"Two hundred and seventy thousand," Dennis warned.

"*Atlantis*, Houston. We predict radio blackout in thirty seconds. We're still without telemetry and unable to send the abort command. We need you to confirm the contingency and stand by for ditching procedures after blackout."

"Houston, we confirm the freaking contingency!" Every second was precious and the last thing Harden had time for was protocol. He looked over to his unconscious pilot and considered Batema's odds. If he had to ditch the shuttle into the open ocean, his pilot's chances of survival approached zero. *There has to be another option.*

"Two hundred and sixty thousand feet. Blackout in fifteen seconds."

A new voice crackled in the comm loop, momentarily confusing everyone—except Harden. "*Atlantis*, how far is your R-V line from Istres?" Harden immediately recognized the voice of his friend and TALCOM, Jeff Burns.

Harden looked down at the range-velocity line. The computer generated arc displayed the energy potential of the world's heaviest glider. "It's about five hundred miles short of Madrid."

"That's okay," Burns said reassuringly. "An OMS burn no later than two-hundred-thousand feet should stretch your R-V line all the way to Istres. But you really have to crank up the angle of attack to get the thrust vector you need. That will increase your range without pushing your velocity past the thermal stress point. It'll get you back on a steep recovery profile. Trust me—I did it in the simulator. It'll work as long as..."

The transmission quickly faded into static as the shuttle plunged through 250,000 feet and the ionized atmosphere surrounding *Atlantis* swallowed Burns's final words. But the cryptic radio transmission had no trouble reaching across the Atlantic and shocking everyone listening back at Mission Control in Houston.

White Flight Control Room

"What in the hell is going on up there, Bill?" the NASA mission manager shouted. "They can't do that. There are no procedures for burning the OMS pods in atmospheric flight. Who's the TALCOM? Get him on the line and tell him he doesn't have the authority to make those decisions. Only I do."

"It's Jeff Burns, sir. And no, he doesn't have that authority, but the mission commander does. Burns just made a suggestion. We'll have to wait and see what Harden does with it," Paxton replied diplomatically. He knew the half-baked plan coming from his TALCOM was nothing short of anathema to NASA management. To him however, it was pure brilliance. His hands were tied. He could not authorize such a radical procedure. But what did Burns have to lose? He would probably never make it into space anyway. Timing was everything in this business, Paxton concluded, and Burns had arrived on the scene just a little too late.

"We're not just talking about a NASA spaceship and four astronauts here, Bill. If they foul this up and drop out of the sky in the middle of Spain, they could kill hundreds. And the property damage would be—"

"Look, they have to dump the OMS fuel overboard anyway before they ditch, per the checklist. They're just dumping it in a different way. Besides, there's nothing we can do about it now. Either they come out of blackout with enough energy to make Istres, or they don't. If they do, we'll just have to trust Harden with the rest."

CHAPTER 4

Shuttle Atlantis
220,000 feet over the Atlantic

ARDEN FINALLY SAW A WAY out of his predicament. Ditching the shuttle had always been his worst nightmare. The plan Burns had come up with was a real roll of the dice, but he knew instantly that it was his only hope for saving his ailing ship, its irreplaceable payload—and his injured pilot. And it was at moments like this that he had learned to trust Burns instinctively.

"Get us set up for a manual OMS burn, Mark," Harden ordered.

"I'll get it," Batema said as he drifted back into consciousness.

"Okay, Russ, if you think you can." Harden looked over his shoulder and whispered, "Mark, back him up just in case he fades again."

"Yes, sir."

"Hey, you hang with us, Russ," Harden said as he struggled to keep Batema's spirits up and his head in the game. "And don't forget, if this crazy plan works and I can get us close enough to Istres, this is supposed to be your landing." Earlier that morning, everyone at breakfast thought Harden was delirious, offering up the last space shuttle landing to a coin toss with his rookie pilot. Although there were no rules governing the decision, the landing was historically the commander's to make. But Harden reasoned that they were both qualified, and besides, he already had a shuttle landing to his credit. There would be no next time for Russ Batema.

"I'll just be happy to get the landing gear down in time," Batema said solemnly. Part of him wanted to believe Harden was serious about the offer, but his priorities had suddenly shifted. Doing his best to mask the mounting pain, Batema flipped the appropriate switches for manual OMS control and waited.

Harden tweaked the hand controller aft, slowly increasing *Atlantis's* pitch attitude to a precariously high sixty degrees. "OMS burn in three, two, one. Mark."

Batema leaned forward and punched the EXEC button on the computer. The thrust was modest, but instant. Harden watched with amazement as the arc of the range-velocity line began to slide slowly to the east. The orbital maneuvering system didn't have enough thrust to push *Atlantis* higher, but it was surprisingly successful in arresting the sickening rate of descent. Harden marveled at the results as their airspeed hovered near 12,000 nautical miles per hour. He knew this would push the thermal protection system to the limits, but it was his only chance to reach dry land— and the medical facilities his injured pilot desperately needed.

And the plan seemed to be working. The range-velocity line now extended all the way to central Spain. But Harden didn't like what he saw as he compared the OMS fuel burn rate with the movement of the R-V line. "Russ, I don't think we're going to get back on the profile before the OMS shuts down."

"It's going to be close," Batema agreed, sounding slightly more lucid now. "But we still might be able to stretch the glide to a straight-in approach if we set up for the minimum entry point profile."

"We'll have no margin for error," Harden said as he made eye contact with his fading pilot. "So make sure I don't fuck this up."

"Roger," Batema replied as he forced a painful smile in return. *Just make the commander look good... and don't forget the landing gear.* Of his remaining tasks, he wasn't sure which one would be harder. If the landing gear had been damaged in the explosion, Harden's heroic effort would be wasted. Either way, he could feel his own odds slowly slipping away.

"Stand by to terminate the OMS burn," Harden said. With one eye on the fuel gauges, he stretched it as far as he could. "Shutdown!"

Burns's raspy voice suddenly punched through the final seconds of the communications blackout. "*Atlantis*, TALCOM. Over."

"TALCOM, *Atlantis*. We read you loud and clear. How's the weather looking in Istres?" Harden asked, the optimism in his voice evident even across the great distance.

"Warm and welcoming, *Atlantis*. The skies are clear, and you're cleared to land on Runway 33."

With the OMS thrust gone, Harden gently decreased *Atlantis*'s pitch attitude to intercept the maximum lift-to-drag profile and stretch out the glide as much as possible. They were already through the region of peak thermal stress, and if the wings hadn't melted off yet, he doubted they would.

When he finally took his eyes off the instruments and looked out over the nose of the spacecraft, a beautiful land mass came into view. At 100,000 feet the curvature of the earth was still quite pronounced. Harden couldn't make out the landing strip yet, but he was able to use the familiar contour of the

Mediterranean shoreline to help funnel his eyes toward their hopeful sanctuary.

"TACAN locked on," Batema said. "Looks like we're still a little low."

Coming all this way to end up ditching in the Mediterranean was not something Harden wanted to think about. "Yeah, I'm going to have to cut the corner a little bit."

"*Atlantis*, we have you in sight," Burns reported from the Learjet. "I'm going to set up for the rendezvous and join to your left, on the inside of the turn."

"Rog." As the *Atlantis* sliced through 50,000 feet, Harden decided it was all or nothing. Preparations for bailout normally started at 60,000 feet and had everyone out of the orbiter by 30,000 feet. With the reduced crew complement, even at this altitude he knew he could still drive straight up the Mediterranean, pop the hatch, slide down the escape pole, and parachute to safety. But Batema would probably die in the process.

Harden pushed the thought away. "I have the field in sight," he advised his friend in the chase plane. "I'm going to set up for a short straight-in."

Burns spiraled up to meet the *Atlantis* as it plummeted through 30,000 feet. He scanned the distance-measuring equipment. *Twenty miles from Istres.* "It looks like you might want to start your turn now."

Harden responded promptly. "Coming left." The shuttle's turn radius at their current speed was a gigantic three miles, and he couldn't afford to overshoot the runway in an unpowered spacecraft.

"How are you doing, Russ?" Harden asked, his eyes glued to the critical information on the heads-up display.

"I might be able to manage the gear handle, but the landing is all yours, boss."

"Okay, Russ. I don't blame you. I did manage to drop us off a little low. Looks like I bought this one." Plunging through 20,000 feet, *Atlantis* was still well below the recommended altitude gates. But when Harden rolled out on final, he was relieved to find his ship's energy state slightly higher than expected. As he began the pre-flare maneuver at 10,000 feet, less than three miles separated *Atlantis* from the beckoning concrete oasis of France's 125AB. "Stand by on the gear."

Batema's pain was spiraling out of control. His left arm tingled, his fingers numb as he reached toward the landing gear handle to complete his final task.

"Landing gear down!"

Batema's teeth ground together as he wrenched the landing gear lever out of its detent. Staring blindly at the three gear indicators, he moaned, "One...two..."

"Shit! The main gear isn't coming down," Bernegger yelled.

"*Atlantis*, your right main is stuck," Burns confirmed from his unique vantage point in the chase plane.

Harden, focused intently on the landing zone, gently lowered the nose. Pat Dennis's heart sank into his stomach. *We're not going to make it!*

"Pull up!" Burns yelled into his microphone.

Harden snapped the control stick aft. The abrupt maneuver wrenched the orbiter's already weakened airframe, applying nearly two-g's to the gigantic glider. But the added force proved to be just what the stubborn landing gear needed, and the right main wheel snapped down into position.

"Three down and locked!" Dennis shouted.

Inside the chase plane, Burns was equally amazed by the miracle he had just witnessed. The shuttle was safe on deck, parachute deployed in the warm Mediterranean sun. He glanced over at his white-faced copilot and smiled. Then, cranking the yoke hard left, the former fighter pilot took what he figured would be his last victory roll and sang out into the open mike, "Yeehaaaw!"

White Flight Control Room

With the data and telemetry links down, the mission control team in Houston could do nothing but listen—and wait. When Burns reported that the *Atlantis* was safe on deck in France, the quiet room exploded in a wave of cheers and thunderous applause.

General Patrowski just stared at the blank video feed. He racked his mind to come up with some way to get his program back on track after such an unimaginable setback. He kept coming up empty.

Paxton turned to him and said, "General, cheer up. At least the crew is home safe, and your bird will live to fly another day."

Shuttle Atlantis
Istres, France

Atlantis rolled to a stop. Jack Harden's legs were still quivering as he set the parking brake and dropped his heels to the floor. Leaning his head back against the headrest, he closed his eyes and drew in a deep, cleansing breath.

The horror was over.

But the relief was short lived. Reality quickly crashed in around him as his priority shifted to his injured pilot. "Hang in there, Russ. Help is on the way," Harden said as he reached for Batema. Stopped short by his seat restraints, he quickly unfastened his harness, removed his gloves, and tossed his helmet to the side. "Russ?"

There was still no answer.

Harden twisted the quick release on his pilot's harness. Batema slumped forward against the instrument panel. Pushing Russ back into his seat, Harden took his first good look at the bloody mess behind the shattered faceplate. He quickly removed the smashed helmet and tossed it into the aft cabin. Then, as Harden wiped the waves of deep red from Batema's face with his bare hands, he was met by the emptiness of two wide, lifeless eyes. He pressed two fingers against Batema's swollen neck. Nothing. Russ Batema was dead.

CHAPTER 5

CIA Headquarters
Langley, VA

STEPHEN AUSTIN PICKED UP THE phone, dialed a long distance number, and waited. As he took a seat on the corner of his desk, he couldn't help but notice the small roll forming around his midsection. Closing in on 190 pounds, the South Carolina native loved good food—and the results were beginning to show. He suspected he weighed at least a dozen pounds more than he did in his college days. He had already decided to do something about it but just couldn't seem to find the time to start. It was hard for him to believe how long it had been already since 9/11 and his sudden decision to leave a well-compensated job as an investment banker to join the CIA. And the years, he was finally beginning to realize, had exacted a toll. His hair was noticeably thinner, and his eyes hid behind a pair of wire-framed glasses that suddenly seemed to need a new prescription. He suspected that the increase in paperwork production in recent years had something to do with that. But the recent turn of events seemed to roll back the clock and suddenly reopen what had so far been the most exciting chapter in his too often mundane CIA career.

Somewhere in San Francisco, a voice with a Chinese accent rattled off a terse greeting. Austin typed in a six-digit code and worked through several prompts to retrieve the only message left on the phone since he had last checked. The anonymous caller was notably shaken as he made several obscure references regarding the recent "national tragedy" before requesting a meeting at one of their previously agreed upon locations. Austin made note of the information and then deleted the message. He stared blindly at the concrete walls as he tried to make sense of what was nothing more than a few tiny grains of information. He finally returned the phone to its cradle and moved quietly across the room.

Austin stopped at the far wall, tilted his head back and peered down through the bottom of his glasses. He hadn't been able to shake the feeling he got when he first heard the rumor circulating about the explosion on board *Atlantis*. Disturbing images began to flash through his mind as he read the plaque given to him by the man who had left the mysterious message. Chong's gift, and its chilling inscription, was a daily reminder that nothing could be taken at face value in the business of national security. To Austin, the words of Sun Tzu seemed as applicable today as when they were first written nearly 2,500 years ago: *All warfare is based on deception...*

The intercom on Austin's desk squawked an announcement, interrupting his train of thought. The DCI was on his way in. The door swung open and Austin turned to greet Dr. Robert O'Grady, Director of the CIA. "Hi, Stephen. I hope I'm not interrupting anything important."

Austin shook his head to clear the fog. "What can I do for you, sir?"

"I just got a call from DNI. Director Nash needs an update on the HAVE FLAME program. It seems that the president wants an estimate on the timeline and

49

capabilities if we were to turn the funding spigot back on?"

"I spoke with Sam Freer not long after the *Atlantis* mishap," Austin replied without hesitating, "and we may not be as far behind as you would think." There was a lot more he wanted to say, but he'd already been down that road with the director. And they had both agreed that the president's spurious decision to cancel the only program capable of bridging the dangerous gap in NASA's manned spaceflight program was nothing if not shortsighted. "He's preparing a full brief on Phase III of the project and the facilities out on Johnston Island. I'll be flying out to Vandenberg Air Force Base later in the week to assess Phase II and the conditions at Slick-Six. I suspect the long pole in the tent may be personnel though. We didn't have time to put together a crew before the president shut us down."

O'Grady sounded impressed. "That's good news. But aren't you the least bit curious as to why the president is all of a sudden interested in the program again?"

"It doesn't appear to be that complicated," said Austin. "He's not willing to authorize another shuttle flight. General Patrowski and the rest of the Air Force brass are pushing really hard to get their HALO constellation up and running. And without a crew to deploy the satellite, their bird is nothing more than a two-billion-dollar orbiting paperweight. This is one of the scenarios we used to get approval for HAVE FLAME in the first place."

O'Grady nodded. "Yes, of course. And I guess the Security Council is finally coming to terms with the reality that we can't expect the Russians to lend us a Soyuz to help out with national defense projects." The director then handed Austin a maroon briefing folder with the letters TS stamped on the cover. "And if word of this ever gets out, the press would have a field day with it."

Austin took the folder and flipped through the pages. The executive summary was signed by General James Patrowski, Commander, USAF Space Command. Austin skimmed quickly at first, but his eyes slowed when he reached the section that O'Grady had just suggested. "Sabotage?" he muttered. Austin's face drained as he read from the summary:

Every rocket launched from American soil, manned or unmanned, incorporates a Flight Termination System, or FTS, designed to destroy the launch vehicle if it becomes uncontrollable. The explosive devices on board Atlantis *were designed to be activated by radio frequency from command centers on the ground. Several tests of the receiver equipment on the shuttle and the ground-based transmission equipment were conducted prior to launch. One test was an open-loop test on the actual command frequency, but with dummy codes to verify the integrity of the system. The other was a closed-loop test conducted with the actual* Arm *and* Fire *codes. It is possible that the codes were either accidentally transmitted during the open-loop test, allowing them to be intercepted, or were somehow compromised during the closed-loop test...*

"No wonder the president is spooked." Austin walked back to the plaque he had been reading when the director came in. Several lines from *The Art of War* came into sharp focus: *when able to attack, we must seem unable; when we are near, we must make the enemy believe we are far away; when far away, we must make him think we are near.* He wasn't sure how yet, but his instincts told him that the recent Chinese mission to land a spacecraft on the far side of the moon was somehow connected to the demise of *Atlantis.*

Austin scratched his head. He had long held suspicions about the Chang'e program, but the data he had seen seemed to support the Chinese claim that the mission was as a failure. Still, as much as he tried to clear the thoughts from his head, the events seemed inseparable. And if so, the corollary was frightening. If there was a connection between the *Atlantis* tragedy and the Chang'e program, HALO might not be the right answer anyway. HALO had been designed to combat threats from earth-based systems. The Chang'e 5 was a lunar lander—and it had been more than forty years since America landed anything on the moon. Austin suddenly found himself with more questions than answers. How would the president react if the Chang'e threat were real? Could America respond at all? Austin feared he would find out soon enough.

City of Shenzhen
Guangdong Province, China

China's Moon Festival was supposed to be a joyous occasion. Along with Chinese New Year celebrations, it had been one of the most important festivals for the Chinese people for thousands of years. The Mid-Autumn Festival, as it was also known, was held on the fifteenth day of the eighth month of the Chinese lunar calendar and marked the end of the summer harvest. It was a time for family gathering and celebration. Dongfan Chong had made the pilgrimage to Shenzhen many times, and this trip had been planned for months. But the cause for celebration had quickly evaporated when a week before his scheduled visit, Chong's mother sent word of the terrible news. What was supposed to be a joyous family reunion was suddenly and painfully eclipsed by a funeral procession for the unexpected death of his father.

Chong also struggled to come to grips with the unpleasant reality that this would be his final visit to China. The decision was perhaps the most painful he'd had to make since he first decided to leave his homeland some two decades ago. But his choices were stark. He could repatriate, reassimilate into his native culture and hope to forget his adopted country and its powerful promise of democracy. Or he could once and for all forsake the country of his birth and deliver the information now in his possession to his friend in the American government, never again to return to the country held hostage by a corrupt communist party and mired in outmoded autocracy.

Chong knew of no other alternative. His father must also have known this when he passed on the seemingly innocuous information to his son; the very information, Chong now suspected, that had led to his father's mysterious death. The burden grew heavier with each subsequent implication. Chong blinked away the tears as he pushed the thoughts from his mind and forced himself to focus on the events unfolding in his family's Shenzhen apartment.

Pictures, personal effects, and even some of his father's favorite foods adorned the hastily constructed memorial in the center of the small family room. But amid the mourning at the makeshift altar, Chong struggled to filter his sorrow from the anger welling up deep inside him. Searching for quiet, he retreated to the balcony of his parents' high-rise apartment to sort through the crippling jumble of emotions. The din faded as Chong closed the sliding door on twenty-sixth-story balcony. Far below, the streets were alive with color. Reds, yellows, and bright moonlit whites begged for good luck in ancient celebrations believed to keep evil spirits away. The pop of fireworks echoed through the dense urban jungle, while strings of paper-shaded lanterns strung across the narrow streets below gave the illusion that the city itself was floating on a vast sea of colorful stars.

Chong's mother, sensing an unusual pain in her youngest son, joined him on the balcony. Quiyue, a vibrant seventy-two-year-old, and traditional Chinese woman, had always impressed upon her son that one could be small of stature but still be large with ideals. This would be the hardest part of his decision. If he was lucky enough to make it out of China alive, he knew he would never be able to return. His father's death had come suddenly, shielding Chong from the pain of knowing that he had already said his last good-bye. But as he looked deep into Quiyue's sagging eyes, he sobbed uncontrollably, knowing that this would be the last time he would see his mother alive.

Quiyue dried her son's eyes with a gentle swipe of her thumb. She then handed Chong a small plate topped with a delicate golden-brown pastry. "This used to be your favorite when you were my young son," she said lightly. "You would eat each *yuebing* in sight if we allowed you."

"Thank you, Mother," Chong replied, choking back the pain. He took the small "moon cake" and nibbled at its edge. But the sweet Chinese pastry no longer held the same magic that it once had. As a small boy, the moon had been a heavenly body—the realm of the gods. Now it was the domain of man and held forth the specter of death.

Quiyue could see that the offering did little to change her son's plaintive expression. She fought hard to be strong for him. "Do not worry about me," she said, and then looked up at her son. The largest full moon of the year, drenched in a shadowy red, floated just above his left shoulder. "I will be fine. I was born on a farm, and I will return to the farm for my last days if I must."

"Mother, you should not accept this," Chong pleaded. "*Hukou* cannot be changed so easily. You should be allowed to remain in the city. This is your home now." The family registration system, or *hukou*, had long been the communist government's way of segregating the peasant masses from city populations. This "resident permit" dictated where one could live and work, what schools one could attend, and what limited government services were available to which citizens. Someone born under rural *hukou* had few chances for a better life and would normally live, and die, in the hinterland. Chong's father had broken the shackles of rural *hukou* only after graduating from the university in Beijing and obtaining a job in the nascent Chinese rocketry program. And throughout his distinguished career as an engineer, he had been forced to turn a blind eye to many Communist Party atrocities that would have cost him everything had he complained. The elder Dongfan had shared this shame with his son soon after the massacre at Tiananmen Square, an event so horrible that afterward could be referred to in China only as the "June 4th incident." He confessed to his son that he did what he had to do for his family, but urged Chong never to let himself be put in that position. His father's words struck a deep chord inside the young college student, and Chong left his homeland the very next year. This was why he couldn't bear to see his mother bend so easily to the provincial party's fabrication of charges against his father.

"They told me that if I leave Shenzhen they will not

charge your father as a spy and a traitor to China. And if I try to stay in the city, they will ruin his name and revoke my *hukou*. I would have to live in the city illegally. I will not even be able to see a doctor without *hukou*. I will be a criminal." Quiyue looked away as she tried to hide the tears welling in her small, dark eyes.

Chong pulled his mother close. As he held her in his arms he knew there was nothing he could do about the suspicious death of his father; but it was clear to him now that he would give everything in his fight against a government that could perpetrate such hideous crimes against its citizens in the name of maintaining social order. His mother had been born under such oppression and knew no better. She had no other choice. Chong did. It was the choice his father had expected him to make when the dying man gave a small box of apparently meaningless effects to his wife of fifty-six years before he collapsed and died in her arms.

CHAPTER 6

Memorial Oaks Cemetery
Houston, TX

THE MOTORCADE CAME TO A stop, and John Blaise Harden stepped from the second in a long line of grey Cadillac limousines. He re-buttoned his jacket and paused briefly as the lengthy funeral procession filed in behind him, headlights still blaring in the bright morning sun. At forty-five, Harden was the oldest of the six men who congregated near the rear of the hearse. Medium in build and height, he was physically unremarkable. In a jacket and tie, he looked more like a successful businessman than one of NASA's most experienced astronauts. A full head of hair still bordered his well-proportioned but slightly weathered face. It was only recently that a few strokes of grey had shown up in the dark brown roots to remind him of the passage of time. His engaging blue eyes managed to defy the aging process, however, still highlighting a quiet confidence that instantly gave those who met him the impression that he was worth having on their side.

Harden grabbed a handle on the side of the polished black casket as it slid from the rear of the vehicle. It was a walk he had made too many times in his career, but this one was perhaps the most painful; the man being buried on this humid Houston morning had died under his command. And the harder he tried to push away the final image of his pilot's lifeless eyes, the more unbearable the tragedy became.

Standing alongside the casket he had just released to its final resting place, Harden was immediately surrounded by Russ Batema's grieving family. Then, in waves of support around them, hundreds from the local community and NASA family had come to pay their last respects. Wails of sorrow pierced the thick canopy of mighty oaks as the minister began the service of committal. Being so close to so much pain was physically uncomfortable for Harden. Muscles in his stomach contorted with every agonizing sob. Yet he knew that his presence provided comfort to those in the clutches of such a deep and compelling grief.

Harden choked back his own tears as he glanced down at the three young boys clinging to their mother, Russ Batema's sobbing widow, Jane. This was exactly why he had wanted to wait to have children. Although his wife had never been keen on the idea of her children's father being a senior citizen when they graduated from high school, to Jack the idea was both logical and responsible. After all, his father was in his forties when he was born. But Stacy Harden had suffered one too many disappointments. Children were always promised to her after the next Navy cruise, the next flight test program, or the next shuttle mission. Only after the unavoidable dangers inherent in his job description were no longer a threat could Harden finally commit.

That day finally came. Following his command of STS-125, and what was supposed to be the pinnacle of his astronaut career, he finally answered the alarm that had been blaring on his wife's biological clock. Stacy seemed to enjoy the pregnancy as much as life itself, and eight months later gave birth to a beautiful baby boy. But the joy was short-lived. Born with a rare congenital heart defect, their son died five days later. Tears cascaded over his quivering cheeks. Even now, he couldn't blame her for leaving him, no more than he could expect her to fully understand why he couldn't turn his back on the country he had long ago taken an oath to defend.

Harden couldn't believe it had been a year already. But besides a few phone calls and voicemails, and her unexpected appearance at Kennedy Space Center last week for the launch, the only meaningful exchange between them since their separation had occurred nearly two months ago at yet another funeral. When Stacy's father finally succumbed to a courageous battle with bone cancer, Harden had arranged for time off from his training at Johnson Space Center and traveled to Dallas to console her. The intimacy of the weekend stood in stark contrast to the chill that had settled in on their relationship since he had agreed to command the *Atlantis* mission. It was a rare moment. A return to the period in life when there was no pain, no conflict between them. He thought the encounter may have been a breakthrough, but the warmth generated by the emotionally charged event quickly faded as Harden returned to Houston and poured himself back into the grueling training schedule.

Harden's attention was finally drawn back to the present as the minister leafed through the flimsy onionskin pages of his King James Bible, speaking familiar words about God and country. Jack struggled with the part about eternal life but found solace with the themes of duty, honor, and country. These were the ideas that had defined the lives of men like Russ Batema, the same ideas that had been summed up so well in a presidential address of an era long since passed. Over a hundred years after they were first spoken, the stirring words of Theodore Roosevelt still had the power to move people to tears, as they had when Harden read them aloud during the eulogy:

> *It is not the critic who counts; nor the man who points out how the strong man stumbled; or where the doer of deeds could have done them better. The credit belongs to the man who is actually in the arena, whose face is marred by dust and sweat and blood; who strives valiantly; who errs, who comes short again and again, because there is no effort without error and shortcoming; but who does actually strive to do the deeds; who knows great enthusiasms, the great devotions; who spends himself in a worthy cause; who at best knows in the end the triumph of high achievement, and who at the worst, if he fails, at least fails while daring greatly, so that his place shall never be with those cold and timid souls who neither know victory nor defeat.*

Harden too, had lived his life *in the arena*. He was one of the lucky few who knew the triumph of high achievement. Yet everything had a cost, and the price of some things required a lifetime to repay. Russ Batema's death was one of them. But his decision was reaffirmed even before NASA "recommended" that he return to his retirement. His astronaut career was over. He had flown his last spaceflight. Never again would orders he gave result in life-or-death consequences. As a successful manager in the financial services industry, whether he was more cautious or had a greater propensity for risk would affect nothing beyond his tax return. Certainly not other people's lives. And maybe, just maybe, Stacy would believe him this time.

When Harden had finally shaken his last hand and given his last hug, he looked around to see if she was still there. He wasn't surprised that Stacy had shown up at the church for the memorial service. He knew she wouldn't let her support for the grieving family be affected by her personal feelings regarding his participation in the mission. But by the time the church service had ended and he found a spare moment, she was already gone. He had seen her face in the crowd again at the cemetery, but as he searched for her now amid the endless rows of granite headstones, it appeared that she hadn't stayed any longer than necessary.

Harden glanced at his watch. The service ended almost an hour ago. He had grown accustomed to trading messages with her answering machine, but he had sorely hoped to have his first face-to-face conversation with her since the accident. Apparently Stacy had a different timeline in mind. Harden surveyed the area one last time and then turned to leave. He had a long flight back to San Diego in the morning, and was looking forward to finally putting some distance between himself and NASA headquarters. He was already halfway to the parking lot before he realized what he had been blindly staring at in the distance. Standing next to one of the life-size marble angels that perpetually guarded the sacred grounds, Stacy was talking to one of the other astronaut's wives. When she noticed Jack moving in her direction she gave the young wife a parting embrace and began walking toward him. Harden paused beneath one of the hundred-year-old oaks as he tried to collect his thoughts.

At thirty-eight, Stacy Harden managed to carry herself with the same grace and beauty she had as a young ballet instructor. Her olive complexion, dark hair and full lips hinted at her southern European heritage; a combination that had always made Harden feel like he married into an aristocracy. He studied her face as she walked. She was radiant, even with the lines of mascara drying in the corners of her eyes. It was clear to him now, that after fourteen years, she was still just as strikingly beautiful as the day he first met her. The knot in his stomach began to slowly relax as images from their last weekend together came flooding back into his mind.

"Thanks for coming," Harden said as he leaned in and gave her a gentle kiss on her still moist cheek.

"I'm sorry about Russ," she said sincerely. "But from what I've heard, it's a miracle that any of you survived that explosion."

"I doubt that Jane would call it a miracle."

"No. Not yet," Stacy agreed. "She's still in shock. And I'm sure that no one will ever replace Russ in her heart...but when she finally comes around, she's going to realize that the real miracle is what he left behind...those boys..." Stacy took in a deep breath as she fought to maintain her composure. "Jack, when are you going to realize that you can't beat the odds forever? That could have just as easily been you they put in the ground back there."

"I know, hon. But I've already told you that this was my last—"

"Stop!" she shouted. Stacy then brushed her long, dark hair back with her hand and glanced slowly around the cemetery. There were still a few small groups remaining, but no one seemed to notice the outburst. She lowered her voice and continued. "I've heard all this before, Jack. You didn't learn anything after you broke your back in that ejection. The *Columbia* accident didn't seem to slow you down for very long. And then you go and volunteer for this. Why should I believe you this time?"

Now it was Harden who looked around before he replied. "You know this isn't the right time or place for this." He then focused his stare on her endlessly deep, brown eyes. "Have dinner with me tonight. That's all I ask. And then, only if you want to, you can come back to San Diego with me. We could sort through all of this over the weekend."

"I can't go," she said softly, and then took his hand in hers. "It's going to take me a while longer to settle dad's estate. I don't feel right leaving mom alone to deal with all the details. I'm all she's got."

Harden heard the words but looked for the real reason in her eyes. He knew he was on shaky ground and that now wasn't the time to push the issue, but something about her actions still confused him.

"Plus," she added as she squeezed his hand and leaned in to kiss his cheek. "I'm not convinced that you're ready yet."

Johnson Space Center
Houston, TX

The sign read "Official Business Only," but the driver appeared unconcerned as he wheeled into the empty parking spot and screeched to a stop in front of the offices of the Flight Crew Operations Directorate.

Jeff Burns figured this was as official as NASA business would get for him. He killed the ignition, silencing the signature rumble of a dual exhaust vehicle built before the age of catalytic converters. The 1969 Chevrolet Corvette, purchased by his father before Jeff was born, was one of his most prized possessions. In a day long gone, it was *the* symbol of a NASA astronaut. Today it was just as much out of place in the fractured brotherhood as he was. Burns gripped the steering wheel with both hands and slammed his forehead against the back of his clenched fists. He tried to clear his head, but the images were too powerful. He thought about his father—the one he never knew.

Lieutenant Commander Robert Burns had actually purchased the car in late 1968, almost a full nine months before Jeff was born. It was his reward for reaching the goal he had set for himself three years earlier when he first applied to NASA. And what a long road it had been. Robert's initial astronaut application had been turned down for what he would later discover had been considered "errors in judgment." The rejection of his second application identified a lack of "operational" flight experience. When Robert told his new wife that both deficiencies could be remedied by volunteering for back-to-back combat tours in Vietnam, she cried for days. But nearly a year later when the Department of the Navy notified Robert that he was a finalist for astronaut selection and granted him special liberty from his second tour to attend the selection board, his wife finally let herself get excited.

Following the final interview, chief astronaut Deke Slayton called Robert to ask if he would like to be a part of NASA's astronaut Class-7. Slayton informed him that training for the class didn't start until the summer of 1969, which Robert agreed was perfect. It would allow him to complete his tour of duty and still have time to move his wife to Houston when he returned home. It wasn't until he was back at sea for two months that he found out his wife was pregnant with their first child. For the young fighter pilot, the promise of a bright future couldn't get any better. But the celebration ended abruptly when his F-4 Phantom II was shot down the next week over North Vietnam,

and the Corvette—along with the dream it embodied—
went into storage.

The sprawling gold hood turned a brilliant yellow
as the sun broke through the low overcast and chased
away the ancient reflections. Burns craned his neck
forward just in time to see the sucker-hole close in
again, replacing the fleeting blue sky with a layer of
dirty grey cumulous that portended rain. He decided
to run inside before he got wet.

The deputy director's secretary looked up from her
keyboard as Burns stepped from the elevator. At an
inch over six feet, the college lacrosse player was more
muscular than his large frame suggested. But a full
head of wiry blond hair and narrow cheekbones made
him look more bookish than athletic. Yet the secretary
found herself as vulnerable as most women to Burns's
hazel grey eyes and alluring smile, an undeniable
charm that led her to ignore the fact that his name did
not appear on her boss's appointment calendar.

With the phone half hidden beneath strands of
silky auburn hair, the secretary gave a quick wave
with her free hand and mouthed "hello" in between
several uh-huhs and yes sirs. "Yes, sir, and Jeff Burns
just walked up. Can I send him in?"

Burns returned the secretary's dimpled smile. If
there was one thing he had always liked about coming
to the administration building, it was Rachel Rollins.
"So what's the verdict?" he asked as she hung up the
phone.

"Mr. Grayson said he'll be right out." Rollins's
smile then turned somber. "We're all really sorry about
Russ. The whole thing was so tragic. It's still hard to
believe. But I heard it was your quick thinking that
saved the day."

"Thanks, but—"

When the door to Scott Grayson's office swung open, Burns was suddenly reminded why he had come. He quickly pushed his sweaty hands deep into his pockets. It was the same feeling he'd had when he entered the deputy director's office for the very first time, during his final astronaut interview.

"Come on in, Pipper. To what do I owe the honor of this visit?" A former Air Force F-117 pilot, Grayson was accustomed to using personal callsigns in informal conversation and hoped it would put Burns at ease—at least for the moment. Grayson had already been warned by the director. The party line called for a reprimand to go in Burns's record. But after reviewing all the facts, Grayson decided that it was pure bullshit. Besides, he couldn't help but like the feisty Navy pilot.

"I was just hoping to get a minute of your time, sir."

Grayson closed the door to the spacious corner office and extended an open palm. As he shook Burns's hand, he could sense the man's discomfort. He offered Burns a seat and struck a more somber tone. "Well, do you want to go first, or would you rather I dispense with the official business?"

"I think I can save us both a little pain if I go first. Look, I had a lot of time to think on the way home. I don't know why it took me so long, but I finally realized that I made a mistake when I accepted this job, and—"

"Whoa, hold on there, Pipper. I wouldn't call it a mistake. If anything you may have been a victim of poor timing and some bad luck. But look, when you get right down to it, that's all that separated Gus Grissom from Neil Armstrong. Those are two of the most fundamental variables in this crazy business. You just gotta cast your lot and do like the rest of us, hope for some breaks."

Burns had heard this speech before. "I know,

Grace. I know. Look, I really have enjoyed being part of the NASA team. And I've learned a lot along the way. But as hard as it is to say this, I'm here to tender my resignation."

This time Grayson waited until he could see that Burns had finished. "I know how you must be feeling, Pipper, and I can't say that I blame you. Everyone here is shaken up over Russ's death. But I have to ask you to reconsider. Take some time and think it over. Don't make this an emotional decision." The deputy director then locked eyes with Burns to make his point. "Jeff, I know my credibility is a little shaky right now, but I promise that you'll be my top pick for the next Station crew. Just think about it."

Burns took a deep breath before responding. He had no enthusiasm for shoehorning himself into a Russian spacecraft for an eventual trip to the International Space Station. That wasn't what he had in mind when he dreamt of becoming a NASA astronaut. "Thanks, Grace, but you were right before. It's all about luck and timing, and I've had my fair share of both, good and bad. It's just that I've finally realized something, maybe for the first time. I don't have anything else to prove anymore."

Grayson studied Burns's face for some insight. He had the dubious honor of being the chief of NASA's astronaut corps during what was undoubtedly the lowest morale that he had ever seen at the agency. Worse yet, he knew he would see more defections before it got better.

Grayson stood and turned toward the large picture window behind his desk. His lofty office came with a commanding view of the park-like grounds of Johnson Space Center. He searched for something uplifting to say to his disheartened colleague, but his mind went blank. He had often drawn inspiration from the relics of a bygone era scattered throughout Rocket Park. Whenever he had a problem that seemed insurmountable, he could always look to the Saturn V rocket display and convince himself that if man could build such a grand machine and ride atop it on a column of fire to the moon—anything was possible. But the massive rocket that would have launched Apollo 18 to the moon in 1973 was no longer visible, forever interred in a flimsy white mausoleum constructed to protect it from the erosive Houston climate. And with that, his inspiration was gone.

"About all I can say then is good luck, Pipper."

"Thanks, Grace."

"And since I can't change your mind, I don't guess it will do any good to hammer you for cutting into the control loop with untested procedures—or the fraud, waste, and abuse of practicing such procedures in an expensive spaceflight simulator."

"No, sir, I don't suppose it will," Burns said with a crooked grin. "But if anyone asks, I'll tell them you were mad as hell." He then stood and unclipped the laminated badge from his shirt pocket. "I guess this is it then."

"Officially, yes. But unofficially," Grayson admitted, "what you did over there was pure genius. I think the whole damn country owes you a debt of gratitude."

"I appreciate that, sir."

"And since you're officially a *former* NASA employee now and this no longer presents a conflict of interest, I have something here to give you." Grayson reached in his top drawer and produced a small white business card. He eyed the card briefly before handing it to Burns. "Before you get too far from the fold, you might want to give this guy a call. I'm not sure what kind of jobs he has for ex-astronauts, but I can almost guarantee it will be more exciting than whatever you have planned to do next."

CHAPTER 7

White House Oval Office

THE PRESIDENT PUSHED A BUTTON on the phone. The director of national intelligence soon appeared in the concave doorway. "Have a seat, Doug," the president said as he motioned to one of two Victorian couches straddling the large presidential seal in the center of the room.

Clutching a large black satchel briefcase under his arm, Doug Nash moved to the couch opposite the president's new national security advisor. Sandy Cummings nodded to convey her consolation. Her homework requirements had also increased monumentally over the past week. Cummings had spent the better part of the last three days outlining to the president the most likely scenarios involving a covert Chinese military buildup and how they would affect US Naval operations in the Pacific theater. But it was her most *unlikely* scenario that seemed to put the president on edge. He, like every other president since Jimmy Carter, had to live by the Taiwan Relations Act. The president's personal feelings didn't much matter at the moment. Until the law was changed, he had to play the hand he had been dealt. And if China did decide to exercise its new military might and pressure the tiny island democracy into an unwanted reunification with the mainland, it would be up to the United States to defend Taiwan.

The president shook off the disturbing scenario. "What did you come up with, Doug?"

"Well, sir, I have everything here that you asked for. I've boiled it down to an executive summary, but in case you want to take a closer look at some of the details, we can do that too." The former Naval Academy lineman reached into his briefcase and extracted several folders before setting the bag down against the leg of one of the chairs next to the fireplace. He squared up the stack of files on the coffee table and continued. "And then some of this is from DCI. Director O'Grady's on the Hill briefing the Senate Armed Services Committee at the moment. This one here is the preliminary update on the HAVE FLAME program that you requested." Nash lifted a thin report from the top of the stack and flapped it in his hand. "But DCI recommended that I bring the author of the report with me as well, in case you had any really tough questions. He's in the waiting room."

"Who's the author?"

"One of the Agency's top officers, sir. Stephen Austin."

"The same Austin who wrote the reclama to the Chinese NIE?" the president asked as he tapped a finger on the report that had been taking up valuable real estate on the Resolute Desk for several days. He had nearly memorized the National Intelligence Estimate, or NIE, on China since the Communist Party began making public overtures toward the Nationalist government in Taiwan regarding reunification. There were still a few interesting kernels he wanted to drill down on, although he didn't need a classified document to tell him most of it. China's ambitions on the world stage were clear. They were finally a world economic

70

power. Their gross national product was even on track to overtake the United States' within the next few years. So they could finally afford to project military power, particularly through their growing blue water navy. And there was no question that the People's Liberation Army intended to pursue a robust capability for space operations. But according to the estimate, the implied threat in their recent rhetoric toward Taiwan far outweighed the PLA's current capabilities. China's military, the NIE asserted, was in the middle of a long, slow transformation that left it ill-suited for offensive maneuvers against US forces, on the ground or in space. But as the president had also learned, the agency's National Intelligence Estimates were rarely unanimous, and the dissenting opinion, or reclama, was often attached so that everyone involved felt they had a voice.

"Yes, sir. One and the same."

The president mashed another button on the phone, "Harriet, send Austin in."

"Please come in, Stephen," the president said when Austin appeared in the curved doorway. "You seem to be a popular fellow these days."

Austin sat down next to Sandy Cummings and shot a puzzled look across the table at Director Nash.

The president continued. "There are a couple issues at hand that I'd like to get your opinion on, Stephen, but let's start with HAVE FLAME."

"Mr. President, I leave for California first thing in the morning. I'll have a much better handle on things when I get back. But I did manage to get some good news this morning."

"Go on."

"Despite the lengthy delay since we pulled out of the program, it appears that there has been significant progress. Freer Industries continued to move forward on Phase III of the project with private funding. They've managed to complete the launch facilities on Johnston Island and have subsequently deployed the first of the Saturn boosters to the Pacific. Short of a live fire test, it could be made ready for launch in a month's time."

The president rubbed the back of his neck. He knew that General Patrowski was over on the Hill testifying to a group of increasingly aggressive senators about how important the HALO system was to national security. In response, they would undoubtedly ask Austin's boss the same question he was about to pose. "I suspect you already know why we're reviewing the program."

"You want to know if it's feasible to launch the HALO node with HAVE FLAME assets."

The president nodded.

"Yes, sir. Early in the program we developed shuttle-compatible mating rigs and payload fairings so that any hardware left in the pipeline after the shuttles retired could still go up. We looked around at the NRO and DOD for other programs that could benefit from the same type of interim heavy-lift launch program, and HALO fell squarely into that category."

The president shifted in his seat. He thought he had heard the last of HAVE FLAME. It was, after all, he who had cancelled the program. He had been assured by his advisors that the budding commercial spaceflight industry would be able to bridge the gap between the shuttered shuttle program and NASA's next generation launch system. But several high-visibility failures involving commercial rockets, coupled with the near tragic loss of *Atlantis*, had suddenly put the president in the untenable position of relying on a cancelled program that he had referred to repeatedly as a "boondoggle."

"What about Phase II? When can we expect a

manned launch of the Delta IV from Vandenberg to coincide with a payload launch from Johnston Island?"

"That's going to be the problem, sir. We don't currently have any astronauts in the pipeline. Hardware will sit around for years collecting dust. People won't. But I doubt we could have a crew ready before the Delta IV is declared man-rated anyway. That effort involved Boeing and effectively ground to a halt when funding dried up."

The president shook his head. "How long?"

"At least six months if we go ahead with the unmanned certification flights. Perhaps as little as three months if we press straight to a crewed launch. The Artemis capsule does have a proven launch escape system, so we consider the risks manageable. Do you want us to turn the funding back on and get a crew ready?"

"That leads me to the next issue," the president said, deftly avoiding Austin's leading question. "I've read the agency's NIE on China. The consensus opinion is that their military isn't ready yet for a direct confrontation with US forces. Your reclama, which appears to be well thought out, seems to disagree."

"Mr. President, I'm not a military officer," Austin conceded. "I don't know that I'm qualified to—"

"I've read your bio, Stephen. A major in economics, a minor in Chinese history, and six years on the China desk. I've heard everything I need to hear from the military. What I want now is the opinion of someone who knows the culture. And you make a very convincing case against the Chinese claim that they are seeking a *peaceful* rise to power." The president flipped through the intelligence report on his desk and read the passage from Austin's reclama that he had highlighted earlier. "Here you say 'they would not hesitate to launch an offensive attack on Taiwan

73

if they decided the moment was ripe and the means at their disposal were sufficient. While their naval capability could be countered by our carrier strike groups for the near future, recent advancements in anti-ship ballistic missile technology will negate this quantitative advantage by the end of the decade. Their more fundamental problem, however, is that they have yet to achieve anything close to parity in their space-based operations. But given the current lack of transparency in both funding and operations within their space program, they may be much closer than our current analysis suggests.'" The president looked up at Austin. "Now that sounds like more than a layman's position to me. Explain."

"Mr. President, I believe that the writings of many of today's top Chinese military scholars give us insight into their goals and aspirations as a nation, just like statements by top Japanese military commanders in the 1930s gave us a window into what the emperor was thinking before WWII. Chinese military scholars make the argument and lay out the framework for a scenario in which a weaker military could overcome a stronger one by deploying asymmetric forces. Leading Chinese theoreticians refer to this as the *Shashojian*."

"The *what?*"

"The most appropriate translation, sir, is the Assassin's Mace."

"I haven't heard of any such weapon system." The president rocked back in his chair and studied the other faces in the room to see if he was the only one bewildered by Austin's assertion. He was relieved to see similarly puzzled expressions on the faces of both Cummings and Nash.

"It's more of a concept than any single weapon system, sir. It means that applying a small force where an opponent is weakest will have a similar effect to applying a large force where he is well protected. It's the basic principle of asymmetry. A lesson they learned well from the former Soviet Union is that they could not compete with us directly in a Cold War-style military buildup, so they looked to strategies that would provide the greatest effect for a limited force. Their doctrine identifies, among other things, our economy and our reliance on space-based assets as critical vulnerabilities. Our military commanders call these points 'centers of gravity.' Since the first Gulf War, space has become our most vulnerable center of gravity, and the PLA knows this. Most of our space assets are unhardened against electromagnetic attack. They are also highly predictable in their orbits, which makes them extremely vulnerable to kinetic attacks.

"One of the PLA's top military strategists, Colonel Jinming, describes a two pronged approach whereby enemy satellites are either destroyed or temporarily blinded by terrestrial weapons in the opening throes of a conflict, while China's space-based strike capabilities are kept covert and used 'only if necessary.' This tactic is reinforced by the strategic doctrine of General Lui, who teaches *shei neng kongzhi yuzhou shei jiu neng kongzhi diqiu.*" Austin paused before translating, "He who controls space, controls the world.

"It is also interesting to note that a recurring theme in many of their military journals is that promoting a good image of China abroad is critical to international acceptance of their actions in a time of crisis. I suspect they would look to begin any confrontation with an apparently innocent clash where we were made to look like the aggressors. They've learned to do that well over the years. The EP-3 incident on Hainan Island comes to mind..."

The president's furrowed brow let Austin know he was still digesting the analysis and wasn't in the mood for a lengthy history lesson. He then reached into his top drawer and pulled out another folder. He opened the cover on the days-old President's Daily Briefing binder and flipped to the dog-eared page. He skimmed the text to refresh the details of an incident that he had yet decided how he should react to.

Yesterday, while operating in international waters in the South China Sea, the 5,300 ton ocean surveillance ship USNS Impeccable *was monitoring PLA Navy submarine activity with a SURTASS active low-frequency sonar array. The Chinese frigate* Yuncheng *approached close aboard and then shadowed the* Impeccable *south of Hainan Island for thirty minutes. An unannounced maneuver by the frigate placed the Chinese vessel within 100 yards of the* Impeccable's *bow, forcing the crew to slow below the minimum SURTASS operational speed of 5 knots, or risk collision. When it appeared to the captain that the Chinese frigate was setting up for another encroaching maneuver, he ordered the SURTASS to be reeled in. The 5,000 foot long cable had just started to take up when the* Yuncheng *circled around behind the* Impeccable *and passed close enough aboard to sever the tether. The SURTASS unit has not yet been recovered. No injuries were reported. Cost of the sonar unit is estimated at...*

The president closed the report. "Okay, Stephen, you got what you came for. Get HAVE FLAME back up and running. The *Nimitz* is already underway to pick up HALO from Istres Air Base. When it gets to Johnston Island, let's press to get HALO up into orbit as soon as we can. You can work on getting a crew together, but I see no reason to shortcut safety at this

76

point. Just the mere fact that HALO is in orbit should be a fairly significant deterrent. We can wait to deploy it until the Delta IV is certified for manned flight."

Redirecting his gaze to the director of national intelligence, the president continued, "Doug, I want you to put every asset we have into getting me some actionable intelligence. I want every idea run down. I don't care how crazy it sounds. I don't like the sound of this Assassin's Mace crap."

CHAPTER 8

Freer Industries
Canoga Park, CA

I T HADN'T EVEN BEEN A full week since the *Atlantis* mishap, and Harden was already feeling directionless. His astronaut career was over, the status of his marriage in serious question. The resulting emotion left him confused about just what he needed more at the moment—focus or distraction. He had already planned on returning to his trading desk at JB West next week, but suddenly felt as if he needed a release. And when Sam Freer called unexpectedly last night, Harden welcomed the invitation. The reason for the get together was still somewhat cloudy, but Freer's paternal condolences regarding the death of Russ Batema were comforting, and Harden accepted the offer without reserve. He hadn't been to the secretive facility in years, though, and as he made his way through the San Fernando Valley, he couldn't help but wonder what was suddenly so important.

Harden could see the enormous manufacturing facility rising up out of the 45-acre complex before he even turned the corner onto Canoga Ave. Looking like a time capsule next to the modern shopping mall across the street, the gunmetal grey buildings at the heart of Freer Industries appeared as if they hadn't changed all that much since they were erected in the late 1950s.

The windowless structures were weathered, but wore their age well thanks to the kindness of the Southern California climate. It had always reminded Harden of some Hollywood movie studio backlot, filled with dozens of soundstages that offered no hint of what interesting scenes might be playing out inside. But as Freer had explained to Harden during his first visit, the sprawling industrial complex was actually once the production facility for a startup company contracted to develop and build rocket engines for the US Army. The small company grew exponentially in the fertile years of the early 1960s, ultimately becoming the primary thrust behind America's moon program. Rocketdyne eventually went on to develop all of the Saturn V's engines—the H-1, J-2, and the most powerful liquid fueled rocket engine ever produced, the F-1.

Harden stopped his vehicle at the lot entrance. After a quick phone call to verify his clearance, the chain link fence rolled away and the security guard waved him through. When he arrived in the east parking lot, his host was already waiting for him. Freer was easy to spot. The brown felt fedora he wore low on his brow had often drawn comments from people who said he reminded them of the legendary Alabama football coach "Bear" Bryant.

Beneath the fedora, Freer was a compact, but sturdy man. At sixty-seven, his 5' 9" frame was perhaps an inch shorter than it had been in his thirties, but his stamina was remarkably unchanged. He still played within a few strokes of Harden on the golf course, never once having given into Harden's suggestion that they should rent a cart. And mentally, Freer maintained the same drive and determination he had as a young engineer, a fact that was lost on no one who worked for any of his ventures.

"When are you going to let me talk you into driving

a car with some class?" Freer asked as Harden stepped out of the aging blue Chevy Tahoe.

"I guess when I can afford to have someone else work on it for me," Harden replied, lamenting perhaps the one shortcoming in his father's otherwise excellent tutelage. Benjamin Harden, an optometrist by profession, didn't even know how to change his own oil. So when Jack was young, the family car had always gone into the shop for repairs, and Harden learned to play golf instead.

"You can't find an original one of these around anymore," Freer said as he waved his hand over the Shelby Daytona Coupe parked next to Harden's crackling Tahoe. "This is the car that beat Ferrari at Le Mans in '64, and eventually went on to win the World Manufacturer's Championship in 1965."

Harden had seen the exotic racecar before, but it wasn't much to look at then. In what Freer referred to as an "aggressive state of restoration," it had been scattered across three thousand square feet of garage floor at his Pacific Palisades estate. "Wow, it looks great. When did you finish it?"

"A few months ago. All told, I have over nine years in the restoration. Every nut and bolt, and every piece of sheet metal is either original or remanufactured to original specs. Everything's original except the paint. You know, Jack, with enough time and money, you really can bring history back to life."

Harden shrugged. "Yeah, I guess."

"You don't sound convinced." Freer gave him a sly smile. "Let's go on inside. I've got something I want to show you."

Harden closed the door on the bright afternoon and followed Freer into the shadowy facility. It had been years since he first entered Freer's strange world of "technological philanthropy." Initially confused by the billionaire engineer's motivations, Harden thought Freer was just another Howard Hughes— some eccentric genius with an unquenchable thirst for aviation extremity. But he quickly realized that the enigmatic stereotype didn't fit. During Harden's first flirtation with retirement following NASA's *Columbia* disaster, he decided to finally put his business degree to work and started JB West, his own private wealth management company. His first investor seemed to come out of nowhere. Yet after much courting on the golf links, Freer had somehow managed to turn the tables on Harden—and instead, the savvy engineer convinced Harden to sign on to one of his secretive projects as a consultant. Harden had spent many long nights on the upper floor of the mysterious facility, feeling guilty at times that he was actually getting paid for his services.

"Any new mods to the simulators?" Harden asked as they passed the double doors labeled CM SIM and LM SIM.

"Not in a while."

"Where are we going then?"

"Into the workshop," Freer said, and then swiped his ID in the scanner next to the door labeled Authorized Personnel. Harden followed closely as Freer made his way into the expansive clean room facility. Standing on the grated steel scaffolding suspended above the factory floor, Freer found it hard to believe that his friend hadn't connected the dots already. But from the look on Harden's face, apparently he hadn't.

Harden's mind raced through the years of events that linked his first meeting with the affable billionaire to this moment. It all seemed to make sense now as he suddenly found himself staring at two life-sized spacecraft, the heart and soul of NASA's moon program—an Apollo Command Module and the spidery Lunar Module.

"You look surprised," Freer said.

"Those look incredibly realistic. Are they new simulator housings?"

"Actually, those are FTAs."

"Flight Test Articles?"

"Well, they were back in the 1970s," Freer explained. "Since then they have been restored to original condition and certified for flight by my SLATE team. The flight certification process was the culmination of decades of work. It allowed us to finally consolidate the knowledge retention program that we've been working on all these years."

As he stared down at the incredible spacecraft, Freer had trouble remembering exactly when it was that his original venture sparked to life. Perhaps it was when he acquired his first aerospace company back in the late 1970s. The company had been a subcontractor to Boeing during the Apollo program and supplied some of the tooling used to manufacture the first stage of the Saturn V rocket. Some inexplicable impulse had led Freer to catalog and warehouse the obsolete hardware. But as he acquired more and more of the thousands of parts suppliers that had collectively launched NASA— and America—to the moon, Freer's meager collection of Apollo artifacts grew into an impressive assemblage of space history.

As failing companies scrapped the relics of the moon program over the course of the next decade, Freer snapped them up like some Sunday morning picker at a space-age garage sale. From tools and jigs, to testing and service equipment, to actual flight hardware that would have supported the moon missions beyond Apollo 17, he rescued the aging artifacts that the country seemed all too eager to throw away. Then, to make sense of his enormous collection of seemingly random equipment, Freer began collecting the intangibles of the moon race—the talented and dedicated men and women who built, launched, and controlled the machines of the country's first lunar voyage. He had personally recruited every person who would eventually make up his SLATE team, offering them a job in retirement that gave them a unique opportunity to relive the excitement of their youth. As the years flew by and the men and women grew older, he saw the need to pass this legacy on to a new generation and began recruiting SLATE candidates from the best colleges around the country. NASA, it seemed, was on a different course, a course that would require them to relearn the lessons of the past, to start from a "clean" slate. Freer thought his SLATE was a better approach.

The eclectic group actually began its existence as the Legacy of Apollo-era Engineers and Technicians. Its members, some of the most astute minds in America, couldn't help but notice the acronym that resulted from rearranging the order of "technicians" and "engineers" in the group's title. Some of the older members took to calling themselves the LATE group—too late to be an influence on America's future in space, the future that they themselves had ushered in.

Perpetually driven, although not without a sense of humor, Freer eventually began referring to the group as the Society for the Legacy of Apollo-era Technicians and Engineers—noting that the order of importance of the two subcultures was finally and appropriately recognized, and that they would henceforth be referred to as the SLATE.

"Wow," Harden finally whispered, still mesmerized by the sight.

"Come on," Freer motioned as he shook off the reflection. "Let's go take a look."

Once on the factory floor, Harden was overwhelmed by the sheer size of the lunar module, or LM. The simulator he had trained in was merely a mockup of the LM cockpit and failed to convey the sense of scale of the entire vehicle. The beautiful machine towered nearly twenty feet above the factory floor. "Is it all right to climb up?"

"Sure, but watch out for that first step. It works a lot better in one-sixth gravity."

Harden grabbed the side rails of the ladder and leapt high above the clean-room floor, barely making the first rung with his right shoe. He scrambled to the top of the LM ladder and knelt down on the small porch on the face of the vehicle. Looking down, he saw Freer slide a wooden three-step platform over to the base of the ladder and follow him up. Harden opened the square hatch and crawled beneath the instrument panel into the lunar module cockpit. Freer followed him in. Harden stood at the commander's station and peered through the strange triangular window onto the clean-room floor far below. In his mind's eye he imagined a rugged grey terrain, cratered over millennia, curving toward the horizon.

"I give up. Where did this come from?" Harden finally asked as he caressed the controls and stared longingly at the gauges of the sleeping giant.

"This LM is actually an amalgamation of several lunar test articles combined with actual flight hardware that never made it off the ground. We used every possible original part we could find, and where parts were missing or not flight ready, we crafted them by hand. These were all handmade spacecraft to start off with, you know. Every LM was different from the others in some form or fashion. Each one was unique. We built this one from the ground up, restored it, if you will, just like I did with that Shelby outside. These things are worth preserving, Jack," Freer said wistfully, "and for more than just life as museum pieces."

"What about the command module?"

"Same thing. It's one of a kind."

"Everything works?"

"Just like it did in 1972. Every system and subsystem has been checked and is flight rated. All we need to do is top off the tanks."

"So when do we launch?" Harden quipped.

"That was never the goal, at least not initially. My objective was the preservation of the Apollo system, to include the architecture and the knowledgebase to support it. And on that, we were very successful. Our junior SLATE members, who are now getting hired by NASA, may one day be able to use this knowledge to help get us back to the moon."

"If we ever go back," Harden countered, and then pivoted to address Freer directly. "Why did you invite me up here, Sam?"

"Well, first I wanted to show you how far we've come in the last few years. And then I hoped you would be willing to meet with an acquaintance of mine who might be putting together a team that can use our program knowledge in, shall I say, a more direct application."

"Sam, I've already told you that I'm out of the space business. How much more direct are we talking here?"

"That's not up to me to decide. All I ask is that you meet with him up at Vandenberg tomorrow."

"I was really looking forward to some down time, Sam. This tour was incredibly exciting, but..."

"Good. I'll tell Stephen you'll be there."

CHAPTER 9

Santa Maria Airport
San Fernando Valley, CA

C URRENTS OF WARM AIR ROILED through the hills of
the LA basin, rising up in invisible columns to
buffet the small single-engine aircraft. Harden
bounced along in the blue and white Cessna 172 some
8,000 feet above the smog layer as it tracked northwest
toward the Santa Maria municipal airport. It wasn't
easy to maintain a precise altitude in the turbulent
air mass, but with a cruising speed of just over 100
miles per hour, and the ability to over-fly the endless
traffic jams of Los Angeles, he figured this would easily
cut his travel time in half. Not to mention that the
isolation and relative quiet of the small cockpit would
give him time to reflect on yesterday's revelations—the
tantalizing offer set forth by Sam Freer and what a
meeting with Austin might lead to—and the unusual
message left on his answering machine last night.

Stacy's brief mention of an upcoming doctor's
appointment seemed to be coupled with a new peace
offering, perhaps one last chance for him to make
things right. Harden was at least a bit uncomfortable
when she said that she wouldn't bother him again
until after the test results came in, but in some small
way he found it a relief that he could get his own life

back on track before dealing with what he sensed was yet another life-changing event coming his way.

The landing was a nearly unconscious effort. The chirp-chirp of the Cessna's main wheels on the concrete was Harden's only memory of the long, graceful, straight-in approach. He finally managed to push yesterday's distractions from his mind as he taxied the rented plane to the local fixed-base operator and lined up with the yellow parking stripe. He quickly scanned the ramp and spotted a man in a dark charcoal suit standing just beyond the chain link fence. Harden shut off the engine, climbed out of the flimsy aluminum shell, and kicked two chocks against the left main gear. Another man in denim coveralls walked out of the FBO's small hangar, wiping his oily hands with a red mechanics rag. Harden wasn't sure who was older, the mechanic or the rickety building he emerged from, both apparently of 1950s vintage.

"Want me to tie her down?" the man asked.

"That would be great. And if you could fill her up with 100 low lead, I'd appreciate it. I'm not sure how long I'll be gone, though. What time do you close?" Harden produced a credit card and handed it to the old man.

"Don't worry about it, son. I'll take care of her. We close at sunset though. After that you're on your own," the mechanic said, and patted Harden on the shoulder. "You look lost. Need a ride somewhere?"

"No thanks," Harden said, pointing to the man at the fence.

Harden, sporting a worn pair of blue jeans, a light blue polo shirt, and white tennis shoes, approached the man loitering at the fence. "Hi. My name is Jack Harden. I'm looking for Stephen Austin."

"Nice to meet you, Jack," Austin said, and then

87

closed the gate behind them. "But most people just call me Steve. How was your flight?"

"A little bumpy," Harden confessed. "But beats the hell out of fighting LA traffic, especially two days in a row."

"Nice landing there, by the way," Austin said, and then motioned to the black Continental at the edge of the parking lot. "We have a short ride to the base. Here, you might want to take a look at this while I drive." Austin then slid an envelope across the Lincoln's vinyl roof. Harden grabbed it and followed him into the idling sedan. While Austin drove, Harden removed both layers of brown wrapping from the package. He had seen this type of packaging before on other "black" programs; programs that were not supposed to exist, and would be vehemently denied by the government even as you were tried and convicted for merely acknowledging their existence. His suspicions were confirmed when he removed the maroon folder inside the special wrapping. Stamped on the front cover were the letters TS/SCI. Top Secret/Sensitive Compartmented Information. Harden took a deep breath as he slid his thumb under the paper tape and broke the seal on the folder. He quickly flipped past the legal disclaimers and non-disclosure agreement and read the single paragraph on the last page:

THE DIRECTOR OF CENTRAL INTELLIGENCE AUTHORIZES FUNDING AS REQUIRED TO DEVELOP HEAVY-LIFT LAUNCH CAPABILITY INDEPENDENT OF AIR FORCE EELV GENEOLOGY AND PROVIDE FOR AUTONOMOUS ACCESS TO SPACE ON MAN-RATED DELTA IV HEAVY. THE FOLLOWING CRYPTONYM IS CLASSIFIED TS/SCI:

HANDLE VIA
<< HAVE FLAME >>
CHANNELS ONLY

Harden closed the folder. "So how is Sam Freer connected to all of this?"

"Freer Industries has been the technology driver for the whole program," Austin explained while he drove. "Years ago when I was cutting my teeth with the Agency, I was assigned to monitor a Chinese immigrant who was working for one of Freer's small aerospace operations. His name was on a long list of potential spies suspected of stealing US technologies and exporting them back to China. Dongfan Chong not only turned out to be clean but eventually became a great asset to the Agency. Anyway, in the process I stumbled across an odd pattern of information accumulation regarding the Apollo program. Sam's name kept appearing over and over again. I was eventually tasked with finding out what his motives were and what government he might be working for. DCI thought I was crazy when I finally told him Sam wasn't working for any government, and that he was simply enjoying his fortune the same way many other entrepreneurs were doing at the time.

"Then when *Columbia* came apart over Texas, the question came up again: could America afford to be without access to space if the shuttle program ended before a new launch vehicle could be fielded by a public agency like NASA? I remembered Sam's project and got authorization to subsidize part of his operation through In-Q-Tel, the non-profit venture capital arm of the CIA."

Harden's eyebrows rose when he heard the name. "Wait. I've heard of them. Mike Griffin used

89

to head up the organization before he became NASA Administrator."

"That's right. And they normally target nascent information technologies, but we broke the mold with Freer Industries. Sam was already investing tens of millions in his preservation venture when we teamed up with him. Our goal was to create a new, reusable spacecraft based on proven Apollo technology. Once we were satisfied that he had a team in place and the knowledge base to draw from, we signed a contract with him to build a prototype capsule and two flight articles. It was actually quite amazing. We gave him an incredibly tight thirty-month delivery deadline, and he finished in twenty-six. Even for a Skunkworks-style operation, it was amazing."

Harden sat in silence for the remainder of the drive as he tried to absorb the sudden influx of information. He needed time to process what he had learned so far, and to consider what role he might be offered in such an incredible project. More important still, he wondered as the rolling hills swept by just beyond the tinted glass—was what role he would be willing to accept.

Space Launch Complex Six
Vandenberg AFB, CA

SLC-6, or Slick-Six as it was affectionately referred to by base personnel, had been under development since 1966 when ground was broken on the secret Air Force launch facility. But the Manned Orbiting Laboratory, the Air Force's early attempt at a manned space station, was cancelled before a single launch took place, and the site remained dormant for nearly two decades before extensive modifications were made to accommodate space shuttle launches into polar orbits. Then, only months before the first scheduled launch from the four-billion-dollar complex, the *Challenger* explosion brought NASA's manned space program to a standstill. When the shuttle eventually returned to flight status, budgets and politics forced the still unused launch complex to be mothballed yet again. Finally, after nearly thirty years of preparation, SLC-6 was retooled one last time to accommodate the Air Force's Evolved Expendable Launch Vehicles, or EELVs. In the end, no launch site in history had cost so much, been under development for so long, and had so few successful launches as SLC-6.

Austin brought the Continental to a stop alongside the enormous building at the center of the oceanside launch site. The structure reminded Harden of a shrunken version of the Vehicle Assembly Building at Kennedy Space Center, complete with an oversized American flag painted on its side. Harden exited the vehicle and followed his guide inside the towering hangar. Austin flipped several breakers on a panel next to the door. High above the dusty concrete slab, a crisscrossing array of metal halide lights flickered to life. The skeleton of the launch tower was first to appear, its ghostly latticework supporting an odd arrangement of three vertical rocket boosters.

"That's a Delta variant," Harden noted. He slowly craned his neck back to take in the whole machine. The two outside boosters stopped just past the halfway point in the stack, the central core booster continuing upward, unfolding in what had always reminded Harden of a giant three-fingered salute.

"That's right. This one's a Delta IV Heavy," Austin said as he led Harden to the elevator and selected the Gantry button. "The vehicle itself has been around for over a decade in various forms, but this upgrade to the

91

Heavy is new. It's on track to be the first man-rated rocket since the space shuttle."

The men emerged from the elevator twenty stories above the base of the launch pad. The only sound in the cavernous facility was the creaking of metal panels, blustered by the stiff ocean breeze outside. Austin smiled and followed closely behind Harden as the shuttle commander gravitated toward the open hatch of the shiny, sleek capsule. It was clear to Harden now that the payload occupying the top of the powerful stack was a variant of the Apollo Command/Service Module, or CSM. As he laid a hand on the side of the spacecraft, he struggled to comprehend the impossible scenario. A Skunkworks-style operation, commissioned by the most secretive arm of the US government, had reengineered an historic spacecraft as an insurance policy that would pay off only if America's national security was threatened—and the government couldn't otherwise muster a timely response.

"Go ahead. Climb on in," Austin whispered.

Harden crouched down and peered inside the open hatch. The soft hum of fluorescent lighting inside the spacecraft was inviting. He instinctively grabbed the handhold above the inner hatch rim and slid his body in feet first, coming to rest gently on the center couch.

"Sam calls this one Artemis," Austin explained from his crouched position next to the open hatch. "It's the first Advanced CSM manufactured by Freer Industries based on the original Apollo spacecraft. As you can see, it's quite an upgrade from the original design. All of the systems have been reengineered, taking advantage of the technological advances since the last Apollo flew. Pretty slick, huh?"

"Yeah, you could say that," Harden replied, clearly in awe of the equipment hovering above his head.

Situated at arm's length, nine flat panel displays replaced the outdated "steam" gauges of the original Apollo command module. Apart from a handful of toggle switches and knobs, and a few round-dial "backup" gauges, this machine was cutting edge. Buried beneath its gleaming silver skin were several generations of upgrades, blending the best technologies from both eras to create the perfect hybrid spacecraft.

"Why don't you slide over and check out the mission commander seat."

"Look, don't jerk me around!" Harden snapped. He quickly pulled himself out of the cramped quarters and confronted Austin on the gantry. "Why don't you cut to the chase? What's the mission here, and where do I fit in to this project?"

Austin took a step back. "Okay, okay," he said with his hands raised in defense. "I need to put together a crew who can pilot the Artemis on orbit and deploy HALO once we get it up there."

Harden suddenly felt as if the panels of the creaking building were closing in on him from all sides. He eyed Austin for a long moment as he tried to size up the strange sounding government man. He looked like a straight shooter, but if it hadn't been for Freer's referral, Harden would have just written off the man's gesture as pure folly. He wanted to laugh. Instead, he listened intently as the man in the charcoal suit continued his pitch.

"HALO will soon be on its way to our launch facility in the Pacific. We'll launch it as a package from Johnston Island with one of our heavy-lift boosters. Then, once the Delta-IV/Artemis stack is man-rated, we'll send it up from Slick-Six here at Vandenberg. A crew will rendezvous with HALO on orbit and conduct the required EVAs to deploy it. I'll admit it's a long shot, but we need a mission commander who can make things happen. And Sam said you were the man for the job."

Harden shrugged indifferently. "Why me?"

"None of the other shuttle commanders have any experience in this type of spacecraft. And you do...sort of. Sam says you've logged a considerable number of hours in his original Apollo simulators, which makes you the most qualified man for the job."

Harden pondered the revelation. How long had Sam been setting him up for this? And what made this CIA officer so sure he would say yes? Harden stared at the humming capsule, unsure if he wanted to know more. After a long pause, he turned back to Austin and spoke. "Have you filled any of the other crew positions yet?"

"We were hoping that you would help us pick a second crewmember from this list." Austin retrieved a wrinkled piece of paper from his breast pocket and held it between two fingers. "If you decided to take the job."

Harden grabbed the paper, unfolded it and read silently through the list. His eyes came to rest on the last name. "Jeff Burns, the NASA astronaut?"

"Ex-NASA astronaut. I haven't met him yet. I spoke only briefly with him yesterday, but he resigned earlier in the week. He said he finally realized that there were more important things in life than NASA."

Harden was dazed by the revelation. It had been only three days since the memorial service. "I guess he could read the writing on the wall. I can't say that I blame him. I just wish he would've talked to me first."

"Do you think he might be interested?" Austin prodded.

The question didn't even require an answer. Anyone who knew Burns knew he would jump at the offer. In the Flight Test Division back at Pax River, the more dangerous the assignment, the more likely Burns was to raise his hand. "I could probably persuade him to help you out. But I don't recognize any of the other names."

"That's fine. We only need one additional crewmember with piloting skills. The third seat has to go to one of your two mission specialists, Dennis or Bernegger. They have both been trained on HALO already. I haven't talked to either of them yet because, quite frankly, that's the easy part. Nobody goes anywhere if we can't get someone to fly the mission first. And it looks to me like you might be willing to help us out."

"Whoa, let's not get ahead of ourselves, Steve. Look, I already told Sam that I'm retired. I've got some promises to keep, and that requires my feet being planted firmly on the ground. I'll talk to Pipper about this if you'd like. If there ever was a pilot who could make shit happen, it's him. I can help him along through the training while you find someone else to—"

"You don't understand, Jack," Austin interrupted. His eyebrows rose slowly as he spoke. "We need people who can work *together*. If you don't take the offer, we'll have to find another mission commander. And if we do, there's no guarantee that Jeff will get the third seat."

Harden seethed beneath a calm veneer. Suddenly, out of nowhere, this stranger shows up with an incredible offer and seems to know all the right buttons to push. But as much as Harden hated being put on the spot, he also understood Austin's position. "Steve, I'm just not sure this is going to work."

"Can I at least tell Burns that you're on the fence and have him meet you in San Diego tomorrow? I can arrange for the two of you to tour Pad 39C and the rest of the facilities out on Johnston Island. You both need to see the operation we have there, and the trip out should give you enough time to discuss the matter."

"No," Harden finally conceded. "Don't tell him who he's going to meet. Just tell him that he will be briefed when he gets to San Diego. Tell him to meet his contact tomorrow night at McP's Irish Pub, 2100 sharp."

CHAPTER 10

Golden Dragon Restaurant
San Francisco, CA

USTIN REALIZED LONG AGO THAT an open friendship with Dongfan Chong had become too dangerous for either of them. So contact was maintained through anonymous voice messages and the occasional meeting at various public parks in and around Chinatown. The locale provided the perfect cover for his Chinese contact, while Austin could pretend to be just another tourist in search of some good Peking duck. He would rather have shared the dim sum with Chong than eat alone, but the number and strength of Chinese agents in the United States had grown exponentially since the Chinese government embarked on what had been termed a Revolution in Military Affairs. And since a major goal of the RMA was to actively prepare for space and cyber-warfare, any Chinese-American with access to US military or civilian aerospace technologies came under the close scrutiny of the Chinese government, who saw it as the expatriate's solemn duty to export America's secrets back to the PRC. Few did, but the cumulative results had been devastating nonetheless. Dongfan Chong had been approached more than once for information but had somehow always managed to turn the encounters into new leads for his old friend at the Agency.

Austin checked his watch. His meeting with Chong was in less than fifteen minutes. He cleaned the last bit of pork *siu mai* from his plate and followed it with a sip of green tea. He then opened the brochure for Portsmouth Square that he had picked up in the passenger terminal at LAX. There was a marker identifying the spot where the first American flag was raised during the Mexican-American War, when Captain John Montgomery of the USS *Portsmouth* seized Yerba Buena in 1846. Another marker identified the site of the first California public school. But it was near the next landmark that he knew he would find his old friend. Austin looked at his watch again. He still had ten minutes to make the short walk down Washington Street to Portsmouth Square. The exercise would be a good counter to the dim sum.

Austin exited the restaurant to find that the low overcast had finally burned off. But the unusually bright midday sun did little to warm the cool ocean breeze that whisked through the vibrant Chinese enclave. The streets this morning were busy, but not overcrowded. As he made his way toward the square, he couldn't help but notice the brilliant mix of colors lining the streets. Multi-tiered towering pagodas dotted the skyline, accentuated by a myriad of signs displaying the history and artistry of the Chinese language. Without even realizing it, Austin had the tourist look perfected.

When he reached the corner, Portsmouth Square unfolded from Washington Street to the south, and the financial district, centered around the Transamerica Pyramid, grew out of the landscape to the east. Austin spotted the statue at the far end of the park and made his way to the bottom of the grassy knoll. The Goddess of Democracy statue was barely taller than some of the women Austin had dated. But standing on the squat pedestal, it was still almost twice as tall as the short Asian man perched reverently at her feet.

"I never told you, but I was there in 1989," Chong said, his English still choppy from his recent visit to China. "I was one of the lucky ones, I guess. I lost many friends."

Austin looked down and read the plaque at the base of the statue. It was a replica of the original thirty-foot statue erected by Chinese students of the Democracy Movement in Tiananmen Square. Austin remembered watching the disturbing events on CNN, when columns of tanks and armored personnel carriers rolled into the large plaza in Beijing to break up the month-long protest and destroy the hastily constructed statue. But by the time the masses were dispersed, the square was littered with the bodies of dozens of students who had been ground beneath the cleats of the PLA's tanks as they rolled mercilessly through the square.

"But you made a difference," Austin said reassuringly.

"No, I gave up and emigrated. I left my parents behind, and ran from the things I could not change. Now, I hope with this I can truly make a difference." Chong handed Austin the newspaper that he had tucked under his arm. "Go sit down and read this. I will come join you shortly."

Austin went to a nearby bench and unfolded the yellowing copy of *China Daily*, one of the few state-run Chinese newspapers printed in an English-language edition. He adjusted his glasses and skimmed the front page. The paper was almost three weeks old. None of the headlines caught his eye. Austin crossed his legs and casually leafed through the pages. Deep into the front section a headline jumped from the page. The article was titled *Chang'e 5 Lost to Houyi's Arrow*. He unfolded his legs and sat erect as he read the article. It described the destruction of the Chang'e lunar lander as a great national loss, blaming an uncharted crater and the lack of real-time communication as causes for the accident. It then compared the loss to the myth of Houyi the Archer and his wife Chang'e, Goddess of the Moon. *Houyi can finally live with Chang'e again as two immortals, forever happy on the far side of the moon,* it reported. The uncharted crater would be forever known in Chinese textbooks as Chang'e Crater.

When Austin refolded the paper, Chong sat down beside him on the bench. "I just returned from China. From my father's funeral. He hid this paper and made my mother promise to give it to me if anything happened to him."

"I'm sorry. I didn't know. Was it sudden?"

Chong looked away. "Very sudden. I think he was poisoned."

"Is there anything I can do?"

"No, there is nothing you can do. The government killed my father. And the government *is* the law in China. Just like in Tiananmen. If you want to help me, you can find out why they are lying about the Chang'e."

"You think they're lying about the Chang'e 5 crash? You think the landing was successful?"

"No, I mean the communications satellite. I think the Chang'e 4 might be hiding in the shadow of the moon," Chong said as he scanned the park for signs that Austin had been followed. "And it's pronounced *chang-uh*, not *chang-ee*."

Austin made note of the correction. "What leads you to suspect a cover-up?"

"For one, the Communist Party does not freely print information that makes China look bad. And two, how would they know the landing had failed without the Chang'e 4 to relay the data?"

Austin paused, thinking through his rationale that had seemed solid until now. According to intelligence, the Chang'e 4 had merely been a communications relay satellite in orbit around the moon. Its circular orbit was to be altered to a high-dwell-time elliptical orbit prior to the Chang'e 5's lunar landing attempt so that data could be continuously relayed back to controllers on Earth. But the CNSA reported that the Chang'e 4's engine had burned too long, forcing the satellite into a hyperbolic orbit that eventually escaped the gravity of the Earth-Moon system and fell into orbit around the sun. "Is there something you're not telling me, Chong?"

"Look at the article again. There are three letters and a number that my father underlined faintly in the text."

Austin scanned the article quickly. "There's an E, an L, the number 2, and the letter M."

"Yes. And there are exactly twenty-four possible ordered combinations. I think the most logical combination is EML2."

Austin had an excellent mind for logic, but he knew the mathematician sitting next to him already had the answer. "Okay, Chong. What does that mean?"

"EML2 is a Lagrange point. More specifically, the second Lagrange point of the Earth-Moon system. It's a special point in space beyond the orbit of the moon that is gravitationally stable—and forever hidden from Earth. A satellite placed there could hover above the moon's far side just like a satellite in geosynchronous orbit appears to hover above the same spot on Earth. The Chang'e 4 could be hiding there in the moon's shadow, and no one would ever know. Have your people check its last known trajectory. If I am right, then the PLA is hiding something. Maybe the Chang'e 4 was designed to be more than *just* a communications

101

satellite. If it's hiding at L2, it could be a very bad omen for us all."

Austin wasn't familiar with the Lagrange terminology, but he trusted his friend. His mind twisted as he tried to sort through the possibilities, but there were too many to consider without more information. "Can we trust this? Do you know where your father got this information?"

"Yes, we can trust it. I believe it came from one of my father's old professors, Tsien Hsue-shen."

The name registered with Austin's distant memory. While researching the Chinese space program, he recalled that one name stood out above the rest. It stood out for two reasons. The first was that Tsien was often credited as being the Father of Chinese Rocketry. The second reason was that he was also listed as one of the co-founders of JPL, NASA's Jet Propulsion Laboratory. "Is he the H.S. Tsien that—"

"Yes, your FBI tried to have him deported from the United States in the 1950s in what you call the 'Red Scare.' He eventually returned to China and became the head of its ballistic missile program. He trained Chinese engineers in the techniques he had learned at MIT and Caltech. My father was one of his first students, eventually becoming a colleague and one of his most trusted confidants."

"It sounds to me like Tsien would have had no love lost for the United States after being treated like that. Why should I trust this?"

"My father always said that it was Tsien's work that was most important to him, not his politics. Like my father, he knew that the Communist Party would never willingly allow its citizens to enjoy the freedoms of a true democracy. And they both knew that any blow to democracy would, in the end, be a blow to the Chinese people. My father said it was best that Tsien died when he did. That way he would never have to see his most destructive inventions come to life."

"Thanks. I'll have my people get to work on this immediately." Austin stood and then glanced back at Chong before adding, "Again, I'm sorry about your father."

CHAPTER 11

McP's Irish Pub
Coronado, CA

THE FACT THAT CORONADO WAS part of an unusually shaped peninsula—its remote connection to the mainland some ten miles to the south—never stopped the locals from referring to it as an island. It may have been that most of Coronado's residents commuted to and from San Diego across the Coronado Bay Bridge. Still, it may have been that the city of Coronado had some of the most expensive real estate in Southern California. Either way, no one questioned the moniker. And as Jeff Burns crossed the lofty two-mile span, the exclusive title seemed justified as memories from a chapter in his life that had long since closed suddenly came flooding back to mind.

Burns parked his rental car behind the small Irish pub he had stumbled out of too many times to remember. Flanked to the north by Naval Air Station North Island, which occupied the majority of the land mass, and to the south by the Naval Amphibious Base, home of the legendary Navy Seals, McP's had a steady stream of thirsty sailors, who for decades had made their way to the island bar to either celebrate their return from lengthy Navy cruises—or forget they were about to embark on one.

As he exited the isolated parking lot and turned the

corner onto Orange Avenue, Burns peered through the ornate ironwork topping the chest-high stucco wall surrounding the pub's spacious courtyard. Several small groups congregated under tall, umbrella-shaped gas lamps. Everyone sported Coronado's standard autumn evening wear: short pants and sweatshirts. His contact must be inside and would likely stand out like a sore thumb in a crowd of locals. *But why would he pick this location?*

Inside, the crowd was small, even for a weeknight. Burns noted two men sitting at the bar and one man at the jukebox with his back to the door. The men at the bar sported short military haircuts, obviously sailors from one of the local bases; and the man at the jukebox had on a pair of khaki shorts and a worn Old Navy sweatshirt. Burns checked the time. He was still five minutes early. His contact must not be here yet.

The muscular man behind the bar was drying a tall glass tumbler and spoke without looking up. "What can I get you, pal?"

"Black and tan," Burns replied out of habit. Behind him, the jukebox suddenly roared to life, its volume obviously set for a larger crowd.

The barkeep raised his voice to compensate. "Sorry, but we're all out of Guinness tonight. Can I set you up with some Captain Morgan's instead?" he said, and clunked a bottle down on the bar in front of Burns.

He thought he must have misunderstood the man over the blare of the music. *How can an Irish pub be out of Guinness?* Burns then paused as the words to the song playing on the jukebox slowly sifted into his consciousness and registered a familiar feel. The soft island sounds of Jimmy Buffett resonated with distant memories as Burns put it all together and began to sing along, "*...ran into a chum with a bottle of rum, and we wound up drinkin' all night!*" Burns spun on his heel to find the man in the Old Navy sweatshirt standing directly behind him, singing along in harmony.

"Blaze! What in the hell are you doing here?" Burns roared.

"You're meeting your contact here, aren't you?"

"Wait, you're my contact? You've go to be shitting me! What kind of project could they have put you in charge of anyway?"

"We'll get to that, my friend. Let's go have a seat and catch up first." Harden grabbed two ice-filled glasses and two cans of Coke from the bar. He nodded to the bottle of rum.

Burns smiled, hoisted the bottle with the pirate-bedecked label, and followed Harden across the room. "Yeah, I was wondering when you were going to thank me for saving your ass."

The two old friends found a table against the far wall. Each man poured a healthy shot of rum over the distressed cubes and topped it off with a splash of Coke. Harden raised his glass, eager to close the door on a painful chapter.

"To Russ Batema."

"To Russ," Burns added, and took a long draw from the glass.

They raised their glasses a second time and clinked them together in a silent toast to the years of friendship they had shared. It was hard for Burns to recall a time before the men were friends. Ever since Aviation Officer's Candidate School, where the two young civilians who yearned to be carrier aviators first crossed paths, their lives had been fatefully intertwined. Before NASA, there was Test Pilot School. Before that, they had flown combat missions together in Iraq. Even through basic flight training they had been inseparable—all three of them. Burns's thoughts drifted to the last time they were all together. Graduation day from flight school was a joyous occasion for the three newly-minted aviators. Burns, Harden, and Pete Mitchell had each secured their first choice of assignments to the fleet. Burns and Harden would end up as fledgling F/A-18 Hornet pilots, while Mitchell finally earned his chance to become an F-14 Tomcat driver. But it would be the last time their friendly competition would have such favorable results.

"So have you heard from Mitch, lately?" Harden asked.

Burns's face flushed as he tried to shake off the memory. The rum was definitely beginning to have an effect.

"Mitch?" Harden repeated.

"Uh, well, it's probably been a year or so now. He's still working for Grumman, I think. The last time we talked he was working on carrier suitability for their UCAV program. It sounded like he was doing pretty well." Burns paused and took another long slug of the stiff drink. "Still, I somehow got the feeling he wasn't quite satisfied with the work. I guess you can't blame him, though. Building *pilotless* drones for the Navy does sound like an awfully cruel punishment for a former fighter pilot." Burns suspected there was more to it than that, but he had never quite been able to put his finger on it. As the only Naval Academy graduate among them, Mitchell had always been the one with full intentions of making the Navy a career. Yet not long after Mitchell's falling out with Harden, something seemed to change.

"Can't argue with you there." Harden still exchanged Christmas cards with Mitchell, but the two hadn't spoken in years. Burns instead had operated as the conduit for the estranged friends who hadn't made a conscious decision to avoid one another, yet still couldn't seem to find the common ground that they once had.

"You know, you guys really need to talk more," Burns admonished his friend, then hoisted his glass and took another large gulp.

"I'd love to," Harden finally said. "I just don't think he wants to. Hell, I would've given him my slot if I could have. But Captain Wright assured me that Mitch would get picked up for the next TPS class. I guess everyone just assumed he would apply for the next class." Test Pilot School had long been the entry point for any military flier with the ambition to become an astronaut. But the pyramid was brutally tight at the top, and the final test in a long string of competitions had ended unfavorably for Mitchell. All three men applied for the coveted position, but there were only two slots to be awarded—and they had gone to Jack Harden and Jeff Burns. Pete Mitchell was congratulated for applying and asked to try again next time. Mitchell never re-applied.

"Who knows, maybe he was the smart one..." Burns added, his voice trailing off to a whisper. "Maybe Mitch just grew up a little sooner than I did. What do I have to show for my efforts so far? At least you made it off the ground."

Harden looked away. A long silence followed as he stared deep into his drink. He had pushed as hard as he could to get Burns on the *Atlantis* mission. He had no reason to feel guilty. He had done more than anyone else could have to explain how Burns was the right man for the job. And he meant it. Russ Batema, he had agreed with Grayson, was more than capable. But Burns knew the shuttle better than most of the men who had flown it; and given the nature of the mission, Harden wanted the best man for the job, not the best behaved. Burns may have been one of the most unorthodox astronauts ever to grace the halls of Johnson Space Center, but he was by far the most talented aviator Harden had ever known. Still, he was confused. He didn't owe Burns anything. But how could he live with himself if he turned down Austin's offer and someone else was recruited to go in his place?

Burns finally broke the lengthy interlude. "So how was the debrief?"

Harden was slow to pull himself back to the present. "Huh? Oh, it was brutal. The public may be making me into some kind of hero, but the Monday morning quarterbacks at NASA don't necessarily agree. Management's tactful position is that Russ would still be alive if I hadn't ordered him to unstrap and leave his seat during powered ascent." Harden had no problem admitting when he was wrong, but he had relived the horrible event a hundred times since the abort and couldn't find any other option that made sense, even the option that seemed to be management's consensus—doing nothing.

"You did what you had to do," Burns said flatly. NASA's book of regulations reminded him too much of his brothers in blue. In the Air Force culture, the regulations only told you what you were *authorized to do*. The Navy culture he had grown up in took quite the opposite approach, where the regulations instead only told you what you were *prohibited from doing*. The latter approach, he decided, allowed for more flexibility—but also made for tougher decisions. The more Burns thought about it, he knew exactly what his friend needed at a moment like this, and it wasn't consolation. What Harden needed to finally bring closure to the painful ordeal was someone between a bartender and a priest. So Burns poured them both another stiff drink and sat quietly as Harden relived the flight one last time.

When Harden finished, he began to feel the weight that had smothered him for the last week, slowly lift. "So where did you run off to after the memorial service?"

"Well, I went back to..." Burns began and then paused, his eyes drifting nervously. "Look, I have something I need to tell you."

"Yeah, I heard you resigned from NASA."

"How could you possibly know that?" Then it hit him. "Steve Austin?"

"Yeah, we've met. So anyway, you're giving up on the dream to do what, go to *law school?* Are you sure that's what you really want to do?"

"At least I'll be accomplishing something. I just can't burn another decade of my life chasing some dream that's never going to happen anyway. There's no way around it, man. NASA is crippled. Talk about one step forward, two steps back. Look, I know deep down that I could be a great astronaut. And knowing that may just have to be good enough. I'm done trying to prove myself."

Harden nodded. There was nothing else that needed to be said. He smiled inwardly as he realized that Burns had finally made the decision on his own terms.

Burns paused for a moment and then smiled. "So if you're my contact, what's this job opportunity that you're supposed to tell me about?"

11,000 miles above Beijing

The golden, cube-shaped satellite, flanked by a pair of seventeen-foot-long solar panels, soared through space on long, slender, silvered wings. The Navstar GPS satellite, known internationally as USA-213, had traced the same predictable orbit since its launch from Cape Canaveral some three years ago and circled the globe faithfully every twelve hours, continuously transmitting the radio signals to earth that allowed modern society to function. Its precision time signal, health status reports, and positional data—or ephemeris—were used by hundreds of millions of terrestrial receivers in everything from TomTom and Garmin navigation devices to the ubiquitous cell phone. And that was just in the civilian spectrum. Nearly every military vehicle, whether it flew, floated, rolled, or submerged, had incorporated the critical information transmitted in the GPS signal into every aspect of its operations. But like most US satellites, it was designed to operate in the sterile environment of space and had no defense against threats from below—or above.

The transfer orbit of the kinetic-kill-vehicle had been closely tracked by giant antennas at the Xi'an Satellite Monitor and Control Center since it was launched from the Chang'e 5 some three days ago. Controllers at the XSCC had already issued two mid-course corrections and were preparing to initiate terminal guidance as soon as the projectile passed through geosynchronous Earth orbit. Conjunction of the two space-borne objects was timed to occur high above the sovereignty of mainland China, far away from the prying eyes of the US Space Surveillance Network. The resulting collision would litter the already congested orbit with thousands of additional fragments, making reconstruction of the event extremely challenging for the orbital forensics team at Air Force Space Command.

The impact occurred at a closure rate of nearly five miles per second. The two-meter-long projectile tore through the central mass of the 4,500-pound GPS satellite, ripping out its electronic guts in a tiny

111

fraction of a second. Shards from its Kapton thermal blanket exploded into the surrounding vacuum as the flimsy silver wings folded in on themselves like crumpled pieces of paper, spraying flakes of gallium arsenide into the rapidly expanding cloud of debris.

CHAPTER 12

Oahu, HI

HIS EARDRUMS REGISTERED THE PRESSURE change in the cabin as soon as the pilot pulled the throttles back to idle to begin their final descent. Burns rubbed the sleep from his eyes and slowly lifted the flimsy paper shade next to his right shoulder. Oahu was barely visible at the front edge of the small window. Still groggy from the six-hour flight from Lindbergh Field in San Diego, he wrote off the image to sleep inertia. He stretched and yawned before looking once again to confirm his theory. The realization finally sunk in. *We're landing on the wrong side of the island.* Honolulu Airport was on the west side of Hawaii's most populous island. The only landing strip he knew of on the east side of Oahu was the Marine Corps Air Station at Kaneohe Bay.

Burns leaned over and rousted his friend back to life. He charged through several sentences before Harden's brain fully reconnected with his senses.

"Huh," Harden mumbled.

Burns abandoned the explanation. He had already unclipped his seat belt and was headed for the cockpit when he felt a thump from the landing gear as they extended and locked in place. *We're definitely landing at the wrong field.* He pounded a fist on the cockpit door while twisting the door knob with his other hand.

It was locked. *Damn.* The cabin intercom suddenly came to life, "Please be seated, gentlemen. We'll be on deck shortly."

Burns was already on his way back, recapping the past thirty seconds for Harden when his still groggy friend finally looked out the window. "Why in the hell are we landing at K-Bay?" Burns asked as if he were interrogating Harden for a crime.

"Maybe we were supposed to land here," Harden said matter-of-factly.

Burns paused as he searched for something else to support his claim. All Harden had told him last night was that they would change planes in Hawaii for the final leg to Johnston Island.

"I didn't say which airfield we would land at, did I?"

"You said we would transfer to another jet on the ramp and not have to waste time going through the terminal. I remember that much." Burns instinctively shifted his weight forward as the Lear's pilot flared to land. He grabbed a seat back on either side of the aisle and braced for the impact, but the landing was barely perceptible. *Definitely not a Navy pilot.* When the aircraft finally came to a stop, Burns made his way back to the cockpit. The small door swung open just as he arrived. One of the pilots pointed through the windscreen to the far eastern corner of the military ramp. On it sat a lone F/A-18 Hornet. "Sorry, gents. This is as far as we were chartered to take you."

USS Ronald Reagan, *CVN-76*
100 NM West of Hawaii

Admiral Frank Willard scanned the horizon from his lofty perch high on the Flag Bridge of the *Ronald Reagan*. A thin veneer of silver-blonde locks draped across his tall forehead was the only indication of
114

Willard's true age. His weathered face was a product of long hours at sea and years of fun in the Southern California sun. But the years had treated him well, and the splotchy red patterns on his face looked more like faded freckles than aged sun spots. Yet when contrasted against a pair of transparent grey eyes and wild silvery eyebrows, it was obvious why his peers called him "Red."

The *Reagan* was operating in the western Pacific and designated the surge carrier for Seventh Fleet Operations. But when the news cycle suddenly became dominated by Chinese aggressions in the Taiwan Strait, even the lowest ranking sailor on the mighty warship could make the connection. It would only be a matter of time before they got the call that would send them on their second Westpac cruise in the last fourteen months. And in preparation for the looming crisis, carrier qualifications for the embarked Airwing were scheduled to begin in two hours. But there was no such thing as idle time for such an important national asset, and there was other business still to attend to.

"Admiral, do you think it's going to work?" Petty Officer Ryan asked the strike group commander.

"Yeah, I've got a feeling it will, son," said Willard as he watched the jet blast deflector rise out of the sprawling steel flight deck and lock into position behind the strange delta-shaped aircraft.

"How long do you think it will be before something like this becomes operational?" the petty officer asked.

"Sooner than you think." Willard had been a Tomcat pilot and TOPGUN instructor long before pinning on the stars that adorned his crisply starched khaki collars, and regarded the exotic machine with mixed emotions. "The next war will be fought by remote control. So if your kids want to be fighter pilots when they grow up, you'd better let them play their video games whenever they want. Otherwise they won't stand a chance."

Ryan chuckled. "Oh, they'll love to hear that, sir."

Willard hoisted his binoculars to get a closer look at the unusual vehicle as its launch bar lowered into the catapult shuttle. He was as curious as everyone else on the ship to see if this marvel of engineering was going to work as advertised. Willard had seen a lot of firsts during his years in the Navy, but this he knew, was truly historic. He was about to witness the first launch of an Unmanned Combat Air Vehicle, or UCAV, from the flight deck of an operational aircraft carrier. And if the flight went well, he would also witness a much more delicate feat—the first attempt to land an unmanned aircraft on a warship at sea.

Johnston Island
Pacific Ocean

"It'd be nice if they had a TACAN," Burns mumbled into his oxygen mask.

"Then I guess everyone would know where this place is," Harden said.

"This place" was Johnston Island. Seven hundred nautical miles southwest of the Hawaiian island chain, the isolated atoll was named after its discovery some two hundred years earlier by Royal Navy Captain James Johnston. Back then its strategic value consisted largely of guano deposits. Loaded with potassium nitrate, or saltpeter, the excrement was in high demand at the time for its uses in, among other things, fertilizer and gunpowder. Jurisdiction of the lonely spit of land changed hands numerous times over the ensuing two centuries, from the US Department of Agriculture that had once administered it as a bird refuge, to the Department of the Interior,
116

to the US Navy, who had fortuitously carved out the first landing strip on the island only months before the start of WWII.

Then in 1958, under the direction of Wernher von Braun, Johnston Island had surreptitiously served as the launch site of one of the German rocket scientist's V-2 derivatives, the US Army Redstone rocket. The objective of the secret project, code-named Teak, was to test the effects of an exo-atmospheric nuclear detonation. The Redstone lofted the nuclear device to an altitude of 250,000 feet before it exploded brilliantly in the night sky. The world's first electromagnetic pulse, or EMP, was so powerful that it knocked out streetlights hundreds of miles away on the Hawaiian island of Oahu. Communications were interrupted for several hours over a widespread swath of the Pacific due to the large amount of radiation injected into the lower ionosphere. The test program was short lived, however. Once it was realized how devastating the forces of an EMP blast could be to a sufficiently advanced society, the tests were promptly banned.

"I think I might have something here," Harden said as he pushed a button on the radar display. At their current altitude and airspeed, there would be a narrow window of opportunity to find the small island in the vast expanse of water below; and the high flying fighter would be in this envelope for barely a minute.

"I sure hope so," Burns said as he eyed the fuel gauge. "Because if one of those clouds is covering the damn thing, we might both be going for a swim." Burns hadn't been behind the controls of an F/A-18 since Test Pilot School. The unexpected flight was thrilling at the outset. When he'd won the coin toss to see who got to drive, he felt as if he'd just won the lottery. But the idea of getting lost and running out of gas in the middle of the Pacific was beginning to dull the initial

117

excitement. He could only imagine that the flight was more than a little stressful for Harden too. The last time his friend was in a tactical aircraft, it had left him with a broken back following an emergency ejection. Ironically, Burns thought, it was his ejection from an F-14 during a Navy test flight that had wrecked Harden's original career plans and led him to consider applying to NASA in the first place. Luckily for Harden, the space shuttle didn't have ejection seats.

"Wait a second." Harden stepped the radar to EXP 2, an expand mode of the radar that yielded a higher resolution picture, but at a much narrower field of view. He cupped his right hand around the display to block the sun's glare as he studied the image.

"I think you might have it," Burns said, and then disconnected the autopilot.

"Almost there. I'm going to go to Expand 3." Harden selected the highest expansion mode of the APG-65's air-to-ground radar and worked quickly. "Here goes nothing." Harden knew this was the equivalent of looking for their tiny target through a skinny soda straw; if the radar wasn't pointing directly at the small island, he would never see it.

"That's it!" Burns shouted, and then ripped the throttles to idle. He popped the speed brakes and rolled the fighter into a steep overbank. Nearly inverted in the thin air high above Johnston, the fighter's nose sliced though the horizon until they were pointing almost straight down at the island like an enormous grey lawn-dart. The Hornet fell from the sky at a nauseating 50,000 feet per minute. Burns smiled as he noticed the targeting diamond in his heads-up display superimposed neatly over the lonely strip of terra firma. "Nice work."

Comfortable now that he had a place to land, Burns eased back on the stick and corrected their trajectory
118

to a much more survivable descent profile. He surveyed the waves to get a cut on the wind direction and spiraled down toward the southwest corner of the island to line up for the carrier break. "Here we go, my friend. It's time to dump some gas." Burns slammed the throttles past the military detent and set both afterburners ablaze. At full power, the ferocious GE engines quickly pushed the Hornet past 500 knots as he lined up on the narrow runway.

"There's five bills," Harden said. "You don't have to do this to impress me."

"I'm just gonna let them know we're here. That's all." A shock-cone formed quickly on the nose of the fighter as the heavy ocean air was squeezed to the point of maximum compression. The roiling mach-vapor then drifted back along the fuselage until finally attaching itself to the Hornet's wing root. "This runway looks questionable."

"I see that," Harden agreed, noting several large X's painted down the center of the small landing strip.

The airframe suddenly shuddered around them. When the supersonic shockwave detached from the Hornet's composite wing, it smashed into the island with a rumbling concussion of sound. "Now they know we're here," Burns announced, and eased back on the throttles. At the up-wind end of the runway, he rolled the jet into a crisp 90-degree bank and broke into a hard left turn. The Hornet's stubby wing tips warped noticeably under the intense load as the fighter ripped through the thick ocean air. Burns's g-suit inflated violently. The pressure felt good. *What a release!*

Harden's vision began to blur around the edges as he struggled to focus on an unusual structure below on the ground. The revetment was covered with the same type of camouflage netting he had seen before in Iraq; material that hid tanks in the desert from the prying

119

eyes of orbiting satellites and other reconnaissance platforms. "Don't land long."

"I got it," Burns grunted. He then eased the g-load and quickly rolled out on downwind. "How long do you think the runway is?"

"Five thousand feet, maybe six," Harden estimated. "That's *if* you include the area under that camouflage."

"Yeah, let's not include that." As the speed bled off, Burns leveled the Hornet briefly at six hundred feet and dirtied the aircraft by lowering the landing gear and flaps. After one last glance over his shoulder, he started down in a gentle left hand turn, the same way he had approached the carrier hundreds of times before. "Too bad there's not an arresting cable down there."

The jet slammed down on the short runway in fine Navy tradition. The brakes glowed cherry red as the Hornet rolled to a stop near the end of the crumbling asphalt. Less than a football field separated them from the strange camouflage netting they had spotted from above. *What could they possibly be hiding out here?* Burns wondered.

CHAPTER 13

USS Ronald Reagan

"**B**oss, the Salty Dog is ready to come aboard," Pete Mitchell announced as he pressed the phone up against his chest. On the other end of the muzzled line was his controller in CATCC, the *Reagan's* Air Traffic Control Center, where the futuristic vehicle was being controlled.

Commander McKnight scanned the sky around the carrier. The AirBoss owned the airspace surrounding the powerful warship, and no one dared commence an approach to the flight deck of an aircraft carrier unless approved by this man. "Three more aircraft to recover. Expect a clear deck. Your signal is Charlie."

Mitchell put the phone back up to his ear and relayed the news to the drone's operator buried seven levels below in a windowless steel compartment. "Brandt, your signal is Charlie. You're cleared for the approach, Mode One-Alpha." The Grumman manager nodded at the reply and cradled the phone. "Boss, Salty Dog is commencing. She'll be crossing the ramp in six minutes."

"It damn well better be, mister. That bastard of a machine will never make it out of Op-eval if it can't integrate with my manned recoveries," McKnight said. The historic launch and short flight of the X-47B UCAV had gone off without a hitch, but the most important test for a potential carrier aircraft was just minutes away.

Mitchell, in his sharply pressed khaki trousers and monogrammed Northrop Grumman polo shirt, fought his natural urge to snap back with a witty reply. But he had spent many hours in Pri-fly, the carrier's version of a control tower, as a navy lieutenant and knew intuitively that the last person on an aircraft carrier that you wanted to get into a pissing contest with was the AirBoss.

Peter Mitchell might have been a civilian for the past eight years, but he hid it well. His solid six-foot frame was trim and fit. He was proud to maintain the same waistline that he had in his twenties, and his dirty brown hair, tapered on his nape and tight over the ears, was a military habit he just couldn't seem to break. A quick change into a Navy-issue flight suit, and he would not have looked out of place in any of the squadron ready rooms on board the massive floating airfield.

"Salty Dog five-zero-two, we have ACLS lock-on at five miles," the young petty officer in CATCC reported over the *Reagan's* land/launch frequency. Commander McKnight reached above his head and adjusted a tiny black knob on the tower's low ceiling. Voices emanating from the hidden speaker grew louder until eventually drowning out the low murmur of idle conversations.

"Needles show on and up," reported the voice from deep inside the ship.

"Concur. Stand by for Mode I discrete," the controller responded.

"Command and control selected."

"Mode One-Alpha." The ship's SPN-42 Automatic Carrier Landing System was now sending commands to the flight control system of Salty Dog 502. If all worked correctly, it would direct the unmanned aircraft to a precision landing on the angled flight deck just in front of the third cross deck pendant, or three-wire. At least that's what Mitchell was hoping.

When the red phone rang, McKnight snatched it off the hook before the bell stopped vibrating. *Only the admiral could manage to call at such an inopportune time.* "Yes, sir. Boss here."

"Ron, you only get one shot at this. Tell Mitchell if he doesn't recover his aircraft on this pass, we're going to Bingo the bird to Hickam. We just got orders from Seventh Fleet. We're to proceed to the South China Sea, maximum warp. And before he asks," Admiral Willard said flatly, "No, we won't be able to COD him off the ship."

"Yessir," McKnight acknowledged, and returned the phone to its brass sheath below the window ledge. "Mr. Mitchell, stand by to Bingo that thing if it doesn't trap on this pass. Looks like we're headed west. And you get to come along for the ride, free of charge."

Mitchell could already feel the cavitation rumbling through the steel deck plates as the *Reagan's* screws battered the mighty Pacific. White froth mushroomed in the wake of the warship as it struggled for speed. Carrier aviation always was a tough business, he reminded himself. Every launch was an emergency procedure waiting to happen. *Damn, it's a wonder that it ever works at all.* He would find out what the emergency was soon enough, but right now it didn't matter. Salty Dog was already inside of a mile on the approach.

Mitchell refocused his binoculars on the wedge-shaped aircraft and hawked the flight controls for any signs of trouble. He had witnessed hundreds of approaches during the last two years of field trials, and would be able to smell a "waveoff" long before it ever happened. But the corrections so far were smooth as silk.

Then he spotted trouble. As the aircraft approached the ramp, a last-second lineup correction forced the computer-controlled machine into an aggressive wing dip. *Damn, the burble. We're going too fast.* Mitchell held his breath as the UCAV's single engine spooled up to counter the sudden decrease in lift. This was the one thing that Mitchell couldn't teach a machine: how to anticipate. A computer could only react. It couldn't look down at the wake of the ship. It couldn't read the waves for clues to the wind's direction. And it couldn't hear the LSO's report of axial winds. The machine did the best it could.

It wasn't good enough. The Landing Signal Officer didn't like it either. He pickled the waveoff lights, signaling the unmanned aircraft to go "eat at Joe's." The Salty Dog couldn't see the red lights blaring on the Fresnel lens, but it did receive the discrete data-link command to execute a waveoff. Still, it was too late.

Mitchell squinted one eye as the Salty Dog's engine spooled up to full power. Despite its best effort, the sink rate was sickening. In aviator parlance, the helpless UCAV looked like a turd coming down off a tall moose's ass. The struggling aircraft barely cleared the round down before slamming onto the *Reagan's* flight deck well short of the target point, coming to a quick stop in the middle of the angled deck. Mitchell hung his head in both relief and despair. His Salty Dog was safe aboard, but he had gotten out of the Navy for a reason. And yet here he was once again, embarked on an aircraft carrier en route to the western Pacific. It was the last place on Earth he wanted to be. His head flooded with questions, but one thought won out over the rest. *There has to be a way to get off this ship.*

Johnston Island

Six hundred nautical miles away Jeff Burns flicked a silver switch buried beneath the Hornet's canopy rail. Excess cabin pressure hissed past the deflating rubber seal as their crisply air-conditioned cocoon slowly succumbed to the warm breeze of the balmy Pacific.

"Sure is quiet out here," Burns noted as he surveyed the surrounding isolation for signs of life. Single and two-story buildings dotted the sandy landscape. He couldn't quite decide if the island's infrastructure was in a period of intense reconstruction—or undergoing a much needed demolition. Two Linkbelt cranes, complete with wrecking balls, towered above a small army of bulldozers, backhoes, and graders assembled around one clump of buildings as if to cordon them off for demolition.

The stiff northeast trade wind was spitting sand at the lenses of Burns's RayBan sunglasses when he noticed a man emerging from an outcropping of buildings on the windward side of the island. "Blaze, two o'clock, coming our way. I guess someone knows we're here. Judging by the khaki shorts and Hawaiian print shirt, he must be the island tour guide."

The two pilots quickly hoisted themselves out of the lofty cockpit and swung to the ground by using the Hornet's wingtip missile rail like a chin-up bar. As Burns extricated himself from the sweaty flight gear, he couldn't help but wonder who the strange-looking man in the Wayfarer's was in the grand scheme of things.

"That was some announcement you guys made," the man said with a smile. "I'll take it your trip was enjoyable."

"It sure was," Harden said as he shook hands with

125

the man and nodded to Burns. "Sam Freer, meet Jeff Burns."

"It's great to finally meet you," Freer said. "Jack has told me so much about you."

"Good to meet you," Burns replied, wondering why Harden had never mentioned the man before.

Freer motioned toward the edge of the ramp and turned on his heel. "Come on. I'll show you guys around." Harden and Burns fell in trail, following Freer back toward an aged cinder block building amid a small oasis of grass.

Inside, a wave of cool air washed over them as they walked down the dimly lit passageway. "Has Jack told you about my SLATE venture yet?" Freer asked over his shoulder.

"No, as a matter of fact he hasn't," Burns said, and glanced back at his friend.

"Then I guess Jack must've honored the non-disclosure agreement he signed when he joined my team. Has he briefed you on *any* aspects of the project yet?"

"Not really. But I think it's about time someone starts telling me what in the hell's going on here. All I know so far is that some Agency man asked me if I'd be interested in offering up my services in the name of national security. He asked me to meet a contact, who then turns out to be my best friend. And now I find myself on some godforsaken island in the middle of the Pacific—no offense. So forgive me if I'm not seeing the connection to national security here."

Freer stopped at the end of the long passageway. He typed a code into the cipher lock next to the shiny steel door and waited for the double beep. The magnetic buzz of the locking mechanism reverberated in the empty quiet of the old building. "It won't be long now until you both know as much as I do. Stephen will have to take over from there, since you'll actually be working for him if you decide to take him up on the offer."

Freer rotated the handle and pushed the heavy grey door open. Automatic lights flickered to life as he entered the room. "This is Launch Control. Flight Control is in another building at the other end of the island."

Burns grappled with what he saw. He was vaguely aware that the Army Ballistic Missile Agency had launched rockets from the remote atoll back in the late 1950s, but this equipment was obviously not from that era. And he hadn't noticed any remnants of launch equipment on the island when they flew overhead—*wait, except for the unusual revetment at the end of the runway.*

Freer walked quickly past the banks of computer terminals toward the door at the opposite end of the room. "How did you like the facilities at Vandenberg?"

"I'll admit, I was intrigued," Harden said, following Freer into a small foyer.

"I thought you might be." Freer pressed the elevator call button and the doors slid apart. Inside, he pushed a button labeled 8th Deck S-IC Observation Gantry. The floor jerked suddenly as the elevator began its long descent into the undersea mountain top. In the cramped compartment, Freer couldn't help but notice the confusion on Burns's face turning to anger. "I can see that Jack really has kept you in the dark. You see, Jeff, my SLATE team has designed a spacecraft for the CIA based on the Apollo Command Module. We call it Artemis."

"Like Apollo's twin sister," Burns replied.

"Exactly." Freer sounded impressed. "Only we had no launch vehicle at the time to launch it with. That's why Boeing has been working so hard to man-rate its Delta IV Heavy booster."

"No shit?" Burns murmured as he began processing the first real bits of information he'd received since fielding the strange phone call from Austin. *A covert spacecraft and a man-rated launch vehicle can mean only one thing.*

Burns swallowed hard to clear the pressure in his ears as the elevator plunged deeper into the cool earth. When the cramped metal box finally jerked to a stop, the doors opened to reveal a long tunnel chiseled into the volcanic rock. Burns suspected they were heading in the direction of the revetment at the end of the runway. Motion-controlled-sensor lights flickered on as they moved through the tunnel. The final light revealed a door that reminded Burns of the water-tight hatches on naval vessels. Freer grabbed the large lever arm in the center of the door and threw all his weight at it. Six rectangular dogs arranged around the door's edge retracted from the sturdy frame. He leaned his shoulder against the steel plate and the heavy hatch swung open. A shaft of pure white light poured in from above to reveal Freer's greatest recreation.

CHAPTER 14

Launch Pad 39C
Johnston Island

BURNS FROZE AT THE SIGHT. Three vaulting red letters, stacked one high atop another on a gleaming white backdrop, spelled out USA. He quickly pushed past Harden and Freer as he made his way out onto the small balcony inside the immense underground silo. Burns estimated the vertical shaft to be at least a hundred and fifty feet across, and perhaps three times as deep. His mouth hung open. On display before him was the first stage of what was still the world's most powerful rocket—the business end of the Saturn V.

The only ones he had seen before were the decaying carcasses on display at NASA centers around the country; but they were always lying down, dead, as if interred for eternity. "How did you do this?" Burns mumbled, refusing to take his eyes off the rocket.

Freer shrugged. "It really wasn't that complicated. All the hard work had been done for us already. All the design, testing, and even the manufacturing had already been done. America was just losing the knowhow. Luckily, I was able to build a team to bridge the knowledge gap between two generations of spacefarers—the generation that sent us to the moon, and the generation that will hopefully take us back one day."

Burns listened intently as Freer recounted the history of the project, as well as his reasons for diverting a significant portion of his personal fortune to support it.

"Okay." Burns nodded. The concept seemed sound, but it was the execution that he was most interested in. "So is this an updated version of a Saturn rocket?"

"No, this is actually one of the *original* Saturn Vs— restored, of course, and very nearly ready to fly. When was the last time you paid a visit to Rocket Park at Johnson Space Center?"

"Well, I guess I haven't been there since the restoration project was completed and they closed in the..." Burns paused as he tied it all together. "Wait. This isn't the JSC Saturn, is it?"

"One and the same," Freer beamed. "My company won the restoration contract. We dismantled the entire stack, scanned every part, and put the information into 3D CAD programs. We used the parts that were still serviceable, and the ones that weren't, we manufactured. What we put back on display at the space center is actually a replica. A very good one, I must admit. I'd bet that the average NASA engineer wouldn't even be able to tell the difference."

"What about the engines?" Burns asked, looking down at the monstrous engine bells tucked neatly behind the fairings of the Saturn V's first stage, the S-IC.

"Those were the long poles in the tent. The engines from the display were beyond repair. It really was criminal. NASA had actually looked into the idea of restarting the F-1 production line at the beginning of the Constellation program, but choked on the costs. We got real lucky when I approached Rocketdyne and

130

found out that they had canned fifteen of the originals when the line was shut down."

Burns's eyes followed the corrugated metal skin of the rocket up past the huge first stage to the top of the second stage, where it abruptly truncated. The top third of the Saturn V was noticeably absent. "Where's the S-IVB?"

"Not to bore you too much with the details, but the third stage really isn't necessary unless you're going to the moon."

Burns paused as he tried to take it all in at once. He could now see firsthand how his father could have been so possessed with a machine and its mission that he would have risked his entire career—and in the end his life—just to be a part of it. "Then where are you going with this rocket?"

"I was only contracted to provide for heavy-lift capability to Earth orbit. And with the J-2X engines on the second stage, we can launch 150 tons to low Earth orbit or 120 tons to GEO orbit. It's actually overkill for the missions we're likely to be tasked with."

Harden felt a sudden surge of anger. "So you've been working on this the entire time you've known me, setting me up and assuming I would go along."

"I'm afraid so," said Freer. "I just couldn't fill you in on the full scope of the project until the time was right."

"What if I say I'm not interested?"

"Jack, look, I may have only intended to recruit a new member for the Flight Application section of the SLATE, but you've become a good friend since then. I was going to tell you about all of this some time ago, but with what happened with Stacy and the baby, I just couldn't. And then before we knew it, the president cancelled the HAVE FLAME program. After that, I figured it was too late."

For the first time, the pieces began falling into place for Burns. "Let me get this straight. You're going to use a two stage Saturn V rocket to launch HALO, just like NASA did with Skylab back in the '70s. Then, Jack is going to launch from Vandenberg in the Artemis, rendezvous with HALO, and assemble it on orbit. So who...who makes up the rest of the crew...and when does this science fiction plan blast off?"

"Stephen is planning on tapping Mark Bernegger or Pat Dennis as a payload specialist. That leaves us short one pilot to help fly the command module. We were hoping you would be interested, Jeff."

Burns turned to Harden with a smile as wide as a lifetime. He might finally get to earn that astronaut title after all. "Where do I sign up?"

Harden sighed. Once again he was caught between competing interests—between promises made and debts to be paid. He knew he didn't have forever to reconcile his marriage. But Burns had saved HALO, and the more Harden thought about it, he had probably saved his own life in the process. With each revelation, Harden found it more difficult to come up with a rational response to Austin's proposition.

SLATE Conference Room
Johnston Island

Sam Freer picked up the phone and cradled it against his shoulder. "Hi, Stephen. Yeah, guess who I have here with me? Just got finished giving them the nickel tour. Yep. Sure. I'll go ahead and put you on speaker."

Freer punched several buttons on the STU-III secure telephone unit and the encrypted transmission of Austin's disembodied voice floated down from the ceiling. "Jack, Jeff, glad to hear you made the voyage in one piece. I hope you enjoyed the flight."

"It was great," Burns replied to the overhead speaker. "Do we get to keep it?"

"Just for a while. Long enough to get you guys home, I guess. Look, I'm afraid I've got some bad news from Washington." There was a long pause. "The HALO mission has been put on hold by the president...*again*. It seems we have bigger problems than controlling low Earth orbit.

"We now have reason to believe that the Chinese lunar communications satellite, Chang'e 4, may not have been a harmless communications satellite after all. We suspect it may be hiding in a Lagrange orbit behind the moon. We have no way to confirm it yet, but we have good intel that says the Chinese may be able to use this L2 orbit as a launch point for some kind of deep space weapon." The voice in the speaker paused again. "And the president doesn't want to do anything at the moment to make the Chinese feel threatened, like deploying what they see to be an offensive weapon system: HALO."

"Even to counter one of *their* offensive space systems?" Freer asked incredulously. "In other words, we're backing down from the Chinese. What is it you think they have on us?"

"In the president's opinion, we're not backing down as much as we are giving diplomacy a chance to work."

"That's bullshit, and you know it, Stephen!" Freer shouted, expressing more contempt than Harden had ever seen coming from the normally unflappable engineer.

"I know I'm getting deeper into this than I'm authorized to, but in recent weeks there has been some chatter containing unspecified threats to US national security. And then just a couple of days ago, a Chinese frigate in the South China Sea aggressively squared off with one of our under-sea warfare ships. All this makes POTUS think the Chinese may have the drop on us. Until we know more, or unless we can come up with a better idea, the president wants to move cautiously. And most of the National Security Council seems to agree."

"So we're just going to bury our heads in the sand," Freer said in summary.

"I know how you feel. You should have seen the chairman of the joint chiefs, he was adamant about HALO. And General Patrowski was fit to be tied. Trust me, gentlemen, you aren't the only unhappy campers on this one. But unless we can come up with a better option, we're grounded for now."

"Let me ask you this," Harden broke in. "Does any of that intel point to Chinese involvement in bringing down the *Atlantis*?"

Austin paused as he considered the consequences of releasing information that Harden was supposed to learn through other channels, and only after the *Atlantis* mishap was a distant memory. "Look, I'm not at liberty to discuss—"

Harden slammed a fist down on the conference table and jumped to his feet. "Look, I lost a good friend on that mission, goddamit! If China is responsible for blowing up my spacecraft, you'd better let me know now, because if I find out later—"

"Gentlemen, gentlemen, hold on. Hold on just a second." Freer formed his hands into a T as if to signal a time-out. "Stephen, you said 'unless we can come up with a better option.' Right? What if we had a better option?"

"Sam, you know I can't make those kinds of decisions. But if you have something that's germane to this discussion, let me know, and I'll run it by the right people."

"You think you might have a problem in the vicinity

of the moon. I say that's not an insurmountable problem. I can get us there."

Burns wasn't sure he had heard Freer right. He looked at Harden, who seemed equally confused. Both men shrugged as Freer continued. "All we need is a third stage to the Saturn V, and we're in lunar orbit."

"Whoa, I think you're putting the cart before the horse here. We haven't even confirmed an actual threat yet. And that kind of scenario hasn't been remotely explored."

"It was explored over forty years ago, Stephen. It's really not that hard. We've done it before. We can do it again."

"So you're saying you have a spare S-IVB lying around somewhere."

"It just so happens that I do, right here on the island."

"That wasn't part of the HAVE FLAME contract," Austin muttered.

"My friend, I was working on this project long before you came along, and I continued to work on it even after you guys pulled your funding. As far as I'm concerned, this project isn't just a stopgap measure; it's something that this country can't live without. And if you're worried about the contract—don't. I'll give it to you, free of charge."

Burns had trouble forming his words. "But...but, you said you didn't have a third stage...a third stage for the Saturn V."

"No, I said that you didn't *need* a third stage unless you planned on going to the moon. Looks like our plans may have changed."

Harden's face turned to stone. He knew what else Freer had up his sleeve back in Canoga Park, and for once he was just going to sit back and see how it all played out.

"That's definitely an interesting twist," Austin said. "But if there is anything up there worth worrying about, it may be easier to address with an unmanned probe. Besides, I'm not sure how effective we could be with the Artemis capsule in lunar orbit."

"Forget Artemis. She couldn't make the trip anyway," Freer admitted. "Artemis was designed for Earth orbital missions only."

"Then what else do you have in your possession?" Austin asked in exasperation.

"The two gems of my collection, CSM-115A and LM-14, an original Apollo Command/Service Module, and a fully restored Lunar Module. And those aren't free. Uncle Sam will owe me big time for those," Freer made clear before presenting his case. He had devoted his entire adult life to this vision, and the excitement in his voice was evident as he spoke. "Look, it sounds to me like we're going to need to move quickly on this, and shift gears from an Earth orbit mission to a lunar orbit mission. Forget about Artemis. Forget about HALO for now. We have everything we need to put the whole Apollo stack together and send a crew to the moon. I'm afraid you're going to need to deal with this problem at the source."

Austin broke the long silence. "Wow, you never fail to amaze me, Sam. Helping to bring the shuttle out of retirement was one hell of a show, but if this is your idea of an encore—wow, this *is* intriguing. I don't think we're quite there yet, but I will definitely run this up the chain. I doubt the president will sign off on a plan this radical, but I can't hold back on this kind of information. He has to know. In any case, I suggest you fire up the simulators now and start training. And if we get the go-ahead, we'll need to move quickly to get Bernegger or Dennis in on this."

"Hang on, Steve," Harden shouted, surprising

everyone—himself included. "Look, I'm not trying to be a pain in the ass here, but if you want me to even consider this crazy excursion, I've got to have a say in who the third member of my crew will be."

"I take it you already have someone in mind," Austin sighed.

Burns turned to Harden and smiled. He knew there was only one person in the world Harden could be thinking about. "Pete Mitchell," Harden finally said. "I haven't talked to him in a few years, but I think he still works for Northrop Grumman. I'm sure you can track him down. I won't do this without him." Harden then looked back at Burns and nodded. "I mean *we* won't do this without him."

"I'll look into it," Austin conceded. "I'll call you as soon as I can get an audience with the president. In the meantime, I'll see if I can't hunt down your friend Mitchell."

CHAPTER 15

USS Ronald Reagan
200 NM North of Johnston Island

C APTAIN MIKE METCALF NAVIGATED AN obstacle course of steep ladders and menacing "knee-knockers" between his at-sea cabin high on the O-8 level of the *Ronald Reagan* and the admiral's blue-tile area on the O-3 level. He rapped his knuckles on the ship's only wooden door and was quickly greeted by Red Willard. The admiral, clad in sweaty workout gear bearing the ship's logo, had a white towel draped across his shoulders. Metcalf noticed a thin sheen of sweat on Willard's face as he was led in and offered a seat on the couch in the large foyer that doubled as the admiral's personal gym. The weighted flywheel on the rowing machine was still spinning as Metcalf walked by.

"Mike, I know you're not going to like this," Willard said, mopping the sweat from his brow. "Hell, I don't like it either. But we're going to have to go to flight quarters in about an hour to catch a Hornet on its way out from the beach."

"Who are we recovering, sir? The entire Airwing is on board. Tell me we're not taking on some DV who wants to see what a warship looks like up close. I have enough stowaways on this ship already."

"No distinguished visitors, Mike. Cheer up. We're actually getting rid of one."

"Admiral, we'll never make PIM if I have to make wind for a recovery." The *Reagan*, along with its sprawling steel flight deck—four-and-a-half acres of sovereign American real estate—had less than a week to make it to the South China Sea. The tight schedule, Metcalf had already complained, was nearly impossible as it was. "Who's trying to get off?"

"Mike, you know I've always let you run your own ship, but I just got off the phone with CNO, and he has orders from Command Authority to get Pete Mitchell off this ship before we go blue-water."

"Mitchell? He's one of the Northrop guys, right. Did I miss something? Is he the president's nephew?"

"Mike, I understand your concerns, but the order has come down. Besides, I know this man in the Hornet, and I trust his judgment. Just get him aboard in one piece. I don't want this thing turning sour on us."

"Yes, sir, but can you at least tell me who we're working with here so my LSOs will have some idea what they're up against."

"It's Jack Harden. His callsign is Blaze. Do you know him?"

"Never heard of him. But with a callsign like that, I'm already worried."

"Well, he saved my ass once. That's the only reason I'm even considering this."

"Then do you at least know when his last night trap was?"

Willard sat back and kicked his feet up on the steel coffee table. "I can tell you this much. He's been out of the Navy for at least six years."

Metcalf rolled his eyes. "What's he doing now?"

Willard couldn't pass up such a golden opportunity.

"He's a glider pilot," he said, and then struggled to maintain his composure as he watched the blood drain from Metcalf's tired face. After he had extracted the most from the moment, the admiral smiled and casually added, "He's a shuttle astronaut."

Metcalf laughed as he spun and turned for the door. "That's just fucking great."

Hornet 411
Final Approach

It felt like a dream. Ever since his wheels left the darkened runway on Johnston Island, he couldn't believe it was really happening. Harden had been asleep for barely forty-five minutes when Freer woke him with the news. Stephen Austin had located Pete Mitchell, but by morning the *Reagan* would be out of range.

Harden studied the green glow of information being fed to him through the Hornet's heads-up display. Aircraft attitude, airspeed, and altitude all combined to paint a picture of where he was in relation to the ship ahead—and the ocean below. Nothing else mattered. *Except the tailhook. Shit.* Harden reached out and lowered the tailhook handle with a heavy spring-loaded thunk, releasing the real hook like a prehensile tail into the darkness some twenty feet behind him.

When he finally leveled off at 1,200 feet the TACAN reading told him he was only ten miles out. *Time to dirty up.* Harden lowered the landing gear and flaps and then trimmed the aircraft to fly on-speed: precisely 8.1-degrees angle of attack. As soon as he reached three miles, he nosed the fighter over and began the perilous slide into the abyss. At two miles he caught his first glimpse of the faint yellow lights framing the flight deck.

Lacking any hint of an outside horizon to reference, every minor correction Harden made with the flight controls caused an equal and opposite reaction to the tiny rectangle of lights he suddenly found himself hurtling toward. Approaching a mile, he shot a quick glance at the carrier's primary landing aid, the Fresnel Lens. The amber reference cell, the "meatball," was slightly above a horizontal row of green datum lights.

"Hornet 411, you're at three-quarters of a mile. Call the 'ball," the *Reagan's* head Landing Signal Officer radioed.

"411, Hornet 'ball, 5.5."

"Roger 'ball, 32 knots, axial."

A little high. Can't bolter. A little power off. Power back on to catch it.

"Power," the LSO said slowly, hoping to cajole just the right correction from the mysterious pilot. "You're a little low."

Shit. I'm low. Harden nudged the throttles, wary that an overcorrection could leave him too high to catch any of the cross deck pendants—and the last thing he wanted tonight was to bolter into the inky black.

"POWER."

Harden shoved the throttles forward. *Too much. Ball's going high.* Less than fifty feet from the flight deck and only seconds away from a waveoff, Harden found himself drifting left toward the Fresnel Lens like a moth to a flame.

"Right for lineup."

Twenty feet above the deck, Harden pulled off some power and dipped his right wing to stop the drift. *Don't spot the deck.*

Water finally gave way to solid steel. The Hornet's tailhook skipped across the deck, sending a shower of sparks into the night before finally catching the three-

141

wire and dragging the screaming jet to a stop. After several seconds in full afterburner, Harden finally exhaled and slowly brought the throttles back to idle. *Dammit! How did I let myself get talked into this?*

As the canopy slid open, Mitchell grabbed the rickety aluminum ladder and hiked his boot up to the first rung. But before continuing, he had to know if the unbelievable claim was true. High up in the cockpit, the pilot lifted his visor and unclipped his oxygen mask. Even in silhouette, Mitchell knew that smirk could only belong to one person.

Mitchell climbed the rest of the way up the ladder and carefully lowered himself into the back of the two-seat Hornet. As soon as he got hooked into the intercom circuit, he fired away, "I thought the Navy barred you from flying ejection seat aircraft?"

"First of all, they didn't bar me," Harden said tersely. "They just said that if I ever ejected again I would probably spend the rest of my life in a wheelchair. Secondly, this jet is no longer DOD property." Harden thought about it. Had the F-14 accident not occurred when it did, he would have probably taken the orders he had in hand and joined the Blue Angel's Flight Demonstration team. Instead, he ended up applying to NASA—pursuing the one path that Mitchell had spent his entire life aspiring to.

Outside on the flight deck, a purple-shirted airman removed the refueling hose from the side of the unmarked aircraft while his brown-shirted companion released the Hornet's tie-down chains. Harden nudged the throttles and followed the glow of the light wands for the short maneuver to the catapult. On signal from the taxi director, he lowered the launch bar and hooked up to the number three catapult. Harden ran the engines up to full military power, scanned the instruments one last time, and flicked the master lights switch with his left pinky. The invisible "Shooter" then touched his glowing wand to the deck and pointed toward the bow.

Harden reached up and grabbed the "towel rack" handle with his right hand, backed the throttles with his left, and braced for the punch. Night traps may have been the hardest thing he had ever done in his life, but he hated the night catshot even more. A dozen things had to happen in perfect synchronicity for the catapult to work, and all were beyond his control. Even the rotation to a flying attitude in the Hornet was a hands-off maneuver. Some engineer somewhere decided that it was better that way. It worked, but it was one hell of an uncomfortable way to begin every flight.

The interminable wait ended with a *BANG!*

When the holdback finally broke, Harden rammed both throttles past the military detent. The powerful afterburners lit up the flight deck like some mad Fourth of July spectacle gone awry. Harden and Mitchell were pinned against their seats by the crushing acceleration. In the next instant, the invisible force was gone.

Falling back on instinct, Harden grabbed the stick and pulled it smoothly back into his lap. The forty-thousand-pound fighter settled uneasily into the darkness as its wheels left the safety of the *Reagan's* steel airstrip behind. When he was comfortably away from the water, Harden eased the Hornet onto a southerly heading. "Wow, that was worse than I remember."

Mitchell didn't start breathing again until he saw the altimeter climbing through 1,000 feet. "Yeah, it looks like we managed to cheat death one more time," he said flatly. "But now that we're still alive, *can you please tell me what the fuck is going on?*"

Harden smiled beneath the oxygen mask. At least his old friend was talking to him again. "Let's get this thing on the ground in one piece first."

"And where is that going to be? Not another carrier, I hope. I saw your last landing on the PLAT camera. My heart nearly stopped, and I was only *watching* it."

"No, we're definitely headed for dry land. Assuming I can find it again. Next stop Johnston Island. We shouldn't be more than a couple hundred miles out. Why don't you fire up the radar and give me a hand."

"Never heard of it," Mitchell said sharply. "What's on this island anyway, and why are you taking me there instead of home?"

"Because Johnston Island may very well be the launch site for America's next moonshot. And there's at least a fifty-fifty chance that we'll be going."

CHAPTER 16

Launch Pad 39C
Johnston Island

STARING DOWN FROM THE RIM of the enormous silo, Burns and Mitchell were mesmerized by the mammoth moon rocket being assembled below. Echoes of mechanical labor swirled up from the deep concrete pit. The staccato cacophony sounded more like the worksite of an emerging skyscraper than the assembly facility for a rocket with the heavenly precision of the Saturn V.

Mitchell rubbed his two-day stubble as he considered his predicament. He was still feeling way behind the power curve. He hadn't flown as much as a Cessna in the past five years. And yet just this morning he had been subjected to an exhaustive physical examination, while anthropometric measurements were taken of every part of his forty-two-year-old body. He was told that these detailed skeletal indices would be used to form-fit his couch in the Apollo command module, and custom tailor the individual pieces of his very own pressure suit. He bristled when he thought about it—*a space suit.*

Burns studied his friend's tired face, the tiny crow's feet in the corners of Mitchell's salty blue eyes a subtle reminder of the years that had slipped by since their paths had last crossed. "So give me just *one* good reason why you don't want to go? We need you, man."

"If all you want is one, *then I'll give you one—*" Mitchell shouted over the incessant clanging. "Because I'd like to live to see fifty. And another thing, this little excursion of Blaze's sounds like a suicide mission to nowhere. Your chances of walking away from this are so bad that you couldn't even get a Vegas bookie to give you odds. What good am I to my wife and kids if I end up drifting through space for the rest of their lives in some forgotten tin can with a couple of washed up NASA astronauts?"

Burns knew he had to seal the deal—fast. "Aw, c'mon. Lighten up. Gayle and the boys never kept you from throwing yourself at the back of a moving ship for all those years. This is no more dangerous than a night carrier landing. Besides, we probably have less than a ten percent chance of going anyway. You could at least play along."

"You know, landing on the moon would be one thing," Mitchell shot back. "But this is nothing more than a stupid high-wire act. Flying to some imaginary point in space? On a rocket that used to be a museum piece?"

"You really should cut him a break, Mitch. Trust me. I heard Blaze tell Austin that he wouldn't do this without you."

Mitchell kicked at the golden sand that had piled up against the silo rim. "Sure he would," he said, doubting the words even as he spoke them.

"I'm telling you, you're wrong. I get the strange feeling that Blaze doesn't even want to go through with this himself." Burns paused as he gazed across the gaping hole in the earth. "I think he's doing this for us."

"Humph," Mitchell grunted. "There's probably a

good reason why he doesn't want to go...like it's pure insanity...and he's just using us as an excuse. If you or I decide not to go, then he's off the hook, his conscience clear of letting this Freer guy down."

"Wow, you really have become one cynical son of a bitch."

"Life has a tendency to do that to people."

"If I remember correctly, there was a time when you would have given anything to be a part of a program like this," Burns argued. "You wouldn't have wanted to get into TPS so badly otherwise, would you?"

Mitchell thought he had effectively put that painful chapter behind him. But he was surprised at how easily the scab came off. Being accepted into Test Pilot School was the one goal in his life that he had been unable to achieve. And his wife's affirmation that "things worked out the way they did for a reason" never seemed to provide the comfort it was supposed to.

Mitchell turned to Burns and said flatly, "You guys are fucking insane. You know this is never going to work." He then drew in a deep breath before going on. "But I guess as long as I can't go home, I might as well keep myself busy. Just don't expect me to actually climb atop this circus stunt and strap in with you two idiots. God only knows how I'm going to explain all of this to Gayle."

"You don't have to. She was informed earlier this morning by the Department of the Navy that her husband has been detained on the USS *Ronald Reagan* until further notice—for reasons involving national security."

Burns smiled inwardly. He had his friend exactly where he wanted him. All he had to do now was let Mitchell run out the line for a while. Then, when the time was right, he would just reel him back in and pull him up in the boat. Burns looked up as the sky darkened overhead. A towering cumulus cloud drifted between him and the glowing warmth of the sun. A sudden shiver rippled through his lanky frame. The dirty grey cloud spewed a thin veil of virga across the eastern sky. Burns jumped as the earth suddenly trembled beneath their feet. Accompanied by the hum of powerful hydraulic motors, the armor-plated silo doors inched slowly together. "Come on. We'd better get back inside before we get wet."

Sam Freer's Office
Johnston Island

"It's not you or your hardware I have doubts about," Harden said as he shifted his stare to the peaceful view beyond Freer's office. A warm rain spattered against the long, slender glass panes of the antique jalousie windows.

Freer twisted three separate hand cranks until each section of the horizontal slats was angled perfectly, keeping the rain out while still allowing nature's air conditioner to cool the office. "Well, if it's not the hardware, then what's the problem, Jack? You picked your own crew. And I must say that from what I've seen so far, you couldn't have chosen two better pilots. Pete seems appropriately skeptical for this stage of the game, and Jeff has more than enough confidence for the entire crew. All that's needed now is a commander to provide some direction to those polar, but necessary, qualities of pessimism and hubris—and I think you're the perfect guy for the job."

"You're right, Sam. I couldn't have asked for a better crew. But it's not them. It's me." Harden stood up, walked over to the wall of windows, and jammed both hands into the pockets of his wrinkled khakis. He thought briefly of telling Freer about the message
148

he had gotten from Stacy, but decided against it. Until he knew more about her condition, he couldn't make a rational decision anyway. And the last thing he wanted was to make his painful choice someone else's headache. "I just don't like the direction this program is going. That's all. It feels like the wheels are coming off the train. Last night I found myself staring down the blunt end of an aircraft carrier in the middle of the goddamn ocean with almost no warning. Sam, I'm getting too old for this shit..."

Freer suspected there was more to it than that. He knew most of the Apollo astronauts on a first name basis. The ones who lived through the program all seemed to have one thing in common—they knew when it was time to get out. Harden, he decided, after his recent brush with death, may have been having his own face-to-face confrontation with fate.

The unnerving warble of the STU-III on Freer's desk snapped both men's attention back to the business at hand. Freer quickly punched a button on the phone to stop the noise. "Go secure," he told the caller.

Austin's voice came through the tinny speaker on Freer's desk. "How's my astronaut corps doing today?"

"We're a few astronauts short of a corps at the moment," Freer replied. "Let me get the rest of the crew in here. Talk to Jack for a second." Sam then picked up an older phone next to the encrypted secure telephone unit and made a PA announcement requesting Burns's and Mitchell's presence in his office.

"Good. I'm glad I've got the ear of the commander," said Austin. "We've definitely had an interesting series of events develop over the past thirty-six hours. In case you haven't heard, the Air Force lost contact with one of its GPS satellites a couple of days ago."

"No, we hadn't heard yet," Freer cut in as he hung up the other phone.

"Not surprising. The story went mostly unnoticed in the US since the only signal degradation occurred in a remote area of the western Pacific, and an on-orbit spare was promptly maneuvered to cover the gap. But what quickly became evident was that the satellite had not just failed. It had been completely destroyed. Pulverized by direct impact."

"No hints from previous conjunction reports?" Harden asked.

"Nothing that even came close. All co-orbital satellites at the time were still accounted for. But once Space Command started to build a catalog of the debris cloud, the resulting TLE data began to paint an interesting picture. The impactor was not only exo-atmospheric—it appeared to come from a *higher* orbit."

Harden was familiar enough with the GPS constellation to know that this limited the unknown object to one of the geosynchronous, or GEO, satellites, or a handful of special use satellites in highly elliptical orbits. "Did you look at the Molniya orbits?"

"All Molniya satellites are still accounted for."

"That only leaves the GEO satellites, but I'm guessing they're all accounted for too."

"That's correct."

Harden quickly connected the dots. "Then you're either dealing with a stealthy ASAT or..."

"That's right," Austin replied, "something from beyond GEO orbit. Space Command has so far labeled it with 'medium probability' as an undetected Earth-crossing meteoroid."

"But you came to a different conclusion."

"Yes. I had my people run a trajectory analysis on the Two-Line Element sets that we got from Space Command against an object launched from the vicinity of the moon. The numbers were in the ballpark at first, but it was no smoking gun."

Harden scratched his head. "Did you take time of flight into account?"

"Voila!" Austin shouted. "When we ran it again and wound the clock back three days, roughly forty degrees back along the moon's orbit, we hit pay dirt. The impactor could have easily been launched from the hidden Earth-Moon Lagrange point, L2."

"The Chang'e," Freer concluded, just as Burns and Mitchell, both soaked by the afternoon rainstorm, burst into his office. "How long before you can confirm your theory?"

"That's the problem," Austin replied. "We don't have any way to *see* that particular point in space. It could be quite a while until—"

"See what point in space?" Burns asked, dripping water on the terrazzo tile as he slicked his thick blond hair back with both hands.

"Welcome, Jeff," Austin said, recognizing Burns's baritone voice from their previous phone conversations. "We're trying to get a look at L2. But we're currently short on assets. To say our situational awareness in space is lacking would be an understatement."

"I know we have some pretty powerful telescopes out there," Burns said. "What about the GEODSS telescope on Maui?"

"The problem with terrestrial-based equipment, and even low-Earth-orbit scopes for that matter, is that the moon itself gets in the way and blocks our view of L2. It's not until you get out close to geo-sync orbit that you have a clear view of that piece of space."

"What about the Lunar Reconnaissance Orbiter?"

"We're working on that," Austin said. "NASA was already in the process of altering LRO's orbit to get us some pictures of the Chang'e 5 crash site when I hit them with the L2 request."

The Lunar Reconnaissance Orbiter had long since

completed its mission to photograph the moon's surface in high-resolution 3D and was put into a state of suspended animation following the cancellation of the Constellation program. The spacecraft remained in orbit around the moon but was short on maneuvering fuel and had scant electrical power remaining. Any additional tasking would drain the aging satellite's limited resources, NASA had warned, and was initially met with much resistance. They were eventually convinced to cooperate once the White House got involved, but the complex maneuver required to meet Austin's objectives would take time. And re-tasking would take even longer.

"So to answer your question, Sam," Austin concluded. "It could be weeks before we get the confirmation we need."

Mitchell was still trying to absorb the flood of information that began pouring into his world last night. "How could you not have expected this?" he asked sharply.

"Not that that's not a good question," Austin replied, "but the more immediate concern is what do we do about it now? The president has authorized us to investigate the feasibility of a plan to disable any satellite that does not conform to current treaty. If the Chang'e 4 *is* in a stable orbit on the far side of the moon, it would definitely fall into that category. Sam, you and your team have forty-eight hours to come up with options that will satisfy the Executive Order to dispose of any such existing satellite—and that includes sending a manned mission to lunar orbit."

SLATE Conference Room
Johnston Island

"Our trajectory guys have come up with what they

think is the best way to affect the transfer from a sixty-nautical-mile lunar orbit to a rendezvous with a satellite stationed at L2, approximately 32,000 nautical miles above the lunar far side," Freer said to the small audience gathered in the conference room. The rough plan had begun to circulate within hours of the conference call with Austin yesterday. No one would know for sure if it would work until they got a crew into the simulator to work out the details, but on paper at least, it was shaping up to be an elegant solution. "Instead of using the lunar module to land on the moon, we'll use the *descent* stage engine to boost Jack and Pete to L2 on a Hohmann transfer orbit. When the mission there is complete, they'll use the LM's *ascent* stage engine to lower themselves back down to the nominal sixty-nautical-mile parking orbit." Freer then turned to the chalkboard and drew a curve that represented the path the lunar module would make during the journey.

"That profile looks like it's going to be hell on their fuel reserves," Burns noted. "Would it help if I used the command module to drive them into a higher orbit first, before they detached for the transfer burn?"

"Yes, it is going to be tight," Freer agreed, addressing the newly designated command module pilot. "But there's just not enough fuel in the CSM to get you guys home if we do that. Plus, we would rather hold onto your fuel reserves in case we need to move you into a rescue orbit when Jack and Pete return from L2. They will have cut the LM's descent stage loose by then, and may have trouble getting back down to you in the command module."

Pete Mitchell was taking in a lot of information, but it just wasn't making any sense. Not that it mattered. He had no intention of going through with the plan anyway. But he found the analytical exercise—not to mention the amazing array of hardware on the island—exhilarating. "I know I'm probably the lowest common denominator here, but is it too much to ask how we're going to get *into* lunar orbit before we blast out of it into this L2 black hole thing?"

"Good question, Pete," Freer said, waiving his chalk-dusted hand in the air. "We did skip over that rather quickly. We're going to execute a standard Apollo G-mission profile to get you guys into lunar orbit. Now I know that doesn't help much right now, but I planned on teaming you up with Josh Camden back there on tomorrow's flight to Burbank for a little one-on-one in the area of orbital dynamics." Mitchell turned in time to see the eager young graduate student identify himself.

"Got it," Mitchell said. "Then a description of L2 would go a long way at this point."

Freer flipped the dusty chalkboard over to reveal a clean whiteboard on the back side. He picked up an erasable marker and drew as he talked. "There are five points in space for any two-body system that offer equivalent gravitational attraction toward a third body, whose mass is insignificant compared to the other two. In this case, the Earth and the moon represent the two major bodies, and a satellite represents the smaller mass. Three of the Lagrange points are in line with the axis that joins the two planetary bodies. The first point is the most obvious. It's the point between the Earth and the moon that is gravitationally neutral, here at L1. Not as intuitive perhaps is L2. It lies beyond, or behind the moon at a point where the combination of the Earth *and* moon's gravitational forces balance the satellite's centrifugal force and keep it from escaping into a solar orbit.

"L3 lies along this same axis but is on the opposite side of the Earth from the moon. L4 and L5 lead and lag the moon approximately sixty degrees in its orbit, here and here." Sam stepped back to look at the picture, making sure he had it all right. "And if this were all drawn to scale, you would see that L2 is hidden from direct line of sight with the Earth, forever locked in the moon's shadow."

"Don't worry," Freer said to the skeptical pilot. "You've got the best people in your corner. Okay, let me recap. Pete and Jack will depart the sixty-nautical-mile lunar parking orbit in the LM and rendezvous with the Chang'e 4 at L2. A spacewalk will be conducted to attach an explosive device to the satellite. After reentering the lunar module, they'll discard the LM's descent stage and return to the lunar parking orbit in the ascent stage." Freer scanned the room one last time before adding, "Any questions?"

CHAPTER 17

Daedalus Crater
Far side of the moon

LUNAR DAWN INCHED IMPERCEPTIBLY ACROSS the vast basin of Daedalus. This slow motion spectacle would last two long weeks—the length of a single lunar day—making temperature extremes here as unforgiving as anywhere in the solar system. And without the insulating effects of an atmosphere to moderate the transfer of heat, transition from night to day on Earth's closest celestial neighbor could be brutally punishing to manmade systems. This unfortunate detail had to be ignored, however, by the PLA officer who had just been ordered to launch the next weapon from the secret Chinese battle station.

The command to initiate the pre-launch sequence in the lunar lander-turned-launch-platform originated nearly a quarter-million miles away. Routed by a dedicated landline to the large transmitting dish at Weinan, the signal was then rerouted through a Russian communications satellite in geosynchronous Earth orbit before being beamed to the clandestine Chang'e 4 hovering quietly at L2. The signal then ricocheted down to the far side of the moon and activated the control circuitry in the weapons platform.

The upper half of the Chang'e 5 was divided into three chambers, housing launch tubes for twenty-two separate boosters. Each of the arsenal's outer chambers contained two rows of four tubes canted outboard at forty-five degrees. There was now a forty-centimeter hole in the gold foil on the port side of the platform where vehicle number-5 had been. Inside each of the remaining fifteen outer tubes was a similar single-stage kinetic-kill-vehicle. Tucked away in each KKV was a 20-kilogram warhead surrounded by thousands of tiny tungsten pellets. Each was capable of a 90 percent Pk, or probability-of-kill, for any unhardened satellite within a 1,000 meter range—a statistic that had proven lethal to the GPS satellite USA-213. But the warheads in the six remaining vertical launch tubes were anything but "conventional."

As the launch platform came to life, nitrogen gas was vented through several remote outlets, purging potentially flammable vapors from the tube that housed vehicle number-19. Heaters pre-conditioned the liquid fuel in one of the six "special" delivery vehicles loaded vertically in the Chang'e's center chambers. The process was especially critical prior to a sun angle of thirteen degrees to the lunar horizon. During this thermal soak time, the liquid-fuel rockets were at least as likely to explode in their launch tubes as they were at their target. This detail, as the colonel had outlined it, mattered little to the chairman of the central military commission, who had ordered that the launch proceed at all costs.

When the last interlock finally fired, three thousand pounds of compressed gas rushed into the base of the forward vertical silo. The 275-kilogram launch vehicle erupted from the top of the golden cube on a column of gaseous nitrogen. Gyros inside the projectile commanded a tilt program just prior to the volatile hypergolic fuels mixing in the combustion chamber. The small single-stage rocket belched an invisible flame from its conical engine bell. The two-meter-long missile accelerated away from Daedalus crater, and was quickly traveling faster than a rifle bullet. The spent motor casing detached on command, and vehicle number-19, along with its nuclear payload, began the long fall back toward its target—located somewhere in the fringes of Earth's upper atmosphere.

Washington-Reagan National Airport
Arlington, VA

Except for a quick stop in the DCA terminal gift shop, Dongfan Chong had made good time. By managing to catch an earlier flight and traveling light so he could bypass the long wait at the luggage carousel, he figured he must have shaved at least two hours from his lengthy trip. But darkness was rushing headlong toward the upper east coast, and he knew he would have to hurry. As the glass doors at the end of the concourse slid apart, Chong zipped his jacket up tightly under his neck, wishing he had been better prepared to do battle with the cold front that had swept into the metropolitan area earlier in the day. As he searched the rental car lot for the white Toyota Avalon, he again thought through his rationalization. He still felt bad about breaking the protocol that Austin had put in place, but he knew the lag time in communications wouldn't work for something of such an urgent nature. Yet after all the hand wringing, he had missed Austin anyway and was forced to leave only an abbreviated message with his secretary. None of this mattered anymore; he was now less than an hour away from delivering the contents he had recently discovered in the hidden compartment of his father's heirloom box to Stephen Austin at the CIA.

Chong began to breathe easier as the traffic thinned

and he made his way north out of the city. His thoughts drifted as he followed the slippery yellow arrows and sultry voice of the Magellan digital navigation assistant, focusing not on the road ahead or the cars around him but instead on what the mysterious key went to—and what might be lurking inside whatever it opened. And it was this logic that kept leading him back to the same unsettling conclusion. He would never be able to prove it, but he was sure that his father's murder was intended to keep this key from ever leaving China.

Central Intelligence Agency

By the time Austin got the message, it was too late to stop him. He would rather have had Chong just ship the package to him, regardless of the perceived importance. Having Chong hand deliver anything brought a whole host of complications along with it, not the least of which could be endangering his own life. A person could be tailed much more easily than an envelope or a cardboard box that snaked its way through the bowels of a modern package delivery system. FedEx may not have sounded like a very covert way to deliver something critical to national security, but the old-fashioned notion of couriers delivering precious packages in briefcases handcuffed to their wrists didn't always make sense anymore.

It was just after seven o'clock by the time Austin left his office. At least the traffic would be light, he thought, and the long drive down George Washington Parkway would give him some time to think. He had hoped to be heading home early tonight, but instead he would have to be satisfied with a peaceful drive along the Potomac to help him put the chaos of the past few weeks into perspective.

But what if it isn't bad news at all? What if it's good

159

news? So important that Chong deemed it necessary to abandon protocol and deliver it himself. Austin began to smile for the first time all day. He checked the time. He was still early. Maybe he would have time to stop at a drive-thru for a quick bite before his friend arrived.

LM Simulator
Canoga Park, CA

"Start the event timer," Harden ordered.

"Copy." Mitchell selected the countdown option on the mission clock and toggled another switch to Start. "Two fifty-nine, fifty-eight, fifty-seven. Looks good."

The time had come to validate the short-fused flight plan developed by the SLATE team barely two days ago. But four hours of instruction in orbital mechanics and a one-day crash course in lunar module systems was all that could be afforded to the unlikely lunar module pilot at this point. For Mitchell, the circumstances were anything but optimal, but deep down he was glad to be back in a cockpit—any cockpit. It had been too many years since he was at the controls of a flying machine from the inside. Standing up in front of a small window with barely two square feet of oddly canted triangular glass, he stared out into the blackness of a night darker than any he could remember. But inside, the lunar module cockpit was warm and inviting. Bathed in the warm glow of fluorescent green light, Mitchell was transported back in time to an era when aviators flew dangerous machines in a bold effort to conquer the unknown. And he liked it.

"One minute 'til Tig," Harden announced.

As Mitchell awaited the Time-of-ignition, or Tig, for the approaching rocket burn, he referenced the fireproof checklist Velcroed to the cabin wall just above his right shoulder. His eyes darted rapidly between the pre-thrust checklist and the rows of gauges on the battleship grey instrument panel. Just one misplaced switch or skewed pressure reading could bring an abrupt end to the entire mission.

Standing at the commander's station to Mitchell's left, Harden calmly anticipated the rapidly approaching event. He mentally verified his own checklist for the prograde burn of the lunar module's descent propulsion system, the DPS. The lengthy burn would take them out of their comfortable sixty-nautical-mile lunar orbit and lift them slowly toward the isolated Earth-Moon L2 libration point some 32,000 nautical miles out into deep space.

Harden scanned the DSKY. The *diskey* was an antiquated combination of computer display and keyboard mounted in the center of the LM's lower instrument panel. The number in the PROG register confirmed their machine was ready. "We're in Program 40," the commander announced to everyone listening on the comm loop. "The DPS Thrust program is active, and we are standing by for the external delta-v burn."

"Average-G is on," Mitchell confirmed as the numbers flashed on the display.

When the countdown timer scrolled through zero, Harden verified the result. "We have Auto-Ignition."

"Thrust is good," Mitchell noted. "Throttle's coming up to ninety-two percent." It was the type of flying that Mitchell had grown accustomed to in the world of unmanned aviation; flying by instruments with no way to see what was going on around him. He knew intuitively that the moon was a mere sixty nautical miles below, but there was nothing for him to see as the LM's two small windows were pointing off into deep space. Instead, he monitored the spacecraft's progress on the nine-inch DSKY display nestled between the two sets of pilot controls. The additional thrust from the descent engine was steadily increasing their velocity while simultaneously raising their altitude to a point far above the unseen lunar terrain—and heights never before achieved by man.

"Stand by for the shutdown," Harden announced. "Three, two, one, shutdown!"

A quick fist pump by Harden indicated the results. The burn had gone off without a hitch, and the ungainly spacecraft was gliding quietly toward its objective. Time passed quickly as the men practiced donning their pressure suits for the planned spacewalk. In the cramped cockpit, the process quickly burned up more calories than either man had expected. Mitchell was still sweating as the next critical burn approached. Only this time, as the lunar module pilot, he wouldn't be monitoring engine performance. Instead, as LMP, he would be operating the second most important system required for the rendezvous of two objects in space, the radar.

They were well into the deceleration burn when Mitchell made the first contact. "I've got two lights. Altitude and velocity. Coming through sixty thousand feet. Delta-h is...shit, it dropped out."

"Check the signal strength."

Mitchell looked over at a gauge mounted on the commander's console. The needle twitched erratically. "It's in the weeds. It's going to keep dropping out."

"Yeah. It's not like we're landing on the moon. There's just not that much out there for landing radar to reflect off of. We need a bigger target."

Mitchell reached for a control knob over Harden's right arm. *Landing on the moon would be a lot easier than this.* "I'm going to switch it out of auto for a second," he noted. "There. I got a bump with it in the descent mode. It's up over 1.0 now."

"Good. Now give me your best guess when you think

we're inside thirty thousand feet. If our H-dot is in the ballpark, I'll go ahead and pitch us forward. Then you can switch over to the rendezvous radar."

Mitchell rubbed his heavy gloves against the legs of his pristine white pressure suit and continued to hawk the data as it flickered on the DSKY. The numbers were erratic. How could he be sure? "Thirty-two thousand feet. Delta-h looks good. Stand by." Mitchell counted in his head. "Shutdown!"

"Shutdown," Harden echoed and slammed an open palm down on the manual stop switch. "I'm going to pitch us forward now and see what we've got."

"Roger. I'm switching to Rendezvous."

Mitchell selected hi-rate slew on the rendezvous radar and began his methodical search pattern—up, left, down, right, up, left—guiding the forward-facing radar antenna into an increasingly larger box-shaped search pattern. He studied the signal strength gauge for signs of life.

"We're flying blind here, Mitch. Talk to me."

"Nothing yet."

"We should have started the clock."

"Next time...*wait!* There's something."

Mitchell flipped the Rate switch to Lo. He eyed the signal strength indicator as he fished around for the impossibly lonely satellite. His left hand froze as the tiny needle flickered above three on the scale. Mitchell held his breath as he carefully twisted the mode knob to Auto Track. The green no-track light extinguished and the white needle suddenly pegged at five. Numbers reappeared on the DSKY display. "Lights are out. Numbers look good."

Harden breathed a deep sigh of relief. His decision to bring Mitchell along was beginning to feel less like an impetuous gamble and more like a carefully calculated risk. And for now at least, the risk seemed to be paying off. "That's just what we needed. Thanks, bud."

"Yeah, you bet," Mitchell said, taking his first full breath in what felt like hours. "Now let's get in there and make this rendezvous happen."

CHAPTER 18

Arlington, VA

THE LAST IN WHAT HAD been a long line of red tail lights made the left turn off George Washington Parkway. The northbound lane was clear for the first time since Chong left the airport. But it was also considerably darker. Cultural lighting from the city was gone, obscured by the deep blanket of trees lining the west bank of the Potomac. As Chong slowed to compensate, he scanned the rearview mirror. He was relieved to see only two sets of headlights, and both were far off in the distance. The Magellan GPS indicated twenty-three minutes to his destination at the current speed. He would be at Austin's office by eight o'clock. He only wished that this could be a friendly visit; perhaps he could have avoided the impromptu meeting if he at least knew what the inscription on his father's key meant.

Even as Chong pondered several possible answers to the question, two beams of bright white light lit up the road beside him. Then, like a bullet-train, the vehicle chasing the headlights roared by only inches from his left shoulder. The buffet that followed rocked the rental car violently. Chong swerved across the solid yellow line several times before regaining control. Still shaking from the close encounter, he glanced again in the rearview mirror to see if there were any more crazy drivers behind him. Another set of headlights was closing fast.

But by the time Chong refocused on the road ahead, the bright red lights in his windshield were too big to avoid. Chong stumbled for the brake pedal, but the front of the Avalon was quickly transformed into a crumpled mess of plastic and sheet metal as he piled into the back of the mysterious car that had just roared by. The unlatched seatbelt, dangling loosely by his left elbow, proved useless. Chong's tremendous momentum was quickly transferred to the inflating airbag. The resulting impact carried the punch of a heavyweight boxer, and slammed him mercilessly back into his seat.

He couldn't seem to remember how his car had come to a stop. Recovering from the momentary lapse of consciousness, Chong was confused. The car he hit had already disappeared into the darkness. But the interior of his car was bright as day, the blinding light from the headlights behind him only adding to the confusion. A reflection in the side mirror caught his attention. A dark figure moved slowly toward him. The first sign of help, Chong thought, as he tried to take stock of his injuries. He tried to move, but his limbs were stubbornly uncooperative. Everything seemed to be happening in slow motion. In the mirror he could see a man standing outside his window. The man's mouth appeared to be moving, but Chong couldn't hear anything. He groped for a switch on the door and managed at last to roll down the driver's side window.

There was even more confusion when he heard the voice. The language the man was speaking was foreign, but curiously, one that Chong recognized. It was his native tongue—Mandarin Chinese. By the time he figured out what the man was saying, it was too late.

The mysterious man reached in through the open

window and unlocked the driver's door with his left hand. Chong's brain screamed for action but his body was slow to react. Still in shock from the impact, Chong scrambled for the passenger door, but his assailant was quicker. The stout Asian man grabbed Chong and pushed him back into his seat. Chong clawed at the muscular arm with both hands but was too weak to ward off the attack. The assailant then reached across with his free hand and thrust a sharp instrument into the soft tissue behind Chong's right ear. In one continuous motion, he dragged the shiny thin blade slowly across the width of Chong's throat, stopping only after reaching the base of his left ear.

Chong knew the fight was over. He felt no pain, only warmth as blood flowed from the deep gash in his throat and cascaded down the front of his jacket. Both carotid arteries had been severed. Chong could feel his heart flutter. He gurgled helplessly as the man's strong hands rummaged through his pockets before disappearing into the darkness. As he waited for the inevitable, Chong blindly reached into the console and searched for Austin's package. When his hand came across the gift shop bag, he felt a brief moment of relief before the bright white light that had flooded his world faded, and darkness pulled him under.

George Washington Parkway

Austin finally broke free from the last of the traffic. He wouldn't have time for dinner now, but he still should be able to make it to the airport on time. He had his doubts at first, but when he discovered that the traffic jam was caused by an accident in the northbound lane, he was relieved. He would normally have stopped to see if he could offer any assistance, but tonight he was in a hurry. Ten minutes later, as he headed south

167

toward Reagan National Airport, the vibration in his pocket, followed by a curt National Anthem ringtone, identified an incoming call from his office. He unfolded the cell phone and said his name to the caller. "Are you sure?" Austin replied as a wave of dread rolled over him.

As his secretary repeated the information, Austin made a quick check behind him and then slammed on the brakes. The antiskid chirped against the dirty asphalt. Even as she gave Austin the new inbound flight number and the type of car Chong had rented, Austin dropped the phone to the passenger's seat and performed a dangerous three point turn on the narrow two-lane thoroughfare. Within minutes, Austin was back at the scene of the accident. Flashing lights from several emergency vehicles pushed back the darkness that had surrounded the scene earlier. He exited the car, and with a flip of his billfold, quickly gained access to what was now unmistakably a crime scene.

A criminal investigation team was documenting the bloody vehicle while a collapsible gurney was being loaded into the back of the ambulance. The black body bag gave Austin the answer to one of his questions. He would have to see inside the bag to answer the other.

"I sure hope you didn't know this guy," the police officer said. "It looks like he was in the wrong place at the wrong time. It has all the signs of a smash-and-grab gone bad." The uniformed man unzipped the bag and peeled back the sheet that had wicked blood away from the corpse underneath until the red and white stripes gave it the appearance of a grotesque American flag.

Austin only needed a glimpse to make the identification. He quickly closed his eyes until he heard the officer zip the bag closed. "Did you find anything on him?"

"No, it looks like they frisked him down good. He didn't have any identification either. They must have stolen his wallet and whatever he had in the trunk. We already ran the plates. The car was just rented this evening from the airport. You know, it's only when something like this happens to a tourist that we end up with a bad reputation."

Austin ignored the insensitivity. "Nothing else was in the car?"

"Just a bag from the airport gift shop. Probably a trinket he was planning to take home to his kid or something. Maybe the perp didn't think it was worth the effort."

"Or maybe it wasn't in plain sight until after he left. Let me see it."

"It's a little messy," the officer warned, and produced the only piece of evidence in a large Ziploc bag.

The blood had dried already. Over the faux tarnished-copper finish, it had the appearance of black ink. But Austin had no doubt that the ten inch replica of the Statue of Liberty was meant for him to find. He recognized the souvenir as a bank by the slit on her back and quietly shook the plastic model. He could feel something rattling around in the pointed pedestal at the base of the figurine. "I'll take this and see what we can find out."

"Hey, wait. You can't just walk away with that."

"Trust me, I can," Austin said pointedly. "This 'trinket' may have serious repercussions to national security." He then gave the officer in charge a business card in exchange for the evidence and disappeared back into the night as quickly as he had arrived.

LM Simulator
Canoga Park, CA

"All right, gentlemen, nice job so far. Now we just need to get you home." To Harden, the controller sounded rather nonchalant about what would undoubtedly go down as the most dangerous space walk of all time. Operating without a net, over 271,000 nautical miles above the Earth, the plan was to place an explosive charge on the skin of the Chang'e 4 and destroy what could turn out be the most threatening weapons platform since the Enola Gay. Yet this man just made it sound like it would be a walk in the park. Harden pushed the thoughts aside as he tried to concentrate on the final critical burn that would return them back to the safety of low lunar orbit, and the waiting command module.

Harden knew they would be tight on fuel. He hated leaving the extra fuel behind in the descent stage almost as much as Mitchell did. But he had been even more concerned about commencing the retrograde maneuver with the LM's descent engine, and then having to discard the spent stage before completing the rendezvous with the constant thrust ascent engine. It was just too complex a maneuver, and it had never been tried before. But he had faith in Freer's team, and if they said there was enough fuel to complete the rendezvous with the ascent stage alone, that was good enough for him. Besides, who could argue with their track record? Some of the very same SLATE members supporting them today were there at NASA in 1969, when Neil Armstrong and Buzz Aldrin set down in the Sea of Tranquility with less than fifteen seconds of fuel remaining in *their* tanks. It was just part of the business, and to Harden it offered less risk than separating, or staging, two space vehicles during the final critical maneuver.

"Okay, we're getting set up for the P40 burn with the APS engine," Harden responded to the controller. If the burn went according to plan, Harden would fire the ascent propulsion system, or APS engine, for seven minutes. But since the ascent stage engine didn't gimbal and was not capable of being throttled, Harden would have to use the reaction control system to augment the braking maneuver.

Mitchell nervously tapped the RCS quantity gauge. If there was one thing that stood out in his mind from the pre-flight brief, it was the danger of using too much RCS fuel for the braking maneuver. If they ran out of the precious fuel that also controlled the lunar module's attitude, they could tumble past the command module, or get sucked in by the moon's gravity. Neither option was very appealing. And Mitchell had let Harden know it.

"Three, two, one...ignition," Harden announced as the simple but highly reliable engine sparked to life. "Thrust looks good. Temps are good. Pressure's okay."

"RCS pressure is nominal. Quantity seventy-nine percent," Mitchell added as the tiny craft descended toward perilune, or the low point in their new lunar orbit. The small engine, originally designed to lift the ascent stage and two triumphant astronauts from the surface of the moon, struggled to rein in their incredible velocity. But the numbers quickly began to tell a different story.

"Still a long way to go," Mitchell said.

"Yep, we're a little behind the curve. Velocity's still too high. I'm going to feed in some plus-z." Harden gripped the T-handle in his left hand and tugged gently on the controller. Four tiny rocket engines, one in each quad surrounding the lunar module, fired against their direction of motion. The combined effort of the four small RCS thrusters was only a tiny fraction of the total thrust developed in the APS engine, but Harden noticed the difference. "It's definitely helping."

Mitchell shook his head quietly inside his bulbous helmet. "RCS quantity down to sixty percent. You don't have that much left. We need to save at least forty percent for the rendezvous."

"We only need twenty percent for attitude control if Pipper finishes the rendezvous with the command module."

"Yeah, but it's just not making that much of a difference."

Harden glanced at the fuel quantity gauges. "Oxidizer...thirty-three percent. Fuel...thirty."

"You've got to lay off the RCS quads, Blaze," Mitchell pleaded. "If you don't melt the nozzles, you're going to run us out of maneuvering fuel before the engine shuts down."

Harden scanned the instruments again. Their velocity was still too high. The resulting apolune, or high point above the lunar surface, of his next orbit would be too high for the command module to affect a rescue. He had to get it down below 170 nautical miles if Burns was to have a fighting chance. "It's gonna be close."

"Twenty percent, Blaze!"

"We're still too fast. I've got to..." Harden checked the clock. "Thirty seconds to shutdown. The numbers are starting to converge."

"Blaze, we're going to lose control!" Mitchell screamed. His heart rate skyrocketed as he watched the RCS fuel quantity fall toward zero.

"Okay, okay," Harden yelled and released the controller. "I think we might just make it. Stand by for shutdown in fifteen seconds."

Mitchell tapped the quantity gauge with his gloved finger. The needle on the tapemeter hovered near zero. "You'd better cross your fingers."

"Twelve, eleven...shit!" Harden intoned as he watched the attitude indicator begin to slowly precess to the right. "The Eight-ball's rolling over. How's the RCS look?"

"I told you it's at zero!"

"Shit," Harden swore again. The helpless spacecraft foundered as the thruster quads gasped for fuel. Several jets sputtered sporadically until finally exhausting the remaining propellant from their lines. The LM then began a slow tumble in its decaying orbit. Without attitude control, the final few seconds of APS fuel directed the ascent engine's remaining thrust toward the cratered lunar surface.

The comm loops were quiet as the LM spiraled down into the pockmarked world below. The result was inevitable. The desolate grey terrain grew ever larger, until the light reflecting from the surface filled the tiny cockpit and consumed the fragile spacecraft. The men at the controls could do nothing more than stand and watch.

In the final seconds, a cheerful voice pierced the silence.

"Okay, gents. I'm going to put you on freeze. I guess that one's going to need a little more work." Sam Freer had been monitoring the trial run from the simulator support console outside the LM mockup. "Don't worry. I think you guys did great. We'll get the bugs ironed out before game day. I promise."

The back door to the LM simulator suddenly slammed open. Mitchell, still clad in his bulky pressure suit, stormed out of the trainer and thrust his helmet at a surprised Freer. "I can't work with him, Sam! This whole damned charade is a waste of time. I told Blaze

173

we needed to start the burn with the descent stage engine or we'd never have enough fuel."

By the time Harden emerged from the awkward contraption, Mitchell was gone. Freer moved in front of him, blocking the doorway before an angry Harden could follow. "Give him some space, Jack. He just needs a little time to cool off."

"We don't have enough time for him to cool off," Harden huffed. "I'm sorry, Sam. I thought this would work. I guess I was wrong."

Freer grabbed Harden by the shoulders and squared off in front of him. "He just doesn't trust us yet. And I can't say that I blame him. This whole thing must be quite a shock for him. But don't worry, he'll come around. And we'll get this profile worked out, trust me." Freer considered his next words carefully before continuing. It was no secret that his passion for the space program stemmed from the typical dream every boy has of becoming an astronaut, but few were aware that it was a profound fear of flying that had ultimately steered him down a different path. Becoming an engineer had allowed him to experience the thrill of spaceflight without ever having to leave the ground. "And if he won't go, I will. I may not be a test pilot, but I know the LM systems as well as anyone on the planet."

Harden thought about it for a second. He knew Freer's heart was in the right place, but he also knew that the mission hinged on Mitchell now, and he had sorely hoped that the experience could bridge the rift that had formed between them over the years. But for the moment anyway, Harden needed a dance partner. "All right, Sam. Get your suit on, and let's get at it. We don't have much time to get this profile right."

CHAPTER 19

White House Oval Office

"THEY'RE STILL DENYING EVERYTHING," THE president said to Sandy Cummings as she reentered the room.

"It's not like we were expecting a full confession at this point," the national security advisor replied. She had just passed the Chinese ambassador in the hallway outside the Oval Office, and his polite nod and courteous greeting told Cummings everything she needed to know. "It's doubtful he would be fully aware of the PLA's actions until it was too late anyway."

The president nodded. He knew that central power in Beijing was a long way from the politics of Washington, DC, but he needed to get the ambassador on the record in case further action was required on behalf of the United States. He also knew that the Communist Party was in the midst of a long and complicated transition of power. Unlike American politics, where presidential succession of power was immediate and happened with the swearing in of the new commander-in-chief, the process could take up to a year or more in the People's Republic of China, and the already opaque political system could become downright impossible to read.

As he pondered the ambassador's remarks, the president shuffled between two reports sitting on his desk. The first one was from the director of national intelligence and outlined the case against two Chinese nationals thought to be responsible for downing the *Atlantis*. He skimmed through the highlighted section in the executive report.

> *Evidence thus far points to the Second Department of the People's Liberation Army, the primary HUMINT arm of the Chinese military. Satellite imagery shows that on the day of the attack, several ships were in the area where the destruct signal is believed to have originated. Three days later, one of those ships, the Russian fishing vessel* Elektron, *pulled into port in the Bahamas. Two Chinese nationals were photographed leaving the vessel. From the FBI database, it was determined that one of the men had once worked for a US defense contractor, but under a different name. He had entered the US on a work visa in the mid-1990s but disappeared before his security clearance was properly adjudicated. He later fled the country after attempting to sell a jet engine from an F-16 to an undercover FBI agent. He's had several aliases since then. The name he's currently using is Cheng Mak. He and his partner, Tai Wang, left Nassau one week ago and passed through US Customs in Miami on the 1st of October.*

Cummings could see the wheels spinning in the president's head. "There's only one reason China would get this aggressive, and we both know what it is." Once it was clear to Cummings that the president wasn't willing to complete her thought, she finally added, "Taiwan."

The president looked at the cover page on the second report, *Special Report to the President on*

the Military Power of the People's Republic of China.
It began with a summary of Chinese intentions and
capabilities around the world. But the president kept
coming back to the grim review of what the PLA could
accomplish militarily in a direct confrontation with the
"renegade" Republic of China—Taiwan. It highlighted
the fact that given the current weak state of Taiwan's
ballistic missile defense system, an attack on the
island's industrial complex would be over before the
US could even mount a response. He flipped through
the folder to the charts that highlighted the numbers
and types of ballistic missiles in garrisons on China's
eastern seaboard. The individual variants totaled over
one thousand.

"But our Chinese intelligence estimate clearly
shows that cross-strait relations have been steadily
improving over the last few years," the president said.
"I see no clear rationale for such a provocative move
on their part."

"I agree that the report is rosy when you consider
motive. But I'm sure you haven't forgotten their recent
aggressions in Hong Kong. That was also supposed to
be a peaceful reunification. Mr. President, the most
important thing in Chinese politics is often what's left
unspoken. Given the current state of world affairs, I
agree that both governments would like nothing more
than to keep the status quo. Beijing doesn't want to
risk a move that would isolate them from their trading
partners around the world, and Taipei is happy as
long as it maintains its de facto independence. But
the business cycle is bound to catch up with Beijing
eventually. So the Communist Party may be preparing
for that eventuality by doing exactly what communist
governments do best during periods of uncertainty—
exercise their military power."

The president propped his elbows on the dark

mahogany and massaged his throbbing temples. Protests and demonstrations on both sides of the Taiwan Strait had dominated the headlines for weeks now. But it was the recent buildup of Chinese naval forces in the South China Sea, bolstered by a mobilization of ground forces in the Nanjing military region that had put the president on edge. His options, as his new security advisor had outlined earlier, were stark. If China carried out a limited attack on Taiwan, he *could* do nothing. But if the Nationalist government in Taipei had been anything less than provocative toward Beijing and he did not respond, the US would be seen as abandoning their allies. He could also prepare for the inconceivable, an outright invasion of Taiwan. But if China succeeded in using force to achieve victory in the sixty-plus-year-old campaign and the US provided only limited support to defend Taiwan, the result to his political career would be much the same. He found it almost impossible to believe that his response to the outdated Taiwan Relations Act might actually define his presidency.

The president withdrew the vibrating cell phone from his breast pocket and glanced at the screen. Very few people outside of select cabinet members and the National Security Council had access to the president's personal cell number. He was shocked when he saw that the message was from Stephen Austin. The contents were brief, but the implications were enormous: *L2 mission success questionable. Investigating work-arounds. Will advise if situation improves.*

The president set the phone down and pressed a button on the intercom. "Harriet, set up a conference call with DNI, SECDEF, and JCS. And get General Patrowski on the line too if you can."

Ten minutes later, the president's secretary

informed him that she had everyone but SECDEF patched in and standing by. The president put the call on speaker and addressed the group. "Gentlemen, let's assume for a moment that someone out there *has* fielded a stealthy anti-satellite weapon. Couldn't we just cut off its command and control link to render it useless?" The president knew that none of the men on the line believed the ginned up press release that stated the loss of one of their GPS satellites was caused by a random space rock.

General Patrowski was quick to respond. "That would be the easiest answer to arrive at, sir. But that assumes someone would design a stealthy ASAT and then not incorporate built-in autonomy in the event of a communications failure. When we began working on similar technologies that was one of the first program-critical areas we identified."

"Yes, but it could only attack what it was programmed to attack before the loss of communications, right?"

"That's probably true for any of the threats we could anticipate from the PLA. I assume we're still talking about the Chinese here?" The general continued when he got no reply. "Even the loss of a few satellites could severely affect our capabilities in the region. And if they somehow managed to take out our DSP birds or SBIRS satellites, we wouldn't even be able to *detect* an ICBM launch until it was too late."

"Good morning, Mr. President," the defense secretary announced as he entered the ongoing conference call.

"Welcome, Dick," the president said, clearly not ready to get dragged into the general's doomsday discussion. "So, like I was saying, if we cut communications to this anti-satellite system, and then move our satellites around to confuse it, we wouldn't expect to see as many losses as we would if we just sat here and did nothing."

Patrowski's voice wavered. "You mean redress the entire inventory of US satellites? Not unless we know what the threat is. You've got to be more specific, sir."

"I'll ask you one more time, General. Can we alter the orbits of our satellites enough to enhance their chances of survival against a stealthy threat from space?"

"Yes, theoretically," the general finally conceded. "It would be one hell of a feat. You couldn't do it all at once. We'd have to prioritize, look at the workloads of each satellite, and—"

"Then I suggest you come up with a plan." There was a long silence before the president shot the next question at his national intelligence director. "Doug, where would the most likely communications link to a covert Chinese ASAT system be located?"

Nash was obviously unprepared for the question as it flew in from left field. "Uh, their space program has grown so much in the last five years. They could have multiple sites capable of controlling a space-based weapons system. And our best intel is at least two years old—"

"I'd put my money on Xi'an," Patrowski interrupted. "The control center there is the PLA's oldest and most elaborate...and one of their best protected. The new center near Beijing is too close to the coast to be strategic. If it were me, I'd put it at the XSCC."

"Then how can we take that site down?" the president asked calmly.

"You can't be serious, Mr. President!" SECDEF hadn't been on the line very long, but he could quickly tell that the president was no longer talking hypotheticals. And that meant that there were serious policy issues to be addressed. "That's an attack on
180

Chinese sovereign territory. And official doctrine aside, their military journals are full of threats that any attack on Chinese sovereignty would be met with nuclear weapons."

"I want options, dammit!"

Policy was a matter for politicians, but strategy and tactics were the job of the military. Admiral MacCabe offered his advice. The only Navy helicopter pilot to ever achieve the position of chairman of the Joint Chiefs, the decorated admiral was known throughout the Pentagon as the "Lone Wolf." And running counter to the establishment was his trademark. "The only way I would recommend such an attack would be with an unmanned vehicle, sir."

"Fine, then have a plan ready for my review by Friday. If this thing escalates, we need to be ready to react quickly. That'll be all, gentlemen."

CIA Headquarters
Langley, VA

Austin was amazed that it had taken only two days to get the files from the California Institute of Technology. He had no idea whether the sixty-year-old information would contain anything of value, but the fact that Caltech still had the files was intriguing enough by itself. Still, when he thought about the price that had been paid to ensure these documents made it into his hands, he could only hope that the information would be worth the cost.

Immediately after leaving the accident scene two nights ago, Austin had given Chong's key to the CIA's cryptology department for analysis. As the FedEx delivery woman unloaded the last of six dusty boxes on the floor in the middle of his office, Austin held the mysterious key up and studied the inscription again.

Light from his desk lamp highlighted its worn surfaces. It was definitely old. The analysis team had told him that the key was probably made during the immediate post-war years. The mix of copper and nickel suggested 1948 to 1951, the most probable match being a 1950 Olivetti steel file cabinet manufactured in Italy. He ran his thumb over the serrated teeth and stared at the strange inscription on its broad rectangular head. GUGALAB was stamped above a string of numbers that he figured probably identified the file cabinet.

With access to the world's most ingenious cryptologists and code breaking algorithms, he wasn't at all surprised by how quickly his team was able to decipher the cryptic inscription. What did catch him by surprise though was *how* they had cracked the code. When he asked Alicia Cheever what program she used, her reply was simple: the Internet. He could have done that himself, he thought. By merely regrouping the letters in different combinations, the lead cryptologist approached him with a possible match. When she asked Austin if he thought the key could be from the Guggenheim Aeronautics Laboratory, a light bulb went on. Austin turned the key over and read the reverse inscription: HST. After his brief meeting with Chong in Chinatown, Austin had brushed up on the history of the man his friend had called Tsien Hsue-shen. The initials appeared to be scrambled, but strangely, it made sense to Austin. Chong had once explained the convention that the Chinese use with respect to their formal names. In China, the surname was normally written first, followed by the individual's given name. Since Americans used exactly the opposite convention, he was sure that the initials on the key were Americanized for one H-S Tsien.

During his research, Austin had also learned that Tsien was probably one of the least well known of the fathers of modern rocketry—at least in the United States. The exact opposite, however, was true across the Pacific. In China, he was legendary. It didn't have to be that way, he thought, but the US government had been known to do some monumentally stupid things from time to time. Austin skimmed through the file again.

Tsien had entered the United States in 1935 on a Boxer Rebellion scholarship, obtaining a doctorate degree from Caltech in 1939. After graduation, he stayed on to become the assistant professor of aeronautics under Theodore von Karman, and later became director of the Guggenheim Jet Propulsion Center. His seminal work in aeronautics, rocketry, and hypersonic flow helped lay the foundations of America's early rocket program. During World War II, he had even worked as a consultant to the United States Army Air Force. As the war drew to an end, he was sent to Germany to investigate the progress of their wartime aerodynamics research. It was there that he had interviewed Wernher von Braun, among others, to help determine which scientists should be recruited from Nazi Germany.

Tsien eventually applied for US citizenship in 1949, but as the Cold War heated up, he suddenly found himself accused by the FBI of being a Communist Party member. By that time nearly all of Tsien's work was classified, which made the revocation of his security clearance a double blow. Without access to this critical information, his career as a scientist was over, at least in the West. Yet when he decided to return to China, he was detained. It wasn't until five years later, when someone had decided the information he possessed was too old to be of any military value, that Tsien was finally allowed to leave the US. Barely a year later Tsien founded the Institute of Mechanics in

Beijing. He soon became the first director of the Fifth Academy of the Ministry of National Defense and was ultimately responsible for developing the country's ballistic missile program.

The report went on to say that once the Cold War had thawed, several attempts were made by some of Tsien's former Caltech colleagues to return his research papers to him. Tsien himself was quoted in the report as saying that the school should "keep the papers because American students needed them more than Chinese students." Austin was shocked when he learned that the files were still in the Guggenheim Lab where Tsien had worked for nearly twenty years. He had no idea what he might find, but he had a sinking feeling that whatever it was would prove pivotal to the mission brewing back on Johnston Island.

When Austin opened the first box, the odor seemed to match the age of the dusty files inside. By the time he tore open the last box, his office had an odor reminiscent of his grandparents' attic in the Bronx. The boxes were stuffed with hundreds of musty file folders. He leafed through several of them before a date on one caught his attention. He couldn't believe that they had actually arrived in his office in chronological order. Austin knew Tsien's post-war years were said to be the most fruitful in terms of "high-concept" ideas. Austin figured that a weapons platform in deep space was about as high-concept as it got. He searched the boxes until he found the files with the most recent dates. The folder he picked out carried a thick patina. When he read the cover, he knew instantly he had found something important. Stenciled on the report was the title: *Investigations of the Military Applications to Lagrange Points.*

The report read like science fiction. For the time it was written, the concepts sounded like something that could have been penned by Isaac Asimov. He thumbed through the pages, skimming quickly but with a sharp eye. It didn't take long.

He stopped when he hit the section labeled *Characteristics of the Earth-Moon L2 Orbit.* He dove in to the section, devouring every word, even though he only understood about every fifth word. What he read confirmed what he had learned so far about the unique location in space. It was hidden from earthly view by the moon for "all but the highest attainable orbits." Even Austin knew he must have been referring to what was still considered science fiction at the time: geostationary Earth orbits.

But the next part confused him. Tsien made the assertion that the second Earth-Moon Lagrange point was "unsuitable for a military payload of any significance due to the perturbations of the halo orbit fuel requirements and other dynamic considerations." Austin scratched his head. There must be some mistake. But the puzzled look on his face was quickly replaced with grave concern as he read the next sentence: "The L2 point is more aptly suited to function as a communications relay station for a more permanent base or launch platform located on the lunar far side."

Austin removed his glasses and stared quietly across the room as he thought through the logic. The flaw in their assumptions was now crystal clear. The Chang'e 5 must have somehow survived the descent to the lunar surface. And if so, Sam and his crew were training for the wrong mission. They didn't need to fly to L2 after all. Their unlikely Apollo mission needed to *land* on the far side of the moon.

CHAPTER 20

High above the Pacific Ocean

N O ONE NOTICED THE BRIGHT flash. But the orange glow lingered for several minutes as residents of the Pacific Rim gazed up at the unusual spectacle in the night sky. The colorful manmade aurora was beautiful to behold, but the intense energy released in the high altitude explosion would have devastating effects on every satellite within a few thousand miles. Detonation of the highly enriched uranium fuel set a dangerous chain reaction in motion. Gamma rays radiated from the nuclear blast at the speed of light, creating a very brief—but very powerful—electromagnetic pulse. The extreme voltages created by the EMP and the speed at which they struck proved to be overwhelming to the electronic components that took the brunt of the blast; indiscriminate current surges frying the fragile transistors in at least a dozen unprotected satellites. Much less physically destructive than the Chang'e's kinetic-kill-vehicles, the stealthy nuclear weapon was designed to leave no traceable signature at all, instead inflicting its damage on a microscopic scale. In the end, however, the effects would prove to be even more widespread—and no less damaging—to the US military satellites that had just been attacked.

San Diego, CA

Harden made the drive from Freer Industries in Canoga Park to San Diego in record time. The unexpected call that set him in motion came in a little after midnight. He had just completed a demanding lunar rendezvous simulation and was looking forward to a few hours of much needed sleep when Stacy called out of the blue. She said she had the test results she had been waiting on, but wouldn't tell him any more over the phone. Even stranger was the fact that she had flown in unannounced from Dallas and was waiting for him at his condo in San Diego. He'd had almost three hours to think about every possible revelation and how he might respond to each one, but suddenly his mind was blank.

The clock on the dash read 3:02 am when the iron gate to the condominium complex swung open. He parked the blue Tahoe in its usual spot and took a deep breath before stepping out of the truck. He was running on pure adrenaline now, and the guarded optimism that had gotten him though the last few weeks was quickly turning to worry. He tried to gird himself for the coming blow as he made his way up the steps and opened the front door.

It was dark inside. Harden switched on a lamp by the door and saw Stacy curled up on the couch with a blanket over her arms. He walked quietly across the room and knelt down by her side. In the dim light, her gentle features were beautifully silhouetted against the gold satin pillow. He welcomed the peacefulness of the moment, and for a while just stared quietly at her. When he finally touched her on the shoulder she roused as if from a deep, peaceful sleep.

"What took you so long?" she asked groggily, even though she had no idea what time it was.

"It never ceases to amaze me how much traffic there can be in LA in the middle of the night," Harden answered as he gently caressed her arm. "How are you doing?"

"Fine," she said with a yawn. "But I need to freshen up."

"You want me to make some coffee?"

"I probably shouldn't, but I think we're both going to need it."

When Stacy finally reemerged from the bathroom, Harden had two cups of coffee waiting on the kitchen table. "Sorry, but I'm all out of creamer."

"Yeah, I noticed," she said, sounding a bit annoyed. "There's nothing in the fridge that hasn't already exceeded the expiration date by at least a couple of weeks." Stacy then stopped in the middle of the room while she twisted her long dark hair into a ponytail and tied it up in a loose knot behind her head. "And it doesn't look like the bed's been slept in for a while either. Where have you been?"

Harden had never given his wife a reason to be jealous, and finally began to relax when he heard the lighthearted tone in her voice. "Well, there's no other woman involved, if that's what you mean."

"That thought never crossed my mind," she said with a smirk. "I know you better than that. You don't leave enough time in your schedule for such extravagances."

Harden shrugged, and they both laughed a while. It was in the midst of the warm moment that Stacy decided she couldn't wait any longer. She ran over and threw her arms around her husband's neck. She squeezed him tightly as she whispered in his ear, "We're going to have a baby."

Harden grabbed her around the waist and held her firmly. He struggled for the right words to say, but every second he delayed became an eternity. It didn't take Stacy long to figure it out. When she finally pulled away, she saw the look in his eyes. "What's wrong?"

Suddenly he was speechless. He had thought of responses to every piece of bad news she could have delivered, but this was hardly what he had expected. And given the recent change in destinations for the proposed Apollo mission, he wasn't convinced that he would even be around to raise a child. "I guess you were right at the funeral. Maybe I'm just not ready yet."

Stacy studied her husband of fourteen years. "You're not that good of a liar, Jack. And I'm not letting you off the hook so easily. I want to know what in the world is going on here."

Harden sat down and stared into his coffee mug as he decided how much he should tell her. It was a battle he knew he couldn't win. "You never let me finish telling you where I've been for the past few weeks."

Stacy shrugged. "Well, here's your big chance."

Harden picked up the cup and blew at the steaming black liquid before testing it with a small sip. When he decided that the time for secrets between them was finally over, he looked at her and continued. "I was in Canoga Park when you called."

"That's worse than another woman—Sam Freer?"

"Yes. And he's asked me to do something that I promised I would never do again." Harden watched helplessly as her face grew pale. *"But I had no idea you were—"*

"Would it have changed anything if you did know?" Stacy snapped.

Harden knew what she wanted to hear, but couldn't bring himself to say it. "I don't know that it would've."

Stacy collapsed into a chair across the table. It was this same sincerity that she had fallen in love with

189

so long ago. For years she had prayed that he would change. But suddenly, asking him to be anything other than himself was unthinkable. She grabbed the other coffee mug and spooned in a cube of sugar. Harden sat there quietly and waited. When she was ready, she finally looked up and asked, "What's so important this time?"

"Does that mean you'll be here when I get back?" Harden asked guardedly.

Stacy hesitated. She placed a hand on the imperceptible bump under her night gown and considered the two possible futures for her family. "Yes," she finally answered. "We'll be here."

Harden smiled for the first time all night.

"But can you at least tell me where you're going this time...and when can I expect to see you again?"

Freer Industries
Canoga Park, CA

Sam Freer rubbed his tired eyes. The days, like the grueling training sessions, were blurring one into another. He paced anxiously back and forth between the two consoles as he simultaneously monitored Jeff Burns hone his celestial navigation skills in the command module simulator, while Jack Harden and Pete Mitchell worked through a generic landing profile in the lunar module sim. Freer had been preparing for this for twenty years, yet it seemed as if he were suddenly facing an impossible deadline.

The team he had assembled included some of the most dedicated of the old-school Apollo controllers, and the best and brightest of a new generation of rocket scientists. But his talent pool was extremely shallow when it came to achieving the original goal of the Apollo program: to land a man on the moon, and return him safely to the Earth. He felt confident in his team's ability to operate the complex system of systems that was Apollo. He also knew that with a sound grasp of orbital mechanics and the right combination of keystrokes, he could have flown the L2 orbital mission himself. But that's where his confidence ended. To actually *land* a spacecraft on the moon required a skill set that had long since atrophied—nearly to the point of extinction. That's why the first number he had dialed after hanging up with Stephen Austin was that of a gracefully aging, silver-haired gentleman who still lived in Houston.

A giant weight was removed from Freer's shoulders when the announcement blasted from the overhead speaker: "Mr. Cernan has arrived."

When the Apollo 17 commander arrived at the facility, the result was electrifying. The atmosphere of nervousness in the simulator bay quickly turned to optimism when the imposing moonwalker entered the room. Freer greeted Cernan with an open hand. "Thanks for coming on such short notice, Gene. I can't imagine trying to pull this off without our most famous SLATE member."

"Are you kidding? I wouldn't miss this for the world," Cernan said cheerily. He then slowly made his way around the room, shaking hands with each of the multi-generational gathering of Apollo controllers. "So who are the lucky ones?"

"Do you remember Jack Harden? He's in command of the mission."

"Yeah, I remember Jack," Cernan replied with a grin. "I've followed his career closely. He's an excellent choice. Who's the other lucky bastard?"

"His LMP is Pete Mitchell. He's a rookie," Freer admitted, "but Jack said he wouldn't fly the mission without him. I guess they go way back. You wouldn't

191

know it from listening to them sometimes, though." Freer was just happy that Mitchell was back on the team after the blowup earlier in the week. In the end, he really didn't care why, although he suspected that the opportunity to land on the moon instead of flying circles around it was powerful persuasion.

"What's his background?" Cernan pried. "Mitchell's?"

"He's a former Tomcat pilot. He and Jack met in flight school."

Cernan smiled. "Perfect. I don't care what kind of baggage they may be carrying around. That's exactly who Harden needs right now. Anyone who can land a fighter jet on the pitching deck of an aircraft carrier in the black of night definitely has what it takes. And they have a bond between them that's unbreakable. Might not sound like it to outsiders, but if Jack was sly enough to get him to sign on to your plan, I'll bet that Mitchell will be there like a brother when the shit hits the fan."

"You're probably right," said Freer. "But they're far from being ready to go. We've been working through the landing sequence all day. That's where we could really use some help."

Cernan wrapped his arm around Freer's shoulder and escorted him to the LM's simulator supervisor console. "Let's take a look." It didn't take Cernan long to figure out where they were in the profile. The SimSup gave the long since retired astronaut a quick rundown of the day's training. The crew had conducted three practice approaches and three successful Auto landings to the simulated lunar terrain. All had gone smoothly; no abnormals, no emergencies. On the next run, the SimSup explained, an untimely landing radar failure just prior to pitchover would give the crew their first dry run of the abort procedures.

"I'm going to give it to them right before they get into Program 64," the simulator supervisor said.

"No," Cernan said softly. "Let them pitch over first and *then* fail the radar. That'll test their mettle, and it'll give me a chance to see what they're made of. If they abort, we've got our work cut out for us. If they don't, give them the landing radar back, and let's see what they do with it."

"But that'll kick them into P66. They won't have time to reconfigure for an automatic landing. Harden will have to fly the rest of the approach manually."

"I know." Cernan smiled. "That's exactly what I want to see."

It seemed odd to have three men crammed into the small cabin, but Harden's first attempt at a manual landing quickly highlighted the need for some one-on-one training. And Mitchell wasn't about to watch this approach from the console.

"Now, when you get into P64 and the LM pitches over, you're going to be looking through the LPD, the landing point designator, for a place to set her down," Cernan explained. "The lunar module pilot will be feeding you sight angles from the DSKY so you can see where you're headed. Now, chances are that you're going to need to make corrections. It's just like flying the 'ball at the boat. You've got to get lineup squared away early, and you need to make your big corrections as far out on the glideslope as you can. Watch here."

Descending through 7,000 feet, the flight program changed on cue and the LM began to pitch forward. The lunar surface rose slowly from the bottom of the triangular windows. "There," Cernan said softly. "I can see our landing spot at an LPD angle of forty-five degrees. And let's say that we're four or five thousand feet south of our landing zone. I can use my attitude controller to redesignate the landing point by rolling into an angle of bank. When the LPD marker intersects my new target, I just release the ACA back to the detent. The computer will then fly you over to the new landing site."

"Is there a practical limit to the size of the correction you can make?" Mitchell asked from the second row.

"Oh, she'll rear up on you if pull too hard on the reins," Cernan replied over his shoulder, his love for horses clearly on display even in the most technical of descriptions. "But for the most part, if you can see it, she'll go get it."

The lunar module computer recorded the newly designated landing azimuth and then began making the required corrections. "Now," Cernan continued the lesson, "once you have the big corrections out of the way, you'll want to switch over to Program 66 as soon as you can, which will basically put you into an attitude hold mode. Then you can vary your rate-of-descent with the ROD switch here. Each click up or down will increase or decrease your vertical rate accordingly. But you want to do this early enough so you get your scan up to speed and get into a rhythm, or else you'll end up looking like a dog on a slick tile floor when you try to change directions."

"Got it," said Harden.

Cernan's hands caressed the controls as he zoned in on the moment and brought the lunar module to a low hover above the simulated lunar terrain. When the low fuel indicator on the instrument panel finally lit, he set the craft down gently, reliving in his mind's eye the landing that had defined his life, the opus of a truly brilliant career.

Cernan's trance was finally broken by the chorus of praise emanating from the simulator console. Harden turned and extended his hand. "Nicely done, Captain."

"Don't worry, Jack. We'll get you up to speed in no time."

Harden shook his head. The shadow Cernan cast was long. He knew it would take an unimaginable amount of training to ever come close to that level of expertise. And training took time, the one commodity there never seemed to be enough of. But as Cernan released his firm grip, Harden noted something that made him smile—Cernan's steady hand was wet with sweat. His mentor may have just made a moon landing appear as easy as landing a Cessna, but Harden knew now that nothing could be further from the truth. The old guy was good at the game. It was rare to find men who could walk the walk. Harden then looked over his shoulder at Mitchell, and realized for the first time that he was friends with another one of those rare men.

"Okay, fellas, we need to stay on schedule," Freer announced over the intercom. "Jack, we need you and Pete to man-up the command module sim with Jeff and go through the launch sequence. First things first. If we can't get you to the moon, it won't much matter if you can land on it or not."

"Sam, is it all right if I skip the first run-through?" Mitchell asked. "I don't have much to do during the launch sequence anyway, and I was hoping to spend some more time on the LM systems—that is if Gene doesn't mind. If I'm going to go along with this madness, I should probably get good at it. That is my main job, right, lunar module pilot?"

"I think we can do that," Freer replied. "What do you say, Jack?"

Harden looked at Mitchell. It was clear to him now that his friend had finally made a commitment to the mission. There was still some healing that needed to be done, but a complete reconciliation would take time. "Sure. Why not."

CHAPTER 21

Freer Residence
Pacific Palisades, CA

A T THE END OF A week of long days and short nights, Sam Freer sensed that something was missing from what he had hoped would be a recipe for success. After discussing the situation with his wife, the answer became clear. What his crew needed now more than anything else was a break from the non-stop training schedule, so he invited the trio down to his estate in the bluffs of Pacific Palisades for a few drinks and a hearty home-cooked dinner. Following the five-course gourmet meal prepared by his wife, Freer escorted their guests to his personal library for the event about to take place halfway around the globe.

Freer eyed Mitchell as he walked by. "That sure was one hell of an idea you had, Pete. I think just about everyone in the SLATE is kicking themselves for not thinking of it first."

"Thanks, Sam. I guess? I just hope it works."

When Austin had relayed Freer's estimate of the earliest possible launch date based on lunar lighting conditions for a landing at the specified location, the president balked. To wait another month was out of the question. Escalation of tension in the Pacific theater was spiraling toward confrontation. And when

US military satellites started dropping offline like a string of bad Christmas lights, Freer's long shot gamble suddenly became the president's best hope for keeping America safe. It was true that another electromagnetic "disturbance" in the western Pacific could devastate the military's ability to operate in the region, but an EMP blast in the skies above the United States became unthinkable. There had to be another way, he had told Austin.

"Why can't we land from the opposite direction?" was all Mitchell had wanted to know. The answer was simple. The SLATE team had planned to follow the same script as every other Apollo mission. The route was planned to have the spacecraft arrive at the leading edge of the moon and enter a retrograde orbit around it. The resulting flight path, upon return, would look like a giant figure-eight, with the Earth inside one swoop of the eight and the moon in the other. When Mitchell suggested a trailing edge approach, he knew how Columbus must have felt when he posited a westward route to reach the Far East. But with one irreverent suggestion, the timing problem was suddenly cut in half. The trailing edge flight profile had never been flown—the margin of safety considered too thin—but there was no denying that the bold plan would move up the earliest launch window by two weeks, and that was all the president needed to hear.

"But don't worry, Pete. I wouldn't have signed on to it if I didn't think it would work," Freer said as he swung open the double mahogany doors and led the trio into his home office. Tucked away in the west wing of his Frank Lloyd Wright-inspired home, the spacious library doubled as a teleconferencing center for Freer Industries. Harden gravitated toward a large replica of the moon next to Freer's desk. Burns walked over to the far wall and examined the books in Freer's impressive collection; the expansive section illustrating the history of science included calf-bound editions of works by Newton, Faraday, Maxwell, and Eddington. Mitchell took a seat on the leather couch next to the stone fireplace. A high definition video projector hung from the center of the room. Freer grabbed a remote and pushed the power button. Burns jumped when the elongated trapdoor above his head snapped open and a large canvas screen unfurled from the slot in the ceiling, sliding neatly into position in front of the wall-spanning bookcase he had been quietly admiring.

"Let's see if they are actually going to televise the launch," Freer said as he searched the international TV menu for CCTV-7. Chinese Central Television was the primary propaganda outlet for the ruling Communist Party and Freer had learned long ago that news obtained from this source had to be deeply scrutinized. He found examples everywhere. Some things, though, were harder to fake than others.

Sam didn't expect the launch of Shenzhou 11 to be broadcast live, but he knew that if the launch was successful, the delay would be much shorter than if a cover story was required. If unsuccessful, however, Freer expected much the same treatment that Shenzhou 7 had received. On that ignominious display of deception, after numerous launch delays, an article covering China's third manned spaceflight appeared in print on the Xinhua News Agency's website. The story was quickly picked up by several more mainstream news outlets, including the Associated Press. The article chronicled the Shenzhou launch in detail. Launch time and precise orbital parameters were provided, as well as actual dialogue between the Chinese *taikonauts* and CNSA ground controllers. The only problem with the report was that the date of the article was still two days in the future—and the launch hadn't even taken place yet. The Communist Party's official response was that it was an honest mistake by a confused technician. The launch eventually went off without a hitch, and highlighted China's burgeoning manned spaceflight program. But to Freer, the motives of secretive space agency were still anything but clear.

"Aren't they supposed to rendezvous with the Russians?" Mitchell asked, and took another sip of the vintage Merlot that had accompanied the superbly grilled rack of lamb.

"Basically," Freer said as he made his way to his favorite chair. "If Shenzhou 11 makes it to orbit and successfully rendezvous with the Tiangong 2, the Russians plan to launch a Soyuz from Kazakhstan and join them later at the space lab." Freer's interest in Shenzhou 11 went well beyond curiosity or national pride. Launching a manned spaceflight with another country's spacecraft already in orbit required detailed coordination in the best of circumstances. Add a third spacecraft in the mix and keeping his Saturn V launch covert—and safe—was far from guaranteed.

Freer set the remote down and watched anxiously as the countdown neared its climax. Video from the far-away Jiuquan Satellite Launch Center captured the launch sight vividly, as powerful spotlights bathed the towering white rocket in artificial daylight. Capped by its Shenzhou spacecraft and silhouetted against the night sky, the Long March 2F rocket looked larger and more powerful than it did during the day when seen against the backdrop of the vast Gobi Desert. But to Freer, the CZ-2F rocket, known as the Divine Arrow, and its Shenzhou spacecraft smacked of their Russian heritage. The assemblage was characteristically utilitarian—clunky even—and lacked any of the style and grace of NASA's once powerful rocket systems. "Hold on. I think this is it," he said as flame slowly consumed the base of the rocket. The bright flash against the backdrop of night quickly overpowered the camera lens, and for several long seconds the only thing visible on the screen was the ragged orange plume beneath the booster's eight engines as the rocket pushed past the launch tower. Fire stretched across the sky as China's Divine Arrow arched eastward over the Gobi. And within minutes the image faded to a black as Shenzhou 11 clawed its way into the inky night.

When it became apparent that the launch was successful, Freer clicked the remote and the overhead projector went dark. The last thing he wanted to do tonight was dwell on the mounting complications of launching Apollo 18 through an orbiting gauntlet of Chinese and Russian spacecraft—or the consequences of the widening gap between America's faltering space program and that of a new axis of space-faring nations.

White House Oval Office

Stephen Austin paced the floor of the receiving room outside the Oval Office. He glanced at his watch again for the fifth time in as many minutes. His audience with the president was supposed to take place an hour ago. Austin wouldn't have minded so much if he didn't have a plane to catch. But he hated to think what might happen if he wasn't present at Air Force Space Command in the morning to confirm that the unknown missile being tracked over the Pacific wasn't a submarine launched ICBM targeting North America.

Austin jumped when he heard the voice burst from the overhead speaker. "The president will see you now, Mr. Austin." Stephen opened the convex wooden door and searched the room. He was surprised to see that he was alone with the president.

"Welcome, Stephen," the president said without looking up. "Have a seat."

"Thank you, Mr. President."

The president was still finishing the last entry in his personal calendar. He was finally beginning to realize just how pivotal these days would be for the country—and potentially the world. He secretly hoped that he would one day be able to reflect back on the events of the last few weeks and see them in a positive light, but that was still a big unknown. The classified report on his desk saw to that, as the most recent assessment of the fate of at least three American military satellites was more than a little unsettling. If they had failed, as intelligence now supported, as the result of an electromagnetic pulse, then the implications for America's security were enormous.

An appendix to the report had clearly outlined the effects of an EMP blast in the upper atmosphere above the United States. He had suspected that computer systems and communications equipment would be hard hit, but the larger effects of an EMP on the nation's power grid—he now understood as he studied the shocking graphic—would be catastrophic. Similar to the geomagnetically induced currents that can result from solar flares, the long duration pulses associated with a high-altitude EMP blast would devastate power transmission lines across the entire country. The report estimated that between six and twenty-five million homes across the US could be without electricity for up to three months if a pulse equivalent to the one that had detonated over the Pacific were to occur at the specified altitude over the upper Midwest. Several coordinated EMPs could throw the entire country back into the nineteenth century. He set his pen down and looked up at Austin. "Two minutes, Stephen. What do you have?"

"Well sir, the crew of Apollo 18 has just landed at Johnston. The rocket is being fueled at this moment, and the countdown is on track to launch at 7:27 Hawaii Standard Time. That'll be 1:27 tomorrow afternoon here in DC."

The president rubbed his forehead. "Is that what we're calling it now?"

"It made sense at the time. They're riding on the booster originally slated for the Apollo 18 lunar expedition."

"It doesn't matter," the president said with a wave of his hand. "No one will ever know about it anyway. Continue."

"Yes, sir. We recently received a disturbing piece of HUMINT, um human intelligence, which indicates the PLA may be aware of our mission. What we don't know at this point is if they suspect a lunar landing, or perhaps just another attempt to launch HALO. But either way it highlights an unforeseen threat."

"Jesus." The president reached for the phone, punched the intercom button, and spoke. "Get Admiral MacCabe on the phone," he said, and punched the button again. "I'll see if there's a cruiser or something near Hawaii that can be deployed to the area before morning. We'll have them interrogate any vessel within a five-hundred-mile radius of Johnston...make sure there are no more 'accidents' like we had with the *Atlantis*."

Austin was impressed. That's exactly what he was going to ask for. "Thank you, Mr. President."

"Is there anything else you're concerned about?"

"Well, we still haven't located the Chang'e 5." After successfully identifying the Chang'e 4 satellite hovering at L2, NASA's Lunar Reconnaissance Orbiter had returned to the complicated maneuver to align its orbit with Daedalus crater, now the suspected landing site of the Chang'e 5. But the fuel critical profile would take several more days to complete. "Otherwise, I've looked at all the critical events in the mission plan. Most of the threats to success are internal—mechanical failures, human factors, and the like. There are still a few areas I have to look into, but you've addressed my biggest concern."

"Good," said the president as he made several more notes in his calendar. "Keep me updated on the major milestones. If this train comes off the tracks, I need to know the second it happens; because if we can't find and destroy this Assassin's Mace thing, we could be in deep trouble. And if they do get lucky and somehow pull this off, I'd like to know about it before I commit to a course of action that we may all regret one day."

"Yes, sir." Austin looked at his watch. His two minutes were up.

"That'll be all," the president said, and spoke into the intercom again.

Austin rose and headed for the door.

The president sat back and massaged his tired eyes. He should have seen it coming. There was no doubt that the PLA was becoming more brazen every day. A proliferation of cyber attacks, the deliberate targeting of a GPS satellite, and the attack on the *Impeccable* were all canaries in the coal mine—clear indications of China's intent to systematically target critical elements of America's defenses. The EMP attack had to have come from the PLA. And by all accounts, they now held the high ground. His thoughts drifted back to Austin's reclama to the Chinese national intelligence estimate. *They would not hesitate to launch an attack if they decided the moment was ripe and the means at their disposal were sufficient.* His reaction to this Sun Tzu-like claim may very well define his presidency.

And that legacy suddenly hinged on the success of a suicidal moon mission—a mission that until recently had been lost to the dustbin of history.

Tiangong 2

The lengthy orbital race finally ended. The Russian Soyuz capsule had caught up with and was station-keeping alongside the twenty-ton Tiangong 2 space station as it coasted along at some 27,000 kilometers per hour above East Asia. Also known as the Heavenly Palace, the already cramped Tiangong was about to become a full house. Three *taikonauts* from Shenzhou 11 lumbered unavoidably into one another as they prepared to welcome their two Russian visitors to China's latest space achievement.

Dmitri Popovich smiled inside his helmet as the capture latches retracted, mating his Soyuz workhorse to the small station's unused docking port. To Pavel Budarin, the burly Russian commander had just made the dangerous maneuver appear no harder than parking his tiny VAZ Niva in the empty parking lot next to the berthing facilities in Star City.

But as Commander Popovich prepared to open the hatch and enter the Soyuz's orbital module, he couldn't help but feel slighted. This was a record setting flight. He was the first Russian cosmonaut to have flown in space seven times. The new record bested that of fellow cosmonaut Sergei Krikalev and catapulted him into the ranks of other record setters like John Young, the Apollo moonwalker and shuttle pilot who had secretly been Dmitri's hero since he was a small boy. But instead of his final, record-setting flight being a lengthy stay at the glamorous and spacious International Space Station—now the de facto flagship of the Roscosmos—he had to settle for a forty-eight-hour "inspection tour" of the Tiangong 2.

After confirming an airtight seal in the airlock, the Soyuz commander braced the boots of his Orlan spacesuit against a storage locker in the orbital module and cranked the hatch handle over. Once the pressures equalized, the hatch swung open easily. Hovering at the end of the short tunnel were three beaming round faces, each flush with pride as the Chinese commander extended his hand and muttered his practiced Russian greeting. "Welcome, comrades, to the Heavenly Palace of New China."

Popovich returned the greeting in the universal language of aviation: English. "Permission to come aboard, comrade?"

Pavel Budarin was quick to notice the frown as it fell across the face of the Chinese commander. Dmitri had prepared him for such a response. At least with the ISS, the commander had reasoned, Russia had been brought on board as an equal partner. But in this flimsy alliance, his once proud country had become nothing more than a technology whore who had spread her legs for a mere few billion rubles.

Trailing his commander, Pavel grabbed the handholds inside the orbital module and pulled himself through the small tunnel that connected his Soyuz to the Tiangong. Pavel glided joyfully through the void as Dmitri righted himself in the small station's habitation module. Pavel seemed immune to the cold reception and bitter silence that suddenly permeated the tight quarters. It was the young cosmonaut's first trip to space, and he had no unrealistic expectations that this chance rendezvous would elicit the same détente that the Apollo-Soyuz Test Project once had. He floated carefully past the Chinese commander to the generous viewing port on the far bulkhead. Arresting his inertia with the aid of a handhold, Pavel pressed his face against the cold glass. The world seemed so peaceful, he thought, as whole continents scrolled slowly across his window.

CHAPTER 22

Johnston Island

C LOAKED IN A SHELL OF white Teflon-coated Beta cloth, silver suitcase swinging by his side, Jack Harden made his way out of the launch control center to a nearby crew transfer van. As he rounded the corner of the eroding cinderblock building, he thrust a gloved hand into the air to block the first flash of sunrise. What he saw through his glass helmet was a shock to his senses. Towering above Jeff Burns and Pete Mitchell in the rosy, early morning dawn was the full majesty of one of the lost Saturns. Filled with an exotic brew of liquids—a super-cooled slush of hydrogen and oxygen—the Saturn V seemed to come alive as lazy wisps of condensing gases, illuminated by shafts of newborn light, were slowly exhaled through the seams of adjacent rocket stages. Harden broke the spell that his two crewmembers had fallen under with a gentle pat on each man's shoulder, then shepherded his fellow spacemen into the waiting van.

Now completely free from its silo-shaped assembly facility, the pristine white rocket grew impossibly large as the crew van approached the base of the launch umbilical tower. Harden couldn't help but admire the sheer scale of the vehicle. It was one thing to see pictures of it, or look across its reclining length as an exhibit at Johnson Space Center, but at nearly twice the height of the shuttle stack, it was something else entirely to see the Saturn V upright, fully loaded, cocked, and aimed at the stars.

When the short drive ended, the three crewmen exited the idling van and climbed into the open-air elevator car. Harden grabbed the wall of the wiry cage as the lift lurched into motion. His eyes followed the skin of the launch vehicle upward as they rose; stage by stage, the girth of the S-IC and S-II stages gently gave way to the svelte, but muscular trunk of the S-IVB. He imagined the lunar module, its spidery legs tucked beneath it, hidden behind the panels of the spacecraft-LM adapter. And at the apex, the Apollo spacecraft glistened like an arrowhead against the brilliantly orange morning sky.

Some 340 feet above the ground, the noisy lift jerked to a stop. Harden led the way as he strode toward the lofty protection of the White Room. This wasn't the first time he had walked the gantry and climbed aboard a fully fueled rocket, but this one was markedly different from any he had ever flown before. He was about to ride into space, on a column of fire— in a vehicle without wings.

Harden threaded himself through the open hatch and settled into the left couch. Mitchell followed clumsily and slid to the right side of the spacecraft. Burns took his position on the center couch and immediately began the delicate process of hooking into the command module's environmental control system. When the closeout crew finally finished grafting all three men into the complex life support system, Freer knelt down beside the open hatch and gave each man a firm handshake.

"Enjoy the ride, gentlemen."

"Don't worry. We'll be gentle with her," Harden promised. Then, just as Freer was about to leave,

Harden held out his hand. "Wait, Sam. What was the prayer that Alan Shepard said right before his Mercury launch?"

Freer paused for a moment and then returned the smile. He was sure that Harden already knew the answer. "Oh Lord, please don't let me fuck this up!" Freer then took one last look inside the capsule and stepped back into the center of the White Room. As technicians worked to seal the hatch, he removed the protective shower cap from his head and readjusted his glasses. The hard work, he knew, was about to begin.

Launch Pad 39C
Johnston Island

Jeff Burns shielded his face with the CSM Launch Checklist as the White Room finally retracted and natural light slowly filtered into the dimly lit cockpit. He blinked several times as his eyes adjusted. Even when well lit, the command module felt more like a cramped cone-shaped closet than the spacious flight deck of a space shuttle. The claustrophobia melted away quickly though as his vision returned and he continued with the checklist, eyes walking over every switch and every gauge in his purview. Then, as part of his final pre-launch checks, he touched certain controls and annunciated the results. "Cabin pressure holding. Suit/Cabin delta-p steady at zero-point-eight."

"EDS Power – On, Abort light verified, harness locked," Harden said as he armed the Emergency Detection System.

Burns then reached above his head and rotated the gearbox selector on the center hatch to the latched position. After settling back into his couch, he ratcheted the lever by his right hip and matched Harden's report. "Harness locked."

"Locked," Mitchell echoed.

"T minus twenty minutes," a raspy voice droned from launch control.

"Apollo 18, Johnston Flight," Freer radioed. "Based on the latest data GNC has on the landing site, you're going to need to update the launch azimuth. Advise when ready to copy."

"Flight, stand by while I clear the DSKY," Burns replied. The *diskey* was the compact input/output device for the command module computer, the CMC. It consisted of a *dis*play, which had placeholders for the current operational program, a verb, a noun, and three data registers—and a numerical *key*pad and several function keys through which data was entered. The concept was simple enough, but operation, Burns had learned, could be quite cumbersome. Within certain programs, a verb told the computer what action needed to be taken, and a noun told the computer what parameter, or thing, needed to be acted upon. But instead of the verbs and nouns being words, they were seemingly random numbers. The display's neon-green seven-segment LEDs flickered as Burns typed. The procedure was maddeningly archaic, even by shuttle standards, but he knew that with enough practice he would eventually become proficient with its operation. Still, as a crutch, he continued to verbalize certain steps as he keyed in the commands. "Verb seventy-eight. Enter."

"Your new launch azimuth is 96.27 degrees," Freer radioed.

Burns jotted down the new heading and then confirmed the data against his checklist before entering the information into the DSKY. "Verb twenty-one. Enter. Zero, nine, six, two, seven. Enter. Proceed."

He was visibly relieved as the numbers on the display flashed, confirming the correct entry format.

"I'm glad somebody knows where we're going," Mitchell mumbled as Burns continued filling the simple computer with the required data.

"T minus six minutes."

Harden felt a slight jolt as the gantry arm retracted and swung around to the 180-degree position on the labyrinthine umbilical tower.

Time began to compress.

Far below in the blockhouse, the launch director had spent the last fourteen hours supervising the loading of nearly six million pounds of propellants into the massive moon rocket. Skip Donovan shook his head. It had taken nearly two and a half *hours* to fuel the RP-1 and LOX tanks in the first stage alone—four and a half million pounds of fuel. And five ravenous F-1 engines, generating over seven million pounds of thrust, would suck them dry in barely two and a half *minutes*.

"T minus two minutes."

In the control room, Sam Freer scanned a bank of security monitors next to his console. The image on one of the monitors caught his attention. At the far end of the tiny island, a small group of men and women, a few dozen in all had gathered to witness the event of a lifetime. More than a hundred technicians had labored for months preparing the giant Saturn, but most had collateral duties that kept them inside protected structures for the main event. Those who didn't crossed their fingers and waited nervously for the miracle that would be witnessed by fewer people than attended the average high school football game. Freer lamented that fact, wishing instead that the whole country could watch, and recall a time when America was in control of its own destiny.

"T minus one minute."

Harden located a single pushtile on the sprawling instrument panel and carefully depressed it. "GDC ALIGN." The spacecraft's primary attitude instrument, the "Eight-ball," jittered as it received its final alignment.

"It feels like we're in tension on the catapult again," Mitchell blurted out.

"Just wait until *this* holdback breaks," Harden warned.

Burns flexed his right arm up at the elbow and touched his helmet with a stiff glove before making a snappy salute toward the imaginary catapult officer. "We can't launch without saluting the Shooter."

Harden agreed with his friend's superstition. "Yeah, and we can't afford to have anything suspend this launch."

"T minus twenty seconds. Guidance is internal."

"T minus fifteen, fourteen..."

A low frequency rumble suddenly found its way into the quiet cockpit.

"Fuel manifolds," Harden advised. "I think we're going to the moon, boys."

"Ten, nine, ignition sequence start..."

Massive turbo pumps, each as powerful as ten locomotives, spooled into service forcing kerosene, at the rate of fifteen tons per second, into five of the most complex and powerful engines ever created.

"Six, five, four..."

Bright red flames belched from the enormous engine bells as the final seconds ticked down and thrust built up to a punishing seven and a half million pounds.

"Three, two, one..."

"*Liftoff!* We have liftoff of Apollo 18."

Command Module Phantom

"The clock is running," Harden announced against the mounting vibrations.

"P-Eleven," Burns shouted above the deafening roar. Scanning the DSKY, he quickly translated the data it reported: inertial velocity, altitude rate, and altitude. All the numbers, along with their chances of survival, were steadily increasing.

The explosion of energy released by the Saturn V at full power masked any sensation of flight. Mitchell blinked several times in an effort to bring the instrument panel into focus, but all of his gauges were a blur. If not for the numbers changing on the DSKY, he wouldn't have believed that they were actually off the ground.

"We have a yaw program," Harden reported as the outboard engines swiveled to guide the precariously balanced stack clear of the launch tower.

"Tower's clear!" Freer bellowed.

"Roll complete," Harden confirmed. "We're pitching."

"Oh man, are we moving now!" Burns hollered as he noted their vertical velocity on the DSKY: 150 feet per second straight up. He did the math quickly in his head. They were barely clear of the launch tower and were already traveling at over one hundred miles per hour.

"It feels like a runaway fright train," Mitchell yelled.

"Yeah, on a crooked track," Burns added as the dynamically unstable rocket frantically hunted for the correct path to orbit.

"Coming up on one minute, stand by for Mode 1 Bravo," Harden said, acknowledging a shift in the complex sequence of abort modes.

Burns shook his head as he eyed the clock. "H-pad is eight nautical miles." It was hard to believe that in barely a minute the mammoth machine was already 50,000 feet above the launch pad.

"Three-g's," Mitchell coughed against the mounting pressure.

Harden forced himself to breathe as he closely monitored their progress on the Eight-ball. The black and grey sphere indicated that the Saturn had already pitched nearly forty-five degrees away from its vertical launch attitude. Half of the rocket's acceleration was now being converted into altitude, and half toward increasing their velocity to the magic value: 25,600 feet per second, or 17,500 miles per hour—orbital velocity.

"Apollo 18, at two minutes you are go for staging," Freer radioed.

Three hundred and twenty feet behind the crew of Apollo 18, the base of the rocket was slowly being consumed by waves of expanding exhaust gasses. No longer constrained by thick air and a powerful slipstream, the fiery plume expanded freely in all directions, nearly devouring the Saturn's enormous first stage.

"Center engine cutoff," Harden said as the middle light on the engine status display illuminated. "There's four-g's. Stand by for the unload."

When the raging inferno of the S-IC was finally snuffed, four-g's of acceleration disappeared in an instant. A magnificent fireball raced ahead of the decelerating rocket, momentarily engulfing the entire command module in a brilliant yellow flash. Coasting through the upper atmosphere now at nearly 6,000 nautical miles per hour, an army of explosive bolts quickly unzipped the S-IC from the interstage skirt. Eight retro rockets then fired to back the spent first stage away from the supersonic stack. Its short life at an end, the carcass of the S-IC would still climb another twenty-five miles on its ballistic arc before plowing into the Pacific Ocean 350 miles east of Johnston Island.

Harden finally caught his breath. "Staging." The behemoth rocket was now 140 feet shorter and five million pounds lighter than it had been barely two minutes earlier. Acceleration smoothly built back up to one-g as the second stage came to life, and the brute force acceleration of the F-1 engines gave way to the gentlemanly ride of the S-II. "Ignition." For the next six minutes, the second act of the Saturn's performance was perfect.

"Mark, 16,000 feet per second," Burns reported. "Trajectory looks good. Steering is good at seven degrees. Altitude ninety-three nautical miles."

"Apollo 18, you are go for staging," Freer advised.

"Copy, we have S-II shutdown," Harden noted as the complex choreography began again. This time pyrotechnics peeled the S-II from the still dormant third stage. "Staging. S-IVB ignition."

"Mark, 23,500 feet per second," Burns reported.

"Apollo 18, at ten minutes you are go for orbit, predicted cutoff at eleven plus fifty," Freer announced.

"Wow, look at it kill that altitude," Mitchell noted as he scanned the DSKY.

"Yep. H-dot is minus-sixty," Burns said, nodding at Mitchell's keen interpretation that the S-IVB had actually adopted a nose low attitude with respect to the local horizon, descending slightly in an effort to trim their orbit from becoming overly elliptical. "Pitch steady at minus-ten degrees. Ten seconds to shutdown. Stand by. Velocity 25,600 feet per second...Mark!"

"Shutdown!" Harden shouted as the S-IVB's single

engine concluded its first performance of the day flawlessly. "Right on, no residuals."

"Wow!" Burns exhaled. "That sure was one hell of a wild ride."

"Unbelievable," Mitchell whispered as he glanced through the small window above his right shoulder. The view was decidedly other-worldly. Film and video could capture the image, but there was nothing, he now knew, that could equal the experience.

Harden fought hard to keep his emotions in check. They still had a long way to go before he would find reason to cheer, yet he recognized the significance of the event for the uninitiated and briefly surrendered to the moment, "Welcome to space, gentlemen!"

CHAPTER 23

High above the Pacific Ocean

HARDEN RESET SEVERAL SWITCHES AS he rattled through the Orbital Insertion checklist. "EDS Power – Off. SECS Pyro Arm – Off. SECS Logic – Off."

Mitchell took his cue and elbowed the command module pilot to his left. "Pipper, let's go. SPS Gimbal Motors."

But Burns was hypnotized by the view through the center hatch as the yawning Pacific scrolled slowly past his window. The view was surreal, the world as he had never seen it before. Yet from his lofty altitude, and in the absence of gravity, looking at the world upside down somehow felt natural to him. "Wow, would you look at that," he intoned. "I think that's Hawaii back there."

"Pipper, Gimbal Motors!" Mitchell barked.

But the excitement was contagious, and a broad smile swept across Harden's face. "You know, I guess the view is pretty spectacular," he admitted as he glanced out the small window over his left shoulder. "But let's not get too distracted. There's still a lot of work to do before TLI. So why don't we get ahead of the checklist first, then we'll do some more sightseeing a little later. I promise." Harden shuddered when he thought about it—Translunar Injection. For a shuttle crew, low Earth orbit *was* the destination. For an Apollo mission, this was merely a parking orbit.

"Apollo 18, Johnston," Freer's voice came over the comm link.

Harden thumbed his mike switch. "Go ahead, Johnston."

"We see the telemetry from your noun sixty-two at 25,605 feet per second, and we confirm your orbit at ninety-five by ninety nautical miles. We also have you on radar now thanks to the US Space Surveillance Network. I'll bet there are a lot of pissed off generals wanting to know what in the world is going on up there right now and why they didn't get read-in to the program."

"That's good news on the orbit, Johnston," Harden replied. "And I'm sure you're right about the pandemonium at STRATCOM this morning. Let's just hope that no one else knows we're up here."

Mitchell nodded inside the bulbous helmet. But after four confining hours inside the cumbersome spacesuit, he felt increasingly claustrophobic. Eager for some fresh air, Mitchell was quick to reach for the red locking ring on the neck of his pressure suit. He pinched the clasp between two padded fingers and slid the mechanism to the left. To his surprise, the helmet shot from his shoulders, bounced off the angled bulkhead, and floated to a stop near the instrument panel above his head.

"Holy shit," Mitchell swore as he wiped his face with a gloved hand. He quickly inspected his palm to verify the results. "Is my nose bleeding? That thing really whacked me on the way up."

"No, you're fine," Harden reassured him. "Maybe a scratch. That's all. Hey, a word to the wise. Take a glove off first to bleed the suit pressure before unlocking your helmets."

"Thanks for the warning," Mitchell said sheepishly.

The command module was soon filled with floating gloves and empty glass helmets as each man doffed the bulky equipment. Burns, eager to experience the magic of zero-g for himself, released his harness and quickly went to work on the framework that had supported his couch during the launch. Like aluminum origami, he folded the seat neatly into the stowed position. He then floated clumsily into the void beyond the wide instrument panel, grabbing a hand hold in the spacecraft's lower equipment bay to arrest his motion. The interior of the conical habitat felt strangely different in the absence of gravity. No longer confined to lying on his back beneath the panels of switches, dials, and gauges, the unusual void where his feet had been suddenly became usable space. Filled with storage lockers and lined with the equipment he would need to navigate the uncharted highways of cislunar space, the lower equipment bay was now a spacious back office in the otherwise cramped cockpit.

Within minutes Burns was maneuvering in his new domain as if he had spent a lifetime in space. He gently pushed himself from one side of the spacecraft to the other, floating in different positions each time. He reveled in a freedom of motion that his body had never before experienced.

But the freeness of space didn't agree equally with everyone. Mitchell was one of the unlucky ones. As soon as he lowered his couch and began to float free of the restraints, the uneasiness set in. He didn't have to say anything. The look on his face gave it away. Harden had seen it before and counted himself lucky to have avoided it. "Take it slow, Mitch. If you move your head too quickly, your stomach will get all kinds of twisted up."

"Rog. I think I'll just stand—I mean float here for a

few minutes. I'll try to get the rest of these serials in the checklist done before I move too far."

"Good idea. That'll probably keep your mind off it anyway," Harden said sympathetically. "And what about that daring young man on the flying trapeze down there? Are we gonna get any more work out of him for the rest of this trip?"

"You bet," Burns said with a mile-wide smile. "I'm going to get the optics going first. Then while I'm down here I'll update the inertial platform."

"Sounds good, Magellan. But before you get too far along, why don't you come up here and check this out first. I promised some more sightseeing."

Burns floated up from the lower compartment toward the center hatch window. What he saw was worth a lifetime of waiting. As seen from space, sunset was an ominous event. Day was divided from night with stark precision. Unlike on Earth where twilight slowly faded to black, the transition at high altitude was spectacularly crisp. And in a matter of seconds, the world below was dark.

Beijing Aerospace Command and Control Center

Occupants of a half-dozen tiered rows of computer banks faced four large viewing screens that dominated the front wall of the control room. Technicians in light blue jackets were focused on their individual tasks, each monitoring their respective slice of Shenzhou 11's encrypted telemetry, as CNSA supervisors in white lab coats strolled up and down the red-carpeted rows discouraging any unnecessary chatter. The room was quiet, save for the hum of computer fans. A few senior controllers, along with a handful of uniformed PLA officers, monitored the Tiangong's communication channel on the closed loop.

At the mission controller's console, Colonel Yuan's thoughts drifted to Dmitri Popovich's smug expression. Yuan was well aware that his country had paid Russia the flattery of imitation in many areas of high technology, particularly in the fields of aerospace and military applications. But they had also employed a native ingenuity in improving what they copied, in the end arriving at versions of tanks, submarines, aircraft, and spacecraft that were superior to the Russian models. He also knew the day would soon come when China would no longer need the help of foreigners, the *gaijin*. They had already extracted nearly all of the useful information from Russia's crumbling technology base, and when they did, there would be no more need for the partnership. But American technology, he had to admit, would take longer to exploit. It didn't matter though. At least China would no longer be demoralized by the Imperialists. It was a stroke of good fortune, he mused, that China hadn't been allowed to participate in the International Space Station. It had proven easier to just steal America's technology. And his country didn't have to *kowtow* to western powers to get it. The peaceful part of China's rise was nearly complete. Now, with enough military power, *his* country would get to decide which actions were peaceful—and which were not.

Colonel Yuan was suddenly jolted out of his reverie when Popovich's voice came through on the loudspeaker. "The Americans have just launched a rocket from the Pacific Ocean!"

Yuan quickly signaled the communications officer to cut the feed, isolating the remaining CNSA managers from the conversation. "What nonsense do you speak of, Dmitri?"

"There is a new satellite in Earth orbit. It appears to have been launched from...perhaps a thousand kilometers west of Hawaii. I will have my people look into it." Popovich quickly switched from English to Russian as he explained what he saw to his own controllers who had been monitoring the same transmission.

Colonel Yuan threw his headset down on the desk and motioned to a man in an identical drab green uniform to take over. The colonel stormed through the double doors at the rear of the room and made his way toward the elevator. There was a much smaller control room buried six stories beneath him. There, every console was operated by PLA members. He would soon find out what the Americans had launched. And what had to be done to bring it down.

Earth Orbit

The thin sliver of Earth's atmosphere was suffused with countless hues of indigo and violet that quickly gave way to the burnt orange of morning. "Man, that's awesome," Burns said as the brilliant light spilled into the cockpit. The pages of his checklist fanned out accordion-like as he released the small three-ringed binder to a stable hover and spun around to take in the amazing event. "I think that must be every color of the rainbow."

"Wow, the colors change fast too," Mitchell muttered. But in a matter of seconds the rainbow of color was gone, and the entire cockpit was bathed in pure white light. "What an amazing view...of an amazing event."

"It happens every ninety minutes in the space business," Harden said without looking. "And every one is just that spectacular. Look, we only have two serials left in the checklist before the TLI burn. So let's get the SPS engine checked out, that's Serial 17. Pipper, you take that one. Mitch, you run the docking probe through the checks in Serial 27. We can't go anywhere if that little contraption doesn't work. And I'm going to rehearse the TLI checklist before the upcoming burn. So I don't end up looking like a monkey...well, you know."

As Apollo 18 began its second and final orbit before Translunar Injection, Harden and his crew were not the only busy members of the Apollo team. Ground controllers had been monitoring telemetry from the spacecraft and S-IVB even as the onboard checks were being completed. The booster had been reconfigured from the ground for restart of the single J-2X, and FIDO, the Flight Dynamics Officer, had calculated the precise parameters for an engine burn that would blast the first manned spacecraft free of Earth's gravitational field in over forty years.

"Apollo 18, Johnston, we have your TLI PAD," Freer radioed to the crew. "Advise when ready to copy."

"Let me find something to write with, Johnston," Burns replied. He looked around and grabbed a mechanical pencil that happened to be floating by. "All right, go ahead with the block data, Sam."

Freer proceeded to reel off an impossibly long series of numbers, known as pre-advisory data—the PAD—to Burns who transcribed the information into empty blocks on one of the specially formatted pages in his checklist. Burns then read back the string of data for verification against the original.

"Your read back is correct," Freer confirmed.

Harden put his flushed face up against the small window and glanced down at the lonely Pacific atoll. In another half orbit, on the opposite side of the planet, the S-IVB would be called upon for an encore performance. If all went as planned, he figured this could very well be the last time he would ever see Johnston Island. "Here goes nothing," Harden warned as he flipped the XLUNAR switch to INJECT.

Burns took the cue and began initializing Program 15 in the command module computer. Mitchell read off the block data from the TLI PAD while Burns tapped the keys on the DSKY, entering the parameters into the computer in the form of various two digit nouns. "My laptop has more processing power than this," Burns mumbled to himself. He still found it hard to believe that such a rudimentary computer, programmed with something called "rope core memory," could guide them all the way to the moon. And—he secretly hoped as he punched the Proceed key—back home again.

Wenchang Launch Center
Hainan Island, China

Two minutes after receiving the call from the Beijing Aerospace Command and Control Center, the first missile was rising into the pre-dawn sky. Hydraulic cylinders pivoted the huge protective canister to the launch position. Canisters on two additional Transporter Erector Launchers, or TELs, rose vertically to complete the battery. The SC-19 ASAT garrison was the latest in China's terrestrial based anti-satellite weapons arsenal. Based on the Dong-Feng 21 launch vehicle, known in Western circles under the NATO code name CSS-5, the two-stage, solid-fuel medium-range ballistic missile was originally designed to deliver a 300-kiloton warhead over a range of 1,800 kilometers.

But following the US military's success in the Gulf Wars, the DF-21 had been upgraded with a much different objective in mind. Complemented by a maneuverable warhead and redesignated the SC-19, the ballistic missile was then deployed with the sophisticated terminal guidance system originally designed for the anti-ship version of the DF-21. The combination proved to be perfectly suited for space-borne intercept. The capability had been successfully demonstrated several years earlier with the test firing of the SC-19 against one of China's own outmoded weather satellites. When the Feng Yun 1C polar orbiting satellite was completely annihilated with a single SC-19 launch, the formidable system was quickly pressed into service as the first phase of China's asymmetric warfare plan—the *Shashojian*— the second phase of which would become known in classified PLA circles as the Chang'e.

CHAPTER 24

Apollo 18

"TEN MINUTES 'TIL TIG," HARDEN said as he compared the ground elapsed time to the predicted Time-of-ignition for their Translunar Injection burn. "Launch Vehicle Guidance to CMC."

Several annunciator lights on the instrument panel caught Burns's attention as they flickered to life. "Johnston, we have uplink activity on the CMC."

"We copy, Eighteen. And your ride looks good from down here."

"How do those tank pressures look, Mitch?" Harden queried.

"So far, so good. All delta-p's are within limits. She's ready to fly."

"Outstanding. Now let's make sure that everything is strapped down. We'll probably see close to one-point-five-g's on this burn, and I don't want any loose gear flying around." Bodies collided in the microgravity, and limbs brushed against guarded switches as three figures in bulky space suits set about to secure the stray items that had quickly filled the small cabin after launch.

"Hold onto your hats," Harden said as he armed the rotational hand controller. Then, with a gentle twist, he eased back on the joystick-like device and thrusters in the auxiliary propulsion system, the twin APS modules located at the base of the S-IVB, fired to place the lengthy stack in the proper attitude for ignition.

"T minus two minutes." Burns held his breath as he stared patiently at the DSKY. The display flashed as if on cue. "Noun ninety-five is active."

"Stand by for a little delta-v," Harden warned. Thrusters again fired in the APS modules, this time with a prograde motion to help settle the S-IVB's liquid propellants and ensure a smooth start for the critical engine burn.

Burns was so focused on the approaching maneuver that he failed to notice the instrument panel blossom in white light as morning again flooded in through the command module's five small windows.

"Here comes another sunrise," Mitchell said, shielding his eyes with a handful of splayed fingers.

Harden renounced the distraction with a timely warning, "T minus one minute."

But Burns couldn't resist just one last look at the world they were about to leave behind. "Hey, did you see that flash on the horizon?"

"Eyes inside!" Harden chided. "I need everyone focused for this burn. You can look out the window *after* we're safely on our way to the moon."

Burns fought the urge to look again for the unusual flash. "S-IVB Ignition," he reported when the single engine light extinguished. "Boy, this thing is smooth."

Harden tightened his grip on the rotational hand controller as he concentrated on the instruments. As Apollo 18's velocity increased, the nose of the spacecraft seemed intent on climbing above the local horizon. If left unchecked for the next six minutes this inertial attitude would dangerously alter their trajectory, flinging them to some remote corner of the solar system. Harden gently rotated his wrist aft in short pulses to bring the nose of the spacecraft back in line with the Eight-ball's zero pitch line, and an inherently more survivable trajectory.

"Coming up on one minute," Mitchell announced.

Burns hovered over Harden's right shoulder. "Good, good. That's it. Smooth corrections," he said calmly, but still couldn't shake the image of the flash he had seen on the ground. Instinct told him that something bad was about to happen. But what? His reaction was a hard-learned self-defense mechanism: *Look outside the cockpit. That's where the threats are!* Burns sought out the window above his head and began a methodical search pattern of the terrain below.

"It's more responsive than I thought," Harden said with the steady voice of a seasoned test pilot. "A little nose-heavy, but the feedback is just enough to remind you of the mass that you're controlling, and subtly influences your inputs. It's like she's telling you, 'Be gentle with me.'"

Burns listened with half an ear as he surveyed the horizon. Below, the east coast of Africa slipped from view and slowly gave way to the marbled blues of the Indian Ocean. He could just make out the island of Sri Lanka on the southern tip of India. The rest of the country was hidden under a thick layer of cumulus that pushed inland all the way north to the Himalayas. China was mostly cloud-free except for... *Wait! Hainan.* His eyes padlocked the smoke trail originating from the large island province off China's southern coastline. "Shit, that's not good!" Burns shouted. The growing white exhaust plume correlated precisely with the flash he had seen earlier.

"What's wrong?" Harden asked calmly as he continued to pitch the spacecraft along the arc of a rapidly expanding ellipse.

Burns made a quick check of the burn performance before turning to Harden with the unsettling news. "Something just launched from Hainan Island, and I think it's headed our way."

"*What!*" Mitchell shouted as he spun around to catch a glimpse of the reported threat.

"You've got to be mistaken," Harden said. "Check again."

Burns slipped his ground communication switch to the Vox position and searched again for the exhaust plume. "No. There's definitely been a launch of some kind from Hainan. Sam, are you aware of any other Chinese launches scheduled this month besides Shenzhou 11?"

"Negative?"

"Well, we just passed over Hainan Island, and there's a growing rocket plume that appears to be arcing to the east. It looks like it's actually pulling lead on us."

Everyone on the comm loop tried to digest the information. Freer collapsed into his seat and rubbed his eyes in disbelief. He thought he was ready for any emergency. But this wasn't just another mechanical problem that could be solved by engineering a work-around for an ailing system. For the first time, he feared for his crew.

"Three minutes." Burns continued with the reports. "Looks like we're picking up a little yaw. Blaze, try not to twist your wrist when you pitch up."

"No, wait!" Mitchell shouted. "That's it. Can we do a Level-S?"

Harden was concentrating so hard on maintaining the proper attitude that he thought he was hearing things. "You mean like roll ninety degrees on the horizon and pull out of plane?" Harden knew the procedure well. He had spent years practicing such defensive maneuvers that were designed to defeat surface-to-air missiles *inside* the atmosphere.

"Yeah! He's right," Burns agreed. "That'll work. But don't bother rolling. Just keep the yaw coming. We're in space, remember. No lifting surfaces. Pure yaw will change your lift-vector just the same. Give me a thirty-degree correction to the left for thirty seconds."

Sweat beaded on Harden's forehead as he gripped the hand controller tightly and twisted it further to the left. "This big stick doesn't like to fly sideways, boys. This had better work."

Freer thought he understood the plan. If they could displace their flight path enough, the enemy missile would have to make energy-hungry corrections to its trajectory, possibly bleeding off enough of its limited energy to force an overshoot. The result might put the mission in jeopardy, but his crew would still be alive. "Jeff, can you tell me if the rocket is still trailing smoke?"

"Four minutes. Steering looks good," Burns said, and then returned his attention to the hatch window. "The smoke trail is still growing, Sam. I can't see the missile itself, but whatever it is, it's still coming our way."

"Jeff, listen," Freer said, putting all his expertise to work on the problem at hand. "That smoke trail will disappear as soon as the booster leaves the atmosphere. You won't be able to track it visually after that. From that point you have three, possibly four minutes before any missile can reach your altitude. And you have only two minutes left on this burn. Once the S-IVB shuts down, you'll be a sitting duck."

Burns agreed. "That's why we have to defeat this thing right now, while we're still thrusting. Blaze, reverse back to the right. Thirty degrees right yaw for sixty seconds." Burns wrenched his body around for a better view as he searched the sky again for the menacing missile. It was gone.

"Sam, you were right. The smoke trail has stopped, but I can definitely make out a kink in the flight path. It looks like we forced it to correct. I think we're causing it some grief."

Controllers sequestered on Johnston Island stared at the projection of Apollo 18's flight path on the large Mercator map in front of the control room. The plan suddenly became apparent to each controller, regardless of his or her discipline, as they watched the spacecraft's orbital path scribe out a huge S-shaped curve over the ground.

"There's sixty seconds," Harden said. "Coming back to the left. I'll bring her back on course in thirty seconds."

"That's the idea," Burns agreed.

"How long till shutdown?"

"Fifteen seconds. Ten, nine..."

Harden wrested the massive stack back to its original course and hawked the DSKY as the velocity-to-go counted down to zero.

"SECO," Burns shouted as the J-2 shut down for the last time.

"How'd we do?" Harden panted.

"Altitude 180 nautical miles. Inertial velocity 35,540 feet per second."

"Good burn, Eighteen," Freer piped in. "Your trajectory is slightly out of plane, but nominal. We should be able to shape it up later."

The busy command module suddenly fell silent. Maybe they had overreacted. Maybe they would die any second. No one knew for sure. "I guess we should just hold our breath for the next sixty seconds. Then we'll know," Burns said dryly.

Unseen in the blackness of space, the second stage engine of the Dong Feng missile burned its last grain of fuel. Steered by a thrust vectoring nozzle, the missile was now bound by the same laws of orbital mechanics as its helpless target.

Three sweaty astronauts glared into the void. But without an atmosphere to propagate light, an explosion in space would be impossible to see unless witnessed directly.

They didn't have long to wait. Thousands of tiny fragments suddenly bombarded the skin of their fragile spacecraft like rain pelting an old tin roof.

Mitchell instinctively reached out for something solid to brace himself on. His pulse pounded in his ears as he held his breath and listened intently for a hissing sound. He silently prayed that the command module's thin skin would be strong enough to protect them from the certain death of space.

Harden was quick to conclude that if his ship hadn't exploded yet, it probably wouldn't. But he also knew how agonizing death would be if just one piece of shrapnel had penetrated the hull of the spacecraft.

Suddenly the fate of three lives was being written by a tiny needle that measured the oxygen pressure in their delicate ecosystem. If the hull were breached, it would only be a matter of seconds before a burst of cabin air shot out into space and triggered an explosive decompression.

Sam Freer finally delivered the news—his tone one of relief—and exaltation. "Command module pressure holding steady at 5.2 psi. Looks like you guys are on your way to the moon. We'll be standing by for TD&E whenever you're ready."

"Damn, that was close," Burns sighed.

"I guess we owe you one for that, Mitch," said Harden.

"I think we just got lucky."

Harden patted his friend on the shoulder. "If that's the case, sign me up for lucky every day of the week."

CHAPTER 25

Cislunar Space

A POLLO 18 RACED TOWARD THE waxing moon at over 20,000 nautical miles per hour. A rendezvous with the elusive orb was now a mathematical certainty. But it would still take fifty-seven long hours before they would reach that invisible point in cislunar space where the moon's gravitational pull would tip the scales and exceed that of Earth. Until then, for Harden and the crew of Apollo 18, most of that time would be spent monitoring spacecraft systems. And waiting.

The next hour, however, would be anything but boring. One critical evolution was still required to complete the complex assembly of lunar spacecraft and render the Apollo stack operational. Without the next maneuver, Apollo 18's trip to the moon would be nothing more than a sightseeing tour. Without it, landing on the moon would be impossible.

The lunar module *Intruder* still lay cocooned inside the spacecraft-LM adapter, sandwiched between the spent S-IVB stage of the Saturn V booster and the cylindrical service module. Transposition, docking, and extraction, or TD&E, was the delicate procedure that would mate the command and lunar modules and cut away the now useless remnant of the spent Saturn booster.

Harden and Burns worked closely together to complete the multi-paged procedure required to extricate their spacecraft from the top of the LM adapter. During the process, Harden maneuvered the Apollo stack to the proper extraction attitude. As they were only coasting through space now, this new attitude had nothing to do with navigation, but instead established an optimum sun angle for docking; highlighting the alignment target on top of the LM without blinding the CM pilot with the harsh sunlight of space.

"Ready to swap seats?" Harden finally said to his command module pilot.

"I thought you'd never ask," Burns replied.

Harden moved aside as Burns floated in front of the flight controls and double-checked several switch positions. "THC – Armed. RHC – Armed. Ready for separation."

"Okay, Buck Rogers, the ship is yours."

"Stand by for SEP," Burns warned as he pushed a button on the elapsed timer and eyed the display. "Ten seconds, CMC MODE – Auto. Translating plus-x." Burns then pushed in gently on the translational hand controller. One of two controllers, the THC allowed him to translate—or slide—in any direction. Pushing in on the T-shaped handle added thrust in the forward, or plus-x, direction. Pulling out, fired the appropriate thrusters to slide the spacecraft backward. Up, down, left, or right on the controller would slide the CSM in the appropriate direction while keeping the nose of the spacecraft pointing at the same fixed point in space, or inertially stable.

Harden lifted the protective guard on a switch and counted down, "Two, one..." He toggled the switch and held it up until he felt the jolt. A powerful guillotine slammed closed with a loud bang, severing all connections between the service module and the S-IVB. Then, as the spacecraft began to slowly drift away from the spent booster, explosive detonation cord sliced the LM adapter into four separate panels that peeled away from the lunar module like the petals of an ethereal flower.

"Okay, we're free. One, two, three, four, five. Release." Burns returned the THC to the neutral detent. "Johnston, we show zero-point-five feet per second."

"Copy, Eighteen."

"Fifteen seconds, standing by for the PRO," Harden announced as the DSKY flashed "Verb 50 Noun 18," prompting him to proceed with the automatic maneuver.

"Any chance I could get a verb thirty-seven instead?"

Harden thought about it for a second. "What the hell. I'll probably foul up the keystrokes anyway. Okay, verb thirty-seven. Enter. Noun forty-seven. Enter. There's your thrust monitoring program. Just don't screw it up."

Burns gripped the rotational hand controller, the RHC, with his right hand and tweaked the pistol grip aft. The spacecraft responded by pitching up slowly.

Harden had the widest angle view through the large window on the center hatch and was the first to glimpse their target. "I have one of the adapter panels in sight. It's just floating there above the Earth. Spectacular. Wait, there it is. I can see the booster now among the ejection debris. And there's our beautiful *Intruder*, waiting patiently on its perch."

Mitchell's attention was drawn to an altogether different image. Through one of the smaller rendezvous windows, he witnessed the glowing blue horizon of Earth bending sharply in an ever tightening arc as it strained to meet itself in full circle. He could easily see the entire continent of North America in one glance. He followed the Mississippi River north to the Missouri and the bend that identified his hometown of St. Louis. He couldn't help but wonder what his boys were doing today. He looked at his watch. On a Wednesday afternoon, he suspected that his wife would be standing in for him at football practice. He shuddered when he thought about it. The most important things in his life were all down there somewhere—and slipping further out of reach every minute.

"It's coming into view through the rendezvous window now," Burns said, and then ratcheted forward on the rotational controller for a long count. The pitch rate slowed as expected. "I can see the LM's docking target drifting into the COAS." He pulsed several more short bursts with the rotational controller as the crosshairs of the crewman's optical alignment sight, the COAS, centered up on the sighting target mounted high atop the roof of the *Intruder*.

"Still drifting away." Burns pushed in again on the translational controller and waited patiently for the visual cues to catch up with the instrumentation.

Harden read the Entry Monitor System. "EMS shows sixty feet."

"Yep, I think we're gonna get there. Looks like forty feet now."

The small rendezvous window was soon filled by the multifaceted metal roof of the lunar module. Burns tugged on the translational controller and fired two short bursts of RCS fuel to slow his approach.

"Not too much," Harden warned. "Twenty feet."

"I'm on it, boss." Burns then gently leaned on the rotational controller. "Just taking out a little roll error." As the *Intruder* grew larger, the raised crossbars of the docking target highlighted small positional errors in their alignment. Both hand controllers were moving in concert as Burns made the final critical corrections.

"Ten feet."

"DOCK PROBE EXTD/REL switch – Extend," Harden said calmly.

"Three feet," Burns noted. "Two, one..."

The docking probe screeched loudly along the wall of the drogue as it slid toward the center of the funnel. Three tiny fingers on the articulated probe tip snapped into position as the device found its way to the center of the hole.

"Contact!" Burns announced as the aluminum roof panels on the *Intruder* wobbled from the shock of impact.

"Talkbacks are barber-poled. We have soft dock." Harden then flipped another switch on the instrument panel. "Retract." Nitrogen gas powered a mechanism inside the probe that pulled the two spacecraft together with a loud wail. As the docking rings seated properly, twelve preset capture latches snapped sequentially into place with a series of loud bangs. There was no doubt that the two spacecraft were now one. "And we have hard dock."

Construction of the Apollo spacecraft was finally complete. For two and a half orbits, what remained of the Apollo/Saturn stack had been a sleek, bullet-like spacecraft racing swiftly around the Earth. Following TD&E, the previously gorgeous machine was unrecognizable, the resulting pair of disparate spacecraft now lumbering slowly toward the moon.

Air Force Space Command
Colorado Springs, CO

Austin stared into the blank screen on the far wall of the spacious conference room. Nursing a cup of tepid black coffee, he waited patiently for the president to appear on the other end of the video teleconference.

General Patrowski stuffed a plug of tobacco into the empty bowl of his Maplewood pipe and lit it with a small silver torch. He was perhaps the largest military officer Austin had ever seen. Nearly every inch of his chest was covered in ribbons. And his polished bald head drew eyes to it like a lighthouse beacon on a stormy night. The entire package was grossly intimidating as Patrowski glared across the table at Austin. Smoke engulfed the general's face as he talked. "I still can't believe that the president signed off on this lunacy," he said as if determined to finish the conversation he started shortly after the launch. "That booster was our last best hope. And we just wasted it on some paranoid plan to scout the moon for Chinese mystery weapons."

"General," Austin said in a fresh attempt to mollify Patrowski, "I have a feeling that your HALO program will eventually get the attention it deserves, especially given the urgency of recent events. But at the moment, your defense constellation doesn't stand a chance against a deep space threat like the Chang'e."

Patrowski pulled the pipe from his mouth, but before he could reply the top of the president's head appeared on the wall-sized screen in the front of the room. "Evening, gentlemen," the president said without looking up. When he finished signing the last document that had been slid under his pen, he aimed his tired face at the camera. "How'd we do today? And please tell me its good news. I really could use a break right now."

"Well, sir," Austin answered honestly, "there's a little of both."

"Start with the bad news."

"It appears that the PLA launched a ballistic missile at our crew today during Translunar Injection, evidence that the Chinese were indeed aware of the launch, if not the details of the mission itself. And there's no way to tell at this point how they might respond."

"And..."

"Well, sir, the good news is that the crew of Apollo 18 is safely on their way to the moon. The TLI burn was ultimately successful, and the docking maneuver went off without a hitch. They should be in a position to attempt a landing within the next ninety-six hours."

"Well, they'd better damn well hurry, Mr. Austin. Our options down here are quickly dwindling. Is that the best they can do?"

"The flight plan is already very aggressive. The tighter we wind the watch, sir, the more likely the spring is to break."

"Tell me something I don't already know," the president said, his voice betraying the tension he was under. "Like what are their odds?"

"Realistically, I'd estimate mission success at twenty percent." Austin felt the general's eyes land heavily on him as he spoke. "The problem's not getting there. Or even getting back. I give them a fifty-fifty chance of making it home in one piece. But finding another lunar lander on the far side of the moon is a mighty tall order." NASA's Lunar Reconnaissance Orbiter had finally achieved the correct orbit to photograph Daedalus crater but had so far found nothing. And a review of the JAXA seismographic data had identified an event that occurred less than four minutes from the recorded "crash" of the Chang'e 5, but the signal was so weak that it was washed out by reverberations from what Austin now suspected was a decoy event.

"Weren't you listening, Stephen? I said I wanted good news." The president rubbed his already bloodshot eyes. He had not slept well in days and suddenly felt a cold coming on. "If you're right and the Chinese are aware of the mission, you'd better find a way to speed things up. The length of an Apollo mission is certainly no secret to the PLA. And regardless of their actions so far, if they think they may lose their advantage in ninety-six hours...well, I suggest you come up with a way to neutralize this *Shashojian* in the next eighty-four."

CHAPTER 26

Apollo 18

"YOU GOT IT, JOHNSTON. PROGRAM 52, coming right up." It would be his first navigation platform alignment since leaving Earth orbit, and Burns rolled up the sleeves of his flight suit like a mechanic about to open the hood and get his hands dirty.

Burns's previous astronaut training at NASA had included a cursory introduction to the sextant and celestial navigation, but it was a skill set that he never imagined he would use since the space shuttle never left Earth orbit. Yet when navigating to the moon, if communication with the ground was ever lost, it would be up to him to find the way home—which was why he had fallen asleep every night for the past several weeks with a star chart on his pillow.

Burns drifted into the lower equipment bay and initialized the command module computer for the upcoming procedure. After working methodically through the checklist, he popped the dust covers from the sextant and the scanning telescope, and repositioned several selectors on the Optics Control Panel. "Mitch, can you copy some numbers down for me? I don't want to lose my night vision once I get started."

"Sure. Give me a second."

"Hey, can you guys do that off the intercom loop?" Harden requested. "I'd like to get the morning briefing out of the way at the same time."

While Mitchell assisted Burns with his navigational duties, Sam Freer went through several housekeeping chores with Harden. He then went over the news clippings that were meant to bolster crew morale, but that didn't take long. "Look, I don't want to alarm you with this next item," Freer continued, "but this comes straight from the source. Stephen has informed the president that the PLA may be aware of your existence...and he's beginning to pick up chatter about an attempt to sabotage the mission."

"Of course they know about us!" Burns said as he backed away from the sextant, his round face turning beet red. "They've tried to kill us once already."

"Look, fellas," Harden said flatly. "Right now we need to focus on what we can control, not the things we can't." He looked out the small rendezvous window into the depths of space and added, "Besides, I don't think anyone can touch us out here."

"And, perhaps even more unsettling," Freer added, "it appears that the satellites lost over the western Pacific last week were most likely the result of an electromagnetic pulse."

"An EMP," Burns whispered to Mitchell. "Shit."

"Okay, Sam, I agree that's a serious situation, but what does that mean to us up here?" Harden asked.

"To be blunt, the president has to assume that your mission may not be successful. And the specter of an EMP blast in the skies over North America can't be ignored. So he's ordered a preemptive strike on China's Xi'an facility." A long silence followed. "And when you put all this together, there's no way to predict what the backlash might be."

"We'll keep that in mind, Sam," Harden said pointedly.

When Freer finally heard the chatter of checklist operations begin again, he decided it was best not to dwell any longer on the subject.

In the lower equipment bay, Burns pulled a patch down over his left eye and pressed the other up against the scanning telescope. The one-power device had a fairly wide field of view and when brought into focus produced a broad star field. He adjusted the scope until he found a star he recognized, and then centered it in the crosshairs. "I've got one star under the pipper. It looks like Theta Centauri."

Mitchell flipped through his checklist, found the star table, and cross-referenced the number. "That's star number thirty."

"Roger." Burns then slid over and sidled up to the sextant. He cupped his right eye against the rubber shroud and carefully maneuvered the landmark line-of-sight of the twenty-eight-power scope until he could see Theta Centauri in the narrow field of view. He identified the star to the computer with the push of a button. "Mark." He then spun the sextant on its axis and adjusted the trunnion angle until he had a second recognizable star in sight. Light from Beta Leonis reflected off the trunnion mirror and was superimposed over Theta Centauri in the eyepiece reticule. Burns made several more fine adjustments to bring the two stars in direct alignment and hit the button again. "What's the number for Beta Leonis?"

"Twenty-three."

The DSKY continued to flash cryptic combinations of verbs and nouns as Burns referenced the checklist and then entered the codes for the two marked stars along with the shaft and trunnion angles from the sextant. The command module computer knew what the angle should be between the two marked stars and compared that to the marks that Burns had taken. It then displayed the resultant error as Noun 5: 00000 in register one. "Five balls!" Burns shouted.

"Nicely done, Jeff," Freer radioed across the void. "I think the commander owes you a beer for that one when you get home."

"You got it, my friend," Harden agreed. "Keep 'em coming."

"Now that's what I call a tight platform," Burns said with obvious pride. "That kind of precision will get us to the moon, I do believe."

"Its not getting there that I'm worried about anymore," Mitchell muttered.

USS Ronald Reagan
Yellow Sea

He knew it would be soon. But not this soon, Red Willard thought, as he stared down from the Flag Bridge onto the darkened flight deck below. It was a strange sight. The bow of the carrier was packed with aircraft but the landing area and waist catapults were wide open, the remainder of Carrier Airwing 14's aircraft tucked neatly down below in the hangar bay. The admiral couldn't see the number three elevator from the bridge, but he knew what was on it. The X-47B UCAV was on its way up to the flight deck; ordnance crews standing by with eight GBU-39s, the small-diameter bombs ready to be loaded into the aircraft's enclosed weapons bay and armed for combat.

The *Reagan's* arrival in the South China Sea several weeks ago had brought tension in the region to a fever pitch. Which is why for much of the last week, the battle group remained well clear of Chinese territorial waters, conducting limited operations near the US

Naval Base in Yokosuka, Japan. But the only chance the unmanned strike aircraft had of reaching its target deep inside the borders of China's Shaanxi Province was to launch as close to the Chinese coast as possible. The *Reagan* had arrived in the Yellow Sea earlier in the morning to conduct what was announced to be routine exercises with the South Koreans. But the sun had barely gone down when the *Reagan* turned west and prepared for another first in carrier aviation—the launching of an unmanned combat aircraft on a live strike mission.

When the ordnance crews finished loading the X-47B, Brandt Sivley emerged from the island superstructure with a green helmet bag in his hand. As Pete Mitchell's assistant program manager, Sivley had the unwelcome duty of supervising the dubious UCAV mission. He had no idea where Mitchell had escaped to, but as his number two, he had suddenly been tasked with planning a strike mission that stretched the operational capabilities of a weapons system that was still in the midst of a lengthy test and evaluation program.

As he approached the aircraft, the former Air Force F-16 pilot was met by a plane captain and two of the *Reagan's* ordnance men. "How's the loadout?" Sivley asked as he crouched down and duck-walked beneath the smooth wing toward the weapons bay.

"It's right and it's tight, sir," Petty Officer Claymore assured the pilot. "She's got eight SDBs, armed and ready."

"Yeah, roger that," Sivley answered the eager ordie. He grabbed each bomb and shook it vigorously against the sway-dogs on the rack. The small-diameter bombs were only 250 pounds each, but with a GPS guidance unit attached in the tail cone, the highly explosive weapons were deadly accurate—and devastating against unhardened targets like the antenna dishes and communications equipment they sought out tonight.

Satisfied with the brief preflight, the pilot removed the memory unit from his helmet bag and placed it into the receptacle on the underside of the aircraft's smooth belly. All of the mission planning elements for tonight's operation: the pilotless drone's flight path, airspeeds and altitudes, target coordinates, frequencies for failsafe control, were all loaded into the tiny electronic brain. The binary pilot had arrived, and Sivley held it in the palm of his hand. Not long ago it would have been his ass strapping in to an armed aircraft in preparation for the dangerous strike mission. The face of warfare was changing rapidly— and he wasn't sure he liked it—America's future security suddenly entrusted to a bunch of robots. A shiver rippled through him as he zipped the empty helmet bag and made his way back to the protection of the *Reagan's* island superstructure.

Back at his console in CATCC, Sivley quickly brought the stealthy craft's systems to life, tested each one for degrades, and confirmed the data download from the memory unit to the mission computers. Then, with the aid of a small camera located on the nose landing gear strut, he carefully maneuvered the pilotless jet onto one of the *Reagan's* waist catapults. Once the craft was hooked securely into the shuttle, he clicked the box labeled TAKEOFF and watched the power indicator roll up toward takeoff RPM. When he was satisfied that all systems were within parameters, Sivley activated the small green light on the rear of the nose strut. Up on the flight deck, the Shooter raised his hands, scanned the area one final time, and pushed the button on his deck edge console. The Salty Dog was quickly engulfed in a cloud of steam as it raced down the flight deck and disappeared into the darkness.

Sivley monitored the velocity vector on his cockpit display for aircraft rotation and noted the positive rate of climb. He moved the mouse to the green box labeled LANDING GEAR. He clicked it and waited for the box to turn white. The aircraft was clean. Passing 500 feet, he selected the stored flight plan and engaged the autopilot. His job was done. The mild tension created by the night launch faded quickly as the UCAV climbed through one thousand feet and rolled into an easy right hand turn. For the next four hours he could do nothing but wait. It would be at least that long before his bird would return. Until then, the mysterious mission would not be controlled from his panel in the *Reagan*, but somewhere far away. His guess was Langley, Virginia.

CHAPTER 27

Apollo18

"WE'RE OVER THE HUMP," BURNS noted as they reached that unique point in space, the equigravisphere, where the Earth's gravitational influence, and the moon's, cancelled each other out. "Get ready for the downhill slide, boys. There's no turning back now."

Mitchell had been copying the proposed procedural changes from the master flight plan into the one he would use in the LM during the descent to the lunar surface. He released the checklist in mid air and glanced at the numbers on the DSKY. Burns was right. Their velocity was increasing for the first time since leaving Earth orbit. "You know, these changes to the flight plan are still a little confusing. If we miss a step somewhere..."

Harden stretched and yawned from a largely unsuccessful attempt at a nap. Actually, he hadn't had much luck sleeping since the launch. And as much as he hated to think about it, the flight plan changes would make tomorrow a very long—and very challenging—day. But there was no way around it. To fly a quarter-million miles only to show up too late to stop the Chang'e was unacceptable.

"All right then," Harden said in the middle of

another yawn. "Let's run through these changes one more time."

Mitchell drifted below the instrument panel and met Harden in the lower equipment bay. Harden reviewed the new procedures again for his copilot. The original plan had been to conduct two deceleration burns with the service propulsion system. The first Lunar Orbit Insertion burn, LOI-1, would put the conjoined spacecraft into a 60-by-160-nautical-mile elliptical orbit around the moon. The second burn, LOI-2, would circularize the orbit at sixty nautical miles. Only then would Harden and Mitchell enter the lunar module and prepare for undocking. But when the order came down to cut twelve hours out of the flight plan, something had to give. Cutting out a rest period wasn't going to be enough. They still needed four more hours. That was when Burns suggested that crew transfer to the LM begin two orbits earlier; which meant that Harden and Mitchell would have to transfer to the lunar module immediately following LOI-1—and leave the second critical burn in the hands of the solo command module pilot. The idea was quickly voted down.

That was until everyone realized there was no other choice.

"Is that all there is to it?" Mitchell said, and released the flight plan into a dizzying spin that mirrored his thoughts exactly. "And I thought this was going to be hard."

Goldstone Deep Space Complex
Mojave Desert, CA

Cheng Mak entered the communications complex three miles to the east of his objective in the small hours of morning. Light from the quarter moon had kept the darkest part of the night at bay until he was within a few hundred meters of the largest antenna; but as the waxing moon dipped below the local horizon, his progress slowed considerably.

Mak and his accomplices, currently carrying out identical missions on three separate continents, were part of an elite new breed of intelligence operatives. Members of the Second Department of the People's Liberation Army, known in US intelligence circles as the 2 PLA, they were part of a clandestine group who specialized in military and industrial espionage—as well as counter-espionage—which had on occasion been known to result in the suspicious deaths of those they had under surveillance.

With only the faint scintillation of distant stars to light the way now, Mak rotated the night vision goggles down over his eyes and flicked a small switch on the side of the bracket. Still, his aging eyes made the task much harder than it would have been if his younger partner was leading the way. But not long after their mission was complete in Langley, Virginia, Mak's accomplice had been ordered to complete a task similar to the one Mak was now conducting—in Madrid, Spain. Mak stumbled through the desert rubble hoping that he and the other agents would be successful in this final attempt to undo the bold American mission. If they could successfully sever the thin electronic umbilical between the Apollo spacecraft and its terrestrially-based navigation equipment, the PLA just might be able to preserve the *Shashojian*. But he had to hurry, time was running out.

It wasn't the type of mission he relished. He preferred to have time to plan, time to prepare. He preferred to have a partner with him. Mak and Tai Wang had had two months to prepare for the clandestine attack on the *Atlantis*, and almost three weeks to conduct their surveillance on Dongfan Chong. Now he was working alone and was given less than a week to carry out his latest assignment. And his odds of success, he suspected, were about the same as him making it back home alive to see his family again.

Mak chased away the unnerving distraction as he tried to focus on the task at hand. When he finished setting the final charge, he collected his gear and began the long trek back to the main road. The aging operative desperately wanted to make it to the car before sunrise. He started off in a gimpy jog, but the equipment clipped to his work belt seemed to come alive as he picked up speed. Mak eventually settled into a slow trot that helped minimize the racket, as well as the pain in his right knee.

Still more than a kilometer from the car, the orange glow of dawn began to slowly overpower his NVGs. Mak switched off the light-sensitive goggles and ratcheted them away from his face. His eyes were still adjusting to the change in light level when his steel toed boot snagged the tripwire strung stealthily across his path. The desert floor rushed up quickly to meet him.

Mak tried desperately to break the fall, but he was too slow. His face smashed into the loose rock stratum that littered the desert floor. The powerful blow sent waves of pain crashing through his skull. But the pain was short lived as his eyes slammed shut and he quickly fell out of consciousness.

Apollo Flight Control Room
Johnston Island

Lunar Orbit Insertion.

Sam Freer bristled when he read the title page covering the next section of the flight plan. The tired engineer sighed as he took off his glasses and gently rubbed the indentions in the bridge of his nose. He leaned his head forward and put his elbows on his knees as he considered the pivotal nature of the coming procedure. *We've done this before.*

The goal of the LOI burn was simple enough: pass behind the moon at a precise altitude, burn the SPS engine at a specific time, for a given duration, while maintaining the proper attitude—and like magic— lunar orbit would be achieved. But to achieve the desired landing window, and avoid being blinded by the sun during their final approach, Harden and his crew would have to enter lunar orbit from the trailing edge of the moon, as opposed to the relative safety of a leading edge approach. And the serious nature of this constraint was lost on no one, the least of which was the man making the important calculations.

But as with all the flight controller positions at Johnston, there were two men occupying the Flight Dynamics console today. Josh Camden, the twenty-four-year-old graduate student from USC, twisted nervously in his swivel chair. As the young FIDO transcribed the pre-advisory data onto one of the specially formatted PADs, he pressed down hard with his red ballpoint pen to make sure all six copies would be legible. He had always been confident in his abilities, but this was the first time that he had someone else's life in his hands, and he welcomed the watchful eye of the man looking over his left shoulder. Apparently aware that his presence was comforting, his SLATE mentor peered reassuringly over the top of his bifocals as his protégé filled in the blocks. If both men were happy with the data, no words would be said. When the final entry was made, the young FIDO rose and walked the data to the back of the room.

Freer was chewing on one arm of his reading glasses

when FIDO handed him the data card. "Thanks, Josh. Good work." He then radioed the Lunar Orbit Insertion PAD up to the crew and waited. Managing the nervous tension the best way he knew how, Freer worked his way to the corner of the room and poured another cup of piping hot black coffee. He looked around for a spare carafe. The pot was still nearly half full, but that wouldn't last for long. He put a second pot on to brew while he waited. His effort to maintain a stoic façade would get increasingly harder as the day wore on.

Goldstone Deep Space Complex
Mojave Desert, CA

He figured he must have momentarily lost consciousness, because the rattling sound seemed to come out of nowhere. When Cheng Mak finally opened his eyes, he found himself face-to-face with the source of the unnerving noise—four feet of deadly Mojave Rattlesnake. The terrifying serpent was coiled up into a wicked skein, its hypnotic rattle vibrating within arms length. When Mak jerked a hand up to cover his face, the head of the brown twisted knot buried its twin fangs deep in his palm. The pain was instant—but death would come slowly—as the venom would take nearly thirty minutes to completely undo Mak's central nervous system.

Mak struggled to get back on his feet, but traction in the loose gravel proved elusive. He made it to his knees twice before finally collapsing back onto his bloodied face. His breathing became labored as the warming numbness spread into his forearm. Mak eventually managed to roll onto his back, but the small victory was quickly replaced by an overwhelming dread as he accepted the fact that he would never make it back to the car alive. He searched his jacket pockets for the electronic detonator. He might not live to see tomorrow—but neither would the men hurtling through deep space toward the surface of the swelling moon.

CHAPTER 28

Apollo 18

THE PIECES WERE FINALLY FALLING into place for Burns as he carefully entered the lengthy string of data from the LOI PAD into the command module computer. As he tapped away on the DSKY, the green glow of seven-segment LEDs flickered in response to his inputs. He paused to double-check his work when he reached the next value, Noun 47: the combined weight of both spacecraft. To achieve the desired change in velocity, the computer needed this critical figure to calculate how much thrust would be required to slow the linked spacecraft. He then told the CMC what that required delta-v would be in a language it could understand: three axis Cartesian coordinates—x, y, and z—the vector sum of which would act through the spacecraft's center of gravity and decelerate the Apollo stack to the precise velocity for the desired orbit. When he was satisfied with his work, he continued with the remaining values required for successful lunar orbit insertion: Time-of-ignition, or Tig, the burn duration of the SPS engine in seconds, and the apolune and perilune—or high and low point—of the desired orbit. Burns rubbed his eyes as he thought back to the old axiom he learned in his first computer science class at the University of Texas: Garbage in, Garbage out.

The signature *Beep* of Apollo's Unified S-Band radio signal preceded Freer's steady voice as it always had. "I've got a lot of thumbs up coming from the front row, Jeff." A second, book-ended *Beep* marked the end of the CAPCOM's terse transmission.

"That's wonderful news, Johnston." For once the former single-seat fighter pilot was glad to have someone looking over his shoulder, even if it was from a quarter-million miles away. "I'm going to maneuver to the burn attitude now and check it against our sextant star."

As Harden and Mitchell finished up their checks of the LM's environmental control system, Burns drifted into the command module's lower equipment bay for one final check of the spacecraft attitude. Apollo was not only an elegant solution to the lunar landing challenge—it was also an extremely robust one. Apollo's designers had used backups to backups to ensure that mistakes were avoided. With the correct values entered into the computer, Burns peered into the sextant's eyepiece. If their attitude was indeed correct for the upcoming burn, and the sextant was sighted along the prescribed shaft and trunnion angles listed in the LOI PAD, the star Vega would appear centered in the sextant reticule.

"Would you look at that," Burns shouted. "Vega, dead nuts in the crosshairs."

"I guess that means it's time for us to get strapped in," Harden said as he emerged from the LM tunnel to meet Burns in the CM's lower equipment bay.

"Stand by for LOS in one minute," Freer announced. Loss of signal was yet another precisely calculated event in the Apollo Flightplan. When loss of their S-Band radio signal occurred at the predicted time, it provided an additional, critical verification to both crew and controllers that their spacecraft was on the proper trajectory. The radio signal that connected Apollo to the huge antennas on Earth was used for everything from spacecraft tracking to crew communications. But when Apollo vanished beyond the limb of the moon, the all important link would be severed, isolating the crew from their support network on Johnston Island for the first time since the launch.

"So long, Johnston," Burns said. "We'll catch you on the flipside."

Central Intelligence Agency
Langley, VA

It was already tomorrow morning in China, and time was running out for Operation Longbow. The mission had started off well; too well Derrick Schmitt thought. The operational handoff of the Salty Dog between the launch crew on the USS *Ronald Reagan* and his Langley based team had taken place right on schedule. The UCAV was then shadowed by two F-15E's right up to the edge of international waters, where they turned away and lured any unwanted radar coverage away from the black aircraft, allowing it to slip undetected through Chinese coastal defenses.

Then all hell broke loose.

Schmitt had been assigned as the mission pilot for the covert operation. As the company's "man-in-the-loop," he had monitored the mission's progress, along with the rest of his team in the CIA control room, right up to the coast-in point. That's where the stealthy drone had gone dark and retracted the last of its antennas, severing the only control link to the unmanned craft. Its flight programming then took over. The X-47B was expected to fly itself along the preplanned route until just short of the Xi'an satellite communications complex, where its antennas would redeploy and contact would be reestablished. Schmitt would then use the onboard sensors to visually verify the target before consent for weapons release would be given. That was the plan, anyway.

But the time for reacquisition of the control signal had come—and gone. The control room was in chaos. Throughout the building, dozens of technicians clambered to get their myriad networks back to a partially functioning state. No one was sure exactly what had happened, but the building thought to be impervious to cyber attacks was suddenly operating in the modern day equivalent of the Stone Age. At the moment, it didn't matter why the power had gone out or where the attack had come from, although everyone had their suspicions. That analysis would come later. For now, the imperative was to regain the satellite link and reestablish the tenuous connection between Langley and the stray aircraft hovering somewhere over the heart of Communist China.

Apollo 18

The crew had been afforded only a few glimpses of the moon during the lengthy cislunar transit. And the inertial attitude of the spacecraft stack since the last platform alignment had positioned them in a heads-down, tail-first orientation with respect to the lunar surface. It was by all accounts an uncomfortable way to begin the critical maneuver. If the data was off by even a degree, death would come swiftly. But the "good news," as Burns had noted, was that if their approach was off—they would never know what hit them.

Mitchell was the first to see it. "Holy shit!" he said, and then slowly pushed himself away from the glass as if the increased distance would prove safer.

"That's incredible," Burns said, pulling himself

closer to the eerie visage. "Look at the size of that thing."

Harden just stared at the great cratered world. He thought he was prepared for this. He had accumulated weeks in space. He had witnessed the sun rise and set countless times from Earth orbit—but this was different. This was not the moon as seen through a telescope in his back yard. The inviting, tranquil mare were gone, having given way to innumerable umbrageous craters. The moon was now a planet in its own right. And it appeared to be offering warning signs to the unwelcome visitors.

Harden finally tore himself from the window. "Okay. Everybody double-check your switches. We can't afford to screw this one up. One minute 'til Tig," he added as he shook off the image, and instead imagined a successful LOI maneuver.

The DSKY came alive as the final seconds ticked away. "Average-G is on," Burns noted as the numbers flashed on the display.

"EMS Mode is Normal," Harden added.

"You are clear to PRO."

"Okay, 99 Proceed."

"Ignition."

"A and B valves are open. Pc holding steady at ninety percent." Harden carefully eyed the instruments as the engine came up to full operating pressure.

"How are the velocities matching up?" Mitchell asked over Harden's shoulder.

"Eleven-feet-per-second delta between the DSKY and the EMS, but they're converging." As long as the engine continued to operate, these became the most important values to monitor during the lengthy burn. "Five minutes. Pressures look good. Velocities still converging."

"Attitude's holding within the deadband. Steering is good," Burns added. "Give me a countdown."

Harden hawked the DSKY as the delta-v remaining approached zero.

"Ten, nine, eight..."

"Shutdown!" Burns yelled and quickly scanned the DSKY. The numbers were comforting. According to the Apollo guidance computer, their orbit was precisely 59.6 by 160.2 nautical miles, close enough to proceed with the next phase of their accelerated flight plan.

Central Intelligence Agency
Langley, VA

"I've got it!" Schmitt yelled, partly in an attempt to quiet the din that had shattered his concentration. "The link is back up. I just need to find out where in the fuck we are." He didn't realize how tall of an order that would turn out to be.

He had expected the UCAV to be in a holding pattern over an unpopulated area fifty nautical miles east of the target city of Weinan. Schmitt had picked the location himself, a point over mountainous terrain that would minimize the acoustic signature of the aircraft. The big black bird was stealthy in the radio frequency spectrum, but it certainly wasn't invisible, or even quiet for that matter. The plan seemed sound at the time, but he soon discovered the limitation of his logic. Without the aid of a GPS signal, the remote location of the holding point could prove disastrous if he wasn't able to reorient himself over the rugged terrain.

The Mission Manager paced feverishly behind Schmitt, who sat in what its operators referred to as the "mockpit," a device that was a cross between an F-16 cockpit, complete with an inert ejection seat, and a high-tech gaming console. "What's wrong now?" Carrie Manson yelled.

"The GPS signal is trashed. The time synch must be all dicked up. I'm not receiving any satellites. We're flying on INS NAV for now. No telling how far off we might be. Does anybody know what the winds were forecast to be in the target area this morning?"

"Strong out of the north," a voice offered from the crowd.

"Then we must have drifted off course to the south after losing the signal," Schmitt surmised, and looked to the weapon systems operator sitting in the fake ejection seat to his right. "Get the FLIR spooled up, Willie. And can somebody find us some topo charts of the area." Several people scattered, searching for aerial photographs, topographical charts, or anything else that might help the pilot with his orientation.

"Without a GPS signal, how are you going to drop the SDBs?" the mission manager asked.

Schmitt studied the displays as he spoke: "The bombs are actually steered by built-in inertial guidance units. They suck for long times of flight without the GPS signal to continuously update their position. But if I can get a manual update with the FLIR, hand off the new present-position coordinates to the bombs just prior to release, and get low enough to cut the time of flight down to less than ten seconds, we might still be able to achieve a pretty decent Pk."

Carrie Manson wasn't a pilot, but she suspected that getting a sufficiently high probability-of-kill was going to take them well below their minimum authorized altitude for the mission. "I don't care what it takes. Just do it."

CHAPTER 29

Central Intelligence Agency
Langley, VA

A STACK OF CHARTS PASSED THROUGH several hands as they made their way into the lap of Willie Geiss. A former Air Force F-111 Weapon Systems Officer, Geiss found the side-by-side seating arrangement of the mockpit comforting. The retired WSO had always felt better about passing along a weapons solution to his pilot if he could look him in the eye when he did it. Geiss quickly shuffled through the charts until he found the one he needed. "Got it," he exclaimed. "I'm going to find us a good update point. Looks like this river to the north should do nicely. Bring it around to the left. Let's get the FLIR pointed in the right direction."

Schmitt typed in the command, and halfway around the world the black drone dipped a wing and began a slow left-hand turn toward the Yellow River.

"This bend right here," Geiss said as he pointed to the chart. "There's a bridge that should be a good update point. I'll get us a lat-long."

"Pick off coordinates for the far bank," Schmitt ordered. "There should be better relief against the north shore."

"Yup, concur." Geiss typed the latitude and longitude of the update point into the computer terminal and hit

Transmit. The forward-looking infrared seeker head, now exposed on the belly of the orbiting UCAV, slaved itself to the new coordinates. But the infrared image displayed on the black-and-white monitor in the CIA control room was filled with featureless terrain.

"Shit," Schmitt swore. "Go to wide field of view."

Geiss toggled the FOV option on his control panel. FLIR magnification decreased by a factor of ten, but the wider field of view covered a much larger piece of terrain. "There's the Yellow River," he said pointing to the top of the display. "I'm going to slew the seeker head up to the river bend, and then go back to narrow field of view."

When Geiss finally applied the position update to the inertial navigation system, Schmitt saw exactly what he had expected. "Looks like we're about ten miles too far to the south. And we're high as a kite. I'm going to need to get down quick."

Schmitt clicked the autopilot off and gripped the joystick controller. He leaned the stick to the left and pulled the throttle to idle. The whisper-quiet black jet banked steeply, its nose slicing through the horizon as it dug for thicker air. "One quick 360 ought to do it. Then we'll head inbound for the target run. Stand by on the bomb-bay doors."

"Rog. I'll designate the target as soon as we come out of the turn."

"Motherfucker!" Schmitt yelled into the crowded room. The resurgent din was quickly replaced with the quietness of a confessional.

"What did I do?" Geiss shouted.

"Nothing," Schmitt said in disgust. "I lost the fucking link again."

A room full of blank faces stared at Schmitt as he tried to regain control of the errant aircraft. But the pilotless drone performed its final command flawlessly.

For the next two and a half minutes it continued its nose-low left-hand death spiral, finally carving out a huge smoking hole in the forbidden wilderness. By the time anyone would figure out what had happened, the world would be a different place, and the reason for the attack would long since have been forgotten.

Goldstone Deep Space Complex

When the Fort Irwin military police notified Stephen Austin of a security breach inside the restricted area, the Army official emphasized that the breach was most likely caused by the local wildlife. Austin doubted it. He may have flown in yesterday from the chaos of Colorado Springs to the relative tranquility of the Mojave Desert on nothing but a hunch, but he was certain now that his worst fears were being realized. The suspected intrusion, he was told, was just beyond the wash, east of Antenna 3.

A mile-long dust cloud roiled into the dawn behind the speeding pickup truck as Austin raced over a rutted track toward the perimeter of the Deep Space Communications complex. The wild ride made it difficult to see the more dangerous features of the bleak landscape. The dilapidated barbed-wire fence appeared to come out of nowhere, rising from the high desert chaparral like a hideous mirage.

Austin cut the wheel and jammed his foot on the brakes. The truck skidded in a looping circle before broad-siding the loose barbed wire. When the vehicle finally came to a stop, the driver's door was pinned shut by the fence. Austin quickly slid across the wide bench seat and exited through the passenger's door.

Across the wash, Cheng Mak was hauled back from the edge of an approaching coma by the sound of barbed wire screeching on sheet metal. It took him several seconds to realize where he was and recall the dire nature of his situation. His body was almost completely numb from the paralyzing venom. He thought about his left hand for a second. It still moved. He had freed the detonator from his coat pocket but passed out before he could activate the first segment. He strained to lift his head to see the markings on the box, but it was no use. His pulse quickened and his respiration grew shallower with each useless motion. When he heard the sound of rocks crushing under boots, he knew he was out of time. Cradling the device against his chest, he fumbled with the selector knob until he found the correct setting and placed his thumb on the plunger.

Austin was in full stride when the first explosion rocked the desert floor. The manmade temblor undermined his already shaky footing, and Austin tumbled to the ground in a cloud of dust. As he rolled to a stop, he could only watch in horror as the tangled web of steel that had once been a lifeline to the far-flung Apollo astronauts crumbled to the desert floor, leaving nothing but a stump where the two-hundred-foot-wide antenna had been. His mind raced for answers; the solution was quick in coming. He had to stop this maniac before he brought down the second antenna.

Austin was back on his feet and up to speed in no time. As the powerful bass note from the distant concussion ebbed into desert silence, he heard a strange voice bellow in the distance. He quickly zeroed in on the direction and saw a man lying in the dirt. He couldn't understand what the man was saying, but he was sure he recognized the language. It was Mandarin Chinese. Austin unholstered his gun and in mid-stride, fired several shots.

"Long live the *Zhongguo*!" Mak wailed in the ancient

267

language as he twisted the selector and depressed the button again.

Austin stumbled as the desert floor shook, but managed to maintain his footing as he squeezed off several more shots. One of the scattered rounds found Mak's chest. As the bullet pounded its way into his heart, the small black box in his left hand flew clear and skittered across the desert floor. But it was too late. Austin cursed the sky as he turned in time to see the second giant antenna tumble to the ground.

An Army jeep appeared on the horizon just as Austin came to a stop next to the lifeless body. Gasping for air, Austin pulled a photo from his shirt pocket and examined the face. It was a match. One of the two men photographed three weeks ago leaving the pier in the Bahamas, lay dead at his feet.

Austin spun slowly as he surveyed the damage. Black clouds billowed on the horizon. Both Apollo antennas were destroyed; the wreckage scattered across hundreds of yards of barren desert. Several smaller antennas remained, but the two necessary for Apollo navigation were gone. His only consolation came from an obscure brief that he had gotten from Sam Freer barely a week ago. He was glad now more than ever that the Apollo system had been designed during the Cold War, at a time when every sign of national prowess was considered vulnerable. The capability had never before been needed, but at least the Apollo spacecraft had been designed with an autonomous navigation capability. He could only hope that Sam was right, and that Jeff Burns was up to the task.

Lunar Orbit

Alone in the command module, Burns drummed his fingers on the retracted armrest as he impatiently waited for acquisition of signal, or AOS. The isolation was overpowering. He was eager to relay the data from his burn report to Johnston; to finally let someone else in the universe know they were still alive. His headset finally crackled to life.

"Apollo 18, this is Johnston, AOS. How do you read, over?"

"You're coming in weak and barely readable, Johnston," Burns said loudly. "We had residuals of only two feet per second...burned those with the service module RCS thrusters. And my God, Sam, this rock is enormous! You should see it."

"Yeah, I bet it is. Look, I hate to have to tell you this, but we've run into some problems down here."

Burns knew that Harden and Mitchell weren't plugged in to the lunar module's intercom yet, but the urgency in Freer's voice was overwhelming. "What's the word, Sam?"

"Goldstone and Madrid have been attacked. And a similar attempt was interrupted in Canberra...luckily before any damage was done to the antenna there."

"Is that why you sound like crap?"

"I'm afraid so. But that's not our biggest concern at the moment."

"The uplink?"

"Now look, Jeff. We're going to have to take this one step at a time. There's no need to panic yet. Your alignments so far have been on par with or better than ours here in Control. And the numbers we gave you for the PC+2 burn should still be good. That gives you two choices." Freer didn't like either one. "You can burn the Pericynthion-plus-two numbers, and have a good chance of making the emergency recovery window. Or you can burn LOI-2 and circularize your orbit. But once you do that you'll be on your own. We won't be able to track you from then on. And once you change your orbit, there's no guarantee we can get you back."

The ramifications were mind boggling. Burns wanted to stop long enough to get his crewmates on the loop, but another thought won out. "What about the landing? Without a position update and a state vector from the ground, how are they supposed to find Daedalus crater?"

"If they decide to go through with it, you're going to have to transfer the platform alignment from the command module computer to the LM. Now, I know that's not what you wanted to hear, and it isn't easy for an engineer to say this...but that should get them fairly close." The comm link was quiet for a moment before Freer filled the loop with the rest of the bad news. "And the UCAV strike on Xi'an was unsuccessful."

Burns cursed to himself. He knew that short of an overt military action against the Chinese, they had just become the president's last best chance of averting a disaster. "I guess I'd better get the guys in the loop on this."

"Jeff, wait. Before you do, I just wanted to say this. If Jack decides to go ahead with the landing, it's going to be on your shoulders to get them home. Now you know I wouldn't blow smoke up your ass, so trust me when I say this. You're up to the task. And everyone down here agrees with me. You can do this."

"Thanks, Sam."

Freer quickly shifted gears in an effort to keep things moving. "So how's the IVT coming?"

Burns thought for a moment. He was still trying to digest the news, and was drawing a blank on the acronym. *Oh yeah, Intravehicular transfer.* "Blaze and Mitch should be finishing up with the LM checklist any time now. I'll see if I can get them—" But before Burns could unplug his comm cord, a new voice entered the loop.

"Johnston, this is the *Intruder*. How do you read?"

Harden's voice sounded far away. "Three-by *Intruder*, but we're working on it," Freer replied. "How's my LM doing?"

"We're on ship's power now. The batteries in the descent stage check good, and we've disconnected the LM power umbilical. I'm about to start the platform alignment, and Mitch is getting the ECS and cooling systems spooled up right now. We hope to complete the checklist before the next LOS. Then we'll get strapped in and ready for the Circ burn. We'll let you know when we're ready for a state vector uplink and a landing site REFSMMAT."

"I'll tell them," Burns interjected.

"Tell us what?" Harden asked.

Burns unhooked his comm cords and worked his way toward the LM. He maneuvered below the CM's instrument panel and floated through the long tunnel connecting the two spacecraft. He emerged upside down in the cramped LM cabin and gave a quick rundown of the situation to his crewmates. Without the simultaneous connection to at least two of the earthbound antennas that made up NASA's Deep Space Network, it would be impossible for controllers on the ground to triangulate their position; they would literally be lost in space. The one good DSN antenna in Canberra, Australia, could provide communication with the ground during roughly half of the Earth's rotation, but navigation calculations, he explained, would be impossible.

Harden just shook his head. "What does Johnston recommend?"

"Sam said it's up to us. But I'm all in. I know I can find my way home if I need to, with or without those

271

antennas. So it's really up to you two. You're the ones who are going to have to land on the far side of the moon with nothing more than a transfer alignment and the seat of your pants; and then you're going to have to trust me to get us home with nothing but a sextant and a forty-year-old gyro." Burns paused before voicing the second option. "Or we can burn the PC+2 numbers and get the hell out of here while we still have an even chance."

Harden looked at Mitchell and waited. He studied his friend's expression for any hint of doubt. "No pressure, Mitch. If you want to punch out, now's the time to say so. Because once we start down the chute, you know we're on government time."

Mitchell met Harden's poker face with his own blank stare. It had been a long time, but he had been on dangerous strike missions before and knew exactly what Harden meant. Mitchell finally shrugged and said, "What the hell. We've come this far. It'd be crazy to turn back now."

CHAPTER 30

Lunar Orbit

A POLLO 18 RACED AROUND THE moon in a steep elliptical orbit. The conjoined spacecraft had just reached apolune—the high point in their lunar orbit—160 nautical miles above the Sea of Tranquility, when Harden finished his first lunar module platform alignment. He steadied himself on the tubular yellow framework that guarded the LM's alignment telescope and waited for Mitchell to finish his part of the cockpit setup.

Mitchell held up a page from the LM checklist. Pictures of circuit breaker panels identified which breakers should be pushed in and which ones left open for certain flight sequences. Black dots identified breakers to be pushed closed; white dots were those to be left open, or unpowered. He quickly scanned the panels on the slanted bulkhead next to the LMP station and set them according to the code in the checklist.

"While you finish up with that, I'm going to button up the tunnel," Harden said. He then maneuvered into the aft cabin and grabbed one of the four small pouches labeled Lunar Sample Collection. He transferred something from his leg pocket to the small bag and resealed the flap. As he floated back through the long tube one last time, he noticed that Burns was busy with his own navigational chores in the lower equipment bay. Harden Velcroed the sample collection bag to the CM bulkhead and floated through a tight pirouette.

"What's that?" Burns asked.

"I don't think we're going to have enough time to collect that many samples while we're down there," Harden said, and then extended an open hand.

Burns looked at the bag and then back at Harden. His expression was alarmingly grim. "You guys had better not screw this up. Because I'm not going home without you." He then shook Harden's hand like it might be for the last time.

Harden met his friend's worried glare with a thoughtful grin. "I know you're going to do the right thing when the time comes—and get the hell out of here—with or without us. But I don't want you to look at that as an order. I'd rather like to think of it as a favor instead." Harden then tightened his grip and added, "Look, you got us here. You've done your job well. I'm sure your dad would be proud."

"Just shut up and get your asses back here in one piece."

Back inside the LM, Harden took his place at the CDR's station. He scuffed the toes of his boots into the thick weave of Velcro on the cockpit floor and flipped the Master Arm switch on the panel labeled Explosive Devices. No longer shrouded by the panels that had protected it during a violent penetration of an atmosphere in which it had not been designed to operate, the *Intruder* was finally ready to stretch her legs. Harden toggled another switch and fired several explosive charges. Beneath his feet, the large saucer-like landing pads that would cushion their fall to the lunar surface, swung out on the ends of four sturdy aluminum alloy struts and thunked firmly into place. "Johnston, the *Intruder* has wheels."

"That's good news, *Intruder*," Freer replied. "Now all you need are wings."

"Roger," Harden replied with a chuckle. "We're going to get strapped in for the Circ burn and stand by for LOS."

Mitchell took the cue and began clipping into the complex system of pulleys and lanyards attached to the deck of the lunar module. Harden did the same as they were about to find themselves in an unusual position. During the upcoming circularization burn, the direction of thrust in the LM would be exactly opposite that of the command module. As Burns would be pushed back into his seat while the SPS engine was thrusting, the two astronauts standing in the LM would be thrown into the overhead panels if not securely strapped in.

"All set for some negative-g," Harden announced.

"LOS in thirty seconds," said Burns. The tenuous S-Band signal from Canberra died with a short crackle. The instant isolation in the command module caught Burns by surprise. He quickly flipped several switches and activated the VHF radio equipment that served to connect the two spacecraft when out of contact with Mission Control. "*Intruder*, this is *Phantom*. You still with me?"

"You're not alone yet," Mitchell replied.

"Rog. I'll give you a countdown to Tig at one minute. You guys all tucked in?"

"We're hangin' in the straps," said Harden.

Minutes passed quickly as the spacecraft accelerated toward its sixty-nautical-mile perilune—and one more critical link in the fragile daisy-chain that separated them from an improbable raid on the vast crater Daedalus.

"Ignition," Burns reported over the VHF. "Pc is good, pitch is good. Roll is right in the center of the dead band. Ten seconds."

Harden and Mitchell's restraints snapped taught against the inertia that tried to pull their boots away from the floor of the LM. Blood rushed into their heads as they stared out into deep space, hanging on every word of Burns's running commentary.

"Velocities are close. Pc is down to ninety-four. Twenty seconds. Looks good. Stand by for shutdown in five, four, three, two...shutdown!"

"Good burn?" Harden prompted.

"Perfect burn. No residuals. The DSKY has our orbit at 58.9 by 60.2 nautical miles." Burns bounced from one end of the wide cockpit to the other as he shut down systems and safed switches at both ends of the expansive instrument panel.

"You're the best my friend!" Harden said, and then raised his hand to Mitchell for a celebratory high-five. "Give us a few more minutes and we'll be ready for undocking."

Lunar Orbit

Burns carefully maneuvered the mated spacecraft to the proper undocking attitude. The long axis of the stack was now aligned radially with the center of the moon, his CM *Phantom* nearer to the moon's surface, the LM *Intruder* occupying the outside of the orbit. He then toggled the Probe switch to Extend. The cyclical wailing of the release mechanism howled through the lonely cockpit as the probe cycled to full extension.

Harden was keen to the loss of rigidity between the spacecraft. They were no longer one firm unit, but two separate flying machines with only the most tenuous of connections. The precarious arrangement was unnerving for Harden who had grown accustomed to being in the driver's seat. "Okay, buddy, you can cut us loose any time now."

Burns lifted the Probe switch again, this time holding it until the tiny latches on the probe tip fully retracted. Tugging aft on the translation controller, he fired a short burst from the RCS thrusters and gently backed away from the lunar module. "You're free."

The two spacecraft flew in close formation as they raced through another orbit. Checklists continued at a feverish pace. Not long after the unlikely mechanical duet swung through lunar high noon, the weak radio connection to Johnston was severed once again.

Harden rolled the spidery *Intruder* until the triangular windows afforded him a view of the battered terrain below. Using the landing point designator, he searched for landmarks that he hoped would help guide them toward Daedalus crater. The LPD was a simple but powerful tool. Scribed into the window at the CDR's station, the crude device was made up of two graduated pitch ladders, each on a separate layer of the multi-pane glass. When Harden adjusted his eyes' line-of-sight to superimpose both markings into one, he would get an accurate pitch reference with respect to the lunar horizon—without having to look at the instruments inside the LM. It was the technological precursor to the modern day heads-up display. The solution was simple, but he loved it.

Burns had an even more challenging task as the CM coasted toward lunar dusk. He needed more than to just locate the fifty-nautical-mile-wide crater—he needed to find the Chang'e itself. He had been hoping for some good coordinates from Austin, but the Lunar Reconnaissance Orbiter had finally exhausted its limited power supply, and the satellite's energy hungry cameras were irrevocably dormant. Now all he had was his twenty-eight power sextant and a tired pair of eyes. The task was overwhelming, but what else could he do? He had to find it. Without precise coordinates for the Chinese lander, Harden and Mitchell's job in the LM would be nothing more than a cosmic crap shoot.

Lunar Module Intruder

"*Intruder*, this is Johnston, AOS, over."

Harden was caught off guard by the voice crackling in his headset. He was fully anticipating acquisition of signal, but it wasn't Sam Freer's voice on the other end of the long distance connection. Instead, it sounded a lot more like the voice of the man who currently held the lesser known title of "Last Man on the Moon." Gene Cernan had landed on the small Pacific island during the radio blackout of their last orbit. Following a quick mission brief by Freer during LOS, Cernan took control of the microphone as Capsule Communicator. The silver-haired Cernan recalled how comforting it was for him to have an experienced astronaut on the other end of the line when he began his descent to the valley of Taurus-Littrow and was quick to accept the offer from Freer.

"Gene-O, is that you?" Harden asked.

Cernan's seasoned voice sounded as if it were still trapped inside the thirty-eight-year-old body that had taken it to the moon over forty years ago. "Affirm, good buddy. How did the LPD calibration go?"

"Uh, fine. I think we're just about ready. One more alignment and it'll be all over but the shouting."

"That's great news. I'm glad to see that all of your training has finally paid off," Cernan said, then added wistfully, "Still, I'd love nothing more than to be up there with you guys right now."

"The feeling is mutual, sir."

Cernan then carefully flipped through the pages of the Apollo Flightplan. He wanted to review the sequence one last time before Harden and Mitchell commenced the descent orbit insertion burn, DOI. He had made the rounds in the simulators over the past few years, but it had been a lifetime since he had participated in a live mission, and this mission was notably different. In many ways it was a mirror image of all previous Apollo missions. Apollo 18 would not land on the near side of the moon in plain view—and radio contact— with its support team. Instead it would land in one of the most isolated craters in the solar system. Cernan leaned forward and buried his face in his palms. He closed his eyes and imagined the profile.

Unlike his Apollo 17 mission, this DOI burn would occur on the near side of the moon. Once the *Intruder* was safely in the descent orbit, it would swoop down to within 50,000 feet of the proposed landing zone. Harden would then use the LM's alignment telescope to search for the Chang'e lander. One orbit later, the *Intruder* would make its bold attempt, a first in manned spaceflight. By igniting the descent engine near perilune, Program 63 would begin the braking phase of the approach, powered descent initiate, or PDI. For nearly ten minutes the descent engine would steadily decrease the *Intruder's* velocity until it reached high gate, approximately 7,000 feet above the surface, where the lunar guidance computer would switch to Program 64. The *Intruder* would then pitch forward and finally bring the landing area into view. From there, Harden would evaluate the landing site and make corrections until low gate, barely 100 feet above the lunar surface.

As Cernan chair-flew the lunar landing in his mind's eye, a quarter-million miles away Harden and Mitchell were ready to commence the journey for real. Harden had just tapped the last keystroke on the DSKY when he called down to Mission Control. Cernan was jerked back from his mental imagery as the anxious voice bore through his dreamy trance.

"Johnston, *Intruder*, we're standing by for DOI."

"Stand by, *Intruder*," Cernan replied as he waited for the signal from Flight Control. Freer then went around-the-horn with his flight controllers and accumulated the necessary Go's needed to send the crew of the *Intruder* down for a closer look. With a short nod from Freer, Cernan's response echoed across the great expanse of space and time. "*Intruder*, you are go for DOI."

CHAPTER 31

Lunar Module Intruder

THE LUNAR MODULE, IN ITS slightly higher orbit, had drifted almost five miles behind the command module. Burns continued to monitor the wandering spacecraft through the CM's sextant. He also maintained the VHF radio link that provided ranging to the LM in the event its descent engine failed to ignite and he was called on to rescue the stranded spacecraft. He was delighted with the clarity of the picture that the sextant delivered even at such a distance. He could easily tell which way the LM was pointing and was even able to make out the details of some of its more prominent features. He watched closely as Harden maneuvered the awkward spacecraft to the proper attitude for the upcoming burn. When the short maneuver ended, Burns found himself looking directly into the *Intruder's* engine bell.

"Hey, I can see right up your skirt, *Intruder*."

"I guess that means we're pointing in the right direction," Harden chuckled as he made one final switch check. "Hey, Mitch, give me a countdown to Tig, would you?"

"Coming up on one minute."

"Descent Engine – Armed."

"Average-G is on," Mitchell said, acknowledging that the Primary Guidance and Navigation System, the *pings*, was in control of the burn and would average out any rapid changes in acceleration resulting from a rough starting descent engine. "Thirty seconds."

"Flashing 99. Proceed." Harden punched the PRO key on the DSKY and awaited the result. "Ignition!"

"She's burning," Mitchell reported. "Ten percent on the commander's gauge." The low thrust setting on startup allowed the PGNS to gimbal the descent engine to direct its thrust through the lunar module's center of gravity. Mitchell felt a mild vibration work its way through the floor and into his boots. "It feels good."

"Throttle up at fifteen seconds. Eleven, twelve... throttle up."

"Forty percent thrust," Mitchell relayed.

"Pressures are good. Attitude is holding."

"Stand by for shutdown at thirty seconds. Twenty-seven, eight..."

"Shutdown! Engine Arm – OFF."

"Engine Arm – OFF. Master Arm – OFF."

"Good burn. Residuals...zero, plus two, minus six," Harden reported.

"We can live with that, gang!" Cernan radioed from his far away console.

As *Intruder* began a slow fall toward the lunar surface, Harden copied down the orbital parameters from the DSKY: 60.5 by 8.9 nautical miles. The LM would reach its new perilune of just 50,000 feet roughly 220 nautical miles up-range from the center of Daedalus. If all went well, they could scout for the Chang'e on the upcoming perilune, and then begin their descent to the lunar surface on the next orbit. Harden referenced his checklist, cleaned up the remaining switches, and for the first time in a long while, drew in a deep cleansing breath.

The situation had the exact opposite effect on

Mitchell, as he suddenly realized there was no guarantee they would survive the next twenty-four hours.

"You know, Blaze, there's something I've been meaning to get off my chest," Mitchell said as he rubbed his bare palms on the legs of his pressure suit. "About Test Pilot School I mean."

"Hold that thought," Harden said, and then unzipped a small pocket on the left leg of his pressure suit. "Things could get pretty crazy from here on, and there's still one important detail we ought to settle before the flight plan gets away from us."

Mitchell's face drained as Harden produced a shiny coin from his pocket. Mitchell had seen it before and remembered its history. Benjamin Harden had given the rare silver piece to his son as a gift when he finally earned his Eagle Scout badge. The small memento had always held special meaning for Harden, who as a young man carried it around in his pocket for good luck. He eventually developed a more practical use for the coin, however, and had often used it as a gesture of good will, a novel way to level the playing field with his friends and colleagues. And then there were, as Mitchell had often suspected, those rare occasions when Harden actually used the coin to let fate make certain decisions for him. "What are you doing with that?"

"I probably shouldn't have waited so long, but I never really thought we'd make it this far anyway." Harden then took the silver piece and gently hung it in the zero gravity field between them. As it floated in the middle of the LM cabin, he flicked it on one edge with his finger. He moved an open hand below the spinning coin and stared at his old friend. "Give me a shot of plus-x."

"No, wait, Blaze. You don't have to do this." But

283

Mitchell knew it was too late. The coin would continue to spin until the outcome was clear. He reached for the translational controller and gave it a quick pull, just enough to break the detent. Four RCS thrusters released a quick puff and the coin dropped gently into the center of Harden's open palm. He clenched his fist tightly around it and eyed Mitchell.

"It's your call."

Mitchell didn't hesitate. "Heads."

Harden released his grip slowly. Both men gazed at the coin. Staring back at them was the silhouetted bust of a youthful president whose rousing words had challenged a generation—and set the future in motion.

"Heads it is," Harden announced, and returned the 1964 Kennedy half-dollar to his pocket. He then looked at Mitchell and smiled. "You know, it's probably for the best. Half of my landing attempts in the sim ended up aborted anyway."

Mitchell's mouth hung open in the silence. But before he could reply, the quiet reverence was interrupted by the far away voice of Johnston's CAPCOM.

"*Intruder*, Johnston."

"Go ahead, Johnston," Harden replied.

"We've got a bit of a situation here," Cernan said flatly.

Mitchell looked at Harden as if he knew the rug was about to be pulled out from under them. Harden shook his head. It was hardly a month ago that he had fully expected to have made his last life-or-death decision, but it was clear now that he would have to make at least one more.

"We're standing by, Johnston."

Cernan relayed the situation as Freer had laid it out. "Well, fellas, it looks like there's a cabin leak that's bleeding off your Oh-two reserves. Now there's no immediate risk here as we see it, but the long term prospects are a bit more grim."

Mitchell looked at Harden as he processed the information. "A leak?"

The only possible answer bubbled up like acid from Harden's stomach. "It must have been the fucking SAM!" The command module had been designed to absorb hits from small micrometeoroids, but if just one stray piece of shrapnel from the Chinese anti-satellite weapon had impacted the lunar module—as thin as a few sheets of paper in some places—it could have fatally damaged the frail spacecraft.

"Shit!" Mitchell cursed as he spun around and tore a small reference card from a patch of Velcro on the adjacent bulkhead. He quickly rotated a selector on the instrument panel as he compared the quantities of various oxygen tanks against the data on the card.

Harden keyed his mike, "Johnston, we're taking a look at those numbers now."

"EECOM says you have eight hours of breathable oxygen left in the LM. That's barely enough for one three-hour EVA if you touch down at the current ground elapsed time of eighty-four hours and eighteen minutes."

Harden silently cursed the chain of events that had brought him here. "Has anyone run the figures on an eighty-two-hour GET landing?"

Cernan was prepared for the question. "Yes they have, Blaze. A landing one rev earlier should buy you a single five-hour EVA, or possibly two three-hour EVAs—but that's no guarantee. If you decide to take that route, your PDI burn time will be in approximately thirty-six minutes. And you'll lose any hope of spotting the Chang'e on the recce pass at the bottom of this orbit."

"Yeah, I know, but that was a long shot anyway,"

Harden replied. *Hell, this whole damned thing has been nothing but one incredibly long shot.* "Look, we're going to need all the time we can get on this rock if we're going to have any chance of pulling this off. One three-hour EVA is out of the question. We're going to prep for PDI."

"Copy that," Cernan said. "All your numbers should remain the same except for the Tig, and we'll get that up to you shortly."

"I know I don't have to tell you to hurry up down there, but we're coming up on LOS in six minutes, and I don't want to have to do this in the blind."

Cernan had his answer in two minutes. He took the revised Tig and reassured the young flight dynamics officer, "Don't worry, son. I'm sure this'll get 'em in the ballpark."

Cernan passed up the new PDI burn time to the crew of the *Intruder* and waited helplessly for LOS. As loss of signal approached, Cernan voiced one final observation to the anxious men in the *Intruder*. "Gentlemen, fate may have led you both to this point in time, but from here on, you're in charge of your own destiny. And remember, if you want to get a tiger's attention, you don't grab him by the tail—you grab him by the balls. Good luck."

CHAPTER 32

Lunar Module Intruder

D IRECTLY BENEATH THE LUNAR MODULE, the shadows that defined the moon's craters shrunk and disappeared; the surface became a blinding mix of indistinguishable features as the desolate terrain baked under the scorching temperatures of lunar high noon. Yet *Intruder* continued to slip ever closer to the lifeless lunar night.

"How's it coming, guys?" Burns radioed from his high perch. "I show five minutes to Tig, and it's awfully quiet."

"I forgot how lonely it must be up there," Mitchell replied. "We'll go ahead and switch to Vox on the VHF so you can listen in."

"Okay, Mitch. I guess we'd better go ahead and swap positions," said Harden. "Then we can get suited up for the PDI switch check. I don't want to be fumbling with a glove or locking ring when the burn is about to start."

"I guess you won the coin toss, huh, Mitch?"

"Yeah. We'll see how lucky I was soon enough."

Already firmly ensconced in their pressure suits, Harden and Mitchell carefully donned their helmets and gloves to complete the pressurized ensemble. Harden then moved to the LMP station and commenced the final checklist. "Thrust Control – Auto, CDR."

"Auto, CDR," Mitchell replied, and then flipped the appropriate switches on the instrument panel. For the next sixty seconds the checklist dance moved ahead slowly but with purpose as each challenge and every response carried the weight of the entire mission along with it.

When the PDI checklist was complete, the comm loop fell silent. Mitchell's gaze gravitated to the world beyond his window. On the moon's ancient surface the number of craters seemed to multiply, the shadows that had disappeared at lunar high noon now growing longer again with each passing minute. The images made it impossible to ignore importance of the next maneuver. If the descent engine lit off on schedule and burned faithfully until shutdown—he would soon be landing on the far side of the moon.

"Thirty seconds," Harden noted.

Mitchell reeled in his drifting thoughts, lifted a lock-levered toggle switch and ratcheted it forward. "Descent engine – Armed."

"We've got two lights. Altitude and velocity," Harden said calmly, as he knew the lights wouldn't extinguish until they rolled over and pointed the LM's landing radar toward the lunar surface.

"Auto ignition. Throttle at ten percent," Mitchell reported. "Descent engine command override is on. Throttle up at twenty-six seconds. There's ninety-two percent."

"Wow, that's a kick in the pants," Harden said. "Helium pressure is good. Regulator valves look good."

"There's one minute. Getting a little RCS action," Mitchell noted as the reaction control system pulsed to steer the *Intruder* down its long parabolic glideslope.

Harden continued to narrate their progress from the DSKY display. "Five thousand two hundred feet per second horizontal. Mark. Twenty-five feet per second vertical. Altitude 47,500."

"Looks good."

"Okay, Mitch, at the three minute mark you should see the western rim of Coriolis at thirty degrees on the LPD." One of the few easily recognizable features on the pockmarked far side, the Coriolis impact crater was chosen by the SLATE trajectory team to give the crew a crucial visual backup check to the integrity of the archaic computer program that now guided their craft through space.

"I'll be on the lookout."

"Two minutes. Forty-two thousand feet. H-dot is fifty-seven feet per second down."

Mitchell searched the terrain below. He was beginning to doubt that he could actually find the landmark amid the numerous impacts absorbed by the tortured far side over the millennia. The world beyond his window seemed to be forever reinventing itself, as smaller, younger craters continuously blossomed to replace the older, larger ones that seemed to slough off like so much dead skin.

"Coming up on three minutes," Harden warned.

"Wait. There it is. Coming into view at the bottom of my window. Yep, it's definitely Coriolis. I can see the three smaller impact craters on its southern rim."

Harden's window was canted down and angled slightly outboard and away from Mitchell's. He couldn't see the crater himself, but watched closely as the three minute mark came and went.

"Here it comes...Mark."

"Three seconds late," Harden decided. He then turned to Mitchell as if to confirm the obvious. "We may be a little short." Mitchell's expression highlighted his discomfort. They were targeted to clear the crater rim by less than six thousand feet. Arriving at the landmark early equated to being low, and landing short. Neither outcome was desirable.

Command Module Phantom

High in lunar orbit, Burns was busy flying his own spacecraft. He kept one ear tuned to the running commentary from the *Intruder*, while simultaneously prepping the *Phantom* for the upcoming tracking maneuver. He would have only one chance to locate their target before the LM began its final approach. Hovering in the lower equipment bay, Burns called up Program 24 in the CMC. He put his eye up to the scanning telescope and waited for Daedalus to come into view.

The expansive crater would be easy to spot. That was part of the problem—it was actually too big. The Chang'e could be hiding in plain view and he could still miss it. Even Austin had admitted that the coordinates he derived from the lunar seismographs were suspect at best. Burns shook it off. He made one last check of the clock and then went back to the telescope. Daedalus appeared on cue.

With Daedalus successfully identified, he switched his view to the more powerful sextant and began a methodical search pattern. The magnification gave him a much better chance of spotting a manmade object from orbit, but the tiny field of view meant it would take much longer to cover the same ground. And time was a luxury his friends didn't have.

Lunar Module Intruder

The *Intruder* continued its struggle against the incredible momentum that had held it in orbit. Operating at full power, the descent engine still needed another eight minutes to counter the moon's gravitational pull and slow the *Intruder* down enough to make a landing survivable. Anything less would leave the crew with only one option—cut the descent stage loose and abort back to orbit.

"Let's see if we can get the landing radar to lock up now," Harden said.

Mitchell gently twisted the pistol grip in his right hand. One RCS thruster in each quad fired a short pulse, imparting a lazy yawing motion to the *Intruder*. The lunar surface slowly slid out of view as the spacecraft rolled over on its back. Pointed at the lunar surface for the first time, the LM's landing radar probed the rugged terrain below. "I liked the other attitude better," Mitchell said as he stared out into the blackness. "At least before we could see if we were gonna crash."

"Looking good at four minutes," Harden said, as if offering a direct counter to Mitchell's lament. A flash on the DSKY caught his eye. "Altitude light is out. Delta-h is...twenty-four hundred feet. Velocity light is out. H-dot's a little high. I guess it's trying to work off the extra altitude."

"Yeah, but we might need that extra altitude."

"I've got no choice but to accept the deviation. Without verification from Johnston, we're just going to have to trust the landing radar." When Harden's gloved finger hit the Enter key on the DSKY, the lunar guidance computer immediately began reshaping their trajectory based on data from the landing radar.

"How's the RCS doing?" Mitchell prodded. "It's banging around an awful lot."

Harden felt it too. "We're okay. It's just the descent engine gimballing...trying to find a new trim position. Mark. Six minutes. Altitude thirty-two thousand. H-dot's five high. Throttle down to fifty-six percent at six plus twenty-seven."

As *Intruder* plunged toward the giant bulls-eye in the center of the moon's forbidden face, Mitchell took stock of their situation. Halfway through the burn, they were barely thirty nautical miles short of their intended landing site—and on a collision course with the massive mountain wall that rimmed Daedalus crater.

Command Module Phantom

Burns continued his search for the elusive Chang'e. He could only hope that the methodology he chose for searching the large area would pay off soon. The floor of the crater was expansive, but it did have obstacles that should have shaped the trajectory of an autonomous lander. A cluster of peaks in the center of the crater—remnants of the colossal impact that had formed Daedalus a billion years ago—was offset slightly toward the heavily terraced eastern wall. Intelligence reports stated the Chang'e 5's orbit, unlike theirs, had been retrograde around the moon. Burns deduced that such an approach made the area east of the peaks undesirable for a fully automated landing and began his search pattern at the western edge of the crater. But as his scan neared the central peaks, he still hadn't spotted the Chang'e.

He went back to the wide-field-of-view telescope momentarily to reimagine the big picture. The southeastern quadrant looked particularly undesirable. He returned to the sextant and decided to give the northeast portion of the crater a quick review. He knew if he hadn't found the Chang'e by then that it wouldn't much matter, as his friends in the lunar module would be too close to the surface to make the necessary corrections.

Burns had no sooner put his eye back up to the

sextant when he saw a flash on the surface. He jerked away from the eyepiece. *That has to be manmade.* He refocused his eye in the sextant and the sparkle appeared again. It had to be the Chang'e.

CHAPTER 33

Lunar Module Intruder

" I JUST WANT TO TAKE A quick peek," Mitchell warned, and quickly flipped the pitch, roll, and yaw switches to Attitude Hold.

"A peek at...*what the hell?*" Harden calmed down once he realized the method to Mitchell's madness. "You just couldn't wait, could ya?"

Mitchell gently rolled the *Intruder* back to a face down attitude. "Holy shit!" he whispered. The western rim of Daedalus crater spired high above the surrounding terrain. Mitchell leaned forward to look out the bottom of the triangular window. "I can barely see over the top of it."

Harden saw the same thing. "Roll back over. We can't do anything about it now anyway. And if you think it'll help, lift your feet up as we go over."

Mitchell forced a nervous chuckle and quickly righted the spacecraft. "Mode control back to Auto."

"Eight minutes. Fifteen thousand feet on the DSKY. H-dot's right on the money. Pitchover should be at nine plus twenty-one." Harden paused the commentary and held his breath as he watched the altitude readout on the tapemeter begin to decrease at a sickening rate. "We're coming up on the crater rim."

The altitude reading plunged below 5,000 feet as

the terrain surrounding the ancient formation rose to form the crater's edge. The tapemeter shuddered near 4,000 feet before quickly reversing course as the crater rim fell away beneath them. Mitchell didn't start breathing again until the altitude rebounded back above 10,000 feet.

"Damn, that was close," Harden sighed. "Nine minutes. Ninety-five hundred feet. Stand by for pitchover."

"P64," Mitchell exclaimed. "Pitchover!"

The *Intruder's* thrust had been nearly parallel to the lunar surface during the braking phase in an effort to kill off its orbital velocity. The transition to a more vertical attitude not only gave Harden and Mitchell a better view of the area they were targeted to land in, but also put the descent engine to work cancelling their vertical velocity toward a survivable speed of something less than ten feet per second.

Harden punched the PRO key on the DSKY. "We have LPD!"

"Give me a number," Mitchell prompted.

"Forty-seven degrees."

Mitchell shifted his gaze to marry up the landing point designator's two markings on his window and rolled his eyes down the pitch ladder just beyond the forty-five-degree tick mark.

"Shit, that's right on the money," Mitchell shouted. "We're targeted right in the center of the Bermuda Triangle. Can you believe that?" The alignment of three prominent landmarks in the middle of the enormous crater came together to form what Mitchell had referred to in the simulator as the Bermuda Triangle. The massive central peak he had dubbed Mt. Whitney. Two evenly spaced craters to the south and west completed the triangular design.

Burns broke in with the bad news. "Then you're going to land *way* off the mark."

"What!" Harden shouted as he scanned the tapemeter. "Six thousand feet. Down at one-fifty. Three minutes of fuel remaining."

Mitchell responded with slightly more composure. "Talk to me, brother." He knew that if he was going to make corrections, he needed to make the big ones in a hurry.

Burns responded immediately. "All right, let's use the base leg of the triangle as one unit of measure."

"Got it," Mitchell replied as he began building the picture in his head.

"Now let's use the western leg of the triangle as a directional pointer."

"Okay."

"Five thousand feet. LPD forty-two degrees," Harden continued.

"Look one-half unit of measure along that line to the northeast of Mt. Whitney. The Chang'e is just up-sun of an elongated rille. That's your landing zone."

Mitchell stretched his neck forward to the far corner of the window, bumping his faceplate against the center instrument panel. "All right, I can see the area you're talking about. I'm not sure we can get there from here, but I'm going to start heading in that direction."

"I'm passing directly overhead the Chang'e now," Burns noted. "I'm probably going to lose sight soon, when I go down-sun. Good luck."

Harden strained to see what his friends were describing, but the view from his window was blocked by the large vertical strakes protruding from the prominent nose of the lunar module. "Can you give me a little yaw to the left, Mitch?"

"Stand by. I've got to get our vector heading in that

direction first or we're liable to tumble over. I don't think I can fly this thing sideways yet."

"Four thousand. Down at one-twenty. Forty degrees," Harden said, and then checked the fuel quantity gauges. "Fifteen percent fuel. Oxidizer at seventeen."

"I'm going to redesignate with the LPD." Mitchell made two short clicks to the left with the attitude controller, identifying the new landing target to the PGNS. In response, the *Intruder* leaned slightly left of pure vertical and began a yawing motion in the same direction. "We're not going to be able to hack this turn unless we slow our descent rate down. Give me two clicks up on the Rate of Descent switch."

"That's going to put us in Program 66," Harden warned. "We'll lose the auto-land option."

"I know, but we don't have a choice."

Harden thought about it. He figured it was probably the hardest decision he would ever have to make, and he had only seconds to make it. He scanned the instruments once more to buy time. "Three thousand. Rate of descent is shallowing out at fifty feet per second."

"Do it!"

Harden reluctantly toggled the ROD switch twice. "I don't think we're going to have enough fuel for this."

"Then I'll get us as close as I can." Mitchell leaned hard on the attitude controller to adjust their course. The *Intruder* reared up and rolled nearly thirty degrees to the left, followed by a commensurate yaw about its vertical axis.

"Easy!" Harden yelled. "Easy with it." But his tone quickly changed from fear to joy as he finally began to see what Mitchell was aiming for. "Wait, I'm starting to pick up Mt. Whitney in my window. You're not going to try to make it over the top, I hope."

"No. We won't have enough juice for that."

"Maybe we could arc around the mountain."

"I don't think so. Hey, Pipper, it looks like I'm going to be lined up to the southwest of Mt. Whitney, on the *opposite* side from the Chang'e. Do you see a viable path through the mountains?"

The same horrible vision flashed through Burns's and Harden's minds at the same time. "You're not going to try and fly *through* the valley, are you?" Burns asked incredulously.

"Negative! But do you think we could get through there with the rover?"

Burns breathed a sigh of relief as he aimed his sextant into the cluster of peaks and tried to scout a possible passage. "I can't be sure. It might be passable on foot, but I'm not sure about a wheeled vehicle."

"Blaze, give me two more clicks up on the ROD."

"That's going to level us off too high. It'll take too much fuel to get a good rate of descent going again."

"For us to get close enough, I'm going to have to ring every ounce of fuel out of this thing," Mitchell bargained. "Trust me."

Harden finally assented and clicked the switch twice more. The *Intruder* nearly leveled off over the flat plain below. "Fifteen hundred. Down at ten. Seven percent fuel. LPD now at *fifteen* degrees!" Harden compared the DSKY sight angle with the *Intruder's* current pitch angle. "That barely puts us on a three degree glideslope. Horizontal velocity picking up. Fifty forward. We're going to have to kill that soon."

Mitchell referenced the fifteen degree mark on the landing point designator. He had stretched out their flight path as long as he could. The base of the central peak now reached all the way up to the twenty degree mark on his LPD. On his current flight path, the *Intruder* would smash headlong into the side of the steep outcropping in less than two minutes. "Don't worry," said Mitchell. "The last thing I want is to have a crater in this godforsaken place named after me. All right. One click down."

Harden willingly obliged. "One thousand feet. Coming down at sixty—no, seventy feet now. LPD twenty-five degrees."

Mitchell liked what he saw. He eased back gently on the pistol grip to help slow his horizontal velocity.

"Five percent fuel. Eight-fifty. Down at forty. Thirty forward. LPD holding at thirty degrees."

"I guess we're go for landing?" Mitchell queried.

"Yes, go for landing, go for landing!" Burns shouted over the radio.

"Low fuel light," Harden said, and started his watch. "Ninety seconds remaining. Six hundred feet. Down at thirty. A little too hot. Twenty forward."

"All right, we're at pattern altitude now. What do you say we bring her on down?" Mitchell was in the zone. He quickly fell into a rhythm as he worked the *Intruder's* controls.

Harden was aghast as the mountain peaks grew taller in his window until they eventually dwarfed the tiny LM. It was suddenly impossible to believe that their landing zone would place that gigantic upheaval of lunar crust in between the *Intruder* and the Chang'e. It would have to do, though. They were about to run out of fuel.

"Five hundred. Down at twenty. Still too hot."

"Three percent fuel!"

"Four hundred. We're too steep now."

Mitchell finally saw where he wanted to land. "I've got a spot to set her down."

"Three hundred feet. Great. Just do it!"

"Two percent fuel."

"Two hundred feet. Ten down. Eight forward."

Evidence of their arrival suddenly began to shoot across the lunar surface like a fan in all directions. "We're kicking up some dust," Harden said with inflection.

"I see it."

"One-fifty. Down at eight. Three forward."

"One hundred. Down at six. Don't drift backward."

"One percent fuel! We're sucking fumes. You'd better round this descent off soon."

"I promise it'll be a good Navy landing."

"Eighty feet. Down at seven. Two forward."

"I'm on the instruments now," Mitchell said as he quickly scanned the cross-pointers and acknowledged his error. "Drifting a little to the right."

"Sixty feet. Down at six. There's ninety seconds! Still at fifty feet." Harden knew that a fall from this altitude, even in one-sixth gravity would spell the end for the fragile *Intruder*. "Let's get it down!"

"Almost there," Mitchell said in his best soothing voice.

"Forty feet. Down at four. Fuel quantity's off the gauge."

Mitchell worked hard to center the cross-pointers while Harden continued to feed him the rest of the picture.

"Thirty feet. Down at three. Attitude looks good."

"Twenty feet. Down at three."

"Ten feet. Contact light." Harden instantly felt the comforting vibration from the descent engine disappear beneath his feet. "Shutdown!"

The *Intruder* fell the last seven feet to the lunar surface with a resounding thud. Harden quickly checked to make sure that Mitchell had punched the

Engine Stop push button. A yellow and black guard still covered the switch. He looked up at Mitchell, his face full of disbelief.

"I didn't do it." Mitchell shrugged. "It shut off all by itself."

CHAPTER 34

Daedalus Crater

THE LUNAR MODULE CAST A long shadow across the vast basin of Daedalus. *Intruder's* metallic face and golden foil skin suddenly became a shimmering beacon in the bleak lunar landscape. Inside the LM, Harden and Mitchell fought back the pounding adrenaline as they quickly reconfigured their spacecraft for its new role as lunar outpost.

"Engine Arm – OFF. Descent Engine Command Override – OFF."

"They're off," Mitchell observed as he activated the controls.

"Master Arm – ON. Descent Vent – FIRE."

"Copy." Mitchell flipped a switch and again armed the spacecraft's numerous explosive devices. Another switch fired several pyrotechnic charges. Supercritical helium vented from the descent stage fuel tanks. One less thing to blow up, Mitchell thought, as he disarmed the system. "Master Arm – SAFE."

"Okay, now keep your eyes peeled." Harden's heart was racing. Without telemetry for the flight controllers back on Johnston to monitor, he knew the stay/no-stay decision was his alone to make. He tried to take it all in at once, every needle on every dial of every gauge. As if the instrument panel were some technological Rorschach test, he studied it carefully, searching for clarity. He knew they had to stay, but how could he ignore a glaring abort indication? After a long minute, Harden finally exhaled, "Looks like we're stay."

Mitchell's eyes had already wandered to the exotic panorama on display beyond his triangular viewport. Transfixed by the unearthly landscape, Harden's words were slow to register. "Huh?"

"Jesus, Mitch! Couldn't you have set her down a little sooner? Next time—"

Mitchell was still unable to process the words. "What was that about next time?"

"Forget it. Let's clean this thing up. Can you reach the landing radar circuit breaker?"

"Uh...yeah...okay," Mitchell mumbled as he fought to bring his breathing under control. His hand reached for the circuit breaker even as his mind grappled with the stunning reality—he would soon be walking on surface of the moon.

Johnston Island

Sam Freer tapped a pencil on his console as he stared at the blank telemetry blocks on the computer screen. He checked the ground elapsed time on the mission clock against the predicted acquisition of signal for Jeff Burns in the command module. The wait was agonizing. It had been the longest forty minutes of his life. More than enough time to consider every possible failure that could undo the complex man-machine symbiosis of *Intruder* during the long fall to the lunar surface.

Freer peeled the headset away from his aching head and hung it on the hook next to his chair. He closed his tired eyes and gently massaged the bridge of his nose under the black-rimmed reading glasses. He remembered telling Jack Harden to trust him, to

303

have faith in the technology that would take them to the moon, the proven technology of Apollo. Now it was Freer who suddenly needed to take his own advice. He replayed the last month in his head: the mission plan, the training, preparation of the spacecraft. What if he had missed something—something that could make the difference between success and failure? Life and death? The speaker on his desk suddenly crackled to life.

"Johnston, *Phantom*," Burns radioed. "The *Intruder* has landed! I say again, the *Intruder* has landed!"

Lunar Surface

Mitchell stared at the oxygen gauge. "Blaze, you're not going to like this. Our little cabin leak? Not so little anymore."

Harden backed away from the alignment telescope when he heard the tone of his friend's voice. "How bad is it?"

Mitchell cycled a selector knob through several positions so Harden could see for himself. "Damn, it looks like we're only going to get one shot at this."

Mitchell reached for the ECS reference book. "I'll get the charts out and try to get a rough idea of where we stand on consumables."

"Negative. Not enough time. We need to get into the PLSSs as soon as possible. Preferably before the descent stage oxygen tanks empty." Once they were breathing from their portable life support systems, the *plisses*, Harden could secure the LM's oxygen tanks and save the ascent stage consumables for when they were needed most, after the EVA. "We're dead men walking if we can't save enough Oh-two for the rendezvous."

Harden and Mitchell hastily prepared to depressurize

the lunar module, managing to race through the hour-long checklist in less than fifteen minutes.

"I'm just about through here," Harden finally said. "You happy with your part of the checklist?"

"Yep, pretty sure."

Harden frowned. "I said we're only going to get one shot at this."

"The ECS panel is now configured for egress, *sir*," Mitchell said while tossing a choppy salute at the dubious commander.

"Okay, I get it," Harden said, and then motioned to the ascent stage engine cover, a readymade circular tabletop in the center of the small cabin. "You first."

Mitchell unstowed his extravehicular boots from a compartment in the aft cabin and sat down on the engine cover. He ran his fingers across the ribbed soles and imagined the imprint they would make in the lunar soil.

"Come on, man. Get those things on. We gotta keep moving."

Mitchell finally managed to get the boots on after a bit of a struggle and then laced them up over the pressure garment boots that would keep his suit pressurized during the upcoming EVA.

"Now stand up, and let's get this mother on." Harden lifted the bulky life support system up to Mitchell's shoulders and clipped it to his PLSS harness. Shaped like a giant white box of cigarettes, the PLSS weighed in at a hefty eighty pounds on Earth, but Mitchell hardly noticed its thirteen pounds in the weak lunar gravity.

With the PLSS secured, Harden assisted Mitchell with the numerous connections: oxygen hoses, an electrical umbilical, and water lines for his liquid cooling garment. He separated the jungle of hoses by their brightly colored anodized connectors and hooked them to Mitchell's pressure garment—blue-to-blue and red-to-red. While Harden finished assembling the complex space suit, Mitchell removed his glass helmet and fitted it with the protective extravehicular cover. He held up the bulky unit and stared into the empty faceplate. He hesitated for a moment when he saw his distorted reflection in the gold visor, hoping they hadn't missed anything important in their haste. He then lifted the EV helmet to his head and twisted it into position until it successfully mated with the suit collar. He slid the locking ring until he felt it latch with a click. He then repeated the procedure for the gloves, and his Apollo Extravehicular Mobility Unit, the EMU, was complete.

Harden followed the same procedure. Once both suits were checked and pressurized, he gingerly rotated the lunar module's oxygen flow knob to the OFF position. Mitchell carefully monitored the pressure gauge on his wrist cuff for any decrease in suit pressure.

"I'm going to hit the dump valve now. Start your watch." Harden then dropped awkwardly to one knee. Careful not to bang into any of the controls they would need to fly the LM later, he crouched down beneath the instrument panel and rotated a lever arm in the forward hatch. When the embedded pressure relief valve finally unseated, the leaky *Intruder* vented the last of its precious oxygen with a silent hiss.

"Here goes nothing," Harden said, and with a stiff tug broke the hatch seal.

Mitchell's eyes widened as the small door rotated inward and the eerie glow of lunar twilight spilled out onto the floor of the LM. He didn't even realize he was holding his breath until he noticed the cabin pressure gauge plunge to zero. He finally took in a gulp of cool, moist air from the PLSS, checked his cuff gauge again, and reminded himself to continue breathing. Like watching a silent movie in an empty room, the only sounds inside his helmet were the whir of a circulating fan, and his own ragged respiration.

Harden shuffled around on his knees until his boots faced the small porch on the chin of the lunar module's ascent stage. All movement proved clumsy in the weak lunar gravity. Standing in place with a depressurized suit was one thing. But maneuvering the pressurized EMU underneath the LM's instrument panel and through the small hatch would require more finesse than he had expected. The PLSS seemed to bounce off of everything except the ceiling as Harden tried to thread himself backward through the two-foot-square opening.

"Looks like you're clear now," Mitchell said.

Harden continued to inch backward until he reached the edge of the porch. He gripped the handrails and slid his right knee free of the ramp-like platform. He slowly rotated his body upright and fished for the top rung with his right boot. His left leg followed, and he carefully stood up on the top rung of the ladder.

Harden knew how high he was and that any misstep would be disastrous, but there was no time for practice. He flexed his legs gently at the knees, took in a deep breath, and sprang himself clear from the firm foothold. But his aim was perfect, and both feet landed squarely on the next rung. He continued with the hopping technique until he reached the bottom rung. Without pause, he sprang up one last time and fell three long feet to the lunar surface.

"I'm on the footpad," Harden said, and then drove his left boot into the regolith. Dust shot in all directions before quickly disappearing into the startling clarity of the airless void. "Well, what are you waiting for?"

"I guess I was waiting for you to say something."

"We don't have time for big speeches. Hurry up and get your ass down here."

"That's good enough for me!"

On the surface, Harden was struck by the stark beauty of the landscape surrounding him. He surveyed the anti-oasis with an eye toward the upcoming traverse. The rugged expanse of rock and regolith in the middle of the vast ocean of space was utterly incapable of sustaining any form of life. He glanced down to his RCU, the small remote control unit on the front of his pressure suit. All indicators were in the green. But that he knew, wouldn't last forever. He looked back up to the LM and pushed away the thought. Unless they returned to this remote ecosystem soon, his and Mitchell's lives would ultimately be measured by the needles on the gauges of his RCU.

CHAPTER 35

Lunar Surface

A LONE IN THE LUNAR MODULE, Mitchell began threading himself through the small hatch. He shuffled backward onto the porch and was carefully searching for the top rung of the ladder when he heard Harden's voice enter his helmet. "Hey, Mitch, don't forget about the D-ring."

Damn. Mitchell's mind was racing. He had almost forgotten to release the rover. *Calm down.* He took a deep breath and reached for the D-shaped release handle mounted on the right edge of the aluminum porch. Without the Lunar Roving Vehicle, the LRV, their chances of finding the Chang'e in time were virtually nil. And even if they could find it without employing the rover, Mitchell knew that they would never make it back to the life-sustaining lunar module without it. "I've got the release. Say when."

"Stand by," Harden said as he tore the crinkled gold foil from the side of Quad 1, the five-foot-square compartment immediately to the right of the descent stage's forward landing strut. Beneath the foil, he retrieved two long flat strands of flexible Mylar tape that had been Velcroed to the lower framework of the compact lunar rover. "Okay, go ahead."

Mitchell tugged on the handle. With an inaudible click, an ingenious mechanism of levers and rods sprang into action. The upper frame of the rover then rotated neatly away from its storage compartment and laid taught against the release cable.

"Now get down here and give me a hand."

Mitchell's boots landed firmly on each rung as he hopped down the ladder. When he finally stepped clear of the footpad, he spun around to get his first ground level look at the barren landscape. The view was many things, but seemed to have been summed up quite well some forty years ago by the previous "last man" to walk on the moon. The view was truly "out of this world."

Mitchell would've traded anything for just a few more seconds to savor the experience, but Harden was already working hard to extricate the rover from its descent stage garage, and there was no time to spare. He snatched the limp end of the deployment cable from the rover's frame and pulled it taught.

"Here it comes," Harden announced as he pulled the Mylar tape from the double-braked release reel.

Mitchell smiled inwardly as he tugged on the cable and backed slowly away from the base of the LM. The engineer in him couldn't help but appreciate the beautiful complexity of the operation as the rover's chassis unfolded from the lunar module like a drawbridge over a waterless moat.

Finally free from the confines of the LM, the aft section of the rover sprang open from its stowage position and snapped firmly into place, instantly increasing the vehicle's length by three feet. The rear wheels simultaneously unfolded and swung into position, bouncing several times against the tethers that had secured them during the transit.

"There. We're halfway home," Mitchell said.

The moon buggy continued to rotate slowly away from the LM until the wire mesh of the rear wheels skidded lightly onto the regolith. Then with a stiff tug on the cable, the front suspension unfolded and snapped into position. Harden continued the process with the second tape until all four wheels came to rest on the surface. Mitchell then pulled two ball-lock pins to release the deployment cables and announced, "The rover's free."

"Great. Now get the HED from Quad 2 while I fire this thing up."

As Mitchell embarked on his first lunar foray, Harden set about preparing the rover for lunar operations. He lifted each of the orange fenders into position and carefully pinned them in place. Next he raised the seat backs and unfolded the footrests, toeholds, and handholds. Even the instrument panel and steering controls needed to be erected from their stowage positions. Nearly everything on the LRV had a pin and a "Remove Before Flight" lanyard attached to it. When Harden finished, the area surrounding the rover was littered with shards of shiny gold foil and more than a dozen ribbon-like red flags—the detritus of any successful lunar mission.

Around the side of the towering LM, Mitchell wrestled to free the HED from its stowage receptacle. Affixed to the side of the descent stage on Quad 2, the hypergolic explosive device was the quickest and safest solution that Sam Freer could conceive of when tasked to create a deep space explosive device on such short notice.

The HED consisted entirely of spare parts from already well-understood LM systems. Casks originally used to carry fuel for Apollo's Radioisotope Thermal Generator power supply were filled with the same fuels that burned in the LM's main propulsion system—a mixture of unsymmetrical dimethyl-hydrazine and nitrogen tetroxide. This Molotov cocktail, Freer had promised, was perfectly suited for a "safe" explosion in the vacuum of deep space. With spare valves and solenoids from the LM's reaction control system coupled to a simple VHF receiver, the ingenious device could be remotely activated from a range of up to two miles.

"How's it coming, Mitch?" Harden asked his friend through the radio link. "You need a hand back there?"

"I'm on the last latch now," Mitchell replied with a labored grunt. He thought he was in the best shape of his life, but he had obviously underestimated the effort required to work against the pressurized suit for several minutes with his hands above his head. When the package was finally free from the side of the LM, he hefted it down to chest level and began a quick shuffle back to the rover.

"Whoa, take it easy with that thing. If you trip and fall you'll end up blowing us both to smithereens." Harden then took the device from Mitchell and carefully slid the package onto two mounting poles behind the rover's seats. After securing it to the framework with a spring-loaded locking lever, he announced, "Let's roll."

Harden shuffled to the driver's seat and lifted his right boot up to the floorboard. He couldn't help but notice that his space suit was already beginning to look like that of a dirty coal miner from the knees down. The last thing he had time to worry about now though was suit contamination. He grabbed a handhold and hoisted himself onto the tube-framed seat's nylon webbing. "Where are you going, Mitch? Get in."

"Not until I back us away from the LM," Mitchell said, and strode to the front of the rover. "I had a bad experience once with a finicky shifter. Drove straight through the back of my old man's garage. The LM wouldn't be much use to us if you started the rover up in gear and accidentally drove into one of the landing struts. It'd be kinda hard to get back into orbit with the *Intruder* lying on its side."

"I'd take that advice if I were you," Burns interrupted from his high perch.

"Good call, Pipper." Harden smiled, comforted by the voice that had been absent from the comm loop for the past hour. "Let me release the parking brake," he said, and then ratcheted the T-handled controller inboard. Mitchell, still huffing in his bulky suit, bent over the front of the rover and gave it a firm shove.

"I hate to break this to you guys," Burns announced on the comm circuit, "but Sam passes new numbers on your Oh-two leak. Advise when ready to copy."

"Just give me the *Reader's Digest* version," Harden said as the rover rolled safely away from the LM.

"Expect no more than three hours of life support in the LM on power up." Burns paused, but there was no reply. "That ties our hands to a direct rendezvous."

"Yeah, well we'll cross that burning bridge when we get to it," Harden said flatly. Most of the rendezvous simulations he had practiced used the more forgiving co-elliptic rendezvous sequence. With the direct rendezvous, he'd get only one chance to rejoin with the command module, and there would be no room for error. Worse yet, he'd get little help from his copilot, who had missed that part of the training when Freer stood-in for Mitchell during the emergency rendezvous procedures training.

When the vehicle came to a stop, Harden set the parking brake again and began the power-up sequence. Mitchell strapped himself into the right seat as the dormant LRV slowly came to life. The radio-luminescent coating on the control panel provided an eerie blue background glow to the numerous switches and dials as Harden reset the four main bus circuit breakers.

As with everything in the Apollo program, Mitchell was amazed by the level of redundancy of such an austere design. Two batteries attached to the front of the rover powered four separate electric motors, one on each wheel. Any or all wheels could be powered by either battery through the appropriate busses. Both front and rear steering was provided for, but the vehicle could operate with either system alone if the other was unserviceable. The navigation system provided multiple means of telling the astronauts where they were. Unfortunately, as Mitchell recalled from the preflight briefing, the primary navigation system required input from mission control to properly align. Luckily, a secondary feature gave the astronauts a simple but effective range and bearing display that, if reset prior to driving off, could be used to guide them back to the stationary LM. He decided that knowing how to get back to the lunar module was infinitely more important than knowing precisely where he was on the moon at any given time.

"Volts and amps are good, temps are in the green," Harden said as he rotated a selector switch. He pushed in four more circuit breakers for the steering and drive-motors, and toggled several switches to connect each motor to the appropriate power supply. He then thumbed a large button on the Nav panel. "There," he said, pointing to the compass display. "Range and bearing reset to zero."

Mitchell looked to the horizon and tried to orient himself in the midst of the enormous crater. "Steer to the left of Mt. Whitney," he said, pointing to the tallest mountain in the nearby cluster.

Harden nodded inside the bulbous helmet, then grabbed the T-handle on the center pedestal and rotated the controller forward. The rover rolled smoothly across the regolith, slowly at first, then faster as Harden increased the force on the stick. When he completed the turn and rolled out on course, Harden glanced back over his left shoulder. The V-shaped tread design of the rover's wire mesh wheels left a wake of chevron-shaped tracks in the loose lunar soil—a clear indication to future explorers that the chariots of Apollo had once again returned to haunt the moon.

CHAPTER 36

Lunar Surface

THE LRV BOUNDED ACROSS THE hummocky lunar terrain. Rippled with hills and littered by the shattered remains of millions of impacts over billions of years, the crater floor was much rougher up close than it had appeared during the descent. As Mitchell bounced against the seat restraint, he realized that no more than three of the rover's wheels were ever on the ground at any one time.

"This sure is one tough machine," Harden said after the left front wheel ricocheted off of an apparently unavoidable moon rock.

"Maybe we should slow it down a little then," Mitchell suggested. The modified rover was actually moving across the lunar terrain at a healthy fifteen kilometers per hour, a full 25 percent faster than the original, he recalled, thanks to improvements made by Freer's team. "It's kinda hard to see some of the smaller rocks until it's too late. My eyes keep playing tricks on me. I see what looks like a small rock up ahead and then it turns out to be the size of a house by the time we get there."

"It's the lack of depth perception. There's only one thing out here of known size to reference."

"Yeah, I guess you're right." Mitchell then turned

around to see if the LM would be useful for comparison. "Holy shit, it's gone!"

Harden slammed the T-handle against the aft stop and cranked the control stick hard to the left. All four wheels locked up, but gained little traction in the loose lunar silt. The rover spun in a circle before skidding backwards to a stop. Harden's eyes followed the shadowed tracks all the way back to the edge of the lunar horizon.

The LM was gone.

"Shit, Mitch!" Harden shouted when he finally realized what had happened. "The LM's not gone, man. It's just over the horizon already."

Harden pointed to the luminescent blue window that displayed the range and bearing to the lunar module. "We've already traveled over five kilometers. This isn't Earth, man. The horizon just isn't that far away on this godforsaken rock."

"I don't remember getting briefed on that," Mitchell mumbled, apparently embarrassed by the oversight. "That'll make it real easy to get lost out here."

"No shit. It's also going to make finding this Chinese battle station more than a little challenging, too. But we gotta keep moving. From Pipper's ballpark math, we could still be an hour away at fifteen kilometers per hour." Harden put the rover into reverse and completed a crisp three point turn before slowly advancing the throttle to full speed again.

As the rover plowed on through the late lunar evening, Harden noticed the shadows growing longer on even the smallest rocks. Barely a few degrees above the local horizon now, the sun's rays drew dangerously close to being eclipsed by the mountainous western rim of the crater. It would then be fourteen long Earth days before sunlight would again spill into the isolated, frozen hell of Daedalus.

Harden cursed his luck as he drove. Ninety percent of Daedalus was relatively flat real estate, yet the only major obstacle in the enormous crater just happened to lie between the *Intruder* and the Chang'e. And the detour around the mountain range was eating into any spare time they might have had. His arm flopped at the shoulder as he tried to read the digital display on the Omega Speedmaster strapped to his left cuff. Time was everything now. The LRV's lifespan was measured in Amp-hours. The EMU's lifespan, and by extension his and Mitchell's lifespan, was measured in hours. And to the best of Harden's knowledge, the time remaining until a potential nuclear weapons launch against the United States was measured in hours—and time was running out for all three.

Traveling to the northwest for forty-five minutes at top speed, the rover was finally closing in on the far western edge of the imposing massif. "I was starting to think we would never get here," Mitchell said. "All right, let's cut the corner. Come right about thirty degrees and I'll see if I can make out any of the landmarks that I saw during the descent. It's going to be a lot tougher than I thought, though. Everything looks so different from down here."

"That's not what I wanted to hear, Mitch."

As the rover forged ahead into uncharted territory, Mitchell was beginning to think that finding those landmarks might be too tall an order. "It feels like we're on a treadmill." He gestured at several landmarks. "Except for those peaks and the crater rim, everything looks the same. Big rocks...little rocks. Big craters... little craters. And regolith as far as the eye can see. I don't think I'm going to be able to recognize anything unless we get to a higher vantage point."

"Keep looking," Harden said, and then glanced down at the battery temperature gauge.

"Whoa!" Mitchell yelled, and instinctively grabbed the handholds beside his seat as the rover sailed over the edge of a rimless crater as wide as a football field. He braced for the impending impact, but the crater was shallow—having been filled in over the ages with ejecta from innumerable impacts—and the rover's suspension and wire-mesh wheels handled the collision like a Baja racer. Still, having bounced to a landing more than thirty feet beyond the crater rim, Mitchell was shocked when the rover didn't slow down. He grimaced when he saw the speedometer peg the scale. The rover was suddenly barreling downhill toward the belly of the crater at more than twenty kilometers per hour.

"What are you doing?" Mitchell screamed.

"There's only one way out of this thing now. And that's the same way we got in. Hold on!" Harden leaned forward in the straps and pushed the throttle hard against the stop. The rover quickly reached the bottom of the crater and raced uphill toward the far rim.

"Are you sure?" Mitchell asked incredulously.

Harden didn't have time for an answer. The lithe rover shot from the shallow depression like a cosmic cannonball. Then, just as the rover's trajectory crested above the lunar surface, Mitchell saw a sparkle in the distance. Several chaotic bounces later, the moon buggy settled back down to its normal rhythm—no more than three wheels on the surface at any one time.

"Give me the controls," Mitchell demanded, and pushed Harden's hand clear of the control stick.

"Hey, Mitch. I'm sorry. Trust me, it was the only way out of that thing. If we didn't keep our momentum going, we'd have been stuck in there forever."

"No, you're right. I just don't want to loose this bearing. At the top of our trajectory I saw a flash over the horizon."

Harden turned and stared at Mitchell. "It's gotta be the Chang'e!"

Xi'an Satellite Monitor and Control Center

The PLA controller switched on the Chang'e 5's remote sensing cameras for a routine operational check. The first time the cameras were activated was when Colonel Yang had used them to soft land the Chang'e in Daedalus more than a month ago. Since then, the cameras had been activated twice as a means of visually verifying each weapons launch. The results had been spectacular. Images beamed back to the control room provided a huge boost to morale for the men who had worked on the program. Tangible results of a job well done. But no one was prepared for what the cameras were about to reveal this time. Almost no one.

Lunar Surface

Dangerous features on the lunar surface were easy to see from certain altitudes and sun angle combinations. But from the low grazing angle of the rover, the chances of spotting a crater before it was too late depended on the prominence of the crater rim. Mitchell, sensitive to this dangerous phenomenon after their recent excursion, leaned the T-handle controller gently to the right and deftly maneuvered around what turned out to be a deep and unforgiving crater.

Harden again checked the health of their lunar transport. The reading on both batteries was just above the mid-range level on the gauge. He was fairly sure they could lengthen the batteries' life spans if they were able to return to the LM at a slower speed. But that would depend on the amount of life support remaining in the PLSSs after the explosive device had been set. And until their mission was accomplished, he knew they would have to put their own survival on the back burner.

"There it is," Mitchell shouted when he saw the first glint on the horizon.

Harden saw it too. As they barreled across the rugged terrain, the Chang'e 5—standing guard over Deadalus like a glimmering lunar sentinel—rose ominously out of the regolith. "I wonder if they know we're here."

Xi'an Satellite Monitor and Control Center

In the front of the control room, four images flashed on the large screen in quick succession. Divided into quadrants, one camera pointed in each of the four major sub-cardinal directions. Three of the cameras relayed images of the immense lunar starkness. The feed from the fourth camera, however, appeared to capture a curious phenomenon. The eerie image from the Chang'e's southwest quadrant electrified everyone in the quiet control room.

"Pan down and zoom in on camera 3," the PLA colonel ordered.

As the operator complied, the colonel struggled for an explanation to what he saw. Waves of regolith were being pushed high into the airless sky as if by some unseen force. He then saw several quick flashes from what appeared to be a metallic object. Even though he had been told to expect this, he still couldn't believe it was happening. He had also been told what to do next if this situation arose.

He gave the order without delay.

The young corporal's hands trembled, fingers stumbling across the keys as he input the final command sequence. Most of the fifteen remaining conventional weapons had been targeted against select

American military satellites occupying geosynchronous orbits above Eastern Asia. The remaining few would take out key Western spy satellites in lower orbits. But it was the special ordnance targets that had made the corporal wince as he input the final command. The remaining five nuclear payloads were all targeted for atmospheric detonation above the continental United States.

Lunar Surface

Mitchell eased back on the T-handle and slowed the rover to just under ten kilometers per hour. With their objective in sight, the last thing he wanted was to damage the only transportation capable of getting them back to the *Intruder* alive. And the ride was much smoother, he noted, at the slower speed.

Harden unbuckled his seat belt to prepare for a quick exit. Mitchell squinted as he struggled to make sense of the strange illusion. He blinked twice, straining to bring the image into focus.

"Is that smoke?"

"No, not smoke," Harden said, and brushed Mitchell's hand from the rover's control stick. "They're purging the launch tubes with nitrogen. Dammit!"

Harden glanced at his watch again. *So much for intelligence.* His mind raced through the options. They weren't going to have enough time to set the HED. And even if they did, they would never be able to get outside of the blast radius in time to activate it before the Chang'e launched its deadly payload. Harden remembered Mitchell's story about the finicky shifter. He rammed the throttle forward and the LRV leapt back to full speed.

"Blaze, wait! There's gotta be another way. I could throw the HED under the Chang'e and we—"

"Negative! There's only one way to take out the launch platform now. I'm going to aim for the right leg."

As the distance closed, the Chang'e continued to purge successive pairs of opposing launch tubes. The image was chilling. As he tweaked the hand controller and refined his bearing, Harden tried to ignore the ghastly image of a giant lunar dragon exhaling nitrogen through nostrils on both sides of its golden faceted face. He focused instead on drawing a perfect bead on the right landing strut. When the impact was imminent, he leaned inboard and sought cover behind the rover's control console.

"Hold on!"

The front of the rover crashed into landing strut just above the footpad. Still attached to the base of the strut, the saucer-shaped landing pad rose up like a giant claw beneath the rover's chassis. The tubular leg gave way to the crippling side forces and crumpled at the knee. But before being completely severed, the Chang'e's footpad flipped the lithe rover like a coin tossed into the weak gravitational field. Harden was thrown clear and tumbled across the hostile terrain. Still belted into the wildly spinning machine, Mitchell rode the vehicle through a series of corkscrews before it smashed to the ground and slid to a stop on top of him.

The Chang'e listed precariously in the direction of the sheared landing gear before finally succumbing to the instability of its remaining three legs and toppled over, crashing slowly into the lunar regolith.

But deep inside the launch platform, computers continued to send commands to the weapon sequencers.

Half of the conventional launch tubes were now pointed toward the center of the moon; the remaining ones aimed vertically into deep space. And the six tubes holding nuclear tipped launch vehicles lay flat on the surface—aimed directly at the astronaut who had come to rest only twenty yards away, the bright white of his space suit covered by a grey, dusty film that camouflaged him against the colorless backdrop.

The conventional weapons' sequencers fired in salvos of two, one on each side of the toppled vehicle. The skyward aiming projectiles belched from the launch tubes on columns of expanding gas. Their solid rocket motors ignited like roman candles, launching them into highly elliptical arcs that would not escape the moon's gravity but instead return to add to the countless craters of the battered far side landscape. The opposing projectiles had no means of escape, trapped in their tubes by the thick lunar crust. When their rocket motors ignited, the Chang'e began to burn, consuming itself from the inside. In less than a minute, the conflagration had heated the casings of the remaining warheads to the critical point of detonation. They cooked off one by one in rapid succession. The powerful explosions sent thousands of tiny tungsten pellets ripping through the shell of the exploding Chang'e like an omni-directional shotgun blast.

Mitchell couldn't see the Chang'e from his sheltered position beneath the upended rover; and without an atmosphere for the concussion to propagate through or sound waves to warn Mitchell of the ensuing cataclysm, the only indication he had of the devastation beyond his pinned position was the bright flashes of rocket motors as they lit against the black lunar sky. The images were clues that he had at least survived the crash. But he had no such hope for the only other person in the universe that mattered to him at the moment. He groped for his friend in the darkness. He knew he had to find Harden, but his battered body refused to cooperate, and he slipped quietly out of consciousness.

CHAPTER 37

Xi'an Satellite Monitor and Control Center

"THE TIME HAS COME TO decommission the Chang'e 4." It was clear to the PLA colonel now that their mission was a failure. But in China there was still one thing worse than a failed mission: a failed mission that became public.

The corporal again followed his orders. He selected the Orbital Maintenance menu and input a delta-v correction that would lead to a decaying orbit for the now useless communications relay. Far above Daedalus, small thrusters on the satellite fired, condemning the Chang'e 4 to premature destruction—and ensuring that the entire Chang'e program would be forever erased from existence.

Lunar Orbit

Burns put his eye back up to the telescope. *Damn.* He cursed himself for not taking a mark when he spotted the Chinese lander the first time. But he never expected that a sun angle change of just a few degrees could make that much of a difference. What else could it be? What else could cause the Chang'e to disappear into the monochrome regolith? If it had been blown to pieces by the HED, there should be a new crater, and a large enough debris field to be seen from his altitude. But the glint he had witnessed on his first flyover was nowhere to be found.

Burns shook his head as he considered the situation. He knew that Harden and Mitchell were already halfway through the nominal lifespan of an Apollo EMU. If they weren't on their way back to the LM by now, they would quickly eat through any safety margin that had been built into the plan. And if they weren't back at the LM on his next orbit, any chance of a second EVA would be out the window. *Shit.* Burns pulled back from the telescope and checked the ground elapsed time. He would soon be in contact with mission control again. And he didn't like what he had to report.

As he backed away from the optics control panel, Burns's blank stare landed on the lunar sample bag that Harden had Velcroed to the bulkhead before sealing the LM tunnel. At the time, it had struck him as odd that Harden would be worried about the number of sample bags he would or wouldn't need on the lunar surface. Far side rock samples would be a nice bonus, but that contingency was such an afterthought that it wasn't even written into their hastily developed flight plan.

Burns finally snatched the bag from the Velcro weave. As he suspected, the bag was not only weightless, it was massless too. But why would Harden go out of his way to move an *empty* bag from the lunar module to the command module before descending to the surface...*unless he never planned on coming back!* Burns tore into the bag as he put it all together. He reached inside and pulled out a small section of checklist pages that had been taped together to form a makeshift envelope. Burns turned the lightweight pages over and saw a message penciled on the other side. He knew instantly that it was meant for him to read. In Harden's handwriting, the message read: You'll know what to do with this when the time comes.

Lunar Surface

Mitchell's eyes opened slowly. He had no idea how long he had been unconscious; he lay motionless, struggling to recall the sequence of events that had brought him here. The view through his golden helmet visor was ethereal. The sky was incomprehensibly black, yet he could hardly find an empty piece of space in it. It was as if every star was connected to another, the adjacent space around the brightest stars filled with the light of dimmer stars impossible to see through the filter of Earth's atmosphere. Then the light slowly began to fill the cracks in his memory. And the final images came flooding back in painful detail, sending a rush of adrenaline coursing through his body.

Trapped beneath the mass of the crumpled rover, Mitchell struggled to lift his head, but the effort was in vain. He clawed frantically at the seat restraint until the latch finally released its firm grip and he slumped to the lunar surface. Then, as blood returned to his lower extremities, an intense wave of pain followed. *Move.* Mitchell grabbed the rover's square framework and grunted against the invisible knife in his side. Even in the weak lunar gravity, the weighty LRV seemed impossibly heavy. But with one final labored wail he was able to lift the rover from his chest and slide his legs clear of the twisted metal.

Mitchell's breathing grew shallow as he tried to process the impossible scenario. He knew he had to get moving. He tried to raise himself to a sitting position, but the pain was unbearable. It took several more failed attempts before he understood the problem. He lacked the strength to sit up with the bulky PLSS backpack strapped to his back—yet it was impossible to remove. It was also impossible to comprehend how after coming this far, he might actually die here in this unimaginable vacuum. His eyes welled up as he considered how it would all end.

An answer finally crashed through the fear. As a mechanical engineer, Mitchell understood his problem was clearly one of leverage. He had to get off of his back before he could get back on his feet. An idea formed quickly in his head. He knew it would be painful, but so would dying from oxygen starvation.

He began the maneuver by rocking his body side to side several times before letting go a powerful scissors kick and violently twisting his torso in the opposite direction. Pain tore through his battered body, but the inertia proved to be just enough to flip Mitchell over onto his chest. His upper body suddenly became useful again, and he was finally able to use his arms to reach the push up position. He then kicked his legs to bring his knees under his center of mass and stumbled clumsily to his feet.

Still dizzy from the disorienting maneuver, Mitchell eyed the overturned rover for clues. His breathing became even more ragged as he surveyed the damage. He could see that the front steering was severed, its left wheel akimbo. But it would be impossible to assess the damage to the most delicate part of the rover—the control panel—unless he could right the upended vehicle. He could feel his broken ribs grind together as he bent down and grabbed the edge of the square frame. Mitchell screamed into the darkness as he lifted the rover and flipped it back over onto its wire mesh wheels. When the vehicle finally came to rest, Mitchell was aghast. The rover's center console was crushed, the left seat-back a mangled mess of anodized tubing. *That's where Blaze was sitting at impact!*

Mitchell quickly examined the perimeter of the crash site. He saw the hulk of the crippled Chang'e, its crumpled tanks still out-gassing into the lunar vacuum. But Harden was nowhere to be found. He widened his search pattern. He eventually spotted the HED amid some debris in the distance. Sam's unbelievable claim was true—it was a "safe" bomb after all. It must have been torn from the LRV when it impacted the Chang'e, but the ingenious device was still intact. Mitchell kept searching. Finally, some fifty feet beyond the twisted wreckage, he spotted the dirty ball of a spacesuit lying motionless on the ground. He called out through the comm link as he bounded over to Harden, but there was no reply. He knelt down next to his friend and gently rolled him onto his side. Mitchell's worst fears were allayed when he saw that the fragile glass faceplate was still intact. But Harden's eyes were closed; his body limp inside the rigid suit.

Mitchell screamed into his mike as he shook Harden violently, but there was still no response. Through sixteen layers of suit material, he couldn't tell whether the man in his arms was alive or dead. He closed his eyes and screamed again. The situation was hopeless. The rover was smashed—and his friend was most likely dead. He would die soon, too. Only his death would be an agonizing asphyxiation as he choked for oxygen like a helpless fish on the beach.

"My back..."

Mitchell opened his eyes when he heard the strange words. "Blaze? Thank God you're alive!"

"I don't know for how long, though," Harden moaned. "I think my back is broken again."

"Shit, we've gotta get you back to the LM." Mitchell quickly assessed the remote control unit on the front of Harden's spacesuit. The RCU's oxygen gauge read one-quarter. Mitchell checked his own tank. His was still over half full.

"How bad is it?"

"500 psi!" Mitchell's heart pounded. His friend was in real trouble. Harden's suit was leaking and impossible to patch. If he didn't get him back to the LM soon, the suit would decompress, and Harden would suffer the most horrible death he could imagine. "You must have picked up some shrapnel when the warheads exploded."

"That makes it easier on both of us," Harden mumbled. His head bobbed lazily on his shoulders as he tried to find Mitchell's face. "You've got to leave me. Get back to the LM before it's too late."

Mitchell ignored the feeble plea. "I'm not going anywhere without you."

"Mitch...it's all right," Harden said as his eyes finally found Mitchell's face. "I'm gonna die here...no matter what. Even if I could get back to the LM...I'll never make it up the ladder."

"Fuuuck!" Mitchell screamed inside his helmet as Harden lost consciousness again. His fear was spiraling out of control. Inside his lonely cocoon, Mitchell thought about giving up. He thought about Harden's plea. Was there really any sense for both of them to die here? But could he even make it back into orbit on his own? And if he did, could he live with himself knowing he let his friend die like this? Mitchell pushed back the fear. He knew he had to keep moving. And the rover was his only chance.

He laid Harden down gently on the rocky surface and shuffled back to the rover. He sat in the twisted driver's seat and pulled the controller into reverse. He was shocked when the vehicle suddenly lurched backward. It was his first ray of hope since the crash.

But he would have to fix the dragging left front wheel if they were to have any chance of reaching the LM before the rover's batteries expired. Freer's brief description of the rover's dual steering systems flooded back into Mitchell's head. If he could lock the two front wheels in place, it might be possible to steer with the rear wheels. The rover would operate more like a forklift than a car, but anything was preferable to the alternative.

Mitchell carefully centered the front wheels and pulled the two locking levers. He then climbed back aboard the rover and backed it up next to Harden. As he struggled to lift Harden's considerable mass, he felt the jagged edges of broken ribs stabbing against his side. He tried not to think about how the blood would affect the sterile environment of his pressure suit if a rib had poked through his skin; or worse yet, if there was internal bleeding. There would be nothing he could do about it for the next four days anyway.

Harden stirred again as Mitchell dragged him across the regolith. Staring into the void, Harden mumbled, "I told you to leave me...get the hell out of here...you're wasting time."

Mitchell knew Harden was right about one thing. Of all the unknowns that could have killed them so far on this mission, time was now their biggest enemy. And Harden's time was running on a different clock than his. "Stay alive, you son-of-a-bitch!"

"Mitch...it's all right...you have a family. I had my chance..." Harden squeezed his eyes tight as he thought about the future. "Tell Stacy..."

"Tell her *what?*" Mitchell looked down when he got no answer. "Blaze?!" Harden was out again. *Shit!* A red flag labeled H2O suddenly popped into view on Harden's remote control unit. The suit was failing. Not only was it leaking oxygen, but the suit was no longer circulating the water necessary to remove excess heat from his body. If his liquid cooling garment failed, even if Harden didn't die from asphyxiation, his body would cook itself from the inside out. Mitchell's body went rigid when the reality finally sunk in. Jack Harden was going to die.

CHAPTER 38

Lunar Orbit

"PHANTOM, JOHNSTON, AOS. OVER."

"Johnston, you're weak and barely readable."

"That's what we expected, Jeff," Cernan replied as he looked at the graphic on the computer screen next to his console. The only remaining DSN antenna dish in Canberra, Australia, was about to go below the horizon and sever all communication. But in the minutes before that happened the tenuous S-Band radio signal would have twice as much atmospheric attenuation as it did when the moon was directly overhead. "Have you heard from the crew yet?"

"Negative."

"Anything visual to report?"

"Negative."

Even with the poor connection, Cernan had no trouble inferring Burns's concern from his clipped responses. "Well, they've still got another orbit to work with."

"That's not very comforting, Johnston," Burns revealed.

"It has to be, my friend," Cernan insisted. "That's all we have at the moment."

Cernan then caught a glimpse of Freer out of the corner of his eye. Sam was making an exaggerated hurry-up gesture with his hands. Cernan looked at the mission clock again and then picked up the data card from his console. "In the meantime, though, we have some numbers to pass up to you before we lose the Canberra antenna."

"What numbers, Johnston?"

"We have your TEI PAD."

"TEI? That sounds a little premature, Gene," Burns said, obviously displeased with the suggestion. "If I remember right, Transearth Injection comes *after* the rendezvous."

Freer jumped on the line when he sensed the exchange heading in the wrong direction. "Jeff, I know we never addressed this contingency directly, but we all knew it was there. I just don't think we can avoid it anymore. Look, we're working on finding a suitable relay station for the S-Band signal, but until then we've only got the one antenna. Once Canberra sets, we won't be able to pass these numbers to you for another twelve hours. And we just don't think it's a good idea for you to hang on for six additional orbits if there's no chance of a rescue. Besides, without your telemetry our numbers for TEI get worse with each successive orbit. Then we risk not getting you back either."

Burns put his face up to the main hatch window. The crescent Earth hung in the emptiness of space like a shattered blue marble against a curtain of black velvet. Sam was right. There had been no reason to address the issue during training. The underlying assumptions were well understood. But there was no way to avoid it now. Burns turned from the window and floated into the lower equipment bay. He snatched the lunar sample bag from its Velcro mooring and retrieved Harden's makeshift envelope. He peeled the checklist pages apart and held it upside down as if something might fall out. When he remembered that things don't "fall" in zero-g, he stuck his hand down in the envelope and retrieved the contents.

Inside was a clean white envelope sealed with a NASA gold seal. He turned it over and read the writing on the front side. *Why would Blaze leave behind an envelope addressed to himself?* It took a minute to sink in, but Burns's eyes went wide when he read the name again. The letter was addressed to John Blaise Harden, Jr.

Burns was floored by the revelation. Why hadn't he told anyone? But as he eyed the pristine white envelope in his hand, Burns was sure now that he understood the intent of Harden's earlier request. For his entire life, Jeff had wished that *his* father could have done the same thing for him—find some way to reach across time and offer him insight into exactly what it was that Robert Burns had died for.

Burns finally keyed the mike and said, "Johnston, *Intruder*, I'm standing by for the TEI PAD."

Lunar Surface

Weaving like a drunk driver in the wounded rover, Mitchell cursed the rugged terrain. He cursed the fact that he was still alive, and that Harden was going to die here—alone. But Harden was right...*wasn't he?* Did it make any sense to haul a dying man all the way back to the LM just to leave him there at the ladder and blast into orbit without him? Mitchell looked at the empty seat next to him. His brain ached with indecision. Logic was telling him one thing, but the knot deep in his stomach was telling him something different.

Mitchell shook his head inside the bulbous helmet. He wanted to scream, but the silence was deafening enough. Instead, he tried to focus on survival; he was suddenly operating in what Everest explorers referred to as the "death zone." Not only was his body running out of the oxygen that it needed to survive, he feared that his mind was succumbing to the most dangerous threat of such extreme environments—impaired judgment.

Mitchell tried again to clear his mind. He scanned the remains of rover's instrument panel for some kind of positive reinforcement. Most of the indicators had been smashed in the collision. The luminescent blue range and bearing display on the backup navigation system was shattered and useless. Luckily, the rover's shadowed tracks were still visible in the regolith as a guide back to the Intruder. And the battery gauges still functioned. But when he compared the power drain on the batteries at his current speed against the charge remaining, it was clear that he would have to slow down—or finish the journey on foot. He slowly eased back on the throttle and took stock of his own life support system.

He studied the RCU on the front of his suit and then glanced at his watch. Without knowing the exact range to the LM, getting an accurate hack on his suit's lifespan required a bit of Kentucky windage. His best guess was that he could still make it back to the Intruder on foot even if the rover died before he got there. But his analysis revealed another, more terrifying revelation. He had reached the point of no return. If he continued on his current course and speed, he may make it back to the Intruder alive—but Harden would be forever interred on the far side of the moon.

Mitchell slammed the throttle against the aft stop. The rover's brakes locked up and the vehicle skidded to a stop. No matter how hard he tried, he couldn't clear his mind of one single overriding thought. He was finally convinced, beyond any hint of a doubt. Harden would never have given up on him. Not as long as there was breath in his lungs. *There has to be another solution.*

Lunar Orbit

Burns stared blindly at the data card in his hand. The numbers on the TEI PAD blurred together as he considered his dilemma. The Canberra antenna had gone below the horizon; he would be cut off from communication with Johnston Island for the next twelve hours. And he hadn't heard anything from his friends since they left the lunar module. They could have fallen victim to any of a thousand tragedies. And if something had gone wrong, chances are he would never know what happened—no one would.

He stowed the checklist and returned his gaze to the main hatch window. His first glimpse of the moon up close had filled him with a sense of wonder. Suddenly, the image in his window was full of foreboding. If he didn't hear from Harden or Mitchell on his next orbit, he would be left with only one option: enter the data that Freer had radioed to him, and program the command module computer for Transearth Injection. Then, on the subsequent far side pass, he would have to do the unthinkable—initiate the TEI burn and put the moon in his rear view mirror. At least that's what everyone expected him to do. *Damn!* Approaching things rationally really wasn't his strong suit.

Xi'an Satellite Monitor and Control Center

As the countdown clock reached 03:00:00 hours, the PLA colonel gave the order. "Activate the search mode."

Several keystrokes later, the Chang'e 4, hurtling undetected toward the center of Daedalus crater, began the one subroutine that its programmers thought would never be needed—the one designed to detect and guide the hulking robot satellite to an existence-erasing collision with the Chang'e 5 lunar lander. Seventeen minutes into the scan pattern the corporal was alerted to the presence of a metallic object that exceeded the threshold of the satellite's detection software.

"The radar has picked up a return," the nervous corporal reported.

"Good," the colonel said. "Activate the track."

"Should we run a complete scan of the crater first, colonel?"

"Negative!" He did not need a corporal to tell him what he already knew. A full scan of Daedalus from the Chang'e 4's current altitude would take too long. It wasn't his fault that no one had envisioned the need to sort through multiple targets when the program was written.

Lunar Surface

The drive back to the crash site had given Mitchell just enough time to come up with a new plan. It seemed strange, but things suddenly became clearer when he gave up calculating his own odds of survival, and focused instead on Harden. He had reached his own abyss, and somehow broke through. The hurdles were still just as daunting, and there was no guarantee the plan would work. But he had made up his mind.

He would save them both—or die trying.

The Chang'e was still out-gassing when Mitchell crested the horizon. Looking back on the scene as an outside observer was surreal. Like being trapped in a recurring nightmare, the setting he found himself in was eerily familiar. He could only hope that his short-fused plan would work, and that this time the outcome would be different.

Mitchell parked the rover next to Harden, exited the damaged vehicle and shuffled over to his side. He tried to roust his friend back to life, but Harden was still unresponsive. He examined Harden's RCU and quickly realized that even if his friend was still alive, it wouldn't be for long. Gritting his teeth against the pain in his side, Mitchell hefted Harden up to the rover and was finally able to wedge him into the right seat. He fastened the restraint around Harden's waist and climbed into the driver's seat next to him. He then reached behind Harden and removed a set of hoses from a pouch labeled Backup/Secondary Life Support System. He quickly connected one end of the hoses to his own PLSS and the other to Harden's suit. It was a million-to-one shot, but he had to try. The connection would now allow cooling water from Mitchell's PLSS to circulate through Harden's suit and keep his body from overheating.

But Harden's suit was still leaking oxygen. Mitchell needed a way to keep his friend breathing during the lengthy traverse back to the lunar module. He recalled yet another backup system built into the amazing Apollo design. He reached over and pulled the OPS actuator ring on the side of Harden's RCU. But the oxygen purge system would add only thirty minutes of oxygen to his leaking suit. There was no way they would be able to return to the LM the same way they had come. The circuitous path would take too long. If there was any hope of Mitchell's long-shot gamble paying off, he needed a more direct route. He needed to find a way *through* the mountains instead of *around* them. He recalled Burns's warning about the mountain pass. For the first time in his life, he hoped Jeff Burns was wrong.

CHAPTER 39

Lunar Surface

MITCHELL FORCED HIMSELF TO FOCUS. Everything now hinged on his decision to navigate through the immense unknown before him. And any error would be fatal. The path he had chosen narrowed as the steep walls from two rocky massifs closed in on both sides, creating a saddle that grew steeper as he drove.

And the deeper he penetrated the peaks of Daedalus, the darker his world became. A full third of the sun's sphere had been swallowed by the western rim of the crater when they left the floor of Daedalus. The remaining arc of the sun's limb was now occulted by the steep mountain walls, and only a faint scintillation of light found its way into the steadily deepening chasm.

Mitchell lost all track of time. Minutes passed like hours. Compounding his problem was the fact that the rover continued to move ever slower as the terrain rose higher. He looked again at the control panel as he navigated the precarious path. It was as he had feared. The steep climb was draining the batteries at an alarming rate. Mitchell prayed that he would reach the crest of the saddle before the rover exhausted its power supply and stranded them in the deadly isolation.

Another twenty minutes of his life support had

expired when Mitchell's world went completely dark. He pulled back on the throttle and brought the rover to a short stop in the inky black. It was suicide to continue without being able to see the terrain ahead. But making it back to the LM was impossible in the total darkness. He thought quickly. There was only one way he could continue. He groped for a zipper on the leg of his pressure suit. From the pocket, he removed a battery-powered flashlight and held it high in his left hand. The narrow fan of light penetrated the darkness barely ten feet ahead. The traverse would be slow, but he had to continue.

When the sensation of speed increased for the first time since leaving the crater floor, Mitchell observed the air bubble in the rover's inclinometer. He was elated to see that they were actually heading downhill for the first time in over forty minutes. The rover's batteries were nearly drained, but the reduced electrical load from the drive motors just might be enough to deliver them from the mountainous maze.

When the peaks finally fell away on the south side of the pass, a dim glow began to reappear as sunlight again shafted through the craggy terrain and diffused against the ancient grey rock. Mitchell was just about to put the flashlight away when he noticed a break in the path. He directed the beam on the black void and quickly realized his error. He slammed the T-handle back against the stop, but the brakes failed to slow the errant rover. The battered buggy continued to slide down the steep grade until the front wheels skidded over the edge and back into the darkness.

The rover careened downhill out of control.

Mitchell grabbed for a handhold while trying to hold Harden back in the seat with his right arm. He could see the slope flatten out below, but with the

343

dangerous lack of depth perception, the drop could've been twenty feet or two hundred.

His answer arrived with a crash.

The rover's front suspension crumpled on impact. Mitchell was nearly thrown from his seat as the vehicle bounced several times before skidding sideways to a stop. When he looked to see if his friend was still there, Mitchell was shocked by the image over Harden's right shoulder.

Instead of clearing the mountainous plateau as he had hoped, the rover came to rest on the edge of a lofty precipice. The crater floor was still far below—but the rover's path ended here.

Mitchell moved quickly. He released Harden's lap restraint and slid his body out over the side of the rover. He then climbed out after Harden, trying not to kink the hoses that connected the men like twins on the same umbilical cord. He dragged his friend to the edge of the steep slope and prepared him for the descent. Mitchell saw only one solution to his dilemma—an unusual method of transport he had learned during his days as a hiking guide in the Sierra Nevada's. It worked best on moderately packed snow, but he had also practiced it on the talus strewn western slope of the real Mt. Whitney, and while not as comfortable, he knew it would work on lunar regolith as well.

Mitchell sat Harden down on the top of the slope and then straddled his friend with both legs. He latched on to the sides of Harden's PLSS backpack, and with one final push they became the first men to glissade on the moon. Mitchell struggled to see over the top of the backpack as the two men skidded down the steep slope on their butts. He used his legs to try and guide them to a safe landing, but their path was nearly a straight line as they accelerated toward the crater floor.

Halfway through the long descent, Harden stirred for the first time since leaving the crash site. He struggled to understand his situation as he careened down the terrifying gradient. He wasn't sure how he had gotten here, but he knew his chances of survival were improving by the second as he glimpsed the beautiful lunar module waiting in the distance. Harden finally spoke, and in a weak but discernible voice said, "Do you have any idea how expensive these suits are?"

Mitchell's face lit up behind the glass faceplate. "Welcome back to hell!"

"Hang on," Harden grumbled. "This is gonna hurt."

The glissade ended in a train wreck at the bottom of the mountain as the two astronauts disjoined and tumbled out onto the open plain of Daedalus. As Mitchell rolled to a stop, the pain in his side was overcome by the image at the edge of the horizon. The lonely LM was the most beautiful thing he had ever seen.

Lunar Orbit

"*Intruder* Base, this is *Phantom*, over," Burns radioed. But the response was the same—pure static. His heart pounded beneath his sweaty flight suit. Harden and Mitchell had been living on the limited PLSS consumables for over four hours. If they weren't within range of the LM's radio transceiver on this pass, they wouldn't have enough life support to make it back to the lunar module. The mission clock showed less than five minutes until he would be going over the hill for the third time. And on the next orbit, it would be time to leave.

Lunar Surface

"Come on, let's go. We're almost there," Mitchell said

as he struggled to loop Harden's arm around his shoulder. He had carried his friend along at first, but the searing pain in his side made it impossible to continue. He then switched to a light shuffle that he hoped Harden could match, a gentle lope that forced the semi-conscious commander to focus. Harden tried to keep up at first, but it didn't last long. The vertebrae that had been fused in his back following the ejection from the F-14 had separated again, and even the weak lunar gravity pushed the pain past any normal human threshold. Mitchell soon found himself dragging Harden's boots through the regolith. "Damn it, Blaze! Get your ass moving. We're both going to die out here if you don't stay with me."

High above the scene, Burns heard Mitchell's voice break into his headset over the LM relay circuit. "Where in the hell have you guys been? Do you know how close I was to leaving your sorry asses behind!?"

"Man, it's great to hear your voice," Mitchell replied.

"How's the boss doing?"

"We're running out of time. Here's the deal. The Chang'e is out of commission, but Blaze got banged up pretty bad in the process. He keeps fading out on me. I think I can get him back to the LM, but I'm not sure if I can get him inside. And even if I do, there's no way he can fly the rendezvous."

"I'm all right," Harden mumbled.

Banged up? Burns didn't have time to find out when the plan had changed, and what had gone wrong. "Quickly, I'm almost at LOS. What's your ETA back to the LM?"

"Maybe fifteen minutes," Mitchell posited as he looked at his watch. "Then I've got to try to get him up the ladder."

"Just get the inertial platform up and running, and stand by for a Tig when I come around the other side.

If you can get the LM into a stable orbit, I'll come down and get you guys. *Phantom*, out."

Mitchell hoped it would be that simple. The rendezvous was the one part of the profile that confused him the most, but he trusted Burns. If he said he could conduct the rendezvous from the command module and rescue them from a low lunar orbit, then Mitchell would bet his life on it.

Mitchell checked his watch again. It had actually taken only twelve minutes to reach the lunar module. "Here, hold on to the ladder," he said as he detached the hoses that connected him to Harden's pressure suit and discarded them beneath the LM. "I'll open the hatch and be right back down. Think you can pull yourself up the ladder if I get underneath and push?"

"I don't have much choice, do I?"

Mitchell hopped up to the porch and pried the hatch open. When he returned, Harden was still holding himself up, but his eyes were closed again. "All right, Blaze, I'd love to stand around and take it all in, but we've gotta get out of here."

To Mitchell's surprise, Harden opened his eyes and turned away from the ladder. Ignoring the pain, he grabbed Mitchell by the arm and stepped off the footpad. "No, I think we can spare just a few more seconds... because I'm sure that we'll never see anything like this again as long as we live."

CHAPTER 40

Lunar Surface

MITCHELL FOLLOWED STEP BY STEP as Harden pulled himself up the LM ladder and maneuvered through the narrow hatchway. Inside, he secured the hatch and helped Harden into the aft cabin. Sitting him down atop the ascent engine cover, Mitchell leaned Harden against the bulkhead and quickly repressurized the cabin.

"As soon as you get the ECS up and running," Harden said with some effort, "you're going to want to get into the emergency liftoff section of the lunar surface checklist. It's in the flight data file."

"Okay, but I'm going to need your help with that, so stay with me."

As soon as the cabin came up to operating pressure, Mitchell connected his suit to the LM's environmental control system and doffed his bulky helmet and gloves. Relief from the overwhelming claustrophobia was immediate.

As Mitchell read through the checklist, Harden tried to brief his pilot on the highlights of the emergency procedure. "You're going to have to get the PGNS up and running and then do a P57, Option 4. That'll give you a solid platform to navigate with, but you'll skip the stellar alignment and align everything to local vertical. The rest of the systems prep should be pretty straightforward. You'll need to get the Ascent PAD data from Pipper when he comes back around the corner. Then you can run Program 12, the powered ascent program."

Mitchell did his best to make sense of it all as he once again configured the circuit breakers on both side walls of the LM to match the diagrams in the checklist.

"We're only going to get one shot at this," Harden reminded his friend. "But as long as we can get this baby into orbit, Pipper can handle the rest. Hell, I think he's actually looking forward to this."

Mitchell worked feverishly as Harden slowly regained his strength. With the platform finally aligned, Mitchell brought the ascent stage batteries online and configured the flight controls for liftoff. He then fired the explosive valves in the ascent stage helium lines and quickly checked the propellant tank pressures. "Okay, that does it. We're just waiting for Pipper to feed us the liftoff data now."

"You're doing fine," Harden replied. "Now why don't you help me doff this PLSS? Then maybe I can help you out of yours."

"Just a sec," Mitchell said as he configured the VHF comm panel for the rendezvous. "All right, turn around here and let me get this thing off of you."

Finally free from the PLSS backpack, Harden returned the favor.

Burns's voice crackled in the comm loop. "*Intruder* Base, *Phantom*. How's it coming down there?"

"Perfect timing, Pipper. Go ahead with the numbers. We're ready to copy." Mitchell scribbled the long string of numbers into the empty spaces on the fireproof checklist as Burns read off the data. "Copy all. Stand by for read back."

Burns confirmed the information, and then relayed

several amplifying remarks. "Those numbers are for insertion into a nine-by-forty-five nautical mile orbit and a direct rendezvous; but disregard the TPI time. I'll make the terminal phase burn with the SPS engine and finish the rendezvous in the command module."

"We were hoping you wouldn't change your mind," Harden said with a pained chuckle. "And be advised, we're PGNS only. No AGS backup. We'll be flying with one eye closed, so keep a close watch on us."

"I'm all over it. And I'm showing seven minutes 'til Tig. Mark."

Chang'e 4

The three-metric-ton titanium-alloy arrow hurtled toward the imaginary bulls-eye in the center of Daedalus crater. Thrusters on the Chang'e 4 gave the satellite one final trajectory correction. All systems were functioning perfectly. In less than ten minutes, the communications platform would complete its final task and completely obliterate the poorly defined target being tracked by its onboard radar.

Lunar Surface

Cut off from the rest of the universe, it was impossible for the men inside the *Intruder* to know what was happening in the sky above them. While Mitchell rapidly entered the liftoff data into Program 12, Harden monitored the progress from his perch atop the ascent engine cover. As Tig approached, Harden stood up and began the painful process of hooking himself into the restraint cables at the LMP station. He then pulled a checklist card from its Velcro mooring on the right edge of the instrument panel for reference. "Let me know when you're ready, and we'll run through the APS start card."

"Great. Because I couldn't be more ready to get the hell off this hunk of rock."

"Amen, brother. Stand by for ignition in one minute."

Mitchell then looked out the left window of the *Intruder* for the first time since reentering the spacecraft. The landscape surrounding the LM had been plunged into total darkness. Only the upper portions of the towering mountaintops were still visible. A grim thought entered his mind as he realized where their flight path would take them. "I sure hope we clear those peaks on ascent."

Harden looked out his window and muttered, "Yeah, me too." The blink of the DSKY display caught his eye and alerted him to the impending launch.

"Abort stage," Mitchell said as he began the liftoff sequence. He reached forward, lifted a protective cover, and carefully depressed the square pushbutton beneath it. Four explosive bolts fired to finally divorce the ascent stage from the base of the lunar module. The remaining pyrotechnics then drove powerful guillotines through several bundles of cables—the descent stage's last remaining duty to serve as a spartan launch pad for the voyage home.

Burns's voice came on the loop, "I'm marking the top of your position...now."

"Copy. We're on our way," Harden replied.

"Engine Arm – Ascent," Mitchell reported. "Flashing 99. Proceed."

"Five, four, three, two, one...*liftoff.*"

Chang'e 4

The spacecraft that the Chang'e 4 had been targeting for the past three hours suddenly split in two. As the lunar module's ascent stage roared into space on a

351

column of invisible flame, the two spacecraft converged on a constant bearing and rapidly decreasing range. Seconds separated the two spacecraft from collision.

Lunar Module Intruder

The *Intruder* rose smoothly into the lunar dusk. Mitchell hawked the Eight-ball as the tiny craft yawed smartly to align itself with the correct launch azimuth. He then scanned the thrust-to-weight indicator. The needle on the tapemeter hovered just above the 2.0 mark, slightly better than a two-to-one thrust-to-weight ratio. Mitchell breathed a sigh of relief. The *Intruder* was on her way.

"We have pitchover," Harden announced. Barely a hundred feet above the lunar surface, the *Intruder* pitched away from the vertical and began its quest for horizontal velocity. When it did, the landing site came into view through the triangular windows.

"What the fuck!" Mitchell yelled when he saw the explosion. Barely a few hundred feet below, the Chang'e 4 disintegrated before his eyes as it plowed into the LM's abandoned descent stage.

Harden just shrugged and ignored the disturbing image. Why should it matter now? *We've been only seconds away from the grave for the last four days.*

Mitchell shook it off and went back to the instruments. He monitored the little engine closely. But its performance was perfect. In less than four minutes, the ascent stage had climbed through thirty thousand feet on its way to a predicted cutoff time of seven minutes and change, and an insertion altitude of nearly sixty-thousand feet. The ride was much smoother than he had expected; the only sense of motion was the periodic firing of the RCS thrusters as the faithful craft guided itself to orbit.

"Shutdown," Harden announced. "The PGNS shows our orbit to be 8.9 by 45.6. And since we can't compare that with the AGS velocities, we're not going to burn the residuals."

"Copy that," Burns replied cheerily. "I'll plug those numbers in, and be on my way."

Harden took a deep, satisfying breath. He then turned and offered his hand to Mitchell. "Hey, I wanted to thank you for coming back to get me. It was about to get really cold down there."

Mitchell reached out and shook Harden's hand. But his blank stare said a mouthful. He had just assumed that Harden was unconscious during his entire absence from the crash site. Mitchell shrugged inside the bulky suit. Not that it mattered. He would have told him one day anyway. But the more he thought about it, now seemed to be as good a time as any to clear the air. Mitchell had known all along that there were safer choices Harden could have made for a copilot—but as the two old friends exchanged glances, Mitchell was finally convinced that Burns was right— and that Harden had brought him along for a reason. "I guess we're even then."

"Even." Harden grinned. "Now let's go home."

Lunar Orbit

"*Intruder, Phantom,* this is Johnston on a relay circuit, how do you read? Over."

"*Phantom,* loud and clear," Burns replied.

"You're a little weak, Johnston," Harden said. "But it sure is great to hear your voice again."

"Welcome back, gentlemen!" Cernan howled across the distance.

"Reading you five-by-five now," Harden said, his physical pain suddenly suppressed by the thought that he might actually live to see tomorrow. "With just a little more luck, we'll be back on the beach in three days—drinking beer and telling lies. I surely hope you can join us, Captain."

"I'll be there, buddy," Cernan promised. "You can count on that."

Phantom and *Intruder* sailed quietly through the lunar night. But flying in separate elliptical arcs around their ancient grey host, a velocity change would be required by one of the spacecraft if their orbits were ever to intersect. To reach the desired conjunction, Burns hastily prepared the command module for TPI, Terminal Phase Initiation.

The lengthy RCS burn lasted thirty-six seconds. When complete, Burns eyed the DSKY readout as the range between the two spacecraft slowly decreased. "Coming up on 1.2 nautical miles. Closure rate twenty-three feet per second."

"Copy, *Phantom*. You're looking good, and we confirm those numbers on the radar," Harden replied.

"Three thousand feet. Eighteen feet per second." Burns crosschecked the error needles on his Eight-ball. "Looks like I'm picking up a little drift. Down and left."

"We concur. We should be level on your horizon. Just drive it on home, pal."

"I got it. Fifteen hundred feet. Ten feet per second. Five hundred, braking to five feet per second."

"Almost there," Harden said softly.

"Johnston," Burns finally announced with a huge wave of relief. "We're station-keeping at one hundred feet."

Harden traded places with Mitchell. Quite sure he would never have such an opportunity again, he ignored the pain and took the controls one last time. He gently pitched the nose of the *Intruder* forward to present her upper docking hatch to the waiting *Phantom*. Gazing through the overhead rendezvous window, he slowly yawed the faithful spacecraft to the left until the two docking aids lined up precisely. Then, with the sun at his back, he looked through the LM's triangular window and was greeted by an entirely different moon than the one he had left behind at Daedalus; its bright face at lunar high noon suddenly a welcoming augury of a long, but successful voyage home.

EPILOGUE

Apollo 18

I T WAS A STRANGE MIX of aromas that had lured Mitchell out of his extraordinary slumber. Still corralled by his sleeping sling after nearly twelve hours, the first smell to register was one that had wafted into the command module two days ago, just before they jettisoned the LM. The acrid smell of space immediately transported him back to his final moments on the lunar surface. It hadn't registered at the time, but the unearthly smell suddenly reminded him of burnt gunpowder. The other smell was much more terrestrial—the unmistakable aroma of roasted coffee beans.

"Sorry," Burns whispered, "but I spilled some of my dehydrated coffee. Looks like it might have floated in your direction."

"Shit, you won't believe the dream I just had."

Burns laughed. "I know. I had the same dream. Now get up topside and grab a headset. Sam's about to give us the reentry brief."

"I'll get some coffee and be right up." Mitchell grabbed the hot water dispenser, squirted some of the steamy liquid into an absorbent cloth and buried his face in it. Then, after mixing a strong bag of coffee to chase down the medication, he glided up into the cockpit and joined the discussion already in progress.

"How'd you sleep?" Harden asked during a break in the conversation.

"Are you kidding? Whatever Sam put in those medical kits is amazing."

"I know. The blue pills almost made me forget the pain in my back."

"So..." Mitchell said with a sleepy yawn, "...we still pointed at the big blue marble."

Harden chuckled. "You'll be glad to know that Pipper's due diligence while we were recuperating has paid off in spades. One of the Madrid antennas came back on line this morning, and Sam just informed us that the cumulative error in his navigation is, quote, 'less than the ground crew could've possibly hoped for.'"

Burns smiled. "I told you to trust me, didn't I?"

"Okay, hold on a sec," Harden prompted with a raised hand. "Yeah, go ahead, Sam. Everyone is on the line now."

"Before we get to the reentry brief, I just thought you guys might like to know that the Chinese have finally acknowledged the launch of a ballistic missile from Hainan Island last week." The communist party's official press release claimed that the test had been conducted to gauge the performance of the SC-19's upgraded propulsion system, not the guidance functions of the warhead; and that by missing its target satellite by a "nominal" distance, the responsible test did nothing to add to the menacing cloud of debris already in Earth orbit.

"Then, in a separate statement," Freer continued, "the CNSA reaffirmed its plans to land a *taikonaut* on the moon by 2020. But in a shocking turnabout, the Chinese have invited their compatriots in Taiwan to share in the historic achievement, citing that under the 'One country, Two systems' principle it's in everyone's best interest at this point to proceed on a course of cooperation rather than confrontation."

"I wonder what changed their minds?" Burns said with a smirk.

"The statement also claims that they will do something that has never been done before—their *taikonauts* will land on the far side of the moon."

"I knew we should've brought a camera," Mitchell harrumphed.

"Any way you look at it," Freer continued, "it appears that your success has had quite an impact on world events. The president has just announced that next week he will ask Congress to authorize a budget increase for NASA—specifically aimed at cutting the development time for the Space Launch System in half."

"That's an interesting development, Sam," Harden said guardedly. "I just hope it's a promise we can follow through on this time." A quick glance at the mission clock reminded the commander that they still weren't home yet. "Before we start whoopin' and hollerin' though, we'd better get ready to thread this needle. Johnston, Apollo 18, we're standing by for that Reentry PAD."

When the service module was finally jettisoned, all that remained of the Apollo/Saturn stack—a towering 363 feet at launch—was the twelve feet of conical habitat designed to deliver its human cargo safely back to Earth. It had taken two full days for the *Phantom* to reach half of its final velocity—a figure that it had doubled again in just the last two hours—as its crew prepared to smash into the atmosphere at an incinerating 22,000 nautical miles per hour.

The DSKY flashed on cue. "P63," Harden

announced. "Johnston, Eighteen. Are we still go on those numbers?"

"Standby one, Eighteen," Freer replied. "Yep, it looks like they're still good. If Jeff is as accurate with the reentry as he has been with everything else so far, you should be within a mile of Johnston at splashdown."

"You'd better fire up the band then," Burns said.

"Entry Interface," said Harden, acknowledging the unceremonious event.

"Point-zero-five-g," Burns reported as a corresponding light flickered on the Entry Monitor System.

"Holy shit!" Mitchell swore as he stared at the rapidly changing numbers on the DSKY. "Thirty-six thousand feet per second."

"Program 64," Burns announced. "The EMS is scrolling."

"Get ready for some g's," Harden warned.

"Two-g's," Burns acknowledged as the pressure began building in his chest. "There's a little left roll, fifteen degrees."

"Three-g's...four...five," Harden grunted. The rapid onset of forces proved punishing to the men who had been weightless for the past week. "Six-g's."

"She's about to roll over," Burns said as he eyed the EMS display. "There she goes. Lift vector down." Burns hawked the instruments closely as he waited to put his piloting skills to work one last time. The *Phantom* wasn't a space shuttle, and a pinpoint landing wasn't a requirement for survival; but the blunt nosed lifting body was capable of being steered, and had routinely splashed down within a mile of the recovery ships.

"Seven-g's," Mitchell croaked as he strained against the crushing force. "Approaching orbital velocity."

Burns spoke in short, terse bursts. "Range profile's good...maybe a little long...I'll fix it after skip out."

Mitchell continued to monitor the numbers unrolling wildly on the DSKY. "There's capture," he shouted, rejoicing in the knowledge that even a skip out of the atmosphere at this point would still end in an earthbound recovery.

"Program 65. She's pulsing back up," Burns announced as the spacecraft rolled 180 degrees about its axis and began climbing again.

"We're back above 200,000 feet," Harden said. "Going ballistic."

"Beautiful," Mitchell murmured as he glanced at the spectacle just beyond his window. As the *Phantom* ripped through the upper atmosphere, the plasma sheath left in its wake was a multi-spectral explosion of color. "It looks like were flying on the inside a thousand-mile-long fluorescent tube."

"Take a deep breath," Burns warned as he watched the g-meter hover near zero. "Here it comes again."

"Program 67," Harden noted as the DSKY flashed its warning. "Get ready to Arm the pyros, we're coming in."

Burns then rocked the rotational controller out of its detent and scanned the DSKY. The target error values on the display changed with each deliberate movement of his right hand. A slight roll seemed to correct left or right errors without much affect on their downrange travel. Larger roll angles had a more noticeable impact on the range error.

"One hundred fifty thousand," Mitchell noted.

Burns quickly crosschecked the deceleration-versus-velocity graph on the EMS. As he continued to pilot the *Phantom,* a transparent green "bug" traced out their progress across the back of the scrolling

361

Mylar tape. *What a way to fly.* "All right gents, here we go. Down the chute."

"One hundred thousand," Mitchell noted. "We're almost on top of it now."

The data on the EMS and DSKY displays finally began to converge. Burns made several more fine adjustments to their lift vector as the range-to-go displayed on the EMS marched steadily toward what appeared to be a pinpoint landing. Then, as their velocity fell below Mach 2, Burns released the controls. The blunt nosed lifting body was now merely a ballistic projectile, subject only to the ever present force of gravity.

"Fifty thousand feet," Mitchell announced.

"Roger," said Burns. "Pyros A and B are Armed."

Harden reached for another pair of covered switches. "ELS to AUTO."

"There go the drogues," Burns shouted as the Earth Landing System began to deploy. The two smaller drogue chutes deployed first to stabilize the spacecraft and ease the shock on the main parachutes. Three powerful mortars then exploded from the apex of the spacecraft, hauling the main parachutes out into the slipstream.

"Contact on the mains," Harden shouted as the *Phantom's* three seventy-five-foot-wide parachutes blossomed into full glory.

"Eight thousand feet," Mitchell exhaled.

Burns smiled as he scanned the DSKY one last time. The display read 0.1—one tenth of a nautical mile—a mere 500 feet from their target.

Phantom plunged toe first into the shallow water. A wall of white foam erupted from the base of the spacecraft; the translucent water around the heat shield sizzling as it shed the intense energy of reentry. Three red and white parachutes drifted lazily above the charred capsule, finally collapsing into the azure blue Pacific like giant flags in the gentle coastal breeze.

Inside the *Phantom*, warm air—and more than a little bit of salt water—poured in on Harden before he could secure the vent valve. "Sorry, gents. That was more of a shock than I'm used to on landing."

"What the hell," Mitchell said, and began unbuckling his straps. "We're all about to get wet anyway."

Burns quickly followed suit. When he had finished stowing his couch, he stood up for the first time in a week and stretched his muscles against the powerful, wonderful pull of gravity.

Mitchell emerged from the lower equipment bay and peered through the main hatch window. "You've got to be shitting me!"

"How'd we do?" Burns asked with a crooked grin.

"We could almost swim ashore from here," Mitchell said as he reached for the gearbox selector on the center hatch. When he finally swung the heavy hatch open, a gust of warm ocean air rushed in and quickly purged the week-old, stale cabin atmosphere.

When Harden finished securing the ship, he stood up and stowed his couch. Mitchell slid over to make room for him in the small hatch opening. The light was bright. Harden closed his eyes and let the glow of the midday sun warm his face.

Mitchell stared up at the clear blue sky as if it were a tall glass ceiling they had just crashed through. It was strange not to see the stars anymore. Or the moon. "Looking up at the sky will never be the same again," he muttered.

Harden's eyes were still closed as he basked in the sunlight.

"No. I guess not."

Made in the USA
Middletown, DE
23 February 2016